FAVOUR FIRE

FIREBORN SERIES BOOK FIVE

VANESSA RICCI-THODE

THODESTOOL FICTION

Publisher: Vanessa Ricci-Thode
Editors: Kristopher Mielke, Sydnee Thompson, Chelle Parker
Cover art & design: GetCovers

Library and Archives Canada Cataloguing in Publication

This is a first edition of *Favour Fire*.

For Aunt Rosa.
You were always the cool one.

Author's Note

Previously in the Fireborn Series

Hello reader! This is the fifth and final book of the Fireborn series. If you're skipping the previous books or it's been a while, below is a spoiler-filled synopsis to get you caught up or to act as a refresher! But this book follows *Firebound*, the fourth book in the series, and *The Dragon Next Door* (a Fireborn series side quest) more closely than the others, and I recommend not skipping those ones. There's also the short story, "Testing the Waters," in the anthology *Farther Reefs* by Space Wizard Publishing (or *The Dragon Next Door* bonus scenes, if you were lucky enough to get those) that acts as a bridge between *The Dragon Next Door* and *Favour Fire*. Also note that Canadian spelling is being used throughout the book.

Dragon Whisperer

Dionelle Joasera was born immune to fire. After moving to her new husband's farm, the ruling nobles in the city force her into the position of dragon whisperer, where she must negotiate with the local dragon population. Dionelle enjoys the work but not the strain it causes with her husband, Reiser, who fears for her safety. Tension mounts between the newlyweds, exacerbated by her sister's jealous rage.

Dionelle disappears and her mentor is murdered, pulling Reiser into the snare of politics surrounding Pasdale's corrupt ruling nobles. He must work with the dragons to find his wife, working particularly closely with the black dragoness who leads the local blaze and has grown fond of Dionelle. Enlisting Dionelle's best friend, a dragon scholar named Ondias, and finding allyship from two court wizards, Zev and Nandara, Reiser discovers that Dionelle's unique pyromantic nature is due to being part fire demon and that her sister is responsible for the death and disappearance, with Dionelle banished to the fire realm.

But the presence of a human in the fire realm is throwing all of the elements off balance, and the world is slowly tearing itself apart with wild weather swings and dangerous earthquakes.

In a desperate bid to save Dionelle and the world, Reiser becomes the first human to visit the dragon city—a towering structure of diamond and obsidian suspended over a valley—where he is enchanted to be fireproof and sent to the fire realm. He discovers Dionelle is alive (and also pregnant), and he is able to bring her home again. The elements stabilize, and Dionelle and Ondias are treated with a trip to the dragon city when Reiser is brought back there to remove the dragons' enchantment.

The story ends with the corrupt nobles removed from power, and the king's cousin is installed as the peaceful new ruler of Pasdale.

Trueflame

Neesha Joasera, Dionelle's nearly adult daughter, is determined to be as unlike her mother as possible, despite also being part fire demon. She's a talented pyromancer intent on gaining entrance to the Wizards Guild and shunning every attempt to bridle her with marriage. An unplanned pregnancy throws a wrench in her plans, leaving her with an impossible deadline to pass her Guild exams before motherhood sidelines her.

The former ruler of Pasdale, exiled just before Neesha was born, has allied himself with a powerful aquamancer named Loch and a handful of traitor dragons, and he is coming to reclaim Pasdale and satisfy his vendetta against the Joasera family.

Neesha uses her magic to defend Pasdale, and with the help of fire demons, opens a portal to the fire realm, wielding trueflame against the flood Loch has made. She vaporizes the waters, saving Pasdale, but the attack on Pasdale was a distraction—the real target is the dragon city. Neesha and her allies don't get there in time, and terrifying flood waters wash away one of the support columns, causing the dragon city to crumble and fall.

Devastated, Neesha goes to the fire realm as her parents once did to send back demons and trueflame to properly combat Loch's magic. The plan works, but Neesha goes into labour, unable to continue her role in the battle. Her daughter, who she names Mita, is fireborn like Neesha and Dionelle.

Desperate and fiercely protective of her daughter, Neesha commands dragons, demons, and trueflame until she and the black dragoness finally push back the flood and secure victory. But Neesha's spirit is lost to the flame. She is preserved in a magical coma in the remnants of the dragon city, while Dionelle has gone silent in her mourning. The king's cousin was killed in the final battle, leaving a power vacuum that Loch sweeps in to fill.

Fireborn

Mita Joasera, a.k.a. Spark, is the most powerful fireborn yet, able to pull fire out of the air. She lives with her grandparents, Reiser and Dionelle, and extended family. The dragon population is slowly being enslaved to drive industry, and the Joaseras are outcast for taking the dragons' side. Loch, now Pasdale's magistrate, sends a blaze of enslaved dragons to attack the Joaseras, destroying Spark's home and murdering her family while she watches helplessly. Dionelle holds them off and forces Spark to run.

The black dragoness scoops up Spark as she flees through the foothills outside of Pasdale and carries her away from the danger while the loss of Spark's family replays in the girl's mind. Spark and her dog, Shadow, make the long journey with the dragoness to the dragon city, which is still recovering from Loch's attack.

In the valley beneath this city lies a small human settlement filled with dragon supporters, including Ondias and Nandara. Spark, who believed her mother was dead rather than in a magical coma, is horrified and enraged when she discovers the truth.

Spark befriends the black dragoness, who she calls Abyss, and dusts off the village's old forge to become the resident blacksmith. Eventually, she also befriends some of the other teens in the village, including Ember and

Nandara's grandson, Jatt. Proximity to Ember sets Spark's pulse racing; a deep crush on the older girl flourishes alongside their friendship.

Spark learns that Dionelle survived and is Loch's prisoner. Driven by desperation, Spark experiments with the dangerous magic that cost her mother, Neesha, so dearly: demon possession. Spark builds all manner of tools and weapons to help the village and the dragons, including lightweight dragon armour and a sling for Abyss to carry Spark in flight. When Loch's ice dragons attack, Abyss is captured and the Dragoness Superior is killed. Spark works with both humans and dragons to free Abyss and battle the ice dragons, summoning fire demons and opening a fire portal to call trueflame to end the battle, much as her mother had years before.

One of the ice dragons is killed and the others injured, while Abyss is freed.

Despite this success, a budding romance with Ember, and building a new family among her friends and allies in the dragon city, Spark aches to revive her mother and free her grandmother.

Firebound

Spark is listless and frustrated, as all she's learning about magic and making gadgets still isn't enough to help her mother or free her grandmother, and news comes from allies, including other dragon riders, that Loch is building a dragon army. He also has one of Abyss's eggs, all of which are close to hatching.

Desperate Spark opens a fire portal for the first time since the previous book's battle and goes to the fire realm, just to see if she can. The act triggers strange magic, finally waking Neesha from her seventeen-year slumber. Neesha is a distraught mess over all the time she's lost, and Spark rushes headlong into rescue plans while the adults are talking in circles, taking a fire portal back to Pasdale to free Abyss's egg and bring Dionelle back.

She's only half-successful, freeing Dionelle but not the egg.

Traumatized Dionelle is not the woman Spark remembers, and bitter Neesha is struggling to catch up and help Spark in any meaningful way. The three of them flounder as they try to rebuild their family under the renewed threat to the dragon city. Spark's half-successful heist in Pasdale leaves the dragon city vulnerable, as they are once again Loch's target.

Spark, Neesha, and Dionelle must confront past errors and fresh traumas, as well as terrifying magic, in order to defend themselves and the dragons. Spark and Neesha even get some lessons from their new dragon rider friends. Sooner than they're prepared for, they learn that Loch's forces are on their way, attacking from the southern plains. They fly out to meet the challenge head-on. And with three fireborn women finally playing to their strengths and keeping each other safe, they drive back the threat, even though Loch escapes. The trio immediately head to Pasdale via fire portal to free all of the dragons and eggs held captive there. Spark is on hand when Abyss's egg hatches, making a new baby dragon friend.

In the end, the three fireborn women have a reprieve to recover from their traumas and griefs and learn how to be a family and celebrate life's joys.

The Dragon Next Door

This side quest brings the adventure to Upalint, a nation on the southern continent, where hero-for-hire Tollar has stolen a dragon egg from one of Loch's underlings, Karthiry. Before it can be returned to its kin, the dragon hatches and imprints on both Tollar and her neighbour and longtime crush, Beenala. Beenala is an anxious pyromancer, and Tollar a demonborn aquamancer, though that's something she's keeping to herself after hearing how being demonborn worked out for the fireborn women.

The baby dragon, who Tollar names Bale, is still in danger, as Karthiry's forces invade the southern continent and plan to move inland to Upalint. Tollar manages to free one captive dragon, its rider Croves, and another dragon egg with Beenala's help, and an inept spy named Draminedes reveals Karthiry's plans in enough time for Tollar to rally her community into defending itself. Following his conscience, Draminedes turns on Karthiry and becomes part of the growing resistance in Upalint.

Tollar reveals herself as demonborn in exchange for help from the dragons in defeating Karthiry. The battle is long and drawn-out, leaving Tollar exhausted, so that when Karthiry is defeated and Loch arrives, Tollar has little reserves left to fight. With support from Beenala and a host of elementals Tollar has trained to harness each other's magic, they liberate their neighbours and protect their own nation, though Loch once again escapes.

This book ends with Beenala and Tollar making a life together with new neighbours Croves and Draminedes, while Bale is in the skies watching over them all. Tollar is recovering from injuries sustained during battle and enjoying the new life she's building, but is still wary of the threat Loch poses.

Favour Fire content warnings: abuse and torture (implied), anxiety, blood, death by dragon, death by fire, demon possession, drowning, environmental destruction, pregnancy in danger, PTSD. And don't worry, the dog lives.

Heat level: low

Some say the world will end in fire,
Some say in ice.
From what I've tasted of desire
I hold with those who favor fire.
But if it had to perish twice,
I think I know enough of hate
To say that for destruction ice
Is also great
And would suffice.
- "Fire and Ice," Robert Frost

CHAPTER ONE

The ground beneath Neesha's feet shook, and she wondered if she should be more concerned than she was to be standing on an actively erupting volcano? Nandara had been taken aback when Neesha told her what she and Spark intended to do, so Neesha hadn't even bothered to mention it to her mother—and especially not Ondias—before she and Spark had set out through a fire portal. She knew exactly the look Dionelle would give her, and Ondias would give her an agonizingly boring lecture about being a responsible adult and blah blah blah.

Besides, Neesha *was* being responsible by coming with Spark instead of letting the girl come alone. Only a fool would believe that forbidding Spark from coming at all would actually work.

Spark was nattering on the way she did, up to her knees in one of the gentler lava flows—they'd both agreed not to mention to anyone else how the fire portal they'd opened had brought them out into a much less gentle flow, not that they hadn't been able to get control of the situation quickly. It was mostly fire, and the rest was very hot earth, and both of them could work with those elements, so what was the problem? They'd made themselves little stone rafts to float to more solid ground.

The ground shook again and Neesha glanced to the summit. The flow was getting heavier, the fountaining fire at the top spouting higher.

Nandara, at least, had given her some useful warnings, primarily about how unpredictable an erupting volcano was. But they lived with dragons. How much worse could this be?

Spark was dragging her fingers through the magma before scooping it up and cooling it into dark shapes that looked a lot like the sort of work she was doing to help repair the dragon city. Neesha hadn't been able to master fusing the obsidian and diamond the way her daughter had, so she didn't get to go up to the city nearly as often as Spark did. Especially now that Abyss had left with her family, back to the mountains near Pasdale.

That was fine. Didn't bother Neesha. No, not at all.

She went to the... riverbank? Lavabank? Whatever. She knelt at the edge, running her own hands through it and watching the bright glowing shapes. Her white skin stood out even more against the dark orange flow. She and Spark both were white like fresh snow, hair and skin alike. But where Neesha had blue eyes with a fiery amber ring at the outside of her irises, Spark's eyes were fire, flickering to reflect the lava right now. And while Neesha was on the short side and tended toward daintiness, Spark was like a dragon, tall and broad and strong.

Neesha scooped up some lava, sifting it between thumb and fingers. It was neat, but she didn't find it nearly as academically interesting as Spark, who was still muttering to herself about composition and compounds and replication and...

Neesha had no doubt the girl would figure out how to make fireproof notes and come back out here to study the lava flow in more detail.

And Neesha really needed to stop thinking of her as a girl. Spark was coming up on nineteen now. It was one of the things that had made Neesha's relationship with Dionelle nearly unbearable back... before. Even now, Dionelle often treated Neesha like she was still a teen.

Of course, Spark had been deeply sheltered most of her life, right up until that terrible year where she'd been exposed to the worst traumas the world had to offer. And now she was back to being insulated. Safe in the bubble of the dragon city. There'd been a time it was necessary, for all of them, to get over what had happened and to figure out how to be a family.

Well, as best as they were ever going to figure that part out.

Neesha didn't think Spark needed quite so much insulating these days. Since they could both go anywhere in the world where there was some fire burning, Neesha had started doing just that—taking Spark on mini adventures.

This particular volcano wasn't even that far away. If Abyss had been around, she could have brought them here within a day. Somewhere northwest of the dragon city. Spark had heard about the eruption from one of the returning scouts and had been immediately fascinated, badgering Neesha to go with her to see it firsthand.

Neesha sat on the bank with her chin in her hand, elbow on knee, feet in lava, watching Spark have a fantastic time. Probably with that dopey dumbstruck mom look Ember had discreetly informed her she had whenever Spark was deeply enjoying something. Neesha didn't think she'd ever get over the bitterness at missing so much of this clever human's life, but that didn't mean she couldn't enjoy it now that they were together again.

And then she realized that the cute little fireproof boots Ember had made her were filling up with lava.

"Ah, shit." One nearly came off when Neesha pulled her feet up. She stood on the bank to dump them out.

Spark looked up at her. "Oh! Oh no…" Standing on one leg, Spark lifted a foot up out of the lava to discover that she was missing her boot. Lifted the other leg to find the same.

Neesha laughed.

"Ember's going to kill me." Spark went hunting around with her hands, trying to find her boots, but they'd probably been swept down the slope out onto the distant plateau where the lava was pooling.

"Ember will delight in making you a new pair, this one a snugger fit."

Ember loved the challenge of working with what limited dragon skin they had to make fireproof clothing out of. Neesha was wearing the suit she'd made out of Neesha's old purple wizarding robes, one with a lot of straps and buckles to tuck in the looser-fitting parts when they were flying with Abyss. Spark's suit was a patchy grey and white, mostly the darker grey patches, a little more utilitarian, but still with some straps and buckles for her flying harness and glider attachment.

Neesha laced her boots tighter but didn't put her feet back in the flow. Spark went back to mucking around in the magma, and Neesha went back to watching her. She'd hoped there'd be something a little more magically exciting to do, something new to practice. But fire portals were routine, and everything else they'd been doing didn't even involve active magic. Fire couldn't harm them.

Nandara had warned that the volcano was more than fire, which was why they'd come in boots. The liquid earth did feel different than walking on the ground of the fire realm, and the bits where Neesha had been walking were sharper, but it was a smoother bed under the flow where Spark focused all her attention.

Neesha hadn't done much magic at all since late winter, when she and Spark had finally completed their full Guild entrance exams, trading in their specialist tokens for Guild badges made of some kind of charmed iridescent gemstone. Neesha had initially been ecstatic to finally be a full Guild member and sincerely hoped someone told Loch about it. But with nothing to actually *do* with her magic out in the middle of nowhere, the excitement had worn off.

The ground shook again, continuous now, and the roar from the summit was all she could hear. Like all the dragons going to battle at once. Wincing against the sound and trying not to let it crumple her, Neesha looked up to the fountaining fire above them to see a horror of flame and smoke and debris. A dark plume raced downhill toward them, and fiery chunks burst from the cloud to land nearby.

"Shit!" she gasped, drawing from the fire all around them and pulling open a fire portal between her and Spark. "Let's go!"

The fire couldn't hurt them. But flying chunks of rock and whatever gases that plume held sure could.

Spark was frozen to the spot, her eyes wide as she watched the plume consume everything before her. Neesha pulled up fireball and threw it at Spark's shoulder. Spark shrieked and nearly fell over into the lava flow—getting swept away was the last thing they needed right now.

Neesha stumbled across the shuddering ground and caught Spark's shoulder near the lavabank, tugging her to the portal. No easy feat when Neesha still had noodle arms and Spark was possibly twice her size.

Neesha wouldn't have expected it, but the roar of the fire realm was somehow a quiet reprieve from the roar of the exploding volcano. Spark staggered to a stop next to her, closing the portal behind her.

"What in all the hells was that!"

Neesha gave her a wry smile. "That, my dear, was a volcano."

Neesha had been sitting in one of the rooftop patio chairs, watching the city and everything around it glitter, when Nandara dropped into the chair beside her. It was a beautiful summer day, the weather perfect. Nandara was in a simple light-green dress, her greying blonde hair swept back into a loose braid.

"So how bad was it actually?" Nandara asked.

Neesha furrowed her brow. "What do you mean?"

"You came back because the tremors were too much? Really?" Nandara arched an eyebrow at her, skewering Neesha with her emerald gaze.

"You'll just tell Ondias, and she'll give me a lecture, and I'll get angry and do something even stupider next time." Neesha gave her mentor a pointed look. "No one got hurt, so what does it matter?"

Nandara sighed. "Nee, you really do need to think things through more carefully. No one got hurt this time, yes. But you know how bad it can get."

She meant that time Neesha had spent seventeen years in a magical coma because she'd been reckless with magic right before and immediately after Spark was born. Like she could possibly forget the worst thing that had ever happened to her. But she knew so much more about her power now. She and Spark both did. They were getting really good at a lot of things—the Guild didn't let just any wizard in.

Neesha shrugged. "I know the risks."

"And I know you're bored. You don't have to stay here."

"I don't. That's what today was about."

"You can go somewhere for longer than an afternoon."

"Go where? And do what? I can't go back to Pasdale. What else am I supposed to do? Spark needs me."

Nandara pressed her lips together and took a breath like she meant to respond, but instead she shook her head and leaned back in her chair to watch the city. They both knew it was a lie, and Nandara knew saying so wasn't going to change anything.

Spark did still need her, just not the way she had when Neesha had first woken up. But it was also true that there was nowhere else for Neesha to go. She could head to Baymouth Shores to see the rest of the family, but even seventeen years hadn't been enough for her oldest brother, Bly, to stop being an asshole, and he still hadn't forgiven her for getting angry and saying it should have been him that died instead of Breen.

Okay, that maybe hadn't been fair, but she did miss her youngest brother desperately.

Neesha had started lurking around the apprentice hall, especially when Jatt was there with other artists, trying to see if there were any side skills she could pick up that would be useful in a place like this. There were a lot of powerful wizards here and not much in the way of actual work. Plenty of leisure time, but the sorts of leisure activities Neesha had enjoyed in her misspent youth were no longer things she was particularly interested in.

Well. More like there wasn't anyone she was interested in being leisurely with—it was all men her father's age and boys her daughter's age. It was a beautiful place, but still small and lacking in options.

But it was safe. Safe for all of them. Somewhere she and Spark could continue to grow.

"I just need more time to get used to all the wide-open space. And maybe someone interesting will come in with the next caravan and keep me amused for a bit."

Nandara gave her the sad smile that made Neesha's stomach roil.

"Nee, not everything requires a lot of space to grow. Sometimes, a rose needs a trellis or it will bloom in the mud."

Neesha glared. Nandara, who they both knew was right, turned to watch the city. At least she didn't gloat like Ondias.

The fact remained that Neesha had nowhere to go. And being a rose blooming in the mud was better than being compost.

The door to the main part of the house burst open and Spark loped out. Both women turned as she called to Neesha, brandishing a pair of the decorative obsidian chunks she'd stuffed in her pockets when they'd fled through the fire portal. Both of them had changed out of their fireproof clothing into regular linen trousers and short-sleeved tunics—Spark's a plain white shirt and grey pants, Neesha's a boring sort of brown pants but a nice lilac top.

"Mamma, where do you think—"

A fierce storm of dragoncries erupted from the city and all around the valley, dragons funnelling out of the tower—much taller now even than when Neesha had awoken two years ago—with a blaze of them flocking east.

Neesha cringed against the sound, but Spark went utterly still, breathing fast and shallow. Neesha leapt from her chair and gripped Spark's wrists, her hands fisted around the decorations she'd brought up.

"Deep breath, Spark." Neesha reached up to touch her face. "Those are our dragons. That's their welcome call."

Spark gasped, still breathing erratically. "Doesn't sound right."

Neesha cocked her head. "It's different, yes, but it's still a welcome. We're okay, Spark. You're safe."

Spark blinked a lot, her expression clearing as she managed to focus on Neesha's face. Spark inhaled, deep and shuddering. Neesha helped Spark ease into the seat she'd just vacated and took her obsidian pieces, setting them carefully aside.

"Oh my," Nandara whispered.

Neesha glanced back, following Nandara's gaze, and she stood suddenly when she saw the large black shard of Abyss flying over the eastern mountains amidst the welcome party that had gone out to meet her. She disappeared into the city with the rest of them. Spark had seen her too, and raced down the stairs and out into the field next to the house where Abyss often came to visit them.

"I didn't think she was due back until midwinter," Neesha said.

Nandara's brow furrowed, and she shook her head slightly. "No, she wasn't."

Neesha's limbs buzzed. "Do you think something's wrong?"

Nandara gave her a grim look and got up to go talk to Ondias. Neesha stayed where she was, watching Spark over the railing as she stayed in the field, watching and waiting. It would be rude to summon Abyss so soon after she'd returned, but the way Spark kept flexing her hands, Neesha knew she wanted to.

The afternoon wore on, with Ember and Jatt both taking turns keeping Spark company in the field and Shadow, the dog, going out to lie next to her for a spell. But as the sun set and night drew in, there was still no sign of their friend. Neesha didn't like it either, and was half tempted to do the summoning anyway.

A quick visit from Abyss would answer a lot of questions and set them at ease. Or not.

Neesha wasn't sure what it meant that she was hoping, just a little, that Abyss would bring the "or not" sort of news.

CHAPTER TWO

T ollar would be in the dragon city tomorrow and there was no way she could sleep. How Croves and Beenala were asleep, she had no idea. Tossing and turning until dawn was on order, but moving at all would upset the delicate balance, what with Croves pressed at her back and his trunk of an arm around her growing waist, and Beenala a handspan away, her fingers entwined with Tollar's.

Tollar released her building sigh in a long slow exhale.

It had been like this the whole week. Eleven days of travelling from Upalint, north down the curve of the world and across the equator, and west into new lands that even Tollar hadn't seen despite her endless wandering. And every night, Croves would curl up at her back and Beenala on the other side of her—Croves because he was getting a touch overprotective and Beenala because she was still a mess from what had happened in Port Sawulxo. Tollar missed being able to sprawl out.

But it was time to take Bale to the dragon city. Time for the not-so-little-anymore dragon, Tollar's adopted daughter, to be properly named by her dragon kin. Tollar had planned on going alone with Bale, but Beenala had insisted on coming along. And then Croves and Shell, who hadn't been to the dragon city in years, decided they might as well come as a formal escort. They didn't know where Loch was, after all, and it was best to be safe.

And between the lingering effects of her illness after the war combined with the effort of growing two babies, Tollar's body was taxed—it affected her magic, making everything harder. She always loved the company, but this was the first time she'd needed it to stay safe.

Tollar would be lying if she said she wasn't delighted to have them along. Balipar, their local dragon whisperer, had insisted the dragon city was a true marvel. They hadn't seen it, but they'd heard stories and seen some art. They'd half-wanted to come along on Tollar's mad adventure. Tollar had promised she'd try to bring them back something special.

Of course, Tollar's mad adventures were plenty infamous and Balipar knew better.

But the dragon city! Now that was an adventure. Tales of a glittering tower in the clouds had lived in Tollar's dreams since the first time Balipar had mentioned it. And tomorrow she'd see it.

Best of all, she'd see something incredible and new and get to share the experience with her best friend. Tollar smiled at Beenala in the dark, the other woman's round face pinched with worry even in her sleep. But there was no sleep for Tollar tonight, so she kissed Beenala's knuckles and disentangled herself, gently prying loose Croves's arm so she could slip out of her sleep mat and climb out from under Bale's wing.

Bare feet on cool stone, Tollar walked the length of Bale's long dark body, providing all the warmth Tollar needed despite the cool mountain air all around them. Shell and Bale had spent their nights in the mountain peaks along the way, leaving the humans to the valleys and forests, where they camped together and slept in the tent-like gondola that Bale otherwise wore strapped to her underside.

But this close to the city, the dragons worried about dangers—especially after the thing with those sea monsters at that volcanic archipelago—and had taken their human companions with them up into the lofty heights.

Bale swung her carriage-sized head around, her black eyes glittering in the starlight, and nudged Tollar with the tip of her vast, soft snout. Tollar leaned against her, stroking her nose. Tollar had dark blue-brown skin but looked almost pale next to the dragon. Most of Bale was as dark as the night around them, endless black like a void but for some lovely amethyst bits on her wings and marbled streaks on her body.

"Too excited to sleep," Tollar whispered.

"Me too," Bale whispered back in her gentle teakettle voice.

"Did the others tell you what to expect?"

Bale tilted her head to the side in a way Tollar had learned to interpret as a shrug. Tollar wondered if it was more secret dragon business.

But there were humans in the dragon city too, a whole village of them, from what Balipar had been able to convey. And Bee always joked about how Tollar could make friends anywhere, but Tollar hoped it would be doubly true here, where she would be surrounded by people who loved dragons every bit as much as she did.

And since no human had ever raised a dragon from egg without ill intent before, Tollar expected the dragon scholars there would have plenty of questions for Tollar and Bale. Maybe they'd even learn what had happened to Bale's parents.

"What sort of name do you think they'll give you?"

Bale tilted her head again. "Do you know that Shell's dragon name is Mighty Alpine Evergreen?"

"Really?" Tollar glanced at the nearby green lump of Shell where he slept. He snorted but otherwise remained silent. "So that's the sort of name they'll give you?"

A glint of large teeth in the starlight indicated that Bale was grinning, something somehow made even worse by not being able to see all of it, though Tollar wouldn't have thought it possible.

Bale went back to watching the mountains around them, and Tollar stood with one hand resting on Bale's warm snout, watching the stars and taking in the beauty—until a whimper from the wing-tent pulled her into action. She swept back to Beenala's side, carefully kneeling between her and Croves to take Bee's hands. Beenala gripped Tollar's hand and jolted awake, voicing a sad little cry.

Tollar stroked Beenala's spiky brown hair and crooned, "It's all right, love. I'm here and everything is safe."

Beenala muttered something slurred and incomprehensible, still half asleep. Croves snorted awake, rubbed his shaggy-bearded face, and asked, "More night terrors?"

"I think so," Tollar whispered.

Croves grunted and rolled over, instantly back asleep. Tollar leaned against his broad back as Beenala snuggled in closer, her head in Tollar's lap. The two of them were probably about equal size around, though Beenala was a head shorter than Tollar and Croves a handspan taller. Croves was like a mountain, tall and solid, with scarred olive skin, shaggy black hair, and one dark-brown eye. Beenala was sturdy and round, with tawny skin and lovely warm-brown epicanthic eyes. Tollar hadn't liked how weary those eyes had been lately, the travel disrupting Beenala's sleep even more than the night terrors alone. She continued to stroke Beenala's mess of short light-brown hair, watching deep into the night until sleep finally claimed her, shimmering dreams filling the time.

Tollar jolted awake when Bale started shrieking. Beenala grabbed her hand and breathlessly whispered, "Come look!"

Beenala instantly had her face pressed up against one of the gondola's porthole window things like she hadn't since they'd been on their ocean crossing searching for the planned rest islands. Tollar hadn't meant to fall asleep on the approach, but that was the price of not sleeping much the night before.

She shifted to look out the porthole next to Beenala's and gasped.

There had been grey mountains all around them when they'd set out that morning—dull and grey and lovely, but just mountains. This, though? Tollar could barely comprehend what she was looking at. Beenala's artist eye was drinking it all in.

The mountains were red. Not sandstone, but red. Like rubies. And they glittered. Perfectly ordinary mountains otherwise. But that red! Tollar had seen a lot, but she had never seen anything like this. She had never seen anything not made by humans that glittered quite this way.

"I'm going to look." Tollar reached for the door of the gondola, but Beenala grabbed her hand.

"In flight like this? Are you sure?"

"I'm feeling okay today."

"There's no water down there if you fall off this time."

"Bale will catch me. And I jumped last time—it hardly counts. Besides, I won't fall off."

Beenala gave her a pinched look, but Tollar pushed open the flap and found the first of the handholds. She knew better than to look down right away, and focused on her climb. Still slower than she liked, but a steady and sturdy pace all the same, until she reached Bale's shoulder, where she could hold onto the spikes and stand despite the rush of wind tugging at her long dark braid.

Shell glided below and to their left, and Croves had done the same—climbed out of his riding sling on Shell's arm to stand on the green dragon's shoulder. Shell cried out and Bale echoed it. A moment later, the wind carried an answering call.

Tollar looked out ahead of them, trying to spot the dragons that were hopefully greeting them—it sounded like a greeting, but Tollar was certainly no expert. Her breath caught when she saw the large glittering shape on the horizon, towering above the peaks.

"Cursed ancestors, Bale! Do you see?"

Shell and Bale called out at regular intervals, their call answered—the cries of the other dragons responding. Tollar could make them out now against the bright red of the mountains. They were dark shapes still, one much darker than the others. But Tollar found it hard to concentrate on them as the bright shape ahead resolved into a shining white-and-black spiral, like a fire made out of gems, towering into the sky.

The dragons approaching were a kaleidoscope of colour, except the one in the lead who was massive and black as the depths of despair, a dragoness the shade of the midnight sky.

When she got closer, Bale's calls grew exuberant, and Tollar had just enough warning—a subtle tilt of Bale's wings—to grip the nearby handholds before her dragon tipped into a spiral. Tollar squeezed her eyes shut while her stomach churned. Hopefully Beenala had had time to grab onto something or she'd be flung all around the gondola. At least they knew to keep most of their things stowed in cargo pockets.

Bale levelled out of the spiral and that black dragoness was upon them, doing a wide flip over them before levelling out to fly next to Bale. The two dragons conversed in their language, none of which Tollar could understand. Then the black dragoness angled upward and dropped back so that her massive head was near Tollar, but she was otherwise far enough away not to collide with Bale in flight.

"You are Tollar," the dragoness said.

"Yes. Pleased to meet you, Mistress."

"We arrive soon. You will be greeted and oriented by at least one human, though newcomers do tend to draw a crowd. Bale will come up to the city with me, but all human-made gear must be removed beforehand."

"Understood. Thank you, Mistress." Tollar watched the black dragoness pitch upward, flying much higher and pulling ahead to lead the way. She was stunning, but Tollar's attention kept returning to the sparkling tower ahead.

Tollar saw that what could only be the dragon city spanned an impressive valley, the structure itself suspended by four arches rising from the very mountains around it. In the midday sun, the light refracted, casting prisms on the clouds and the mountains and the entire valley below. As the dragons angled in to land, Tollar made out the quilted green squares typical of northern-style farming and a scattering of little blocks of buildings that made up the village clustered to the west of the river that ran north–south through the valley.

Then her gaze was back on the city, trying to wrap her mind around the sheer size of it. It was like a sparkling little moon hanging above them. Stunning and intimidating.

As soon as Bale's feet touched the ground—they'd landed in a field outside the village—Tollar quickly set to work unclasping the gondola while Bale crouched so it wouldn't plummet to the ground. Beenala scaled the side to help her finish, and across the field, Croves was getting all the rigging off of Shell.

Once they were done, Bale plucked the pair of them off her shoulder and gently set them in the field before leaving in a flurry of wings and wind, churning up dust. Tollar shielded her eyes to watch her go until Beenala gripped her other hand.

Tollar turned and saw there was indeed a crowd of humans on the other edge of the field, all watching them while an older woman with greying red hair and a soft middle came their way.

Not far behind her, part of the crowd, were three women who were entirely too pale, and as they drew closer Tollar noticed the tallest of them had flame-coloured eyes. She gasped and squeezed Beenala's hand, leaning closer to whisper, "Bee, I think that's the family of pyromancers I told you about!"

As they all drew nearer, it became clear that one of them was indeed older, not quite as pale, with dark streaks through her long hair. The other two were much younger—maybe twenty? Younger than Draminedes back home. The tallest of them, nearly as tall as Tollar, had fire eyes and was white as a glowing bone, with fuzzy hair cropped close.

"Per Tollar," the red-haired woman said in prime with a polite bow. Balipar must have briefed her on their customs, and Tollar was delighted. "My name is Ondias. I'm the resident dragon whisperer."

"Pleased to meet you," Tollar said with a bow of her own. Beenala and Croves did the same as Tollar introduced them both. "What a delight to be here! The city is incredible!"

There was something brittle about the smile Ondias gave her, and Tollar quickly reviewed what she'd said. Had Ondias misinterpreted Tollar's prime? Did they use some dialect she wasn't used to? Tollar held a pleasant expression on her face and scanned the crowd, something getting her guard up.

The tall pyromancer was squinting at her and came forward.

"Ondias, who are they?"

"Help. Hopefully."

Tollar tilted her head, and Ondias gave her a startled look. Had she not realized Tollar understood Prairiean? She'd been pretty good with it even before Croves had started teaching her some of the dialect and the particularly filthy curses. She'd come here for Bale's naming ceremony and hadn't realized they'd needed her for anything. She wasn't exactly in the hero business at the moment, not in her condition.

The tall pyromancer was eyeing Tollar with an appraising eye. Then her expression lit up with surprise, and she gripped Ondias's shoulder.

"She's like me! But..." She watched Tollar, searching. They made eye contact and Tollar had a moment to wonder what the other woman thought of Tollar's silver irises, and then the pyromancer gasped. "Like me but with water!"

And then everything went still, some uncomfortable shifting from the rest of the assembled northerners. Some alarmed muttering. Tollar's limbs buzzed. Had this been a mistake? She didn't have a single weapon on her. Would Croves? Could they start a fight in the dragon city with the dragons' humans?

Tollar extended her senses into the ground below her, finding the water table, the river just near enough she could draw from it if she needed to. But with Bale nowhere in sight, how could they possibly get out of here safely again?

Beenala took her hand. Tollar squeezed back.

"Yes," Ondias said, her voice level, and the look she gave the young one was hard. "Tollar is part water demon—and she's already handed Loch a particularly embarrassing defeat."

The two held gazes for a moment, until the short young pyromancer gripped the arm of the tall one and pulled her back, murmuring. Ondias introduced them all then: Dionelle, Neesha, and Spark were indeed the fireborn women Tollar had heard of. Some of their friends and a mentor were on hand as well, but Tollar, usually good with names and faces and people in general, was still on edge and didn't retain as much as she'd have liked.

"I wasn't aware I was here to help," Tollar said carefully, switching to Prairiean to make it easier for them. "Has something happened?"

Ondias gave her a look. "I understand from the Guild you made a promise to the dragons."

Ah, she had, hadn't she? An awfully open-ended one, in a fit of desperation as she struggled to save her homeland.

"All right, then. There's something they need?"

"We need to stop Loch." This was from the short young fireborn, Neesha.

"That's a big task," Tollar said.

"You're not up to it?" Ondias asked.

"Well, you need a plan. And where even is he?"

"The dragons would like an idea of your power," Ondias said. "This goes far beyond Loch, with elemental fire and water demons at odds, putting the dragons—and all the rest of us—in peril. Your talents might help set some things right."

"Yes, what exactly can you do?" Neesha had come around Ondias, standing a respectful distance back. "All three of us are impervious to fire. Spark can create it from nothing."

Neesha glanced expectantly back at Spark, but she was frowning at the ground with her arms crossed. Neesha sighed and struck a flint, similar to the tool Beenala kept on her belt for starting fires. Neesha let a blaze bloom in the palm of her hand, letting it burn up her bare arm and back down, leaving no trace of injury and no sign of pain.

"Saying I'm impervious to water sounds a bit ridiculous, but it is true. The tremendous pressure and cold of the deep ocean doesn't affect me, though I haven't found the deepest part of the ocean to really test the theory. And I can breathe water."

Neesha seemed suitably impressed with that, and Spark at least stopped staring at the ground.

"Yes, that's all excellent, and you can report it to the dragons when you go up to the city," Ondias interrupted.

Spark gasped. "Ondias, no! How is this a good idea? A demonborn aquamancer? *Here*?"

Tollar felt cold. She hadn't been expecting the sting of rejection in what was supposed to be something of a holiday. After admitting to Beenala what she was, and admitting it to everyone back home, and being welcomed for it, Tollar had half-expected it would be fine in a place like this where there were others like her, albeit a different element.

Ondias's expression went frosty and turned on Spark. "Do you forget that I was here when the city fell? Do you really think I'd endanger it?"

Tollar cast a glance up at the city. Ondias had to mean that metaphorically, didn't she? Balipar said the city had been attacked, but they didn't know the specifics; it had been when they were a child.

"But she's like Loch!"

"I'm nothing like that monster," Tollar snarled, electric heat coursing through her limbs. Beenala took her hand. Right, losing her temper with these people was perhaps not the best course of action at the moment.

"She raised that dragon they came in with," Ondias said to Spark. "Stole it as an egg from Loch's people and kept it safe and appears to have raised it properly. We'll know soon enough. She's a proper Guild wizard, not one of these rogues. Don't *you* of all people question my judgement on matters of safety."

Spark looked ready to argue, but Neesha grabbed her arm and shook her head.

"Beenala is a pyromancer," Ondias continued, "and Croves is a dragon rider. They've all fought Loch and—"

"Wait, Croves?" Spark stood straight, appraising Croves. "Raia's brother, Croves?!"

"Aye, ye've met Raia and Dragon, have ye?"

Spark brushed past her to natter at Croves about his sister, who Tollar had heard plenty about but hadn't yet met, and Tollar's shoulders relaxed a touch. She approached Ondias, hunching a bit to be closer to the woman's eye level.

"All right," Tollar said. "Yes, I told the dragons I'd help them however I can, and I will. But you have to understand we just came here for Bale—for her naming. None of us are prepared for a fight, least of all me. And—"

Ondias waved an annoyed hand to interrupt. "Just let the dragons know what you can do for now. They've been eager to meet you since we heard you defeated Loch. You're right that we need a plan, and we need to take stock of your power before we can do that."

Tollar absently ran a hand over the gentle little swell of her stomach and glanced up at that marvellous city.

"All right, yes," Tollar said. "The Guild knows where to find me—you've spoken to Balipar, and they can help you fetch me back here later, when it's time."

An eruption of dragon noise came from above, a riot of them funnelling up out of the city while a couple dark blots came back down. One was Bale, and the other was that black dragoness who had greeted them—the one Tollar suspected was Bale's kin. She'd mentioned an aunt once.

"Abyss!" Spark called, delighted, as the two dragons landed on the edge of the field. The black dragoness gave Spark a quick nuzzle, but didn't answer any of her questions, leaning forward to speak to Ondias instead.

"She has been accepted. The Superiors find her rather strange, but not as strange as they had expected given the circumstances."

"Eh now, we did the best we could!" Tollar protested, crossing her arms.

"And I will be deeply interested in hearing about that later," Ondias said.

"And Abyss is no stranger when it comes to dragons who are unusual," Neesha added.

The black dragoness—Abyss, Tollar supposed—snorted a fireball at Neesha. Tollar went cold all over and had a ball of water in her hands too late. But the woman staggered back a step, laughing as the flame dissipated around her face. Right. Impervious to flame. Well, that would take some getting used to. Beside her, Beenala had her hands bunched up around her mouth, probably halfway to screaming if she hadn't been holding her breath. Tollar gave her a nudge and she exhaled.

"Up to the city now," Abyss said, holding a hand out to Tollar. "The Superiors are ready to see you."

"What, now?"

Abyss held her large hand out flat against the ground and said nothing.

"Beenala too," Bale said.

Abyss shook her head. "Mistress said this one only. The demonborn."

Bale put on her stubborn face and said something dragonish, and Tollar caught one of the only words she knew in that language—the one for *mother*. She half-expected anger and indignation from Abyss, but instead she tilted her head and looked sad.

"I knew your mother," Abyss said. Then she nodded toward Beenala.

Bale was pleased as she picked up Bee. Tollar cast a glance back at the others just before Bale picked her up as well. Abyss plucked up Ondias and that whole family of fireborn, the rest of the crowd dispersing.

The way so many of them, like Spark, clearly didn't trust her was more upsetting than Tollar could have anticipated. Wasn't she over this? Did it matter what these people thought?

It did matter. And she didn't like it.

But all they wanted was to know what she could do. She could show them, and Bale could get her name, and then they could go home, where she knew everyone trusted her.

CHAPTER THREE

Spark stood nervously next to Nanny, with Neesha on the other side of them—all three with Abyss—watching quietly as Tollar and her friend bowed low to the Dragoness Superior and formally greeted her. The dragons in attendance formed a kind of semicircle around the Dragoness Superior, with Abyss on one side with them, the new dragon, Bale, on the other, and Tollar in the middle. Ondias was off to the side, halfway between Bale and the Superior.

Tollar was perhaps a finger's breadth taller than Spark, with long elegant limbs, wiry muscles, dark blue-brown skin marked with white tattoos, and dark hair pulled back into a thick braid that hung down to her backside. She wore nondescript, utilitarian travel clothing in light fabrics, but for some reason they conveyed "fighter" in a way Spark couldn't quite parse. What had clued Spark into the fact that she was demonborn was her eyes. Where Spark had amber, fire-coloured irises, this woman's were silver, like the rivers through the valleys when Spark flew overhead with Abyss.

And until Spark had gone and upset her by making it clear she didn't trust her, the woman had had an exuberance about her that had reminded Spark of Bren. It made Spark want to trust her, and she felt bad for not being able to.

Tollar's companions seemed normal enough, even if Beenala—about a head taller than Neesha and Nanny but still not nearly Spark's height, and soft and round, though she moved in a sturdy way that conveyed strength, with light-brown skin and warm-brown eyes and plain brown hair that was short and spiky—was very nervous and fidgety. And Croves, though he wasn't with them up in the city, was every bit what Spark would have envisioned of Raia's brother. Taller even than Tollar and broad like Raia had been, he had a scarred olive complexion, shaggy dark hair and beard, and one dark-brown eye—the other covered by a patch. He was like if a mountain and a bear had decided to have a child. But he had a jovial air about him, much as Raia had.

"All right, show us," the Superior said, settling in with her chin on the floor and her focus on Tollar.

Tollar gracefully brought her hands up, cupped in front of her, and a floating ball of water appeared above them, out of nowhere. No, not nowhere—Spark's skin felt tight, and her sinuses complained. Tollar released it immediately, waving her hands, and the water disappeared, the relief instant. Out of one of the deep pockets in her pants, Tollar pulled out a small waterskin and drew the water out in front of her.

So far, she hadn't done anything Spark hadn't seen Nandara do with water, though it still made her uneasy. But then she pulled the water wider somehow, and it gained a shimmer before gushing out from between her hands. Spark gasped and stepped back so fast she slammed into Abyss's leg.

A water portal. Right here in the dragon city. What in all the hells had Ondias been thinking?

Some of the dragons were alarmed too, but the portal was only open a brief moment, all of the water pooling in an orderly blob in front of Tollar, before it closed again.

Nanny had drawn up closer to Spark, but Neesha had edged around to get a better look.

Tollar brought the large blob of water up and sat it around her head, like she was wearing a giant bowl. Her head and face were entirely encased in water. Very calmly and slowly, she inhaled. Water in, bubbles out.

Spark's stomach tightened as the woman stood there breathing water long enough to prove it wasn't some kind of trick. Neesha must have seen something worrying in Spark's expression because she was at her side, a hand on her arm, her amber-blue eyes shining.

"Come on, Spark. You gotta admit that's pretty cool."

Spark pressed her lips together.

Neesha tilted her head, her brow furrowed, and she leaned closer, whispering, "I like Ondias about as much as you do, but I really don't believe she'd let someone dangerous in."

Spark glanced at her mother but went back to watching the newcomer make shapes out of the water.

"I can make water do anything I want," Tollar said.

She made ropes of it, horrifyingly close to the ones that had been used on the dragons in the battle against Loch. She wrapped one around Beenala, who gave her a longsuffering look and then made a show of struggling against it. Then she pooled the water under Beenala's feet, turning it into a solid platform and raising her up on top of it. *And then* she pushed the platform of water around, Beenala with her arms out for balance, going along for the ride.

Impressive control. And, Spark had to admit, it *was* fun to watch.

But then Tollar started summoning water demon after water demon—their shapes shimmering in a semicircle in front of her—and even Neesha's shoulders bunched up at the sixth one. Tollar had gone tense too, but she summoned one more. And they all held. Waiting.

Spark held her breath. Was this it? If she let that many water demons loose on the dragon city, could Ondias, Neesha, and Nanny act quickly enough to thwart it? Spark had never been taught much aquamancy, especially not anything to do with water demons.

There was a lot of nervous shuffling from the dragons, and for a moment even the Superior's expression darkened.

"I can't actually *work* with this many, mind you," Tollar said, her voice tight in concentration, her body trembling with the effort. "Most I ever actually did anything with was five, and you've got to understand that I was driven by desperation and acting recklessly."

The Dragoness Superior smiled, but it was tight. "Yes, we are familiar with the occasional reckless desperation of the demonborn."

Speaking the rainpatter language of the water demons, Tollar began the slow process of sending them all away again.

When she was down to two, the Dragoness Superior asked, "Can you work with demon possession?"

Tollar frowned, banishing the last of them, then tilted her head. "I'm not sure I understand. I've pulled demons out of others, yes."

"Have you let a water demon possess you?" Neesha asked. "To use its power to boost your own."

Tollar stared at Neesha, eyes wide. "That seems foolish and dangerous."

"It absolutely is," Neesha said. Spark just knew her mother was grinning. "Effective too."

"No, I have not." Tollar turned back to the dragoness. "Should I?"

"We are merely taking account of your abilities," the Superior said.

"If I want a power boost, I harness another wizard," Tollar said.

This caught Spark's attention. Nandara had spoken of the skill frequently, but had never taught them. They hadn't had time before Loch's last attack, and it hadn't otherwise been urgent enough or required for Guild entrance, so it had fallen to the side.

"My strength's not what it was," Tollar said. "Took it rough after the fight with Loch and I'm not all the way back up to what I could do before. I've been harnessing others even more."

"Mostly me," Beenala squeaked. "I'm rubbish in a fight otherwise."

"And I've been learning to channel her pyromancy," Tollar said.

"Oh! What could she do if she channelled one of us?" Neesha whispered. "Double demonpower. That, I want to see."

Spark was relieved that Nanny shared her horrified expression. Neesha frowned and turned back to watch. The Dragoness Superior had asked for a demonstration, and the two women stood holding hands. Beenala closed her eyes and tensed while Tollar cautioned the Superior to stand back. Then she glared at the blob of water in front of her, churning it up.

It exploded in a rush of heat and steam, erupting toward the ceiling with a roar.

Spark screamed. She immediately clamped her hands over her mouth and felt her cheeks warming. She'd startled Tollar, and all the water collapsed, raining down around them. Tollar had pulled the heat out of it before it came down.

"Tell them about the boiling wave," Beenala murmured.

Tollar gathered all the exploded water back in front of her and explained how she could make water hot without pyromancy, though it was tremendously taxing, and that was how she'd kept Bale's egg safe—kept the hatchling inside alive—on the five-day river journey away from Loch's forces. And then of course she'd had to let go of Beenala's hand and show the dragons how she could in fact boil water with aquamancy alone.

Spark felt cold and sweaty, like she did after she'd had a flashback of the attack on Pasdale and Pappy's death. She rubbed her arms and stared at her mother's shoulder, Nanny in the periphery, reminding herself that they were perfectly safe here.

This stranger meant them no harm. Ondias trusted her, and Neesha certainly seemed to as well. Spark was beginning to see how a powerful aquamancer like this could be useful against Loch.

As long as she was, in fact, on their side.

"Thank you," the Dragoness Superior said, her tone a dismissal. "That was informative."

"There's, er, there's one more thing." Tollar shared a worried glance with Beenala. "Just because I *can* do a thing doesn't mean I *want* to or that I *will*. But if you're taking measure of what I can do... Well, I can control water, right? And everything alive is made up of quite a lot of water."

Neesha gasped. Spark didn't understand.

"Show me." The Superior's tone was clipped.

Tollar swallowed and glanced at Beenala, who nodded encouragingly. Tollar breathed deeply and focused on the dragoness's large hand in front of her, her own hand outstretched and her face scrunched in concentration.

And then one talon raised up. Awkwardly, like it had been shoved from underneath. The dragoness stood abruptly and snarled, her hand pressed firmly against the smooth shiny floor of the city.

Tollar took a swift step back, dragging Beenala with her, the pool of water trailing her like an obedient dog.

"My apologies, Mistress." Tollar bowed deeply. "I should have warned you first."

And *then* Spark got it, and her head spun. She leaned against Abyss and pressed her hands over her face, trying to breathe evenly, while all she could think about was how Loch had washed her off his water beast and plunged her into the river. How certain she'd been that she would die until she'd gotten a fire portal open despite the water surrounding her.

She could never fight something like this. She wasn't even sure she could fight *Loch* one-on-one, but this was so much worse. And could Loch make someone do what he wanted by dragging the blood inside them all around?

Spark rubbed her face and opened her eyes, and Nanny was nowhere in sight. She cast around and found Neesha dashing off behind Abyss. And there was Nanny, crumpled on the floor, sobbing from memories of her own. So that was a yes on Loch controlling people. Gods, what had he *done* to Nanny?

Spark shook her head and took a deep breath, then sat on the ground, gathering Nanny into her arms while Neesha stroked Nanny's hair.

Blood magic.

Spark glared at Neesha. "How can you say it's safe to have her here? She's dangerous!"

"She's no more dangerous than you or I. And she's on our side, Spark. It's a lot to take in, I understand that. But—gods, I can't believe I'm saying this—I trust Ondias's judgement. Only when it comes to the safety of this city, mind you. But still. I can't explain what it is, but I trust Tollar."

"Mamma—"

Neesha held up a hand. "Yes, it's a little terrifying what she can do. But Spark, that's what we look like to everyone else. You don't think *your* power is a little terrifying to people when they first encounter it?"

Spark glared.

"All right, have it your way." Neesha kissed the top of Nanny's head and got up. "I want to watch the rest."

Neesha was reckless; Spark knew that and had seen it in action plenty. So this was no surprise. But Ondias was not reckless. Ondias was whatever the exact opposite of reckless was. And Ondias had let this woman in.

"Nanny, Ondias is your friend. Do you trust her on this?"

Nanny sat up slowly, staring at Spark with dull eyes. She'd gone deep inside herself like she did sometimes when she was having flashbacks of her own. Spark had only had the horror of one night. Nanny had had that night followed by an entire year of terrors she had told no one about—not even Ondias, who was her best friend.

Spark didn't get up again until the dragons started moving, the Superiors moving off and Abyss turning around to nudge Nanny with her warm snout. Nanny blinked, and some clarity came back to her expression.

Spark repeated her question. Nanny stared thoughtfully and then shrugged, the gesture somewhat helpless. Nanny got up then and went around Abyss to where Ondias was talking with the newcomers. Nanny grabbed Ondias by the arm and pulled her away.

Tollar stiffened as she watched and then backed away, closer to Bale, where Beenala had retreated.

"You missed it," Neesha said when she spotted Spark. "But the Superior got Tollar to call up another demon and talk to this one. Nandara and others have tried, but they've refused—sometimes violently—to answer certain questions. But they listened to her." Neesha gestured to Tollar.

"You mean she talked to them about whatever Loch has done?"

"No confirmation that it's Loch, necessarily, since the demons can't really tell one human from another, except that demonborn stand out. But they told her someone has been directing a lot of their actions."

Spark felt cold again. "Any chance she's lying?"

Neesha tilted her head and braced her hands on her hips. "Ondias was right here, and she understands the demons. She verified what Tollar said."

Spark caught herself going to rub her face again, and took a deep breath to let it out slowly instead.

"Listen," Neesha continued. "She ran into some of those water beasts on the way here and confirmed they're possessed by water demons. That's why they're attacking. She and Beenala and Croves got the demons out of the water beasts so they didn't have to fight them, just got on with their journey. This is what I mean when I say we need her, that it's a damned good thing she's on our side. She's an ally, Spark. We need to treat her like one."

Now Spark did rub her face, but nodded blearily.

"Come on, let's go talk to her."

Ondias was already back from talking to Nanny, and she was there talking to Tollar as well. Tollar had her long hands folded over her abdomen, answering something Ondias had asked.

"—boy and a girl, but two seasons yet to go."

"Well, that will certainly factor into our plans," Ondias said.

"I'll fight him with you, if that's what you really want." Tollar glanced at the dragons. "We drove him off our lands, but there's no reason he won't try again."

"Your dragon's naming will be in two days, at dawn," Ondias said. "That gives us some time to make arrangements. You have accommodations? You understand this is a small village and we don't exactly get visitors—there's no inn here."

Beenala groaned, but Tollar seemed unsurprised.

"The gondola doubles as a tent. We'll be fine."

"What? No!" Neesha protested. "First trimester or not, sleeping on the ground has got to be a misery."

Tollar shrugged. "I was a mercenary until a year ago. I'm used to sleeping on the ground."

"Nonsense." Neesha waved a hand. "You can stay with us."

"Mamma!" Spark gripped her shoulder, hoping there wasn't too much panic in her expression.

"What?" Neesha barely glanced at her. "Jatt's barely around—I can sleep on the cot, and they can have my room."

They? And then a whole lot of what she'd just overheard clicked into place, and Spark leaned her head back, staring up at the sparkling ceiling. The terrifying aquamancer was here with her girlfriend. *And* she was pregnant.

"Thank you, Nee, that's a good idea," Ondias said. "Depending on what the dragons decide, we may need them here a while yet." She turned to Tollar. "We can also see if Stone will accommodate your other friend. He's got some room with both his children moved out."

Oh, Ember was going to absolutely hate that. But maybe all the strangers going to stay with Stone would be for the best. Keep them together and out of Spark's space. But it was too late—Tollar and Beenala were already gratefully accepting a real bed. Of course they were.

Tollar kept glancing at Spark, and that exuberance hadn't returned yet. Beenala kept twisting the hem of her shirt between her hands, like she meant to tear it into tiny pieces, and hadn't made eye contact with anyone since Tollar had done the creepy blood magic thing. Not that she'd been making much eye contact before that.

Right, great. Neesha was taking that whole "treat them like allies" thing a little too far. Spark sighed. She wished she saw whatever it was that Ondias and Neesha saw, that she could see Tollar as anything other than a threat.

CHAPTER FOUR

Neesha left the little storage room with the cot in it meant for Jatt, and headed upstairs to check on their guests. Ember had gone to bed already like a sensible creature, and there was no sign of the dog, but he was probably with Spark in the forge, where she was banging away on something. That she was using a hammer, and so noisily, meant she was still furious at Neesha for inviting Tollar and Beenala to stay with them. Dionelle seemed plenty angry at both her and Ondias, and had been with Nandara since Abyss brought them down out of the dragon city.

Stone had been happy to welcome Croves in, and Neesha supposed they could have all gone there.

But if she was being honest, Neesha was fascinated by the idea of another demonborn, and having Tollar close at hand meant she could learn more from them in the short time they were staying. She tapped on the door and waited a moment, Tollar's voice the one inviting her in.

Neesha peeked her head in the door. "I just wanted to—oh, I didn't mean to interrupt."

The two of them were snuggled on the bed, Tollar sitting with her back against the headboard and Beenala curled up between her and the wall with her head in Tollar's lap while Tollar stroked her short hair. Feeling her cheeks warm, Neesha began to withdraw.

"Please, join us," Tollar said, her words only lightly accented.

Neesha stepped in and closed the door behind her, but didn't move any farther into the room. Tollar watched her expectantly.

"I just wanted to check in on you and apologize for Spark and my mother," she said, switching to prime so Beenala could follow the conversation. Neesha hadn't heard Beenala speak anything but prime.

"It's fine," Tollar said.

"It's not fine," Beenala grumbled, not moving.

"I'm… used to that sort of thing," Tollar said. "I tend not to let people know what I am and what I can do."

"And look how well that did you!" Beenala sat up, giving Tollar a meaningful look.

"Yes, well, everything's fine at home, and we'll be back there soon enough."

"They'll come around," Neesha said. "You don't have to leave right away."

"I don't expect we'll be leaving before Bale is ready. It was an eleven-day journey. Well, twelve, really—we took an extra day once we crossed the ocean. Bale's never gone nearly so far before. She'll want rest."

"*I* want rest," Beenala said.

Tollar smiled. "Yes, thank you for offering us your room. I really am quite used to sleeping on the ground, but Beenala is not."

"That's quite the trip. Eleven days? Pasdale, where I'm originally from, is a five-day flight from here. I did there and back again with little time to stop, right before Spark was born, and it was misery. Learn from my mistakes." Neesha chuckled.

Tollar tilted her head, and Beenala's brow was furrowed like she was trying to solve a particularly difficult puzzle.

"Sometimes the language difference distorts meaning," Tollar said. "Did you just infer that you're Spark's mother?"

"Oh, right." Neesha was startled, so used to everyone just *knowing* that she didn't even think there'd be confusion. "Yes. I spent seventeen years in a magical coma right after she was born and didn't age all that time. I've started aging again now that I'm awake, and it might be a little accelerated? But it's only been two years, so it's hard to say."

Beenala and Tollar had both gone still and silent. Tollar was the first to shake herself out and speak.

"Yes, well, that sounds like an entire story, or several, and now you're going to have to tell us everything. Come, sit." Tollar tucked her legs in to make some more room at the foot of the bed and gestured for Neesha.

Neesha sat and told them about Draxli and his influence on Loch and how the dragon city had fallen despite her efforts.

"I refuse to believe that city has ever been anything but magnificent," Beenala said.

"It used to be a lot taller."

"Well, it's recovered magnificently," Tollar said.

Neesha shrugged. Tollar wasn't wrong, but that didn't make it any less painful to have lost the city even briefly. Sometimes the loss felt like a dream. In a way, it had been. She'd slept through the worst of it and most of the recovery.

"I am a bit surprised your people let you fight. That they dragged you across the world so close to birth," Tollar said.

Neesha rolled her eyes. "I'm sure they'd have preferred I sat around at home incubating the whole time. I got plenty of 'think of the baby' lectures from Ondias. And I *was* thinking of her! I was thinking that she needed to have a future. It was less that I got dragged into battle and more that they couldn't stop me."

Tollar made a thoughtful noise and Beenala watched her warily.

"You came all the way across the world with babies on the way," Neesha pointed out.

"Oh, I wasn't criticizing you doing what needed doing," Tollar said. "Just surprised, given what I know of your people, that they let you. It's tricky—balancing conflicting needs for the future."

"They wouldn't have done it without me." Neesha sighed wearily and steeled herself, finishing the story, how she'd finally prevailed over Draxli and at what cost. "So that's why Spark grew up to be fearful of aquamancers. Please don't take it personally."

"Mmm." Tollar pressed her lips together and watched Neesha. "And what about you?"

"Me? Oh, I know better than to paint entire groups of people with the same brush. Loch's an outlier, and he and Draxli have given aquamancy a bad reputation, but it's ridiculous to assume from that that all aquamancers are terrible people."

"Excellent!" Tollar grinned, her eyes sparkling. "I think that means we're friends now. You look like you could use some of those."

Beenala huffed in what Neesha interpreted as feigned indignation, and Tollar laughed. She had a full, hearty laugh, one that came from her entire body, and Neesha decided that yes, they were friends now.

"Bee is always astounded at how I make friends everywhere I go."

"And you've been *everywhere*," Beenala said. "It's like you know the whole world sometimes."

"And I told you I'd introduce you, but all you can talk about is how there's never any beds!" Tollar chuckled and Beenala said something teasing in Upalan while giving Tollar a longsuffering look that was also utterly smitten. Tollar touched Beenala's face and took her hand to kiss her knuckles, and then Beenala flopped over, curling up against Tollar again.

And Neesha burst out crying.

"Oh!" Tollar gasped.

Tollar and Beenala both sat up in alarm, leaning forward. Tollar reached one hand toward her, palm up, both of them hovering nearby while Neesha couldn't stop crying or feeling like an utter fool and she had no idea why.

"Would you like a hug?" Tollar finally asked.

Neesha nodded and absolutely crumpled against her. What in all the hells? But it felt so good, wrapped up in Tollar's embrace, like it used to when Neesha was little and her mother would comfort her. Of course, Dionelle still offered comfort when Neesha needed it, but it was different as an adult.

Tollar and Beenala whispered to each other softly in Upalan, and Neesha assumed they were talking about what a ridiculous fool she was. But Tollar stroked Neesha's hair and gave her space to collect herself, offering her the basin—well, the water from it, anyway, floating there in front of her. Neesha laughed and shook her head, wiping her eyes on her sleeve. She got up to wash her face in the basin after Tollar poured the water back into it out of the air.

"Sorry," Neesha said. "I have no idea what that was all about."

"No need to apologize. Seems you needed that. Everything okay?"

"I thought it was." Neesha watched Tollar's earnest expression. "I... don't have any friends. Just my mother's friends and my daughter's friends and the man I nearly married, but he's ten years older than me anyway. I'm not sure there's anyone here actually my age. Maybe some of the teachers? I think… maybe I've been a bit touch-starved. And the woman I love lives in a place where we'd never be allowed to be together the way you two are."

Tollar gave her a sad smile and held her hands out, palm up. Neesha had seen her do it before, like a kind of invitation.

"That means something?" she asked, gesturing to Tollar's raised hands.

Tollar grinned and made Neesha sit with her and explained her culture's greeting customs, where the hands-out thing meant it was okay to touch someone. The nods, like they'd given Ondias, were the polite don't-touch-me greeting. There were less polite greetings as well.

So when Tollar offered her hands again, Neesha took them, chuckling nervously. Beenala only bowed when Neesha glanced at her.

"Bee's shy, and gets overwhelmed with too much physical affection," Tollar explained. "And Croves's appetites are far beyond anything I'm interested in."

"Ah, you both sound a bit like Jatt, then." Neesha shrugged. "I expect my appetites are more in line with Croves's, especially if he's anything like his sister."

"I haven't met her, but they do sound alike."

Neesha sighed, "I do think that maybe I let my appetites get in the way of making friends when I was younger. I am perhaps not great at making friends."

"You're doing fine now." Tollar appraised her. "Your hair is lovely. May I braid it?"

Neesha shrugged. Tollar shifted so she could sit closer and gently ran her fingers through Neesha's hair, detangling a bit, offering some advice on oils Neesha could use to tame the frizz, and then dividing it all up and plaiting it. Silent tears streaked Neesha's face while they chatted, a lot about nothing. She learned that Tollar loved books, and that while Beenala was a farmer, she was also an artist and a touch devastated that her paints had been corrupted on the trip.

"My sketchbooks are simply not going to cut it."

"There are a lot of artists here, including Jatt," Neesha said. "He'll probably be around tomorrow, and we can ask him if you can borrow anything."

And they spoke more of their relationship—how Beenala would be considered Tollar's wife, though where they came from no one bothered with anything so formal. And back home, looking after their farms, was a man named Draminedes who would be something like a husband to Croves.

"But he likes men and women, Croves," Tollar said. "So do I, but not to the same extent—like I said about big appetites, he's never wanted to just pick one and settle. Dram's a fine lad and doesn't mind if Croves wanders a bit looking for someone more feminine now and then."

"And that's why he's got you," Beenala said.

Neesha threw her a glance and then over her shoulder at Tollar, who was grinning.

"Like I said, sometimes Bee gets overwhelmed, and sometimes I need more than she wants to give, and so I have Croves."

"Wait, is he...?" Neesha glanced at Tollar's growing belly.

Tollar smiled again. "Yes, Croves helped make this possible. But not like you're thinking. I'm not interested in that sort of... activity. I used some aquamancy. It's simple, honestly."

"Huh." Neesha sat forward while Tollar finished off the braid. "I've never met a throuple before. Is it complicated?"

Tollar laughed. "I'm not sure I'd call it either complicated or a throuple. More like two couples. A solar system of coupledom with me as the sun in the centre?"

Neesha laughed, turning to face her. "You've got quite the ego!"

"And well earned! You've seen what I can do. Is it wrong to embrace it?"

"I don't think so, not at all." Neesha sighed. "Of course, my ego got me into a spot of trouble. Well, I guess it was less to do with my ego and more to do with everyone around me being intimidated by what I can do instead of getting out of my way and letting me do it."

"Oh, I'm sorry, that's terrible."

"Toll's a bit of a bully about it and just sort of makes everyone get out of her way so she can do the thing." Beenala beamed at Tollar.

"Well, yes. It helps that I'm usually the biggest person in a room. And, you know, usually have my sword with me. Though anyone who knows about these"—Tollar indicated the white lines tattooed across her cheeks—"knows well enough to listen."

"Ah, the tattoos mean something?"

And so then Neesha got a crash course in southern warrior culture—that the lines indicated rank, and the little white dots on Tollar's chest, shoulder, and arm represented all the people she'd helped—and Tollar got up to dig her sword out from under the gear they'd stashed near the foot of Neesha's bed.

Neesha could barely lift the sword, much to her own embarrassment and Tollar and Beenala's amusement. Beenala was not a fighter, but she was a farmer, and she couldn't actually do anything with the sword, but she could at least hold it properly.

"Spark made me a dagger for my birthday. I have no idea how to use it, but I should probably learn."

Tollar's face lit up. "I can teach you."

Beenala groaned. "Every time."

"Hush, love. If Neesha wants to stab someone, she should know how to do it properly."

Neesha burst out laughing. "If you want to teach me, I'm happy to learn."

"Ah, yes. You are rather small. And soft." Tollar chuckled and Neesha took the teasing in stride. It wasn't like Tollar was wrong. "I can see why they maybe didn't get out of your way and let you save them."

"They got it right, eventually, but not till after I'd lost seventeen years. Spark convinced them, embracing the fireborn power in her own gentle way. She didn't leave them with much choice. She's gentle, but the stubbornness runs deep in our family."

Tollar frowned. "I heard a bit of what happened to your family. Not specifics like your magical accident, but that your people rejected you. It made me too cautious for too long. Didn't trust my own people like I should have until Bee made me see the truth."

"You're lucky then." Neesha's smile turned sad. "It's good here—we're safe and accepted. But I just don't know about elsewhere. We certainly can't go home."

"You're making a new home," Beenala said.

"Well, trying. You've shown me I have a lot missing."

Tollar squeezed Neesha's arm. "It's okay to want things that are just for you. Sometimes those things overlap with what's best for everyone, and even if it doesn't, taking care of yourself takes care of your community."

Neesha sat back, remembering what Nandara had said yesterday. "Maybe you're right. I just have no idea what that looks like."

"It looks like this," Beenala said, patting her knee.

"You've got a dragon who will take you anywhere. Come visit us sometime," Tollar said. "I expect I'll be back here again before long, given how conversations went today."

"Yes. I don't think we can stop Loch without you."

"But it's okay to enjoy the light between the darkness," Tollar said. "I think it's probably the only way to get through the dark in the first place."

Neesha got all teary again, Tollar and Beenala politely ignoring it this time.

"Thank you. I might take you up on that—your home sounds lovely. If I can get Spark to warm up to you, I'd like to bring her with me. She and Ember have a good thing, but they'd never be allowed to do that back home. She knows that there are places beyond here where she can have what she wants, but it's different to actually see it."

"She's not the only one who needs that, is she?" Tollar arched her eyebrow in Neesha's direction.

Neesha laughed. When had she last laughed this much? "That's another story that will have to wait. I really should let you get to sleep."

Tollar and Beenala bid her goodnight, and Neesha left them. She still couldn't remember when she'd felt so relaxed, when she'd laughed so much. Certainly before Spark had been born. She'd never had friends before, but she could certainly get used to this.

She'd just hit the bottom of the stairs when Shadow, the dog, trotted past and then Spark came out into the front hall, startled that Neesha was still awake.

"Well, if you're just going to bed now, it must be awfully late," Neesha said.

"Mamma, what are you doing up?"

"Making friends."

Something about Spark's expression crumpled, and Neesha's chest tightened. She didn't know how to help Spark get over a lifetime of training that had set her against every aquamancer everywhere. But she certainly had to try, even if it made the road bumpy in the meantime.

IN THE SKIES

Something nudges Bale awake, and she opens her eyes to darkness. She hadn't thought she'd be able to fall asleep in the first place with all the excitement, and now she's being woken up in the middle of the night, which isn't fair at all.

She blinks and realizes that it is not the middle of the night, but Auntie standing over her.

"It is time," Void Behind the Stars says. "Dawn will reach the city in a few minutes, and the other dragons have assembled."

Bale stretches and takes in the view of the surrounding walls of the clan tower. Many of the surfaces, especially where dragons would walk or sleep, are sparkling polished aventurine while the walls and ceilings glitter with crystals. Auntie Void (a name Bale knows she can never say out loud, especially not in this city, even if she really wants to) pushes some old bones and jerky Bale's way.

This is the one thing that Bale is definitely not going to miss about the dragon city. She loves how beautiful it is. She loves spending time with Auntie Void and learning about her parents. She loves the cold wind under her wings and the sunshine on her scales and the way *everything* glitters. But she hates the rations almost as much as she hates Loch. She hates the rations even more than she hates Ocean Deep.

And Bale is pretty sure she hates Ocean Deep even more than Auntie Void does.

Bale crunches on the dry old bones. She nearly coughs on the dry old meat. She's certain she's going to need to go down to the river for a long drink or choke on it. It finally goes down.

Bale misses eating real food. It's only been a few days, but she'd even be glad to eat a fresh monkey or two. She got to eat her first dolphin on the trip here, and after that, having to eat dry awful rations is particularly unfair.

But it's time to get her name.

This is the entire reason they made the long dangerous journey. Bale is curious about what name they'll give her and if she'll remember to answer to it. She's used to the name Toll-mum gave her.

She wouldn't say any of that out loud, though, not even to Auntie Void, because she doesn't want Toll-mum to get in trouble. It isn't really her fault. She hadn't known any better. And Bale likes her name.

She hopes she likes her dragon name.

But Ocean Deep and some of the other grumpy dragons will be there and involved in choosing her name. The whole dragon community decides on names together. Bale really isn't sure about that part.

"They didn't give your cousins any shameful names and they will not give you a shameful one," Auntie Void says.

While trying to reassure Bale yesterday, Auntie Void told her about how some of the council tried to insist Glacial Sunfire didn't get a proper name because she's small and strange. She has no magic and doesn't speak.

Bale is still learning about dragon politics, but she knows Auntie Void is powerful and influential. She gets away with things a lot of other dragons wouldn't. So Bale believes her that she won't be given a terrible, embarrassing name. Auntie Void will make sure it goes well.

She follows Auntie up out of her clan tower and into the cool pre-dawn air. On a loop past the village, Bale checks for Toll-mum, but there aren't many humans up and around yet—just a few in the central market. She's disappointed not to see her, but it isn't dawn yet. There isn't anything to report, and Bale doesn't think she has time to go down and see Toll-mum anyway.

They spiral up around the outside of the city, all the way up to the top. She swoops in behind Auntie and slides down the wide tunnel, down and down until they drift into the centre of the chamber, gliding to land right in front of the Superiors.

There are a lot of introductions to start, with Majestic Sunrise greeting Auntie by name and Bale as "young one." Getting a real name will be nice, because she's tired of them all calling her that. Even if she is young.

"And do you understand what this ceremony entails?" Majestic Sunrise asks.

"Auntie explained."

Many of the gathered dragons hiss and snarl while Majestic Sunrise glares. Auntie Void sighs and stares. The other dragons are always snarling about how Bale has no manners. It makes Bale want to bite them. Auntie Void says not to try biting anyone until she's full grown and knows what she's doing. Auntie Void says she'll do all the biting for both of them in the meantime.

Auntie Void is patient because she knows that Bale *does* have manners, but they're human manners. Meadow at World's End and Devouring Fogbank tried *really* hard to teach Bale dragon manners. They really did. But it was too late. Toll-mum had already imprinted human manners on her before Meadow at World's End could do anything about it. When she really thinks about it, Bale can remember what dragon manners are supposed to be. But human manners always come to her mind first, and it always makes dragon manners seem ridiculous.

It isn't anyone's fault, and the council of Superiors agree that human manners are better than being Loch's prisoner. Well, Ocean Deep doesn't agree, and that is why Bale wants to bite her.

Bale is never sure exactly how to sound like a proper dragon, but she thinks to the way Auntie and Toll-mum have been joking about how the other dragons sound.

Bale bows her head low, almost to the floor, and addresses Majestic Sunrise again.

"Yes, Dragoness Superior. My kin has explained everything to me."

Majestic Sunrise gives a satisfied sniff. Some of the other dragons grumble more and then settle down.

"This young one does not have parents to speak for her," Majestic Sunrise says to the gathered community. "We have accepted the petition of her kin, Void Behind the Stars, to act as her attendant. Void Behind the Stars will open the proceedings."

Auntie steps forward and bows politely to the Superiors.

"I wish to honour the magnificent colouring the young one inherited from my brother and his mate. I put forth to the council and the committee that the young one be named Shimmering Cloudwall."

Bale tilts her head. That's a good one! But the whole council and then the wider gathered community gets to discuss it and offer amendments, and Bale is nervous about that part. She'd be less nervous if Ocean Deep wasn't here, but she is here, and she's got a gleam in her eye that Bale doesn't like at all.

"An excellent choice," Majestic Sunrise says.

"Perhaps Shimmering Stormcloud?" Heart's Blood suggests.

Auntie nods her head. "An apt suggestion that more directly honours her parentage, but I had hoped to distance her from them somewhat, given the tragic nature of their loss."

Auntie has told Bale that her father, Auntie's brother, was a black and white dragon (mostly black) named Summer's Eve Lightning, and that Bale's mother, who was entirely several shades of purple, was Bruised Horizon.

"Distance her all the way, then," Ocean Deep snarls. "Call her Shimmering Dungheap."

Bale's insides get hot like the first time her fire came, and her scales itch with cold, and she twitches to keep from lunging at Ocean Deep to bite her. But Auntie lunges closer to the other dragoness, snapping her jaws. Other dragons are roaring in displeasure.

"You will maintain comportment," Majestic Sunrise snaps at Ocean Deep. "I will not tolerate further juvenile behaviour from you."

Ocean Deep bares her teeth but subsides.

Bale still wants to bite her.

Other dragons make suggestions and others yet debate them, but Bale has stopped paying attention. She keeps glaring at Ocean Deep while her blood courses hot and loud in her ears like magma. What she can tell, when she gives it any attention, is that Auntie and Majestic Sunrise are leading the discussion. Auntie said while preparing Bale for this that Majestic Sunrise will have the final say.

Once the members of the dragon council have had their say, Majestic Sunrise opens the discussion to the entire community.

"I think," a greenish dragon Bale doesn't know begins, "that Heart's Blood was on the right track—perhaps not in connecting the young one with her parents, but in giving her a more traditional name."

"Oh, this lot doesn't hold with tradition." Ocean Deep again. "Just call her Shimmering Fool and be done with it."

The entire assembly of dragons erupts into noise, and Bale actually lunges at Ocean Deep this time, but Auntie spreads her wings to keep Bale back, and not a moment later, Majestic Sunrise and two other Superiors use their teeth to haul Ocean Deep out of the chamber entirely. One of the Superiors doesn't return, to ensure that Ocean Deep stays away.

Bale is angry but also relieved.

"Shimmering Cloudwall is a perfectly acceptable name for a normal dragon," Majestic Sunrise says, "but this young one is far from a normal dragon. As Emerald Starlight has suggested, a more traditional name may be in order to overcorrect for her human ways."

Bale gives Auntie a desperate look. While the other dragons toss around suggestions, Auntie very quietly says, "Traditional just means imperious. They will not embarrass you."

They decide to replace Shimmering with something more impressive. Tremendous Cloudwall, Imposing Cloudwall, Magnificent Cloudwall. Auntie said they aren't trying to embarrass her, but Bale isn't convinced.

"Like her kin, the black colouring makes her foreboding," Heart's Blood says.

Bale worries someone is going to suggest Foreboding Cloudwall.

"She's typically quite cheerful," Emerald Starlight says. "Perhaps Solemn Cloudwall?"

At this, Bale isn't even sure she understands the point of dragon names.

"Something darker than solemn," Auntie suggests.

"Brooding Cloudwall," Majestic Sunrise says.

No one argues and Auntie gives a nod. And that's it, Bale has her silly dragon name, which she still isn't sure about. But all the other dragons erupt in celebratory fire.

CHAPTER FIVE

T he apricot light of the morning sun glinted off the city, casting delicious sparkles over everything and giving Tollar a moment of peace. It was an incredible place, and befriending Neesha had certainly made things easier. But Tollar preferred it when she was alone, or with only Beenala and Croves. Too much tension otherwise.

For the moment, Tollar embraced the calm of dawn and waited in the field next to Neesha's and Spark's home to learn Bale's dragon name. She'd thought that sort of thing might be a secret, but Neesha had assured her it wasn't—it just wasn't something dragons volunteered, and humans generally didn't ask.

Well, Tollar would have to start asking.

Starting with Bale, just as soon as she came back.

The side door nearest to where Tollar stood creaked open, and she tensed until a glance back told her it was Neesha. Which she should have expected, since it seemed like Spark was practically nocturnal, usually awake well into the middle of the night and sleeping until midday. Tollar's shoulders came back down again. And Neesha, her eyes on the city above, hadn't noticed.

She'd been here two years and still walked around staring up. Tollar didn't expect she'd ever get tired of looking at the city if she lived here too. It wasn't just the beauty of it, or how it changed with the lighting—it was the sheer improbability of it. What kind of magic did it take to hold that thing up there? There was no way it was architecture alone.

"How long does it take—do you know?" Tollar asked.

"I think it's a bit different for every dragon, but once it's over, they all stream out of the city to celebrate. This is the fourth naming ceremony I've been here for and the eighth dragon."

"Do you know why they wait a year to name them?"

"Because," Ondias said, coming around the side of the house to join them, "more traditionally—before they started bringing their eggs here for extra protection—it was rarer for them to survive a full year. A juvenile living long enough to be named is as much cause for celebration as when an egg hatches. As far as we've been able to discern, Bale is the only surviving dragon of her clutch, which is unfortunately more typical. And indeed both of her parents are dead."

"Well, her dragon parents, at least," Neesha said.

Tollar smiled and Ondias scowled. Ondias wasn't particularly keen on the idea of humans adopting a dragon, and certainly many of the dragons agreed, though there was no denying that Bale would be dead or broken and enslaved if not for Tollar and Beenala.

Yesterday, Tollar had spent a good chunk of time up in the dragon city with Ondias talking with the Superiors about how they'd managed to raise Bale. There'd been reports from Minty and Cloudy, of course—and Tollar would have to find out their actual names now—but they'd all wanted to learn more from Bale and her humans directly. Ondias had been rapt, more fascinated than horrified, because there was a lot she hadn't known—like the moulting.

And after that, Tollar had spent some of the rest of the day teaching Neesha what to do with the dagger Spark had made her, while Beenala had made friends with both Jatt and Stone. Stone, like his daughter, had light-brown skin and black hair, and was thick around the middle and tall, almost what Croves would look like if he were a normal-sized tall person. Jatt, the artist and Beenala's new best friend, was tall as well and dagger thin, with black corkscrew hair and brown skin a touch lighter than Tollar's. He had the same green eyes as Nandara. Beenala had made more friends than Tollar, and Tollar wanted it noted for the record that she hadn't even teased Beenala about it at all.

If she was being honest with herself—which she tried to do more these days—the fact made her feel like rubbish and not in the mood to joke around.

Oh sure, Ondias wasn't intimidated by Tollar's power—she disliked Tollar for entirely different reasons. Mostly the same reasons Tollar's own mother didn't like her. So that was going great.

Spark still had a sheen of panic in her eyes whenever she tried to be polite and talk to Tollar, and Dionelle hadn't appeared at all since they'd arrived. The air was thick with the tension of Tollar's very presence, no matter how hard Neesha had been trying to smooth it over.

But that friendship with Neesha was the saving grace. Tollar and Beenala both agreed that they should bundle Neesha off with them when they left. She very clearly needed a change, even if she didn't seem ready to accept that yet.

The dragons burst out of the city, shrieking and roaring, startling Tollar. They spiralled up into the sky, looping and circling, calling out in a joyful cacophony. It was a riot of colour, dappled with light from the city, but Tollar had a hard time picking Bale out of the blaze. She and Abyss looked so similar from such a distance.

The side door opened again and Beenala blundered out, yawning and rubbing the sleep from her eyes. She stood next to Tollar, who draped an arm around Beenala's shoulders, and the two of them stood watching with Neesha—Ondias off to one side—until Bale and Abyss circled down to join them.

"Have you got a name, then?" Tollar asked Bale.

"I'm Brooding Cloudwall!"

Ondias gave a strangled gasp that was lost to Beenala's immediate protest, "That's entirely too ominous a name for someone as cheerful as you are."

"Dragon names tend toward the imperious," Abyss said.

"And what about your name, Mistress?" Tollar asked.

"Void Behind the Stars."

"Ah yes, I see what you mean."

Ondias made a sputtering noise, her face red and stormy, while Neesha's entire body shook with silent laughter and she crammed both hands over her mouth. Tollar had no idea what she'd just done to elicit their reactions, but she wasn't getting lit on fire, so it must be fine.

"Do you have a preference for what we should call you, then?" Tollar asked.

"I think it suits to have the humans use my human-derived name. Even Void Behind the Stars is an approximate translation." She said something in dragonish, which of course Tollar didn't understand. "That is my true dragon name."

"Yes, I think you're right. Bale, what does your name sound like in dragon?"

Bale humoured her, growling out something that sounded like every other dragon grumble she'd ever heard.

"Auntie is right, I think. I like it better if you call me Bale."

"Are you all right?" Neesha asked Ondias, her voice still thick with amusement, a hand on the woman's shoulder. "Do you need to go lie down?"

Ondias was rubbing her face. "I think I'm going to need to rewrite a couple of my books." She turned to Abyss. "If you don't mind, Mistress, I'll have some questions later—plenty of them—about how Bale is different from the other hatchlings, including your own, especially Bolt."

Ondias bowed to the dragons and left, leaving Neesha still snickering behind her hands.

"So what was that?" Tollar asked.

"Oh, Ondias has just had her entire notion of dragons rewritten in a brief interaction."

"Human scholars believe dragon names are sacred," Abyss said. "Perhaps because of the ceremony. We don't offer our names, and humans convinced themselves it would be rude to ask. Not until Spark."

"Spark and Abyss have been keeping this from Ondias for two years," Neesha added.

"Ah."

Bale and Abyss left then, in a torrent of leathery wings, stirring up a gale and debris. Neesha moved in closer to the two of them now that everyone else was gone.

"You don't like her," Beenala said. "Ondias."

"She's my mother's best friend, but I've never gotten along with her. I missed a lot, you understand, but when I woke up, there was a cruelty about her that hadn't been there before. It's softened a touch since we brought Dionelle here, but the last two days are the kindest I've seen her since I woke up."

"Well, she certainly doesn't like *me*," Tollar said.

Neesha bit her lips. "I'm sorry. I think she finds you fascinating—both your magic and your relationship to Bale—but your lifestyle challenges a lot of notions she has about how polite society should work."

Tollar rolled her eyes. "Yes, I'm familiar with how certain northern cultures believe families ought to be structured."

"I really thought you'd made that part up," Beenala whispered in Upalan.

"No, they really are this ridiculous," Tollar whispered back.

Beenala also rolled her eyes.

"While I don't actually know what you just said, that's still exactly how I feel about it too," Neesha said.

Tollar had heard about the woman, Yenette, that Neesha was pining for. It didn't do anything to dissuade Tollar's urge to take Neesha with them when they left.

"Well, I suppose it's refreshing to have someone simply dislike me rather than be terrified of me for no good reason."

"To be fair, it's a pretty good reason. It's just not fair for them all to be afraid of you but not of me or Spark or Dionelle."

Tollar sighed. It didn't actually do anything to make her feel any better. It was the blood magic that had really done it. It was a small place and word got around. Dionelle was especially upset about it, with good reason, as it appeared Loch had used quite a bit of that sort of thing against her.

Tollar had started pacing, her jaw clenched, and she took a deep breath, working to calm herself. She was going to hold Loch down—maybe with some ugly magic—and let Neesha incinerate him from the inside out.

"Would you like to practice stabbing things?" Tollar asked Neesha. "I suddenly feel like stabbing things."

Neesha laughed and Beenala rolled her eyes.

"You have fun with your pointy toys," Beenala said. "I promised Stone I'd go consult with him about adding some trees to his plot. He's got an orchard, but it's separate from the rest of his crops."

Stone had already let Beenala in on a fertilizing secret that only the farmers in the valley had known about—using dragon droppings to improve yields—and Beenala was determined to get him using his land properly. Tollar smiled as she watched her go.

"Are you going to get changed?" Neesha asked. "Or do you tend to fight dressed like that?"

Tollar had worn her travel gear to train with Neesha yesterday, but today had chosen the nicer dress she'd brought with her specifically for Bale's naming—the lovely blue one with Beenala's family vine pattern on it in silver stitching.

"Honestly, I don't do much actual fighting," Tollar said. "Mostly my pointy toys are for show and when I don't want people knowing exactly what I can do."

Neesha fell silent for a moment. "Right, yes. I never hid my power, but Spark's done a lot of the same. She doesn't really need tools at all for the blacksmithing, but doesn't want people to know the truth. I suspect for the same reasons. Which makes it more ridiculous that she's afraid of you. And she knows that, and she's embarrassed, and that's of course not helping either."

Tollar smiled politely. They'd spoken of all this yesterday, and knowing it didn't make her feel better. It made her feel foolish, which she wasn't especially fond of. But teaching Neesha to use weaponry made her feel the opposite of foolish, particularly when Neesha was such a good student.

A touch bloodthirsty, that one.

"I guess I should have some pointy toys I know how to use in case I need to hide my power. Or end up somewhere with no fire. At some point, I'm going to need to leave this valley. Dunno where I'll go, but not having people afraid of me—or at least not afraid for the wrong reasons—is probably helpful."

Tollar shrugged and they headed for the house.

"So you've really saved all those people," Neesha said, gesturing to Tollar's tattoos, "without letting them know what you are?"

"Well, anyone who doesn't know that being demonborn is even a thing has no reason to suspect *that*." Tollar followed Neesha inside to retrieve their respective weapons from the upstairs bedroom. "But I often don't go back to places after I've helped, so I don't feel as weird about letting them see what I can do. I can usually downplay it a bit, and I often work with demons. Swibs don't usually know any better anyway."

Neesha was thoughtful as they headed back outside to practice in the field next to the house.

"I want people back home to know what I can do," Neesha said. "I think it might help set a few things straight, after all the damage Loch and Draxli have done. But I can see how it might get me in over my head if strangers knew the truth."

They both paused while Ember let the dog out and gave them a polite nod before disappearing back inside. Shadow bounded over, pressing his backside against Neesha's legs while Tollar crouched down to scritch his ears. She hadn't expected there to be a dog here, but it was nice that there was, especially for Beenala, who missed Ash so badly.

"Yes," Tollar agreed. "My power is impressive, but enough people could overwhelm me if they decided to. Or take me by surprise. Best to avoid that kind of situation."

Tollar adjusted Neesha's grip and her stance, then gave her a watery target to stab. It was a vaguely humanoid blob approximately the size of an average person, and Neesha lunged in with a big overhand swing aimed right at the approximation of a face. Well.

"Not like that, dear. They'll see it coming."

Neesha pressed her lips together, still telegraphing her moves with her body, but at least less with the flailing. Her arms and shoulders were where they needed to be. Tollar let her practice a bit more, gently correcting until her form was less sloppy. She also let the water splash out from each stab in the approximation of blood-spray, but it didn't slow Neesha in the slightest. And Tollar supposed that given everything Neesha had endured, she couldn't really blame her for the angry violence she harboured.

"Have you been taught much what to do without weapons?" Tollar asked.

"Um, light them on fire?"

"I can teach you more, if you'd like."

Neesha put the dagger back in its sheath while giving Tollar a sceptical look. "I'm not very big and about as sturdy as wet bread. Is there really much of anything I can do?"

Tollar brightened. "Oh yes! I can teach you how to use momentum and leverage. You could knock me down."

Neesha's sceptical look intensified.

"No, really. If I can beat Croves in hand-to-hand combat, I think you'll do all right."

"I assume you've had years."

"Well, yes, but giving you a couple of things now, things you can practice with Spark once I leave, will give you more to work with than you've got right now."

Neesha shrugged. Tollar began by teaching Neesha her favourite weak points on the body and then how to twist out of an arm grab. That was about when Spark woke up, noise from the forge alerting Tollar. She finished up the lesson and was grateful Neesha didn't comment on it when she made an excuse and went to find Beenala.

Bee was thankfully still with Stone, and Croves was there as well, though he seemed a touch bored with nothing to fight and no interest in farming or the scholarly pursuits of wizardry. Maybe Tollar should enlist him to help her teach Neesha how to fight.

Stone was kind and welcoming, much in the way Neesha was, and it helped set Tollar more at ease. She sat back and watched Beenala making sketches of how Stone might alter his land use for better yields.

"And this way you're working more with nature than against it," Beenala said. "Especially to conserve water if you get dry spells."

"Well, if that river ever dries up, we'll have quite the problem on our hands," Stone said. "But I take your meaning."

They took their evening meal with him, and Tollar was hesitant to go back to Neesha and Spark's house. Beenala had clearly picked up on it.

"Toll? We could do something else, if you can think of something, to give us an excuse not to go back there right away. But... there's not really a whole lot going on here."

Even the market was a small affair, not much in the way of variety, and most of it alien to Beenala. They'd brought some supplies, but a lot of their fresh food—sturdier produce, mostly—had been ruined along with Beenala's paints when they'd had to spend the night on that volcano while crossing the ocean.

Beenala hadn't complained about the northerners' strange cuisine, but Tollar knew she wasn't happy with the unfamiliarity of it. They had some dried goods from home that had survived the trip, but it wasn't the same.

"If I'd thought of it sooner, we could have gone down to the trading camp in the plains south of here," Tollar said. "From what I understand, we probably just missed flying over it on our way in."

"The dragon city is the best part of being here," Beenala said. "I know we can't go in it without permission from the Superiors, but can we just sort of... let Bale take us for a fly around it?"

"Yes! Brilliant!" Tollar kissed the top of her head and summoned Bale.

They hadn't seen much of their dragon daughter since arriving, as she was either getting interrogated by Ondias and the other dragons, or off spending time with Abyss. And Tollar hadn't had much time to enjoy the views going up to or down from the city, with all the concerns they'd initially had. Flying around just to see it all would be a fantastic use of the remaining daylight—though as far north as they were, there were a couple hours of that left.

Bale drifted down from the dragon city, pleased to give them a tour around the valley and skimming around the spiralling tower of the city. Up close, there were intricate whorls in the gemstones—diamond and obsidian—and it was even more apparent that the shape was meant to mimic flame. It was dotted with cupped balconies, many of them holding dragons as Bale zipped past.

She held Beenala and Tollar in her hands this close to the city. Even though they were used to sitting between the spikes between her shoulders when she flew, that sort of thing was frowned upon by other dragons.

But once Bale set down on a plateau on the eastern edge of the valley, she put the two women on her back and lay down. It was cool despite the summer heat, so it was nice to stay closer to Bale's body. And they had a stunning view of the city and the valley glittering in the late-day light, and watched as the red-orange hues of sunset lit up the city so that it truly looked like flame.

They didn't talk much except to exclaim how lovely it was or point out the few dragons they knew. Abyss and Shell had flown past. As it grew later, the possibility of Abyss being right next to them without them knowing grew likelier.

Tollar sat on Bale's warm back with Beenala pressed at her side, her head on Tollar's shoulder and Tollar's arm draped around her while the city glittered ahead of them, lights flickered in the valley below, and a whole world of new stars sparkled above.

The vaguely familiar constellations brought a past adventure to Tollar's mind.

"When I was last on the northern plains," Tollar began, "the caravan ended up stopping in a village on the edge of this sort of marshy area. I mean the plains are all just kind of flat and grass, and the marsh wasn't a whole lot different, except that the grass had a different sort of quality to it, plus some gaps where there was open water. So anyway, we're on this grassy marshy plain, and it was overcast and kind of damp, and some of the others were pulling out the ale a touch early. But not long after sunset, just as twilight was fading into proper night, the grass in the marsh lit up with thousands of these little sparkles, like a field of stars on a turbulent night."

"Sparkly grass?" Beenala's voice was full of scepticism.

"Oh, it wasn't the grass itself—it turned out it was all these little beetles with glowy arses. They're called glitterbugs. After a while of sparkling in the grass, they fly around, little blurs of light like falling stars. It was a field full of whole new constellations."

"The stars here are so strange."

"I never thought about what the stars at home looked like until I came north for the first time and realized how different it all was."

Tollar pointed out the few northern constellations she knew. "Oh, and that tight crescent of stars there," she pointed, "is the bow of Dutana the huntress."

Beenala remained quiet and Tollar glanced down, but Bee wasn't watching the stars or the city—she was focused on Tollar.

Beenala sat up. "Do you know that your eyes reflect the starlight?" she said, then snapped her mouth shut and pressed her lips into a thin line.

If it wasn't so dark, Tollar was certain she'd see Beenala's cheeks grow pink.

"Do they now?" A fond smile tugged up one corner of Tollar's lips.

Beenala sat taller and leaned forward, her fingertips brushing Tollar's jaw, sending a tingling ripple down Tollar's arms. Tollar steadied both hands on Beenala's waist and Beenala cupped Tollar's face, drawing her near. Beenala's lips were warm, soft, and dry. Tollar's heart fluttered, heat filling her to the tips of her toes. Beenala tilted her head and pressed her lips firmly to Tollar's before gently leaning away to settle in again with her head once more on Tollar's shoulder.

It had been over a year since the two of them had properly come together, but this was only the third time they'd kissed. Beenala's kisses were special little gifts, given with utmost meaning, the deepest of intimacy. The first had been when they'd come home from the war, properly home, properly a family, safe and together. The second had been when Tollar had discovered she was pregnant. And now, in the dragon city with the glitter of strange stars overhead.

Beenala snaked her arms around Tollar and gave her a squeeze before drawing back, one hand splayed across the gentle swell of Tollar's growing babies.

"I'm glad I came," Beenala whispered. "This is much better than that trip to Port Sawulxo."

Tollar laughed. "I told you that wasn't a normal trip."

"Is this what it's always like?"

"No. This is the most stunning place I've ever been. Except maybe home."

Beenala huffed, and Tollar could practically feel her rolling her eyes.

"You ready to go home yet?" Tollar asked.

Beenala watched the stars, caressing Tollar's belly. "No, not yet."

"Well, that really is a change!"

Tollar chuckled when Beenala playfully bit her shoulder and then sat away, taking Tollar's hand and twining their fingers together while she watched the city and stars shine.

"Wait, are you asking because *you* want to go home early?" Beenala sat up straighter again, facing her in the darkness.

Tollar sighed.

"Toll! Really? I know you're uncomfortable, but it's *twelve* days home! And it's so beautiful here!"

"Yes, this place is stunning. I'd like it better if it were only the dragons."

"Not everyone is uncomfortable about your power. Stone doesn't care, and I doubt Jatt does either—you should talk to him. And yes, Ondias is kind of miserable, but that's not about you—she's just stuck like that."

Tollar chuckled. "Yes, but only one of the people like me will even talk to me."

"And she's practically your best friend!"

"You're my best friend."

"I'm a bit more than that now." Beenala squeezed her hand. "You're allowed to have more friends—there isn't a quota, you know."

Tollar resisted the urge to sigh again. "It shouldn't bother me. And I think maybe if it wasn't for... you know," she waved her hands vaguely around her head. "If it wasn't for that, it probably wouldn't. But I'm still tired and grumpy and just feeling a bit raw."

"I know—hormones and all that." Beenala huffed and stared out at the valley as it reflected and refracted the starlight. "We don't have to stay. Or we could stay but not quite as close as we have been. We could camp in one of the valleys nearby, or down with the traders."

"You hate camping," Tollar laughed.

"Well, yes. Maybe I'll stay and you can go camp with Croves. He's bored out of his mind."

Tollar sat with the suggestion. She really didn't want to be here, and hated that she didn't. She'd promised to help them, and felt like there was more she could do here even if it would be a while before they pooled their talents and went after Loch.

"Or, if you don't want to split up, or maybe not leave entirely while we think on it some more, it's only two days to the nearest city, and it was lovely—the beds were *wonderful* there," Beenala said. "We could retreat, but just a little. Give you time to regroup and everyone here to get used to the idea of you without you actually being around."

Tollar drummed her fingers against her chin. She didn't like the idea of giving up, and going all the way home felt like giving up. But maybe some space was in order.

"What do you think, Bale?"

"I can drop you off and come back."

Ah, yes, Bale would want to spend as much time here as she could.

"That sounds reasonable. Why don't we go find Croves before it gets too late and see what he thinks?"

But Beenala was right, Croves was bored, and Tollar expected he'd be as relieved to be elsewhere as she would.

CHAPTER SIX

Spark didn't like the spiky silence engulfing the room as Neesha packed up supplies of food—things that would travel well even though their departing guests would mostly be travelling through settlements and cities, not through wilderness the way Spark was used to going between this valley and Pasdale.

But there was no doubt Neesha blamed Spark for the early departure.

And it wasn't like Spark didn't feel bad about it. A lot of people here had been around when the city had fallen and didn't trust the alleged world's best aquamancer. It wasn't only Spark. But a lot of people saw her as a leader, maybe even moreso than they did Ondias when it came to certain things. And if she'd been more accepting and less nervous, been hanging out with them the way Neesha had, maybe other people would have relaxed too.

She just couldn't. Her brain knew she was being ridiculous, but her heart didn't care.

There was also the way Nanny hadn't left Nandara's house since Tollar's display up in the city. Nandara had been scarce as well, caring for Nanny, from what Spark understood. Spark had gone there to visit, but Nandara had turned her away. Nanny was an emotional wreck, Nandara had explained.

"Mamma, they said it's only for a few days."

Neesha scowled, barely glanced at Spark in reply. "They shouldn't have to leave at all."

Neesha had been learning a lot the last few days, and Spark hated that she felt like she was somehow taking something special from her mother.

"But they're probably right, a quick break will give everyone some time to get over fears."

"They're not going to come back," Neesha snapped. "They say they are, but they're going to go to Big Water until their dragons are ready to make the long journey home."

"You could go with them to Big Water," Spark said desperately, wanting to make it better for Neesha somehow. "I'm sure Abyss would be happy to have a couple more days with Bale to come get you. Or you can just take a fire home. I'll leave the forge burning."

Neesha set down the bundle she'd been preparing and stared down at her hands, clearly considering it. She shook her head.

"It's probably better if I stay here and make sure people actually do what Tollar hopes her absence will allow."

Neesha finished what she was doing, and Spark's stomach was tight as she followed her outside to see Tollar, Beenala, and Croves off. Beenala had been petting Shadow, but he trotted over to lean against Spark's legs as soon as she came out. Ember was standing back while Stone was handing over a couple of jugs of wine to Croves.

"I expect you'll save one for Tollar until she can imbibe again."

Croves chuckled and packed it into their travel structure with more of their gear. Spark was pretty sure she'd heard Tollar call it a gondola, but it looked like a really sophisticated tent. It had folded down to store next to the house while they'd had other places to sleep, but now it was a long, narrow boxy shape with walls lined with cargo netting for storage. And then there was just barely room for the three of them to lie side by side on the floor.

She wanted to go have a closer look, but didn't think she'd get to inspect it long enough to satisfy her curiosity before they strapped it to Bale and left.

Ember came to stand next to her, slipping her hand in Spark's. Ember was loyal and had stayed away from the newcomers solely because their presence upset Spark, but she'd definitely been curious about them. And occasionally reported the things she'd heard from Stone.

Jatt had been a traitor, making friends with all of them—sharing art supplies with Beenala and chatting with Tollar about how they'd both had ancestors from the southern archipelagoes.

He and Ember had both been subtly trying to get Spark to warm up to Tollar. Neesha had been far less subtle.

"You're being ridiculous," she'd said at least once a day. "And you're going to drive away an ally we sorely need."

Neesha had been right, and Spark felt cold as Tollar folded her mother in for a hug, Beenala leaning in too, saying goodbye. Spark forgot sometimes how tiny her mother was, her big personality making up for it, but right now she looked so small. And once she turned away from her new friends, Spark saw that Neesha was also fighting back tears.

Spark's breath caught in her chest.

Tollar must have seen something in Neesha's posture, because she frowned and called Neesha back.

"Croves, bring me the big map," Tollar said over her shoulder. She touched Neesha's arm. "You can travel through fire, right?"

Neesha muttered a response, and Spark didn't like where this was going. But why? Neesha was allowed to have friends and a life outside the city, wasn't she? Spark had friends. Everyone had been waiting for Neesha to grow into herself, but instead she'd spent two years just the same. She'd gotten into the Guild and then just hung out with Spark or Nanny all the time.

But Spark didn't like the idea of her having *these* particular friends.

Tollar had unrolled a large map and spread it out over top of the coiled loops of straps to buckle the gondola to Bale. She traced her finger from one side of it to another. Despite herself, Spark edged closer. It was a world map, and Spark hadn't seen many, but the route Tollar traced had to put their home almost exactly on the opposite side of the world.

Ondias made an appearance, and Neesha retreated then. She didn't go back inside, but rather stood back while Ondias gave some last-minute instructions, telling the travellers which routes to avoid if they didn't want trouble. Croves chuckled like maybe he wouldn't mind a bit of trouble.

Jatt showed up and stood next to Spark. She glanced around and saw that a bit of a crowd had started to gather. Nandara was there but no sign of Nanny.

Tollar, who had looked down all morning, disappeared into the gondola while Beenala and Croves unspooled the rigging.

And then a distant dragoncry went up in the east and an instant later the whole valley erupted with noise. Spark tensed. Shadow barked and ran for the door, pawing at it until Ember went to calm him. The most recent scouting party had left at dawn, so this couldn't be them returning already. It sounded like a welcome, but it was off, the way it had been when Abyss had unexpectedly appeared.

"Ondias, what's going on?" Spark whisper-hissed. "Is something wrong?"

"You know as much as I do." Ondias shrugged.

Croves and Beenala kept up with their work, but Tollar had come out at the noise, watching the skies.

Spark hated how long it always took for the welcoming party to return, and this morning it felt like an eternity. But there was a familiar trio of dragons with them on the return.

"Wait, is that—?" Ember gasped.

"Well I'll be damned," Croves said. He stopped everything and watched the approach.

The trio had been heading for the field where Ondias took her meetings with dragons (and sometimes riders), but changed course to head for the group assembled next to Spark's house. As they drew closer, she could confirm the markings on the dragons. It was indeed Dragon, Flame, and Ice with Raia, Barlo, and Eltir.

"I told ye it was him!" Raia shouted, practically leaping off Dragon before he'd barely had the chance to land. He caught her before she fell to her doom and set her properly on the ground, and then she was running full tilt toward them, leaping at Croves to attack him with a hug. While she had a darker terracotta skin tone compared to Croves's paler olive complexion, they otherwise looked shockingly similar, with a similar build and features.

"Ach, I can't believe it's you!" she said, grabbing his shaggy beard in two fists before bashing her forehead against his in what Spark suspected was some form of affection between the two of them.

"I hear ye made some trouble for Loch."

"We tried to find ye." She sounded desperate and apologetic. "We saw Shell! Got him free, but he took off south again and we couldn't catch up."

"Aye, they took Shell and made him fight," Croves said, expression darkening. "Said they'd kill me if he didn't do what they wanted. I'd wondered. He came back once without chains and made a nuisance of himself till they caught him again."

Raia's jaw worked, her expression searching Croves's. "Ach, look at all the new scars. What'd they do to ya?!"

Croves shook his head. "It don't matter. What matters is they can't do it no more. Ye shoulda been there when we finally took the bastards down. Well, mostly Tollar."

And here, Croves turned to make the introduction, and Raia threw herself at Tollar, sweeping her up in a massive hug. Shadow, the traitor, pranced over to join the fun, clearly recognizing Raia.

Spark's excitement at seeing her friend turned sour, no matter how ridiculous it was. Of course Raia was excited to see her brother and meet his new companions. It was like finally getting Nanny back. That day, having Nanny and Neesha both just suddenly there, had been a lot.

"—going to be an aunt," Tollar said, bringing Spark back into the present.

Raia beamed at her and gave Croves a look. "You went out and found a wife?"

"Nah, got me a nice lad back home."

Croves took a moment to sort the tangle of relationships for Raia, who only laughed some more, slapped him on the back, and went to greet Beenala, who shied away. Shadow trotted to her and she focused on the dog. Raia caught on quick, gave Beenala a polite bow, and went back to her brother.

"I've heard so many wonderful things about you," Tollar said, a hand on Raia's shoulder.

Raia cackled. "Liar!"

"Well, all right, Croves did tell me about the time the two of you had a fight and you left him naked and passed out drunk on a beach infested with sandflies," Tollar admitted, eyes shining. "But I think we've all gotten up to plenty of no-good, except maybe Bee."

Barlo and Eltir joined them and Raia made quick introductions, and she called a quick greeting over to Spark, who thought maybe she'd finally get a toe-hold on this conversation, but Ondias elbowed her way in and cut them all off.

"What are you doing back?" she asked Eltir. "We haven't heard from you in months and weren't expecting you."

"We got the message Croves left for us outside Meeri Bay right before he up and moved to Upalint," Eltir said. "And we were going to head down there to see him and came across some information that couldn't wait."

"We decided to bring it to the Guild," Raia said.

The trio of dragon riders looked back to their dragons, who hadn't left yet, and Spark was startled to see that Ice had been carrying a travel wagon-bucket thing much like the one they had here for supplies. And there were four wizards climbing out of it.

"Oh stars," Ondias whispered. "Grand Chancellor?"

Tollar whispered a curse under her breath.

Wait, that was the Grand Chancellor of the whole Guild? Here? Spark gave her mother a wide-eyed look, and Neesha had her brow furrowed, watching the old wizard's approach.

"The short of it is, we found where Loch's gone to," Raia said.

The wizard Ondias had addressed as Grand Chancellor had joined them. She was very old, with wrinkles on her wrinkles and hair as white as Spark's but in a long braid. She was a smidge taller than Ondias, and her skin was cool brown, and her eyes warm amber.

The Grand Chancellor nodded. "He's with his forces on the equatorial archipelago of Biterna."

Croves cursed and Spark didn't immediately understand why. But as they all continued to talk, sometimes talking over each other and in multiple languages, while Shadow joined in by barking at them, it became clear that this island nation was nearest to the place Loch had most recently attacked, a seaside city on the southern continent, where Tollar and her friends had handed him an embarrassing defeat and chased him off their land.

Tollar seemed particularly angry, though more at herself. "If I hadn't fallen off Bale—"

"None of that," Beenala said, a hand on her arm. "There's no guarantee you'd have been able to do anything but exhaust yourself. You fell off the dragon in the first place because you'd run yourself ragged. The geyser worked and gave us some space and some time."

"Not much time now," Grand Chancellor Dira said. "We've learned some more of his abilities, especially after being able to thoroughly study the fireborn women and their skills—and get a brief accounting of yours."

"Wait, you know why he's so strong?" Neesha said.

"He's really not like me?" Tollar asked.

"He uses demons, but he's not demonborn, no. And that's reason to have hope," Dira said. "But along with confirming that Biterna is where Loch's retreated to, Eltir and his companions discovered that he's also planning to renew his efforts on the Port in the spring."

Tollar groaned and dragged her hands over her face.

"We beat him once, we'll beat him again," Croves said.

Tollar broke away and stood next to the gondola with Croves and Beenala, having a tense whispered conversation. Spark came in closer to the group of wizards around the Grand Chancellor, and Shadow finally came back to lean his butt against her leg.

"That's good news, isn't it?" Spark said. "That means he's not going to be causing trouble for anyone else before then. That gives us almost a year—"

Neesha touched her shoulder and cut her off. "Port Sawulxo is in the south. It's winter there right now."

"And that's cutting it awful close to when these babies are coming," Tollar said, a hand on her belly.

Spark's chest tightened. "So what does that mean? Do we load up the dragons and head there now or...?"

"We've got to be careful," Tollar said, rejoining them. Beenala was coiling up the straps for the gondola again, and Spark had a sinking feeling. "He's overtaken that island and the population is basically his prisoners. Some, like our friend Draminedes, managed to escape. But we can't just wipe it out. We've got to get Loch while protecting the islanders."

Neesha glanced at the other two unloading their things. "You're staying?"

"Seems like we at least ought to hear what news Dira has. And Croves wouldn't mind some time with his sister. It's been a while, you understand."

Yes, all perfectly reasonable, and Spark hoped she kept her expression neutral because she didn't need to upset her mother or the aquamancer any further, nor did she need another lecture from Ondias. She leaned down to pet Shadow and keep her expression concealed. And as the others continued to talk about the situation, it became clearer it would take all of them to dislodge Loch from his seat of power without destroying an entire nation.

Individually, the fireborn and Tollar had handed him defeats, but they hadn't stopped him for good. He certainly wasn't going to stop on his own. Spark turned away from the discussions, Shadow trotting along after her, and she went inside, Ember and Jatt joining her.

"Finally go time," Jatt said.

Spark shrugged. "We'll see. The Guild takes forever to decide on anything. They're even worse than the dragons."

But Spark had a pretty good idea of what they were going to decide, and she didn't like it. How were they supposed to beat Loch when she couldn't trust their allies? She had to learn, clearly—she couldn't be the reason it all fell apart. Spark groaned and dragged her fingers over her face.

Ember put her arm around her. "Hey, we'll figure it out."

Spark sure hoped she was right, or they were all doomed.

CHAPTER SEVEN

Neesha and the others all crammed into Stone's house, of all places, as it was the only place big enough other than the dragon city, but that didn't have any chairs, and Dira and the other council wizards were *old*. They were exhausted from the trip, and Stone, who had been hovering around through the aborted goodbyes and new arrivals, had offered them his space when it became apparent there were a lot of plans to make.

The only thing Neesha cared about for the moment was that Tollar and Beenala had chosen to stay. At least to hear details and start planning. There was no question that now that they knew where Loch was, they were going to get the bastard.

How they were going to do it could take up all the intervening time between now and when Loch planned to attack the port city again.

Neesha agreed with Spark's impulse that they needed to get moving *now*. But she had also learned the importance of having even the vaguest of plans before jumping into action, and any plan was going to involve at least one of the fireborn learning to work with Tollar.

Dira questioned the wisdom of Tollar's involvement while she was pregnant, but Tollar quickly shut that line down, insisting they had to at least explore their options. She would do what was necessary to stop Loch.

Tollar paced back and forth in front of the windows while Dira continued to lay out what they knew. Loch was not demonborn, but it appeared that he could control a demon possession the way Neesha and Spark had learned to. That was deeply troubling. But it meant he and Tollar were evenly matched in power, though hers was stable.

"So what we really need is a plan to get close to him," Neesha interrupted. "We knock the demon out of him and then he's just like any aquamancer."

"Yes." Dira nodded slowly. "I believe that is the end goal to work toward."

"Tollar and I can do it," Neesha said. "I've been pulling demons out of Spark for two years now. I'll do that part, and Tollar can do whatever it is aquamancers do to kick the shit out of each other."

"The island is like a fortress," Raia said. "And he'll be smart enough not to have a fire going. It's likely he knows ye can travel through it."

"Couldn't I learn to travel through water the same way?" Tollar asked. "It's rainy season, not to mention he's on an *island*. Plenty of fodder for a water portal."

"That's far too risky," Dira said. "If you somehow become trapped there, it will spell the end for everyone. The fireborn women can rescue each other, and in a pinch the dragons could do it. You do not have the same kind of elemental allies."

"Okay, but Tollar doesn't need a water portal to travel through the water," Neesha said. "Could she get in alone and—"

"No!" This came from both Beenala and Croves, startling Neesha.

Tollar had stopped pacing to rub her face in an irritated sort of way. Neesha had learned enough over the last couple of days to know that Tollar tended to go it alone and overextend herself, though with the fatigue caused by her pregnancy, the extent of what she could do had changed.

And she'd also nearly died—according to Beenala—when she'd fallen off Bale in exhaustion after defeating Loch and ended up spending an entire day at the bottom of a war-polluted river.

"A year ago, I could have done it," Tollar snapped. "A year from now, I might be able to do it alone."

Beenala moved swiftly from where she'd been leaning against a counter to stand in front of Tollar with her arms crossed, staring down at their feet.

"You're not doing it alone. Not ever again." She gestured at the room full of people. "You have help, and you're going to take it."

Tollar took one of Beenala's hands and sighed a long shaky exhale as she turned to stare out the window.

"This is absolutely going to be a concerted effort," Dira said. "We don't have a year—we have months. The island is a watery fortress, one with a lot of the king's resources behind it. Part of the reason Loch pulled out of Pasdale was that it was more difficult to defend so far from Golden Hill. He's regrouping, but I'm certain he eventually means to retake the city. So the four demonborn need to work together in whatever capacity works best given everyone's abilities and state of health."

Dira was confident that Dionelle would be part of the solution, but she still hadn't left Nandara's house, though Nandara herself was on hand. As was Ondias.

"I've heard the account of Tollar's abilities," Nandara said, standing from her place at the dining table next to Spark, who was staring miserably at the top of the table. "And I've mentored all three fireborn. I understand Tollar and her companions are already quite proficient at harnessing power, and I believe that's an avenue worth exploring."

Dira shared a look with the council wizards before replying. "I believe that's something we're going to have to attempt under the careful watch of the Dragon Superiors."

Neesha sat upright in her seat near Dira. "Wait, is that why Nandara has put off teaching us to harness each other? She's been talking about it for years."

"I was going to teach you," Nandara said. "But when I consulted Grand Chancellor Dira, she had reason to believe the results could be catastrophic."

Tollar turned at that. "How so? I've done harnessing and been harnessed. The world failed to end."

"And I would have preferred studying the effects before you experimented with it," Dira said.

"Then come up to see us more often," Tollar snapped.

"As you've said, you've done some harnessing already," Dira said, ignoring the outburst. "It gives me optimism about the results of more than one demonborn wizard being involved in that sort of spellcraft. We still need to use caution."

Tollar looked like she was ready to snap again, but Beenala was still there, squeezing Tollar's hand to calm her.

"With all due respect, Grand Chancellor," Beenala began, even managing to maintain eye contact, "the caution—or the *over*caution—of the Guild is why we're where we are."

"Aye," Croves grumbled. "Ye had the chance to move on Loch when he was still a pup."

Dira held up a placating hand. "We have been overcautious, yes. I accept that we are past the point of risks being necessary. That being said, we do have some time, and it's wisest that our risks be calculated ones. All four demonborn have taken risks and made sacrifices, and it is best to minimize further sacrifice."

"We should learn harnessing," Neesha said. "If what Nandara has said is true, it would mean Spark and I wouldn't need to use risky demon possession for large-scale magic. It also means we'll all have someone with us—extra support—so that no one has to lose seventeen years again."

Neesha's chest tightened, and she started pacing without realizing it until she was over by the windows with Tollar.

"No one needs to go through that again, least of all you," she said to Tollar. "It was bad enough what Spark went through without me. We're not doing that again."

"*Calculated* risks," Dira agreed. "We have time to be smart about this. The dragon riders' intel gives us an advantage this time. We have time to plan."

"So our first step is—" Neesha was interrupted by the front door swinging open.

Dionelle came in, small and alone, her amber-blue eyes wide and bright, near panic like she had been when they'd first reached Pasdale to kill those sodding ice dragons. Her pale skin had a troubling ashy-grey flush.

Spark gasped and was the first one to her, Ondias and Nandara not far behind, guiding her in and getting her into a chair.

"I should go," Tollar whispered.

"No. We're going to need her, and she needs to deal with this," Neesha said. "She wouldn't have come if she didn't think she was ready."

Spark was already whispering to Dionelle to get her caught up. The older woman's face was pinched with worry, and she stared at the table without looking at anyone. But she was there, and that was a start.

"We have our next step," Dira said. "Ondias, can you arrange with the Superiors for a time tomorrow to have them oversee initial training on harnessing for the fireborn women?"

"Will the dragons come out to battle?" Neesha asked. "With the Guild finally willing to confront Loch more directly, will the dragons as well?"

"Let's get some sort of plan together first," Ondias said.

"Very good." Dira stood. "Is there somewhere I might lie down in the meantime? It is not a pleasant trip from the Guild, even with plenty of preparation. Not at my age."

"I'll be stayin' out with Raia and them," Croves said. "There's plenty room for the council here, no?"

Stone welcomed the council in, showing them to the two spare rooms that had once belonged to River and Ember. Then Stone left Neesha in charge of the house and headed back to work. Croves left to find his old blaze, and Ondias went to arrange things with the dragons. That left Nandara and Beenala with the four demonborn.

Neesha sat across the table from Dionelle and Spark while Nandara hovered nearby. Tollar and Beenala hadn't moved from their place near the windows.

"This is our chance to make him pay," Neesha said, giving her mother a hard look. "But we're going to need you and Spark to cut the shit and work with Tollar."

Dionelle glared.

"Don't give me that," Neesha shot back. "You've had it worst of all. I get this is going to be difficult for you. But you're still demonborn, you're still powerful, and we need you. If Tollar was some secret agent or whatever it is you've worked yourself up into believing, she'd have obliterated us all by now."

"Neesha's right," Nandara said, sliding into the seat next to her. "Harnessing can go very wrong very quickly, even with normal wizards, if everyone involved isn't calm."

"It's advanced magic," Tollar said, pacing around. "It has its dangers at the best of times. I watched one of Loch's people—Karthiry—drain wizards to death, harnessing them against their will." Tollar's voice was hard and her jaw tight as she spoke. "We managed to save most of them, but there's a couple who nearly died that haven't recovered yet. It's like they've got no magic left."

"Dira shared the report with us," Nandara said, looking troubled. "We'd known it could have ill effects from practice gone wrong. I'd never heard of it being used maliciously like that before."

Tollar stopped pacing to stand near Nandara. "Wise Mother, do you know how we can prevent someone from harnessing against our will?"

Nandara pressed her lips together. "I'm sure it's possible. Is it a concern?"

"Karthiry tried to take my power. Any of Loch's people getting ahold of one of us could be catastrophic." Tollar's jaw was still clenched, but she was looking at the tabletop.

This news startled Neesha. Dionelle had her eyes closed, breathing erratically, while Spark stared at Tollar, eyes wide.

"Dira and her people will know," Nandara said. "We'll ask them."

Dionelle exhaled slowly and opened her eyes, but she still looked ready to run out the door. She held her hand out over the table, palm down and swiping it to the side, as if to negate something.

"What?" Neesha glanced at Spark, who also seemed perplexed.

Dionelle shook her head.

"If you weren't going to help at all, you wouldn't be here," Neesha said.

Dionelle sighed, nodding her agreement.

"So you'll practice, but not fight? What's the sense in that?"

"She helped us before," Spark said. "Practicing with us is still helping."

"No one's expecting you to fight Loch," Neesha said. "That's ridiculous. Between the trauma and the fact that your power is diminished, it just doesn't make sense. It'd be like Pasdale, keeping us safe while Spark and I—and Tollar—do the really intense bits."

Dionelle inhaled sharply and sat back, closing her eyes. She nodded very carefully before opening them again and setting both hands palm down on the table.

"You don't have to fight, Nanny. Just help us practice."

"I already know how to harness. None of you needs to work with me," Tollar said. She caught Dionelle's eye and did something with her hands, some kind of deliberate signalling. Tollar seemed perplexed by Dionelle's blank stare.

"Does she not sign in prime?" Tollar asked Neesha.

Neesha sighed and glared at her mother. "No, she doesn't sign at all. She relies on mind reading."

"I could teach her. I can sign in three languages."

"Of course you can," Beenala huffed, managing to sound both exasperated and proud.

Dionelle smiled politely and did the hand swiping thing again.

"Nanny has a hard time putting thoughts into words when she's on the spot like this. It's overwhelming for her, especially when we're talking about difficult things. And the suffering that's made her like this is mostly because of Loch. And when you did the thing with blood magic—"

"Yes, Neesha explained. I'm sorry it frightened you. There are a lot of reasons I don't like using it. It's not all bad, though. I've saved lives by stopping bleeding until proper healers could arrive."

This seemed to startle Dionelle, though Neesha couldn't tell if it was a good thing or not. She really hoped Spark and Dionelle would let it sink in how much of an ally Tollar was—what an advantage her presence was. Tollar was looking at her now.

"So you all just... what, guess at what she means?"

"She used to talk, before my magical accident," Neesha said. "Nandara and I knew the words that used to go with the expressions she makes. Her silence is all Spark's ever known, so she's a master at interpreting it by now."

"And Nanny will write things down when she's alone and has the peace and space to think."

Tollar shrugged and looked to Nandara.

"You know," Nandara said slowly, "I understand that the lack of trust is difficult for you, but right now, these three just need to learn to harness, and you all need to learn to block it, if that is indeed a thing. Harnessing alone will take us a few days at least. It gives you all more time to get used to each other's power."

"Right, not a terrible idea," Neesha said. "But this overcautious thing isn't only a problem with the Guild. You and Nanny and Ondias sheltered Spark way too much. She could have learned at least a little aquamancy."

Dionelle sighed.

"You know it's true," Neesha snapped.

"Yes, and we're working to rectify it," Nandara said. "So we can teach Spark the basics of aquamancy, the three of you can practice harnessing—assuming it's not a catastrophe and the dragons allow for continued practice—and I'll work on blocking with Tollar and the council."

"Thank you, Wise Mother. I appreciate the help. What Karthiry tried has been haunting me for half a year." Tollar gave Nandara a polite bow. "I think that's enough planning for the moment. I could use a bit of rest."

She and Beenala both left quickly. Neesha glared across the table at Dionelle and Spark and hissed "Stop it!" at them both before heading out after Tollar and Beenala.

"That could have gone better," Neesha said when she caught up to them.

"It could have gone a lot worse," Tollar said.

"She keeps *expecting* it to go worse," Beenala added.

"Their behaviour is an embarrassment," Neesha grumbled.

"If it's as you suspect, that Loch used the worst of aquamancy on your mother, I don't blame her for being worried. Or not wanting to be involved in battle. I'd never ask anyone to expose themselves to that sort of torment, particularly not *again*."

"No, she definitely shouldn't be anywhere near the heart of the battle. But she *can* fight. She *has* fought already."

"Then she will if she has to," Tollar said. "Let us hope she doesn't have to."

Neesha walked with them along the dirt track glittering under the midday sun shining off the city. "Why do you use 'wise mother' when you address Nandara?"

Tollar smiled. "It's a title of respect we give to women of a certain age."

"And what about people who aren't women? Or men, for that matter? You've got a friend who isn't either."

"Yes, Balipar. They're our dragon whisperer."

"We use 'wise parent' when appropriate," Beenala said.

"But you called Ondias 'auntie' and she's about as powerful and, uh, old as Nandara."

"Nandara is a fair bit older," Tollar said. "But I daresay Ondias is going to have to let go of the bitterness if she wants the title of wise."

Neesha snorted. "I think she's grown too used to it. I don't think she'd even have a personality if she wasn't bitter and angry all the time."

"Ah." A smile touched Tollar's lips. She stopped on the track and put a hand on Neesha's shoulder, meeting her gaze. "I appreciate your efforts, I really do, but you don't have to keep trying to win them over. Nandara is right. Your mother and daughter don't have to work with me. You and I can work together if we need a powerful mix of fire and water, or if I need the boost to use water to an extent I hadn't considered before."

"What would that even look like?" Beenala asked. "You can already do anything with water."

"I think it's a matter of scale," Tollar said. "My range is still limited. I can't affect the weather beyond this valley. I have to be within a certain distance of that river to use it. Things like boiling water without pyromancy take a lot of effort. And of course right now there's the way the lingering effects from the swamp lung make it hard to breathe water, and the way these babies make everything more difficult. I expect a demonborn boost would make that all quite simpler."

"All right, we'll work together. I'm going to be so furious if the dragons won't let us try harnessing."

"You'll do it anyway, won't you?" Tollar asked. "I've heard about how you and Spark both practice things you shouldn't in secret."

"Yes, and they know that now. Hopefully it means they'll guide us through what we need to do instead of making it a challenge."

One thing was certain: Neesha was going to learn everything she could to stop Loch before he could hurt anyone else.

CHAPTER EIGHT

S park sat on the stool next to the anvil, half leaning on it with her chin propped in one hand, the other flicking a rivet to spin it aimlessly on the anvil's rough surface. She wanted Abyss to bring her to a mountaintop where she could scream herself bloody until it was time to go to battle. Barring that, she mostly just wanted to sleep—to hibernate like a bear until she could be useful.

The door to the forge pushed open, and she jumped to her feet, grabbing her hammer to make it look like she was doing anything at all.

"See?" Jatt said. "She's in here sulking."

"Yes," Ember agreed. "It's bad. Spark, honestly."

"I'm not sulking!" Spark managed not to wince at the sulk in her tone. "I just need something to do."

"Hmm." Ember took the hammer out of Spark's hand and set it aside.

"You could come do things with the southerners," Jatt said. "They're really not that bad."

Spark couldn't help herself and rolled her eyes. "You've only bonded with Beenala because you're both artists."

Jatt sighed.

"Spark, they raised a dragon from egg," Ember said. "You're really not curious about that at all? After the way you were friends with Bolt?"

"Bolt's gone." Great, now she was whiny on top of sulky. Spark looked desperately around, like there was a pit she could crawl into.

"And his cousin's here!" Jatt said. "His cousin who was raised entirely by humans. Come on, Spark—that's pretty cool."

"Yeah, I guess."

"And demonborn harnessing demonborn!" Ember said. "All your magical experiments and you're not interested in that?"

Spark stared at Ember's sandaled feet. "Everything is weird."

"You're not the centre of attention," Ember said gently.

"Because there are adults who know what they're doing," Jatt added. "You know, that thing you were dying for two years ago?"

"*I'm* an adult!" Spark growled in frustration at herself, but Ember giggled and took her hand.

"Spark, you're the most powerful wizard possibly in the whole world, and no one's questioning that. But you're young. We're all young. And there are wizards here with decades more experience taking charge."

"But I still feel so alone," Spark whispered, startled by her own admission.

"Because Di's been hiding with my gran?"

"And because you're having a fight with your ma for the first time?"

Spark blinked back the sudden sting in her eyes and swallowed against the hot, tight feeling in her throat at the thought of Neesha angry with her, at the way her mother had snapped at her after the first planning session.

"And because Raia's been back two whole days but she hasn't gone dragon-walking with you at all?" Jatt said.

"And Abyss has been back even longer but has barely said a word to you?"

"Yes!" Spark snapped. "All of that, and this godsdamned aquamancer right here in the city like that's not the reason it fell the first time."

Spark caught the quick glance Jatt and Ember shared.

"How much of this is you not trusting Tollar?" Jatt asked. "And how much is you just angry because your friends you haven't seen in ages are ignoring you?"

"Are you scared or jealous?" Ember asked, arms crossed and standing directly in front of Spark.

The tight ache of impending tears got hotter and tighter, Spark's cheeks burning and her insides feeling cold and twisty. She clenched and unclenched her hands, looking around and resenting that her friends had placed themselves between her and the door.

"Um..." Spark croaked, blinking back more tears.

"Your grandparents doted on you your whole life, and you've been your ma's entire world the last two years. Until now, you've been the human Abyss talks to the most. You and Raia were practically best friends." Ember took Spark's hand and squeezed it. "You've not had to deal with this sort of thing before."

Spark clenched her jaw against her lower lip's attempts to tremble.

Jatt came closer and put a hand on her shoulder. "You should probably talk to Neesha about this. She's cross with you, but she'll understand."

"She's busy."

"Right, yes, she has friends of her own for the first time in her life," Ember said. "You've got to learn to share her. But she's always here for you when you need her. You just have to let her know that you need her."

"I just..." Spark cleared her throat. "I figured she knew that."

"Now you're relying on mind reading the way Di does," Jatt said, smiling.

Spark sighed.

"I have a surprise for you." Ember turned suddenly and headed outside.

Spark glanced at Jatt, who was grinning, and followed Ember out into the side field where she was staring up at the dragon city and waving her arms. Way up above, a tiny black shard of obsidian peeled away from the side of the city and drifted closer, taking on the shape of Abyss, followed by another dark shard. Bale's purple markings became visible a moment later. And then Flame, Ice, and Dragon circled in from a different direction. Abyss and Bale landed in the field nearby while the others continued to circle overhead.

"What...?"

Ember giggled. Jatt was still grinning and clapped a hand on Spark's shoulder.

Dragon swooped in near Abyss, angling his wings so he slowed as he went by, and Raia leapt from his tail to the ground, rolling a couple of times before coming to her feet and skidding to a stop not far from Spark.

"Show-off!" Spark called, laughing in delight.

"Aye, well, turns out I've got an impressive sister-in-law to compete with now."

Spark didn't know what Raia saw in her expression, but the other woman laughed, practically crushed Spark in a hug and then nodded.

"I know. Ye don't like her. She's a bit terrifying with that magic of hers, but so's all ye wizards." Raia shrugged. "And ye ain't seen yet what my brother does with that warhammer of his, but ye still like him well enough."

Spark sighed. "Did Ember only convince you to come here to lecture me?"

Raia laughed, her whole body in it, full of delight. "Nah, yer lady caught me in the market this morning and said it's time someone got ye up in the air. So are ye coming?"

Spark glanced at Ember, who was also grinning. Jatt had gone off while they were talking, but Spark spotted him on his way back with one of the harnesses.

"You're coming too?"

"It's been a while," Ember said. "Jatt realized he hasn't gone up since he got hurt. Figured it'd be best to see if he's over that."

Bale and Abyss stood nearby waiting, and Croves and Shell had joined the other three dragons in circling above the house. Bale had moved in around Abyss's side, and Spark noticed she held some of the rigging from the gondola.

"Will you come with me?" Bale asked Spark. "Toll-mum doesn't like flying right now—the babies throw off her balance—so I have no one to fly with."

Spark only realized she was standing with her mouth open when Ember nudged her in the ribs and whispered, "Raised by humans! Come on, Spark!"

"You actually call her your mother?" Spark blurted.

"Toll-mum and Bee-mum raised me. What else would I call them?"

Spark shrugged. "Fair point. Your rigging looks a bit different, so this will take a minute."

But it turned out Bale was very good at helping with the rigging. It had far more handholds than what Spark used, and something like a rope ladder from Bale's underside up to one of her shoulders. Spark presumed it was for ease of climbing from the gondola. Ember helped Spark with Bale while Raia helped Jatt with Abyss's harness.

They'd barely gotten Jatt and Ember secured in the sling when Dragon swooped in shrieking a play call and snatching Raia off Abyss's shoulder. Spark barely had time to register Bale grabbing her and dropping Spark near a handhold on her shoulder before Bale launched into the air, calling after Dragon.

Spark immediately lost her footing, but Bale shifted mid-flight so that Spark rolled between two of the spikes on her back and lodged there. Bale was fast, the wind screaming around Spark as she dragged herself along the row of spikes to the handhold Bale had likely meant for her to hold onto.

The hold was crafted to extend so that Spark could hold onto it while standing. Being Tollar's height, the positioning was perfect. She could stand, face into the wind, and see where Bale was going—and that she was about to slam into Shell.

Spark didn't even have time to scream, Bale tilting her wings at the last moment so that she clipped Shell and sent the smaller dragon spinning off away from them.

Spark had only a moment to be pleased she hadn't lost her footing through the whole thing before Bale pitched into a spiralling roll and Spark's feet were flung out into the sky. Her shoulders strained, but she kept her grip on the hold even as the force of the spiral slammed her around into Bale's shoulder.

"You need practice," Bale chided, levelling out.

"Are you telling me anyone can keep their footing through that?"

"Practice," Bale repeated.

Croves landed next to her and Spark screamed. He laughed and gave her a hand up.

"Bale's ruthless," he said, chuckling.

"Where did you even come from?"

Croves pointed up. Shell wasn't there, having swooped by, but Spark followed the reverse trajectory and he'd have been just above Bale not a moment before.

"Shit, he's fast."

"Aye, and got some years and experience on this one." Croves affectionately patted one of Bale's spikes.

Bale banked into a turn and Spark gripped the handhold tighter. Croves casually leaned into the turn, barely touching the spike next to him to help keep his balance.

"So these handholds are for Tollar and Beenala?" Spark asked.

"Tollar, mostly. Bee don't leave the gondola when Bale's moving. They're handy in a pinch. I'll use 'em in a storm."

Spark nodded and looked around, flinching as Ice zipped overhead so close Spark could have reached up and flicked her claws. She could see all the dragons. She stood straighter, swivelling to get a full view.

"Oh, these are so you can watch Bale's back!"

"In part. Tollar's new to dragon-walking and her balance is off with the babies. She likes to stand up here and talk to Bale and watch where we're headed. But in a fight, aye, it's a good way to keep lookout and not get thrown off."

"I'm out of practice. Abyss left and none of the other dragons will let me walk around on them."

"Well, ye maybe noticed that me and Raia get bored easily, so ye can come up here with us any time." With that, he gave her a jaunty wave, casually stepped right off Bale's side, and fell into open air.

Spark had stopped paying attention to where all the dragons were, so she had a brief moment of sharp terror before he landed on Dragon's back as Dragon swooped by below. Raia promptly put her brother in a headlock, and then Dragon carried them both out of sight somewhere below Bale. Looking up again, Spark spotted Abyss's dark shape above them, circling lazily. She couldn't see Ember in the sling but was startled to realize the little blip moving around near Abyss's shoulder was Jatt.

Spark marvelled. He wasn't even wearing a harness or tether—none of them were—and he'd have had to climb out of the sling and scale the rigging. There were handholds, but they were nothing like the ones Bale had.

"Huh."

Bale spiralled away, chasing Dragon down under the curve of the dragon city. Spark stumbled, but Bale shifted her shoulder to help keep Spark from falling. When they came out the other side of the city, Abyss was there dropping toward them. Spark's stomach clenched, certain the dragons would collide, and then Abyss swooped away and Jatt was falling from the sky and landing hard not far away, near Bale's outstretched wings.

Bale was gliding, holding steady except to adjust so Jatt didn't fall off. Spark quickly made her way down Bale's body to where Jatt struggled to grab onto a spike.

"Did you just jump?"

"Yeah. Wow, that was a bad idea. How do they do this?"

"Practice!" Bale called.

Spark chuckled and pulled Jatt closer to the spikes, but he was steadier now.

"So you're okay being up here again?" she asked.

"Oh gods, no. I mean, it's fun like this." He gestured to where Croves leapt from Dragon back to Shell. "But I don't think I'll ever be able to do it battle-wise."

"Well, at least I'll have more company up here to practice," Spark said. "Apparently I need it."

"Spark, I came here to tell you about Ember. She's freaking out."

"What?"

"She was screaming and threw up on herself. Abyss is taking her back down to the ground."

"Shit. Bale, I need to go back down."

Bale deftly plucked the pair of humans off her back and held them in close as she spiralled into a hard dive.

"I think I see why Ember threw up," Jatt said through gritted teeth, eyes squeezed shut.

Spark's insides sloshed around, a cold shard dropping into her stomach, the force of the dive feeling like she was being mashed into the ground. An impossibly brief moment later, Bale pulled out of the dive and landed in the field next to Spark's house.

Jatt immediately collapsed when the dragon set them down, while Spark wobbled, waiting for her blood to stop whooshing. Abyss and Ember were both nowhere to be seen. Spark hadn't noticed when Abyss ducked out of flight practice. She glanced up but felt dizzy before spotting Abyss's dark form.

"We'll practice more later," Bale said. The dragon took off again, stirring up dust and debris in her wake.

Spark was about to head inside when the side door pushed open, and Ember came out looking pale but in a clean new shirt.

"What happened?" Spark rushed over and took her hands. Ember shrugged and shook her off.

"I just couldn't stop thinking about all the times you almost died fighting Loch." She shook her head. "I don't really want to talk about it. I need to go help Pa with some chores, but I'll see you tonight."

Spark couldn't get her to stay, and Jatt left not long afterward. Spark looked wistfully back up to the sky, but the dragons and their riders had headed away and she was left alone again.

Spark barely got into the hallway when she heard clanking in the kitchen. It was too late for one meal and too early for the next, and she was worried that maybe Shadow had managed to get into the pantry or something, but stopped short in the kitchen door because it was much worse than that.

"Oh, sorry to bother you," Tollar said, softly shutting a cupboard door and stepping away from it.

Spark shrugged. The only reason this was awkward was because she kept making it awkward.

"Didn't realize anyone was home," Spark said. "Mamma said you'd gone to visit with Raia."

"Oh, that was this morning. Bale brought me up to see her and the others, but I needed a nap." Tollar smiled.

Raia's blaze was using one of the clan towers, so the humans had set up camp on the mountainside nearby.

"Looks like Croves is going to stay with them, get caught up," Tollar added.

"Raia's been so worried about him."

Tollar pressed her lips together, nodding carefully. "It was a bad situation. Shell was very happy to help incinerate a good chunk of Loch's armada."

Spark gestured to the cupboard behind Tollar. "Do you need help with something?"

"I just woke up from a nap and feel like I'm half asleep. I need something to eat but don't really want anything."

Neesha had been doing a lot of oversharing about their new guests, probably trying to help Spark acclimatize to them, and she'd mentioned that Tollar had been having trouble with nausea and fatigue. Spark hadn't really been paying attention, but she supposed the woman had spent a lot of her time here sleeping.

"And sometimes," Tollar continued, "it's my body that's tired and other times it's my thoughts that are tired. I just woke up, so my body is happy, but my thoughts are a mess."

Spark smiled politely but had no idea what any of that meant. "There's some rice. I like just plain rice when my stomach is being weird. Would that help you?"

Tollar shrugged but smiled. Spark showed her where the sack of rice was, and there were beans and spices too, so Tollar got a bit of it all into a pan. Spark had no idea where the water suddenly came from, but it was gone nearly as quickly while the rice fluffed inexplicably.

"Did you just magic your snack?"

Tollar gave her a startled glance. "Sorry, I wasn't thinking."

"But you did. You used aquamancy to… cook the rice? It's not cooking, though."

"It's more of a rapid soak." Tollar hunted around the stove and Spark realized she must be looking for a way to light it. With a houseful of pyromancers, they mostly used sparks from a flint, and since Spark didn't even need that, she had no idea where the flint even was.

"Do you just want it heated now? I can do that if you like."

"Oh, thank you." Tollar stood a polite distance back, remaining very still.

"Where's Beenala?" Spark realized she hadn't seen the two of them apart for very long, and usually if it wasn't Neesha playing host to both of them, Beenala had been preparing food for Tollar.

"She's gone to help Stone, I think. I'm not sure how long I was asleep."

Spark cupped the pan in her hands and poured heat into it while Tollar watched with open fascination.

"I've been watching Beenala do pyromancy my whole life, and she's pretty good at it when she wants to be. She saved me from dragonfire once after Bale first hatched—not Bale herself, you understand, but the dragons I'd called to come take her back to her kin. I didn't realize then that she didn't have any kin. Anyway, all that to say, I've seen some fire magic in my time, and watching you and your mother does not cease to amaze me."

Spark set down the pot and got Tollar a bowl. "Well, you're the best aquamancer in the world, and I'm the best pyromancer. Mamma's been impressed with your magic since you got here."

"It's the pulling fire out of the air, right? No one but you can do that."

"Yeah." Spark slid into a chair at the table, wishing she could find a polite way out of the conversation but knowing she'd been rude enough to this woman already that she couldn't keep doing it. And Spark wasn't even sure anymore if the issue was that she still didn't trust Tollar, or if it was that she resented how angry Neesha was with her all the time now. Spark and her mother had gotten along since the day Neesha had woken up, and Spark didn't know what to do with the sudden discord.

Ember's comment about jealousy picked at her thoughts.

"There are things only I can do—not just the breathing water thing—and I'll tell you the same thing I told the dragons in Upalint when I convinced them to help me save the port: *no one* can do quite what I can, not even Loch. I *can* beat him. I *have*. And I will again."

Spark nodded and didn't say anything, and Tollar ate for a moment—slowly, like it was a chore. Then she pointed her spoon at Spark.

"There is one thing I can do that I bet you can too. Not with water, but with fire. Well, maybe if they'll let us harness each other, you can do it with water, but that's getting ahead of myself. Can I show you something?"

Spark watched her expectantly.

"Oh, not here. Give me a moment to finish. Will you come with me to the river?"

Spark had been curious, but the suggestion made her cold.

"I can start with a bowl of water if you want, but it's just not impressive that way. I like to show off."

Spark cracked a smile despite herself, and Tollar grinned like it was a victory. Okay, Spark had probably deserved that.

"All right."

And so once Tollar had finished eating and cleaned up her dishes, the two of them stood on the riverbank at the shallows near the workshop. There was no bridge and locals forded the shallows to cross, except in spring. They had a sort of floating bridge thing when snowmelt made things trickier.

Tollar took off her sandals and stepped into the water.

"It'll be easier if you take your boots off," Tollar said. "Unless you want to use your hands, but that would make it awkward."

Spark hesitated. Was it some kind of trick? Tollar hadn't said exactly what they were doing, and getting into a river with the world's most powerful aquamancer seemed like one of those poor life choices Ondias was always accusing Neesha of.

Spark toed off her boots and stepped in, barely more than her toes in the water. But that seemed good enough to please Tollar. She held a hand out to Spark, waiting. Still hesitant, Spark took her hand and braced for something weird, but Tollar's grip was firm without being crushing and her hand was pleasantly cool.

"Um, you're not going to make the river level rise or anything, are you? I don't know how to swim."

Tollar gave her a sad look. "After this, I'm going to teach you how to swim."

It wasn't a question. Spark was too nervous to be annoyed. And Tollar still wasn't anywhere near as bossy as Ondias.

"We're not supposed to harness without supervision, but this is more... a gentle transfer, all right?"

Spark nodded but glanced around. Should they be doing this without help? What if something went wrong?

"You still need to be calm, though. Can you be calm? I know my power is unsettling. It has been my whole life. But I think you'll find this interesting if it works."

"What if it doesn't work?"

"Well, you'll have wet feet, and I'll feel like a fool."

Spark smiled again, feeling calmer. She nodded that she was ready, and then her body flooded with a cooling sensation that would have been alarming if it wasn't so invigorating, and then Spark was suddenly *aware* of the river. Not the whole thing from headwater to delta, but easily the entire bit of river in the valley. Every eddy and whirlpool and bit of debris and every stone along the bottom.

She gasped and jerked back, breaking the grip. And then it was just the two of them with wet feet on a warm summer's day.

"What in all the hells...?"

Tollar had been watching Spark with guarded hope, but frowned now.

"Sorry, was that—"

"What did you just do?" Spark asked.

"You saw it then? Or felt it, or whatever?"

"It was the river. It was like my feet grew to take up the whole riverbed from the northern slopes to the southern canyon."

"Yes!" Tollar grinned, her eyes glittering. "I can sense any body of water for leagues. I don't know how many, exactly, but it's a lot. I'm betting you can do something similar with fire."

"I..." Spark thought of how Neesha had put herself into the fire, had been aware of it through demons, in order to beat Loch on the southern plains. How she had lost herself to it. She shuddered. "Yes, I think you're right. But is it safe?"

"Best not to overextend and try to see farther than you're capable of. I tried to sense the entire ocean once and nearly passed out."

Spark gave her a look, but Tollar kept grinning. Yes, she was probably telling the truth. It sounded like something Neesha would try, and the two of them were certainly alike when it came to risk.

"Do you want to try it with fire?" Tollar's excitement waned slightly. "I suppose you'll have to light a pretty big fire."

"Thank you, but that's enough for now."

"Of course. I'll show your mother too, and then the two of you can practice it together. Now, get your boots and we'll go to those deeper pools near the start of the rapids. Good place to teach you how to swim."

"In rapids?" Spark's voice squeaked.

"*Near* the rapids. Where the water is deep and calmer. But it really doesn't matter, you know. I can stop the river and turn it into a large pool. Or build up a column of it right here. But I suspect that will not help with this thing where you're afraid of me. So, the pools?"

Spark's cheeks warmed at the casual way Tollar spoke of the problem. Tollar stood gesturing downriver, an easy smile on her face and her eyes sparkling. Spark appreciated her efforts, even if they weren't quite working. But Spark did kind of want to see Tollar stop the entire river.

Spark's stomach still churned, but Tollar had played to her curiosity, and Spark very much wanted to learn whatever Tollar would teach her.

CHAPTER NINE

Tollar felt a bit dizzy trying to see up into the heights of the cavernous shining room where the Dragon Superiors held council. She was going to have to figure out a reason for Bale to keep coming north so she could see more of this place. Though it was looking like her stay here was going to be somewhat extended. Beenala wanted to go home, but it looked like Tollar would need to stay where she was until it was time to find Loch and put an end to his treachery.

Beenala was not with Tollar now, and she rather regretted it. But they couldn't risk Bee panicking with this, and besides, she wouldn't be involved in any sort of battle unless it somehow made its way to her farm. That had been agreed upon almost immediately.

Besides, with the fireborn women, Tollar had all the fire magic she'd ever need.

If they could get this to work.

Nandara had, apparently, tried to go through some of the theory with them last night. But out of an abundance of caution, Tollar was the only person in the room not completely fireproofed. She *was* wearing some fireproof clothing Spark had loaned her and had a good-sized barrel of water at her command.

The real problem was the potential for a fire big enough to pull all the oxygen from the room. Tollar, still trying to comprehend the sheer size of where she stood, really doubted that would be a problem. But they needed to be prepared for all eventualities. Big magic came with big consequences when it went wrong.

At the moment, Neesha was having a one-sided argument with Dionelle while Spark was trying to get more guidance from Abyss. None of them had been able to do what Nandara had taught them. Or had tried to teach them. Or whatever.

"What if I harness one of them?" Tollar asked the room in general, turning her attention back to the proceedings. "I know how to handle fire magic from working with Bee. As I understand it, you're just looking to see what the amplification effect is of demonborn harnessing demonborn?"

The Superiors grumbled at each other in dragonish for a moment, and then the Dragoness Superior gave Tollar a nod.

"We wish to see the effect, yes. And also how well it can be controlled."

Tollar had heard a bit about what had happened when the fireborn women lost control while working with demons. She didn't think it would be the same with this, but all of this was new.

Neesha quit arguing with her mother and came to stand next to Tollar. Another argument ensued when the Superiors tried to insist that Tollar work with Dionelle first, as she was the weakest of the fireborn and would be safer. And then Tollar had to explain that if Dionelle panicked, the fire magic could potentially harm Tollar. Worst-case scenario was incineration.

And it was a lot more possible than Tollar liked.

"What does Dionelle want?" Tollar asked, turning to the woman.

As she expected, Dionelle still had a hard time meeting Tollar's gaze and quickly shook her head, crossing her arms tightly around herself.

"There. She's not ready. Neesha is. Let's get this over with."

"I just have to stay calm, right?" Neesha asked.

Tollar put her hands on Neesha's shoulders and held her gaze. "I'm going to take your magic. It's going to feel a lot like how you described it when your essence has been pulled out of your body with a demon. You're ready for that?"

Neesha looked startled. "Well, I guess I consider myself warned."

"It's not a great feeling. You're going to feel empty. And when I let go of it, your magic is going to slam back into you."

Neesha nodded and held out her hands. Tollar took one, took a breath, and tugged, very gently, on Neesha's magic. And Tollar's entire body lit up with heat, every last nerve searing, like suddenly plunging into a hot bath. She gasped. But it wasn't like getting blasted by a geyser like she had that one time. No sudden pain, no need to rapidly cool the water to protect herself.

This was still magic, not yet real fire.

Tollar realized she'd gone stiff and forced herself to relax before anyone freaked out. She glanced at Spark. Okay, before anyone freaked out *even more*.

"I'm okay," Tollar said quickly. "Neesha?"

"I hate this, you're right."

Tollar glanced at the Superior. "I have her magic and the world has failed to end. Now what?"

"Use it." The dragoness puffed out some fire.

Tollar caught it easily. She pulled the water out of the barrel and put it around herself like a shield. They wanted to know the amplification effect, so the best way to figure that out would be to make the biggest fire Tollar possibly could.

So she ballooned the bit of dragonfire she had, drawing it out and pushing it up, an explosive conflagration. The fire was like an extension of her. She could see with it, just as she'd suggested to Spark. The fire was filling the entire city, rushing out wherever there were vents and tunnels to outside.

Tollar held her focus on the size of the fire, not the intensity of it. While the dragons and the fireborn themselves were immune to the fire, Tollar didn't think borrowing Neesha's power would extend that immunity to her, or to the city itself, whose stones beneath her feet could crack or warp or melt if the fire became too intense.

The fire exploded out of the city, filled it, reached up into the clouds. Tollar couldn't fathom the heights it reached and wondered what it looked like from afar. The cold crept in, and she remembered the countereffect of pyromancy. She dropped Neesha's power and let the fire dissipate.

Only then did Tollar realize that the water she'd encased herself in for protection had frozen solid. She turned it back into water with barely a thought and looked around.

No one frozen solid. No one incinerated. So, probably a success.

Well, the barrel was gone—nothing but ash. They'd been right with their precautions.

"That was horrifying," Spark said. "It was like being in the fire realm again."

"Oh, Tollar you should try to open a fire portal," Neesha said, holding out her hand again.

"Yes, that would demonstrate control," the Superior said.

Tollar drew on Neesha's power again, and it took her a few minutes to adjust the magic for fire, but she could open water portals and this wasn't much different. She widened it a tad, and then drew flame from the realm, a vicious column spiralling up to the room's impossible ceiling. Then she closed it.

"The amplification is concerning," the Superior said. "However, you have demonstrated that control is possible. You may continue to pursue this skill, but with caution."

Tollar bowed, hiding her grin. "Thank you, Mistress."

The dragons dispersed, some disappearing down tunnels, others moving to the other side of the large chamber. Abyss and Bale remained nearby.

"We should keep playing to our strengths," Neesha said. "I can work on harnessing with you, and Nandara can continue to teach Spark and Dionelle."

"I'll be okay," Spark said.

Neesha gestured behind her, where Dionelle stood, arms still crossed and her eyes closed, breathing shallowly.

"I think maybe this is enough for now?" Tollar said.

The dragons collected all the humans and brought them back down to the field outside Spark and Neesha's house before disappearing back into the city. Beenala came out immediately to see how it went, the dog trailing out behind her and dashing straight to Spark.

"There was a lot of fire," Beenala said, her hands gripping the hem of her shirt.

"Ah, yes. That was me," Tollar said.

Beenala gasped. "So it worked?"

"I harnessed Neesha and no one died. So now we can keep doing it and hope we don't blow anything up."

Beenala rolled her eyes.

"We should learn to do it with regular wizards," Neesha said. "Learn control and finesse at a regular level and then use risky magic harnessing each other."

Dionelle had left already, likely gone to find Nandara and rest, while Spark stood uncertainly on the edge of their little group, absently patting the dog's head, and watching the direction Dionelle had gone.

"Spark," Neesha said gently. "Do you think you might want to try learning more aquamancy? With Tollar here, we can work on more advanced things safely."

Spark turned to face them, her lips pinched together, flexing her hands.

"I'd like the record to show that I did not in fact drown you yesterday," Tollar said.

Spark's cheeks went pink, but a smile ghosted her lips, and she gave Tollar side-eye.

"Neither one of you mentioned you did anything yesterday," Neesha said.

"Tollar taught me to swim."

"And...?" Tollar prompted.

"And to see using an element. Well, water, because that was all she could do without harnessing me, but we didn't know yet if that was safe."

"Just a little power transfer," Tollar said. "Gave her a tiny bit of my magic so she could sense the river."

"Mamma, it was pretty cool."

"You two were just going to keep that a secret from me?"

Spark stared at the ground between them and went back to petting Shadow, but Tollar laughed. "I did it with that fire up in the city. It was harder because I'm less familiar with pyromancy, but I could still get a sense of all the tunnels the fire was rushing down and that it went high above the city."

"Tollar, it was up in the clouds," Beenala said worriedly.

"Yes, well, Neesha has a lot of magic." Tollar touched Beenala's shoulder. "It was all right; we were being careful."

"It didn't look careful at all!"

"It's pyromancy—does it ever?"

Beenala huffed at her and Tollar laughed.

"Come on, then, let's head to the river if I'm going to teach you some more," Tollar said, turning away.

Beenala went with them, and they started with a bit of harnessing—Spark and Neesha practicing on Bee. They both worked with Beenala's pyromancy, letting it amplify their own.

"It's a lot like working with a demon," Spark said, sounding surprised.

"Easier, though," Neesha said. "And we're not going to get possessed by Beenala."

"The worst likely to happen is whoever is being harnessed will end up exhausted," Tollar said. "But you do need to pay attention to whoever you're harnessing. Remember that other wizards' power isn't endless like ours. Some have rather low limits."

With her earlier warning about how Karthiry had drained wizards to death, Tollar knew they'd take the dangers seriously. But it was still better to practice with someone who knew what she was doing. Beenala eventually got tired and went inside to rest. Neesha was going to have to help find some more wizards to volunteer. Maybe they could get Croves to come help.

Though Dionelle didn't reappear, Nandara joined them while Tollar was in the middle of teaching Neesha how to see with an element. She'd already done it to some extent in former battles against Loch, so she picked it up quickly. Spark had been sitting on the ground, giving the dog a tummy rub with one hand and with the other making some fairly large fires for the two of them.

"Not practicing harnessing?" Nandara asked, watching Spark bloom the fire and sculpt it into different shapes while Neesha, with her eyes closed, told them what it was.

From her angle, Nandara wouldn't be able to see Tollar lying in the shallows and mimicking Spark's fire shapes with water.

"We did a bit," Neesha said. "Bee got tired, and Toll thinks we should get better at it before we try harnessing each other."

"Yes, we all saw the fire coming out of the city." Nandara glanced up. "I was glad when Dionelle came back and indicated it had been a success."

"The fire was controlled, yeah. The Superiors seemed pleased."

"Very good," Nandara said. "Spark, why don't we practice some more aquamancy?"

Spark looked warily at her mentor, hands buried in Shadow's fur. For his part, the dog had fallen asleep on his back at some point, legs in the air, front paws curled and ears splayed out across the ground.

"I'm here to keep an eye on it for you," Tollar said, sitting up out of the water.

Nandara gasped, startled by Tollar's sudden appearance. She rose up on a disk of water, standing with her hands clasped behind her, waiting.

"Yes," Nandara agreed, recovering. "If you're willing to stick around and oversee things, it's a good time for Spark to learn more."

Spark was reluctant, but shuffled closer to the riverbank while Nandara sat on a large smooth stone nearby and started directing her. From working with Croves's aeromancy, Tollar thought that air and water behaved similarly and wasn't surprised when Nandara took that route in helping Spark gain better control of the element.

Nandara started with a warm-up, getting Spark to slosh water around in a puddle and freeze and thaw its surface. Then she got her making shapes with it, moving it around more purposefully.

"Am I really going to need to know any of this?" Spark complained.

"Don't you want to see the extent of what your magic can do?" Neesha asked.

Given how curious the girl normally was, Tollar was surprised that her fear was winning out.

"You could have many uses for it," Tollar said. "Anywhere you use water in daily life. In the forge and cooking, as you've seen me do. And stemming blood loss in serious injuries, helping redirect water in a flood."

Spark sighed. She went back to making little shapes with it. The dog got bored and trotted off toward the village proper.

All the while, Tollar had paced around them on her little wave, circling the edge of where they practiced. She did everything Nandara was guiding Spark through, just to give her mind something to focus on. If they hadn't asked her to stay and oversee, she'd have gone for another nap.

But when Nandara shifted to working with water demons, Tollar went to lie in the shallows again, eyes closed and hands at her sides, splayed across the water's surface. She wasn't doing much listening but putting all her effort into sensing the water and what was going on.

Spark called the demon—it took a bit since her grasp on the water language was weak, barely good enough to meet Guild standards—and something about the energy was immediately off.

Tollar tensed and waited, barely hearing what the other women said as Nandara guided Spark and Spark asked questions. The demon was like a bright point of light in Tollar's awareness. Before it moved, that light intensified and Tollar was up in a flash, lunging from the water to catch the demon an instant before it hurled itself at Spark.

Tollar thought the younger woman's voice had sounded a bit tremulous as she'd tried to instruct the demon. But that didn't matter. What mattered was stopping the demon.

She'd stayed close and moved fast, faster than she could give commands. She dug her clawed hand into the demon and wrenched it away from the other three, opening a water portal and physically stuffing the demon into it. Once she'd stopped it, banishing it with traditional spellcraft would have been faster, but now Tollar was angry. She had no idea what had made her so furious, but physically dominating the demon had made her feel a little better.

Spark was freaking out and Neesha was trying to calm her down. Nandara came over to Tollar.

"What the stars just happened?" she asked.

"I don't know why it attacked like that." Tollar realized she was still dripping wet and drained the water from her dress, smoothing down and drying her hair. "Its energy was off as soon as she called it."

Nandara frowned. "Is it going to be possible for her to learn higher level aquamancy?"

"She's still afraid. She's not going to be able to do it until she calms down."

Spark stomped toward them, jabbing a finger at Tollar. "You did that! Why would you do that?"

"Do what? I grabbed it when it lunged at you."

Neesha got between the two of them. "You moved first."

Had she? She supposed she had. "I felt its energy change."

"Spark, I told you. Why would she make it attack you just to stop it immediately?"

Eyes shining with unshed tears, Spark stomped away, grumbling to herself.

"Well, that was not ideal," Nandara said.

Tollar shrugged. She'd done what she could. But they definitely couldn't teach the girl more without Tollar around. Or without her getting some more control over her fears. It was going to be a long couple of months if nothing about the situation changed. They all had a lot of big magic to learn—individually and together—and it wasn't going to happen if the rest of them didn't learn to trust Tollar.

She supposed she could focus on working with Neesha exclusively, but she liked the idea of having options. Maybe Dira and her council, once they'd recovered from their journey, would have some guidance. They certainly needed it.

CHAPTER TEN

Neesha found herself on the edge of the river not far from the house in the place that she'd come to think of as their practice grounds. But today things were different because Dionelle had come with Nandara. Spark hadn't been practicing with them for over a week, too frustrated with herself and worried about the water demon attack to properly focus. Tollar had given Spark a very thorough tour of the gondola, and as best Neesha could tell from the mess of supplies in the large workshop, Spark was working on making one of her own.

Which was smart. It would make the journey easier for them once it was time to leave. It was over a week's flight from the dragon city to the island Loch had taken over.

Neesha just wanted to go, but they needed to be ready. Needed to be sure they could beat him when the time came.

She and Spark had gotten good at harnessing regular wizards, and Neesha had been practicing with Tollar. But the magic was unwieldy. Not as unstable as working with a demon possession, but still difficult to tame. Both of them loved the challenge.

Spark was frustrated that she wasn't catching on to the magic as fast as Neesha and Tollar. Even when it was just the three fireborn women working together, Spark was still worried and holding back. Neesha didn't know what it would take for her to settle into the magic.

But as long as Neesha and Tollar could perfect their skills, maybe Spark wouldn't need to.

Dionelle had been working with them to some degree, but she wouldn't be in the heart of the battle with them. Neesha had planned on showing Tollar demon possession.

"We've been talking with Dira about Tollar's concerns with blocking an unwanted harnessing," Nandara said.

Tollar stopped pacing to watch Nandara eagerly. "You've found a solution?"

"We've found a starting point."

Tollar flailed and resumed pacing.

"No one knows how to do this?" Neesha balked.

"We really didn't think we needed to know how," Nandara said. "I can't stress enough how fractured the Guild is—how many wizards have turned away from its guidance. The council doesn't always know what those rogue wizards are doing unless someone encounters them the way Tollar has. Her battle with Loch and Karthiry was... illuminating. And disturbing."

"So *we* have to figure it out, if it can be done at all?" Tollar asked.

"Yes, but we're good at that," Nandara said. "We learned how to deal with their out-of-control demon possessions and how to open fire portals. If preventing being harnessed can be done, we'll figure it out."

"So where do we start?" Neesha asked.

"That's what Dionelle is here for. The council believes that suppression spells, or an element of them, might be the answer."

"They want us to try suppressing the harness?"

"Yes. Though the mental safe space Spark perfected for demon possession might be the correct path instead. Or both. Or something altogether different." Nandara shrugged helplessly. "We're going to find out."

Neesha only knew as much about suppression as had been required for full Guild membership. As a specialist, Tollar hadn't been required to learn it at all. There was some debate over whether she *could* do it with only aquamancy, but they hadn't expected her to be able to do magic like summonings either, and she'd been able to.

"It could be that you do have a small amount of talent in other areas," Nandara said. "Overshadowed by your aquamancy, and weak enough to go unnoticed, especially since you never had formal mentors."

"I had plenty of teachers," Tollar snapped.

"Yes," Nandara said carefully. "Just not the kind overseen by the Guild."

Tollar rolled her eyes and kept pacing along the riverbank, but held her tongue. They'd heard plenty from her and Beenala and even Croves about how sour the southern nations had become toward the Guild—how the Guild's neglect of southern wizards was fomenting discontent. The Guild didn't recognize necromancers at all, which was problematic given how culturally important they were, particularly around the lands Tollar called home.

Really, it was no wonder Loch had been able to basically construct a shadow Guild with himself perched on top of it like some soggy king.

Dira had admitted their failings, but enough members of the council were still stubbornly refusing to change anything else about the Guild. The specialist tiers had been enough for them. Neesha was fascinated by what Tollar had said about the necromancers and didn't understand why the Guild wouldn't want to learn more.

There seemed to be a profound lack of curiosity, which was baffling considering wizards were scholars of the world's trickiest secrets.

"Regardless," Nandara continued, "your magic has offered some surprises already, so this is worth exploring. Dionelle is the best suppression wizard we've got in the valley right now—possibly one of the best in the Guild. So she's going to work with you—both of you—and see if we can get this figured out."

"All right, so how's it work?" Tollar asked.

"Do something with water."

Tollar pulled a rope of water from the river and started looping it around itself, until Dionelle got closer and appeared to be thinking really hard at Tollar. The water dropped from the air to splash back into the river.

Tollar gasped.

Neesha had been on the receiving end of her mother's suppression plenty growing up—necessary to keep her from burning down the house or incinerating Bly. Was that why Dionelle was so good at it? Neesha pressed her hand over her mouth to keep from snickering.

It was a terrible feeling, though, like being buried in the sand or trying to walk through deep water. Only it was all made of magic.

"Cursed ancestors," Tollar whispered. "Do it again."

Neesha smiled and Tollar used bigger magic, stopping the river and letting the water pile up behind her like her will was a dam. Dionelle furrowed her brow, and Tollar shook with the effort of resisting. The water wobbled but didn't give.

"Rotting moons! That's incredible control she's got."

Nandara was smiling and rested a hand on Dionelle's shoulder. "I told you she was our best."

Tollar had let the river go back to its own business again, but gave Dionelle a respectful nod. "All right, so she's going to teach me how to suppress magic?"

"That part will be a group effort," Nandara said. "Neesha knows a bit of it already, so she can practice more, and we'll see if you can do it at all."

"Wouldn't it be a better use of time to find out if it will work at all before I try to learn it? I mean, I want to, but we need to prioritize right now, and top of my list is keeping those monsters from taking my power." Tollar shuddered.

"Yes," Neesha agreed. "We should give it a test run before we devote any time to it."

"Could we try to harness Dionelle and see if she can block it?"

But even before Tollar had finished her inquiry, Neesha saw the way her mother's eyes went bright with panic. Dionelle immediately turned and fled.

Nandara gave them an apologetic look and retreated after Dionelle. Neesha and Tollar both stood in awkward silence, watching them go.

"So..." Tollar began. "You can suppress a bit, yes? Why don't you try to block it just to see?"

Neesha sighed. "I'm terrible at it. If it doesn't work, there'll be no way to tell if it's because it's the wrong approach."

"But if it does work, we'll have our answer without having to upset your mother further." Tollar went back to pacing, but more slowly, tapping her fingers against her lips. "Is there no one here who can help heal her mind enough for her to tell you what happened to her? It's got to be better for everyone if you at least knew what her triggers might be."

Neesha shook her head and gave Tollar a helpless look. "We don't have that kind of healer, no."

"But those exist. Surely there's got to be one who would die for a chance to see this place and would delight at the opportunity to come out here and help her?"

"Yes, I'm sure there are." Neesha shrugged. "But they've got to get past Ondias, and she thoroughly vets everyone first. That takes time."

They gave the suppression spells a try anyway. First Neesha practiced by just trying to suppress Tollar's aquamancy—and she was back to doing little parlour tricks with the water. Neesha was at least good enough for Tollar to notice that she was trying.

But when Tollar tried to harness Neesha's power, there was nothing Neesha could do to stop her. Even though Tollar started with only gentle tugs, like she had up in the dragon city, Neesha couldn't even slow her down.

"I'm sorry, Toll. I know you're desperate to figure this one out."

Neesha had gotten the full account from Tollar about what Karthiry had done—and almost done—and how Tollar had had to kill her to stop her. The fear in Tollar's voice, no matter how much she tried to hide it, was palpable.

"We've got some time before we need to head in for lunch," Neesha said. "I could teach you how to work with demon possession."

They'd spoken about that, and Tollar had cultivated a safe place in her mind in preparation.

"Am I really going to need something so dangerous?" Tollar said, crossing her arms.

"If you end up separated from other wizards, it might do in a pinch."

Still hesitant, Tollar agreed.

"I'll start by showing you what it looks like." Neesha used her flint to light a fire and summon a fire demon. She gave Tollar a hard look. "If my eyes suddenly look like Spark's... Run."

Tollar looked half-amused by the warning, though her expression took on a look of fascinated horror once Neesha actually allowed the demon into her.

Neesha had no idea what showed on her face as the tempting, euphoric heat of the demon washed through her and filled her. She held it a beat and then pushed it out and banished it.

"There are so many ways this can go wrong, and honestly you shouldn't be doing it while you're pregnant. The big risk of losing control comes from how enticing the demon is. Think of the most comfort you've ever gotten from water and then multiply it out to unreasonable levels. That's the pull you've got to resist."

"Right. That's why I need to mentally go sit under the mango tree with Beenala—to ground myself and remind me that there are better things than whatever the demon's enticing me with."

"Yes, and it also makes it easier for us to separate you and the demon if you do lose control."

"Ancestors curse us all if that happens." Tollar pressed her lips together. "You know, maybe this isn't such a good idea." She looked up at the city like she was imagining what it had looked like to see it fall. She'd seen Jatt's painting of that day.

Neesha was about to reassure Tollar that the dragons wouldn't let anything happen before Neesha could fix it all, but then she remembered how Tollar had been able to control the Dragoness Superior's talon. She shuddered.

"Um, you know what, maybe not?" Neesha rubbed her face. "We have the dragons to keep us safe, but I don't know what we'd do if you lost control."

"How likely is that?"

Neesha tapped her fingers against her chin. "Not very? It's only happened when Spark or I let it in practice, or when we're using powerfully dangerous magic and lose focus."

"Right. Well, today's a good brain day, so it's as good as any just to see if I can do it at all."

Neesha was less sure, regretting having suggested this at all, but Tollar had already summoned a demon. What exactly could she do if Tollar lost control? Probably die messily.

Neesha swallowed.

Tollar let the demon in and shivered, euphoria flitting across her expression. And then the demon was out of her again and immediately shoved back into the water realm.

"That was a terrible idea, not to be repeated. Particularly not here." Tollar's expression was grave. "I know Ondias said there was an issue between fire and water, but those demons *hate* this place."

"Well, I suppose that's valuable information, even if we already had a notion of it before."

"What about portal travel?" Tollar asked. "There's water everywhere. I could go anywhere."

Neesha was even more hesitant to teach Tollar this one, no matter how useful it would be for her. Neesha reiterated the dangers Dira had already warned of. And Tollar had heard about what happened when Dionelle had been trapped there.

"Right." Tollar looked determined, though. "But Spark was not enticed. Your mother was pulled in with no warning or any idea of what was happening or where she was, and you were desperate to escape your life."

"Yes, Ondias has had some theories about why Spark has been completely resistant to the pull of the fire realm. Given how much more demon essence she has than Dionelle or I, she should be *more* likely to get pulled in."

"Which only lends to the theory that being prepared will help. I've been warned of the dangers, and I'm uninterested in going places Beenala can't."

Neesha had a half-smile, a brief thing ghosting across her expression before the pang of jealousy quelled it. She was getting better at not being quite so bitter about what she had lost and how much better her youth *should* have been if only her parents had learned some important lessons sooner. She *still* didn't feel as secure in herself and her place in the world as Tollar did.

"If you go, you need to be brief. It's going to be fascinating, and you're going to want to stay longer than you should. Try counting, all right? Don't let yourself get past thirty."

Tollar grinned, pulled a bit of water from the river, and pooled it in front of Neesha. "Hold this here, will you?"

Neesha was mediocre at aquamancy, but she could hold a puddle in place. Tollar dashed into the river, opened a water portal, and disappeared into it. Neesha's shoulders tightened, her limbs buzzing, and she started to count. She only got to ten when the puddle in front of her shimmered and Tollar climbed out of it.

"Well, that was educational."

"What did you see? What was it like?"

Tollar's eyes glittered. "It was incredible and deeply strange—a lot like being deep in the ocean. Cold and heavy. But it was bright, like the water itself was glowing. But not evenly. It was light one direction, and the opposite and less so in the middle where I was, and a vast abyss in front of me. The lighter bits looked like they might have structures, possibly made of ice? Just floating there. But then the urge to go explore nearly overtook me, and I knew it was time to leave."

"So you felt a pull, but could resist?"

"To a degree, yes. I don't think this was as dangerous as with the demon, but I certainly can't linger. Especially not when no one can come for me if something goes wrong."

"Well, I suppose in a few years you'll have your children to help, though that's not exactly a burden you should put on them."

Tollar gave her a sad smile and put a hand on her shoulder.

Neesha knew it wasn't entirely her fault that Spark had had to endure what she did, but it was hard not to feel guilty for not being there. Tollar was, of course, older and far more skilled than Neesha had been when things had gone so wrong. And while Tollar liked to show off with big flashy magic that looked risky, she also didn't like failing or looking like a fool.

Hopefully they could figure out how Tollar could resist being harnessed to spare her having to do anything so desperate as Neesha had done.

CHAPTER ELEVEN

Beenala sat across from Ember at the big table in the studio, both of them working in companionable silence on opposite ends of the same dress. It was a stunning shimmery purple-blue that looked more purple in some light and more blue in others. It was a gift for Tollar, and Beenala had wanted to embroider her family's vine pattern and some flowers at the neck and hem, but couldn't decide on the right colour palette. And she didn't really have time for it anyway. It was Tollar's birthday today.

She'd picked up the fabric a few days ago on their trip to Big Water. It had been in part to break up the monotony, and in part to help celebrate. Also something of a necessity as the boredom had really started getting to Croves—he'd been pushing the boundaries of what Tollar liked so that she was snapping at him a lot, *and* he was incessantly flirting with Neesha, who was bored and lonely and had started flirting back. But she also seemed embarrassed and definitely felt guilty, having asked Beenala if she was going to make Tollar jealous or screw things up, so before anyone could make poor life choices, they'd headed for a proper city. They'd barely even seen Croves; he'd spent most of the trip at the comfort house, making the sorts of poor life choices that weren't going to damage any of the good things the four of them had built.

It had been a good break for Tollar as well. She'd gotten to spend the nights in her own bed, sprawled out for the first time since they'd left home, and she'd certainly slept a lot. Beenala had been able to pick up some new art supplies. Big Water wasn't any sort of major city, maybe half the size of Nytaltek, but it was still a trade hub, so there'd been plenty to see and do and supplies to gather. Beenala and Tollar and Croves hadn't expected to still be in the dragon city this long, hadn't come prepared for an extended stay, and all of Tollar's clothing had gotten tight around the middle or had stopped fitting over her belly entirely.

Ember and Beenala had been working on loosening the seams, but it still wouldn't be enough to get Tollar home in the clothes she had. So they'd picked up some new travel clothes and bolts of fabric to make some new dresses. Ember had worked with Beenala on a design for some nice sundresses that would show off Tollar's tattoos and that could be let out to accommodate her growing belly, and then taken back in once they were home and the babies had come.

Tollar knew they were up to something, but hadn't seen the fabric. They'd been keeping the studio doors locked while they worked and the projects hidden in a cupboard otherwise. The other dress was in a lovely crisp white with a striking pattern of silver thread woven through that would contrast beautifully with Tollar's skin tone.

There was a lot of clattering going on in the kitchen across the hall, punctuated by Croves and Raia's big laughs. They were in there with Neesha and Jatt, preparing Tollar's birthday dinner.

Beenala had wanted to make Tollar her favourite of everything, but they just couldn't find the right ingredients this far from home. Croves, at least, had found some coconuts, and Beenala had picked up a bit of the right kind of rice, so if nothing else, Tollar would get her favourite dessert. Neesha insisted they'd have a good spread with a mix of southern and northern dishes. And Croves had also found the right kind of chocolate for drinking, and Beenala had been making it for all of them in the mornings, with a touch of cinnamon.

Beenala startled when she heard an entirely different kind of clatter, followed by Shadow barking. This was from the forge at the end of the hall, where Spark had locked herself away, working on something secret.

"She does that," Ember said, not even looking up.

Spark hadn't come with them to Big Water—only Neesha, Raia, and Croves had come along, with Spark opting to stay back and work on the gondola she was making. It was easily three times the size of the one Abilerit had made for Bale.

Big Water had been a really nice trip. Neesha had paid for just about everything and Beenala still didn't quite feel right about it even if—after swearing the two of them to secrecy—Neesha had shown Tollar and Beenala her hoard of slightly magical diamonds. They were worth about thirty gold pieces each, and Neesha had a whole rice sack full of them. She'd got them a nice suite in an inn overlooking the river rapids and had paid for the luxurious fabric Ember and Beenala now worked with.

Beenala heard Tollar's voice out in the hall and sat up straighter. She reached into the cupboard for the white dress and went to the door. Glancing back, she saw that Ember stood between the door and the table so that her body blocked the view of the dress they worked on. She gave Beenala a curious look, but Beenala slipped out into the hallway without a word.

"Toll! Good nap?"

Tollar turned to face her and smiled, then spotted all the fabric in her hands. "What's this?"

"I know Neesha said they do gifts after dinner, but I thought that since part of my gift was something nice that actually fits you, maybe you'd like it now?" Beenala felt her cheeks grow hot as she held up the dress.

Tollar sucked in a breath, her silver eyes sparkling as she took it all in and ran her fingers over the fabric.

"Oh, is this Glerisian silk?"

Beenala pressed her lips together and looked down. "I haven't a clue. But it's soft and lovely and the exact right colour."

There was a smile in Tollar's voice when she said, "That's all entirely accurate. Thank you, Bee. This is perfect."

Tollar kissed Beenala's forehead and then took the dress upstairs to change. Beenala slipped back into the studio, cheeks flushed and hands sweaty. She needed to wait a moment, breathing carefully, before she could resume her work.

Ember had a machine that was perfect for sewing the seams, but she and Beenala had agreed that an invisible stitch was the only proper option for the hem and neckline, and that was something they had to do by hand. And while Beenala was good at it, she only sewed things more as a hobby, whereas this was Ember's whole life. So she had the much wider hem and still looked to be finished before Beenala.

"She didn't nap as long as we were expecting," Ember said. "Why don't you go hang out with her? Otherwise you know she's going to try to make her own dinner or something."

Beenala snorted. "She's reliable like that. Are you sure?"

"I'm almost done this bit, and there's not much left on the neckline. I'll have it done in no time."

Beenala took her leave, both grateful and guilty. She should be finishing the work on Tollar's gift. But also, Ember was right—Tollar would get in the way and possibly discover the dress before they had it finished. So she headed up the stairs, reaching the top just as Tollar came out of the room they shared.

Beenala froze, gasping.

The dress dazzled, glittering like new-fallen snow, the contrast of it making Tollar's skin look darker and more lustrous than normal.

Tollar laughed. "The two of you did a fabulous job on this dress."

"The silver matches your eyes," Beenala said in an exhale.

"Does it?" Tollar brushed out the skirt, scrutinizing it. "I suppose you knew it would."

"I suspected; Neesha agreed."

Beenala closed the distance between them and took Tollar's hands, kissing her knuckles.

"Honestly, the dress is a very simple design," Beenala said. "It's the fabric that really makes it."

Tollar did a little spin, the skirt flaring out around her long legs.

"I suppose it is something I could either lounge around in, or dress up with some jewellery and the right wrap and sandals to be properly glamourous."

Tollar started for the stairs, but Beenala tugged her hand and gestured to the door at the end of the hall leading to the rooftop patio. As Beenala understood it, Spark had built the main floor herself and the upstairs together with Neesha, and initially had envisioned it as a place where her family and friends could live with her. There was a small bedroom downstairs next to the forge that had originally been Spark's and was now a spare, and upstairs had originally meant to feature four bedrooms instead of the two.

But Spark had suddenly found herself with the entirety of her family before the house was done. Dionelle had taken up residence with Ondias, and while finishing the space for Neesha, they'd made use of the rooftop as a gathering place and decided that feature had to remain. So there were only two bedrooms upstairs, plus the large open outdoor space full of plants in brightly painted pottery with a lot of comfortable seating and cushions and one bench box to store the cushions in bad weather.

And it had a glorious view of the dragon city.

Beenala brought Tollar out to the patio now, curling up beside her on one of the couches, the two of them holding hands with a span between them. Tollar sat back with a dreamy smile, her focus on the shining city and the rainbow of dragons coming and going. Every now and then, a flash of Bale's black and purple went by. Beenala's gaze flit between the stunning, terrifying city and the way the light refracted off it to sparkle on the already brilliant dress and reflect in Tollar's irises.

Tollar caught her looking and smiled.

"This place is lovely," she said. "I'm glad we came, even if I'm not making friends with everyone like usual."

"I do appreciate all the quiet little hideaways to just sit and watch."

"Neesha's lucky to have this place. I can see why she's hesitant to leave, even without any duty she feels toward Spark."

Beenala's gaze went back to the city, beautiful and terrible, and then drifted to the pile of rubble at the northern end of the valley, debris leftover from when Loch had been part of a force that caused it to collapse. They'd only heard a little bit about it—Neesha was the most willing to talk of those who had been there, but even she didn't want to discuss it to any great extent, still feeling guilty for failing to save it. Beenala couldn't even imagine how much more intimidating the place had been before. It had apparently been three times taller than its current height.

"How long do you think we'll be here?" Beenala asked.

Tollar cut her an amused glance. "Ready to go home?"

"Of course I am!" Beenala shook herself and gave Tollar a look. "I'm happy to be here with you, but I wasn't prepared for this. I don't know for sure that my parents and Per Graza will look after the farm. And we're going to be gone for so long."

Tollar touched her face. "We'll be home again before the babies come. And that's maybe only a little longer than the time we spent in Port Sawulxo. If we can get all this magical nonsense sorted out soon, we might be home well before that, even."

"You think it will be that easy to beat Loch?"

"I think once we have all the magic we need in place, and the dragons, and hopefully more Guild wizards... It'll be a lot like it was when we got to Sawulxo. Some build up, and then over quickly. We can't afford to let it drag out more than it already has. I don't know yet what we're going to have to do, but it will have to be something that takes Loch out quickly."

Beenala sighed.

"But that's enough of that for today," Tollar said, patting her arm and smiling. "It's my birthday, and we're in the most beautiful place in the world—besides home."

Beenala rolled her eyes at Tollar.

"This dress really is lovely. Thank you." Tollar's smile was luminescent. "It could have been a sack and I would have been happy to have something that fits properly again."

Beenala nodded. They'd been here well over a month and had expected to be home by now, even accounting for any rest they'd want between their globe-spanning journey.

"Oh, Ember and I worked together on the pattern to make sure we can keep making the dress bigger around the middle." Beenala leaned forward, running her fingers along the seam to show Tollar where Beenala simply had to cut a few stitches to make the dress grow, an inch or so at a time. "From high waist down to the bottom hem is the same width."

Tollar laughed. "I'm going to be wearing a lovely tent by the time these babies come."

"A very lovely tent," Beenala agreed. "And then I can reshape it to whatever your body looks like afterward."

Tollar squeezed Beenala's hand before taking it up to kiss the back of it. "That was very thoughtful of you."

Beenala was still blushing when Ember came up to tell them that dinner was ready.

There'd been plenty of exclamations over Tollar's new dress when they arrived for dinner, but now everyone was silent for the moment, enjoying the meal, while the dog padded around the room waiting for scraps to fall. Beenala wasn't entirely sure what she thought of the rabbit stew, thick with gravy and root vegetables, but the rest of it was excellent. There was some sort of bird, not quite chicken but close, roasted in a buttery herb sauce, with fresh warm sliced bread and little pastries stuffed with tomato and herb-infused goat cheese. The pastries were courtesy of Nandara. There was leafy salad and fruit tarts, and of course the coconut rice with a dash of cinnamon, just the way Tollar loved it.

There were various compliments about the food and a couple of minor, good-natured scuffles toward the end of the meal as Croves and Raia fought for leftovers, Spark occasionally snatching something before they could to pass it to Shadow. As much food as there'd been on the table at the start, Beenala didn't think there'd be anything left by the end.

As everyone finished their rice—Tollar had been given two helpings—Beenala made the after-dinner chocolate, while everyone else presented Tollar with gifts. Jatt had made a small portrait of Tollar stroking Bale's nose that was surprisingly detailed for its size. Spark shyly presented Tollar with a leather pouch a bit bigger than the ones Tollar typically wore on her belt for battle. The pouch itself contained spiky little metal balls.

Tollar gasped. "Filled with water!"

"Mamma told me about the arrowheads you used. I know you brought your sword, but I didn't figure you'd have all your weapons."

"These are fantastic!" Tollar tipped the pouch out and made the spiky little balls hover up over the table and dance around each other.

"Dragonproof," Spark said.

"Everything she makes is dragonproof," Neesha added. "That pouch will be too."

Neesha's gift was not especially dragonproof, though it was certainly dragony—a glittery pendant made from dragon-city obsidian and one of the diamonds from her stash. Croves helped Tollar clasp it on, and it was perfect with the sparkling white dress she wore. Croves and Raia, of course, had been responsible for the chocolate and the coconuts.

"Got enough to make ye some coconut rice two or three more times, depending on whether ye share," Croves said.

"He found some good spices, too," Beenala added, setting out mugs of drinking chocolate for everyone. She'd flavoured them all with cinnamon, but put the hottest spice in the mugs for her, Tollar, and Croves. Neesha tried a bit of Tollar's and decided she liked it, so Beenala spiced hers as well. Spark tried some of her mother's newly spiced chocolate and immediately coughed and wheezed.

Sweating and sounding distressed, she asked, "Oh hells, is this what burning feels like?"

That got a good laugh. The dog barked and sat next to Spark with his head tilted in concern. And then Ember presented Tollar with the blue-purple dress, and showed her the black silky fabric they'd bought but hadn't had time to make a dress out of yet. Tollar's eyes shone as she squeezed Ember's shoulder in thanks.

"It will be good to have clothes that fit. And pretty ones!"

It was the part of the evening when Tollar would normally bring out the first bottle of wine, but since she couldn't have any, everyone opted for another mug of chocolate. Though Beenala was certain Croves and Raia had a flask of something strong they were using to enhance their drinks.

At Neesha's insistence, they headed up to the rooftop again. "A clear night like this simply can't be wasted."

And it was warm and pleasant in the valley, though the sun had retreated behind the mountains. Its amber light made the city appear aflame.

Tollar dropped onto a couch with Croves, folded up in his big arms, and Beenala pulled a chair up next to them. Ember and Spark curled together on one of the other couches with the dog at Spark's feet, while Neesha dropped into the other chair, and Jatt and Raia sprawled out on the cushions.

Jatt and Ember, who had lived in this settlement the longest, told them some of the lore and the best things about living here.

"What's this place called, anyway?" Tollar asked. "Bale told me what the dragon name for the city up there is. Something unpronounceable that she's not allowed to translate to a human language."

Neesha snickered. "We'll have to let Ondias know."

"Sure, why not? She already doesn't like me." Tollar laughed. "But what's the name of this settlement down here?"

"While the dragons don't think of the valley floor very often and didn't have an official name for it," Spark said, "the closest translation of what they do call the valley is Rubyvale. It hasn't really caught on, though. Everyone just keeps calling it the human settlement."

"Ah, very creative." Tollar asked the two present fireborn what they knew about dragon magic, but even in a place like this, with humans the dragons trusted most, they didn't know much about it. It sustained the city, it had kept Neesha alive for seventeen years, it was probably how anything so large could fly, and they could enchant things and make fire portals. But no one really knew how it worked, or what their spells looked like, or the extent of their power.

At some point while Neesha had been explaining a bit about dragons and fire demons, Tollar had taken out one of her little spiky weapons from Spark, bobbing it in the air in front of her, and Croves kept using little gusts of wind to knock it around.

Tollar skewered him with a look. "You're always wasting your magic on pranks."

"What's the most petty thing you've ever used your magic for?" Neesha asked.

Croves chuckled. "Hard to pick just one thing. But probably using wind to put out lanterns at the worst possible time."

"Ye absolute tosser!" Raia said. "He was always putting the lights out on me."

"Aye, and then to my least favourite teacher at school. That man couldn't keep anything lit or any of his papers in order." His expression darkened a moment. "Came in handy when I was in Loch's dungeons. I put out every single light they tried to bring near me till the bastards finally got smart and used jars of glowing mushrooms."

Neesha nodded slowly. "I was always putting out lights on my brother, Bly. But there was the one time I incinerated one of his school projects and blew away the ashes, and to this day he doesn't know."

"I used to ruin Zarro's food." Tollar had an angry gleam in her eyes. She still hated that man after all these years, though Beenala couldn't really blame her. "I'd make things too soggy or dry it out. Only his portion, of course, right in the middle of eating. He'd get one proper bite and then the rest was just total rubbish."

While Croves explained to the northerners what a subfather was—they called it something different—Beenala realized she actually had a story.

"I used terramancy on my brother, the youngest one, when we were kids. He was being an absolute toad, so I buried him up to the knees in the ground."

"Huh," Spark said. "I can't think of ever being really petty with magic. Not on purpose, anyway."

Ember snorted. "There was that time you froze me with dragon venom."

"That wasn't petty, it was necessary! And it wasn't with magic anyway."

"You're only ever petty when it comes to Ondias," Neesha said.

Spark brightened. "I think the worst we've done so far was hiding the truth about dragon names from her."

"I don't have magic," Ember said, "but even then, I can't think of the pettiest thing I've done because I'm just sort of always low-grade petty."

"It's one of your charms." Spark nipped her with a quick kiss on her ear.

"If we're not including magic," Jatt said, "there was this bully of an apprentice when I first got here, and he got drunk and passed out one night, and I painted some rude things on his face and his clothes."

"Oh, I did that to my brother! Same one I sank in the dirt," Beenala said. "He was being a toad again, so I painted his face purple in his sleep."

"Bee!" Tollar laughed. "Poor Erxo. I didn't think you had it in you."

Beenala stuck her tongue out at her.

It wasn't long afterward that Jatt took his leave, the sky rich and dark and glittering above. Ember and Spark followed not far behind him, the dog trotting off in their wake.

"Well, I guess I ought to go summon Dragon to bring us back up to camp," Raia said, heading inside for the stairs.

Beenala helped Neesha stow the cushions in their bin, then looked around for Tollar, only to find her deep in a kiss with Croves. Beenala's face went hot, and she followed Neesha inside to wait.

"It really doesn't bother you?" Neesha asked.

"I thought it would," Beenala admitted. "But I'm confident with my place in her life, and honestly the idea of trying to kiss her like that makes me feel sweaty and uncomfortable."

Neesha grinned, squeezed her shoulder, and headed downstairs. Beenala leaned against the wall outside their borrowed bedroom, and Croves escorted Tollar in a moment later, handing her off and patting Beenala on the shoulder.

"Fine work on the dress." He winked and headed off.

Tollar took Beenala's hand as they headed into their room. "It really was a lovely day. Couldn't have been better even if we'd been home."

Beenala curled up next to Tollar, trying to still her thoughts enough to sleep.

"I've been thinking," Tollar said.

"That's always trouble."

Tollar laughed and gave her a playful swat. "It doesn't look like we're getting a whole lot done with magic at the moment, and the break going to Big Water was wonderful. So I was looking at the maps and we're only a day and a half dragon-flight from Bettar, where I got that pigment you loved. If a dragon will take us, do you want to go? We can probably trade some of the chocolate for more pigment."

Beenala propped herself up on one elbow to look at Tollar in the dark. "Really? Another adventure?"

"We're practically there already, and I'd love to go back. Why not now? It's nearly a two-week journey otherwise."

"Let me think about it." But that was what Beenala had said about Big Water too. And Tollar was right: if they were here and not doing anything, they may as well see as much as they could. She'd much rather be headed home, and they might go yet. Beenala had brought up that she and Tollar should head back home if there was no further magic work for them to do, and Tollar could meet the fireborn women in Port Sawulxo or wherever when the time came to face Loch.

Ondias had considered it and was planning something, though Beenala wasn't certain what. If they couldn't go home, a change would certainly be nice.

IN THE SKIES

Void Behind the Stars stood with the council and the Superiors at the meeting requested by the Guild via Ondias. In part, the wizards were reporting on progress with both planning and practicing, but they also had a request.

As Void Behind the Stars had been present for some of the demonborn training—and if she wasn't, Brooding Cloudwall often was—she had a good idea of the progress they had and hadn't made. Thankfully, Neesha and Tollar were continuing to work well together, harnessing each other and working on different skills, though Tollar was certainly reserved with her magic. Void Behind the Stars understood there had been some issues with water demons.

"The demonborn and the Guild have not yet been able to address Tollar's concerns about harnessing," Ondias said. "We believe we have the correct theory, but haven't found success in practice."

"This is why we need to return to the Guild and bring the demonborn with us," Dira said.

"Dionelle is the only wizard in the valley with the skills we need, but she hasn't been able to teach the others, nor will she let anyone—even Mita—harness her just to see if blocking can be done." Ondias sighed. "She needs care we can't give her here. And beyond that, there are members at the Guild who have a similar skill set who can help."

Majestic Sunrise lowered her head, bringing her gaze closer to the tiny humans before her. "I expect there are dragons enough to ferry you home."

"Indeed, and the trip itself looks to be less taxing than the trip here," Dira said.

"Mita has outdone herself with the new carrier."

Void Behind the Stars barely suppressed a snort. She would be the one ferrying the humans and everyone knew it. Spark had made the carrier specific to her dimensions. There was a second under construction, though no dragon had yet volunteered to wear it. Spark's gondola was much bigger than the one Brooding Cloudwall had used to bring her humans across the world, but it would not comfortably (if at all) fit the Joasera women, Dira and her councillors, and anyone else who decided they simply must join on the quest.

While they'd been talking for some days—possibly over a week now—about going to the Guild for more instruction, it seemed to be an unspoken understanding that they would not be returning to the dragon city until Loch had been defeated.

"Again, that is not something that requires the attention of the full dragon council."

"No, Mistress." Ondias bowed and yielded the floor to Dira.

Dira went through the proper greeting formalities before making her formal request.

"Mistress Superior and dragons of the council, the Wizards Guild formally requests your aid. We would be deeply indebted to have the full support of your kind in facing Loch. As you know, the Guild is on the cusp of a schism. Loch has built a guild of his own, composed of some troublingly powerful aquamancers, some of whom were responsible for this city's fall. We would see justice done and order restored, but we fear we no longer have the backing of enough of our membership to succeed."

Majestic Sunrise gave a troubled snort and conferred with the rest of the council in dragonish.

"This is a human problem. Let the humans find a solution!" Ocean Deep snarled, jumping in first.

"You wish to let enemy aquamancers run free and threaten this city again?" Void Behind the Stars snapped.

"The enemy aquamancers must be dealt with," Heart's Blood agreed. "However, we have taken on far too much risk already. They have low numbers and no plan. Do they expect us to do all the fighting for them?"

"A fair point," Majestic Sunrise said.

Void Behind the Stars wanted to disagree but couldn't. The humans did not yet have the skills they needed to guarantee a victory over Loch. Dragon involvement might tip the scales, and certainly they would be able to free more of their enslaved kin, but at what cost?

"I will of course go with them," Void Behind the Stars said. "I doubt I will be alone."

Ocean Deep snarled wordlessly at her.

"I wish to see the world cured of the blight that is Loch and his odious followers," Majestic Sunrise said.

"I believe the humans are capable of contributing more. Once the demonborn hone their skills, that will bring the odds more firmly in our favour," Void Behind the Stars said.

"That's still not enough," Heart's Blood said.

"No, but seeing what they can do may inspire a shift within the Guild itself," Void Behind the Stars replied. "Neesha and Spark both have been persuasive in the past. Tollar moved an entire nation to battle. And while Dira and her companions frequently overlook the southern wizards, Tollar will not."

"We need assurance of their numbers," Heart's Blood said.

"And that these demonborn can do everything they claim," Perilous Ice Floe added.

The dragons were swiftly in agreement after that, only Ocean Deep and a couple of her naysayers against the idea of any sort of action, even conditional. They were vastly overruled by the majority.

Majestic Sunrise turned back to the two wizards. "You are, of course, free to return to the Guild at your convenience, and dragons will certainly volunteer. We cannot guarantee you full support of the council or of our kind without knowing how many wizards you have on your side and what their skills may be. The demonborn must prove their skill. We expect a report once you've reached the Guild and given them adequate training."

Dira's expression was tight as she bowed and thanked the council. She was disappointed, of course. Void Behind the Stars had hoped for better as well, though she still trusted that her humans would meet the requirements laid out by the Superiors. She knew they could defeat Loch and hoped in time to see their full plan come to fruition.

CHAPTER TWELVE

Neesha pulled more and more water out of the swamps, feeling like she was going to drain them, drain the whole of the ocean, to fuel the vortex of water she churned higher and higher into the air, much like she did with columns of trueflame. The simple point of the exercise was to see how much water she could command with Tollar's power. Was there enough within her reach?

She could no longer both control what that water was doing and also add to it, so she stopped and did her best to hold it. The massive column of water wobbled.

"Oh shit," Neesha breathed.

She eased her pull on Tollar's power, letting some of it back in without totally relinquishing her hold. This was something else they'd been working on—transferring the power back and forth while still in use.

Tollar claimed a sloppy transfer of power was what had led to her falling off of Bale and spending a night at the bottom of a filthy river.

But Neesha lost control of it and all that water, the whole swamp's worth, crashed down toward them.

Thankfully, Tollar was quick, catching it all midair, a shimmering cloud suspended above them. She slowly syphoned it off, redirecting it back into the marsh, her face scrunched in concentration and beads of sweat forming at her temples. Neesha hadn't been able to control it all and also see into it to get a sense of its size, so she asked Tollar about it.

"I can't say for certain, but it's fairly close to the maximum of what I can control on my own."

Neesha frowned. "But if the effect is supposed to be amplified—"

"Power, yes. Control is something else. You just need more practice." She smiled. But her expression was also bleary as she massaged the middle of her forehead. "I think I've had enough for the moment."

Neesha was disappointed about going back, but she remembered how exhausted being pregnant had made her. And Tollar was carrying twins! She also got headaches when she did too much big magic. Neesha would not push her.

Bale had been napping some distance away, only half paying attention now that they weren't sparring, but she got up to ferry them back to camp, farther from the edge of the stinking marshes.

They'd left the dragon city while the Superiors were still discussing scenarios, but everyone generally thought they would support the attack on Loch. It would be foolish for them not to. But a lot depended on what happened when they reached the Guild.

Neesha and Tollar kept their practice away from the others—always with a dragon for support, but no other humans around. They were heading for the Guild at a leisurely pace, leaving well after dawn and the dragons flying only until late afternoon. It had been three days, and they were only at the marshes.

The trip across the ocean, of course, had to be done all at once. It was something they all worried about, though Tollar was confident she'd get them across.

Stopping early meant the dragons remained well-rested in case they did run into danger, but it also gave the wizards time to practice. Abyss was somewhere on the other side of camp with Spark, Dionelle, and Nandara. And while Dionelle would harness, she wouldn't allow herself to be harnessed yet. Neesha hoped the others were right that there would be a healer to help Dionelle at the Guild.

"Hopefully I just need a nap and we can spar more before dark," Tollar said once they'd landed again.

Neesha chastised herself for not keeping her disappointment out of her expression.

Though maybe the concern was shared equally. Tollar was desperate to block harnessing. Failing that, she wanted Neesha to learn as much as possible to help her when the time came. So they'd been sparring. The hope was that if Neesha could beat Tollar one-on-one, then she could beat Loch. Hopefully she wouldn't have to face him on her own, but if she could, then that just improved their odds.

But the sparring was taxing in different ways. Tollar had to give into her worst impulses and try to fight the way Loch would—the way Karthiry had. They hadn't tried to spar with either of them harnessing anyone else, but the fact was Loch would undoubtedly have wizards at his disposal.

Like garbage. Just logs for a fire.

It was clear why Tollar hated him.

But Neesha didn't like that Tollar was practicing things she hated so much in order to beat him. She'd been using blood magic on Neesha in their fights—far away from the others, of course. The last thing they needed was for Spark or Dionelle to see that.

"We've got lots of time," Tollar said, a hand on Neesha's shoulders. "Cursed ancestors, I never thought I'd meet someone as impatient as I am!"

Tollar laughed, and Neesha took the ribbing in stride.

Neesha stood a bit awkwardly at the edge of their camp as Tollar strode over to their tent, where Beenala was sitting with her sketchbooks. Spark and Dionelle were still west of camp, doing some harnessing—Neesha watched a fireball flare in the distance—and Croves was with Raia and the other riders, off practicing. The little dots of their dragons were visible in the skies to the south. Bale's large shape receded as she raced off to join them.

That left them sitting idly in their own tent or going to see what Dira and her companions were working on—probably napping, if she was being honest. They slept even more than Tollar did.

Neesha sighed and headed for the large tent/gondola thing Spark had made them for the journey.

"What are you doing?" Tollar called, sitting down next to Beenala. "Come join us."

Neesha shrugged and went to sit on the other side of Beenala, who was sketching Raia in mid-leap from Flame to Shell. Jatt had offered to send more art supplies with Beenala, but she didn't know when they'd be in the dragon city again to return them so she'd refused. She did have a really lovely painting of the city and the valley wrapped up and tucked into one of the cargo pockets along with the few art supplies she'd picked up in Big Water.

Tollar lay down and stretched out behind Neesha and Beenala, her back pressed against theirs.

"You sure you don't want me to leave you to rest?"

"I might not nap at all," Tollar said. "But I do really need to just lie here with my eyes closed and not move for a time."

Beenala tilted the sketch toward Neesha so it was easier to see, an invitation to give her opinion.

"Honestly, Raia's expression isn't demented enough."

Beenala giggled and Tollar snickered. Both of them had taken to Raia just as quickly as they had to Neesha. Neesha was more hesitant, not quite used to being surrounded by all these tall people. Her father and brothers had been taller than her, yes, but that wasn't exactly an impressive feat. Getting used to Spark's height had taken some time, and then here was Raia the same height but twice as thick, Tollar even taller, and Croves larger still.

Neesha wondered how much that contributed to how nervous Dionelle was. Loch was tall too.

Were they doomed before they even started? Could they overcome all these traumas before the autumn? They had nearly two months, but the pace just seemed glacial. She sighed.

"Tell me something about Yenette," Tollar said, her voice light with amusement though slurred with exhaustion.

"I don't know that there's much left to say that you'd actually want to hear." The bits Neesha had kept to herself were filthy and just not the sorts of things her companions would be interested in.

"You got a letter from her before we left," Beenala said.

"What—How did you—? Stone."

Beenala smiled but didn't look up from her work.

Neesha had been keeping Stone informed on what was going on with Yenette—or more accurately *not* going on. Neesha had received only four letters so far. So far they were talking around their wants, which were at odds. Their letters were full of longing, and Yenette's first with news that she had recently divorced. But Neesha spoke of the dragon city and how beautiful it was and how much she loved it, while Yenette's letters spoke of how much her children loved Pasdale and weren't old enough to be away from their father.

Neesha's smile turned sad.

"It was late winter when she wrote her most recent letter," Neesha said. She wished it were possible to get the wizards to send messages for them, or to convince a dragon to carry them. Instead their messages followed the trade routes, taking as long as they took.

"They were talking about getting a pet. They probably have by now."

"You should write to her," Beenala said. "We'll be close at the Guild—you might get a few exchanges in before we have to head south again."

"And she should probably know about what's going on," Tollar added. "Better to hear it from you than to get it through gossip later."

"I'll have to think about it." It was hard out here in the wilderness, with little privacy. Nandara was supportive and encouraging, but Dionelle was still being difficult about it. Especially lately. Had she expected it was something Neesha would grow out of?

She didn't want to write to Yenette with her mother able to look over her shoulder at any moment. Spark was starting to get weird about it too. Some kind of weird jealousy or possessiveness. Fear wasn't the only reason Spark didn't like Tollar.

A moment later, Neesha spotted the shape of Abyss returning and realized how much the light had shifted. It was late afternoon, winding into early evening. Croves and the others would be back soon as well. Neesha stood to greet Spark, Dionelle, and Nandara as they returned with the dragon.

"Leaving already?" Tollar murmured sleepily.

"I should see how it went. Maybe they've got some good news. And Spark will need a break from Dionelle, even if she insists she's fine."

Tollar turned over and gave her a sad smile. "You can be supportive without wearing yourself out."

"I'm fine." Neesha shrugged.

Tollar let it go, shifting around until she lay with her head pillowed on Beenala's soft thigh.

Neesha really *would* like to spend more time with her friends—especially time when they weren't practicing magic, Tollar wasn't napping, and Raia and Croves weren't off doing whatever it was they did all day. When they'd still been in the dragon city, their evenings had often been free, and Neesha had gotten used to the idea of having actual friends.

But Jatt and Ember hadn't come with them. Both were nervous about the idea of being in battle again, and Stone really needed Ember's help on the farm. There was also the possibility of Ember running into her brother on the wrong side of battle, though none of them really spoke about that. Spark did not have friends with her, and after two years of the three of them being inseparable, it was hard on her. She hadn't said she was lonely, but it was obvious in the way she clung to Neesha and Dionelle. But especially Neesha.

Neesha still didn't fully understand what her mother had been like in the seventeen years she'd missed, but whatever had happened in her year of imprisonment, everyone agreed she wasn't the same anymore. Whatever relationship Spark and Dionelle had had in Neesha's absence had been altered in ways Spark didn't like and wasn't coping with. It hadn't been too bad in the dragon city, and in a lot of ways Dionelle had been getting better—or seemed to be, anyway. But with Tollar's presence reminding Dionelle of the worst of it, she'd relapsed severely.

So Neesha greeted them and got the overview from Nandara—harnessing was going well, but blocking it still wasn't. Spark was developing some remarkable control while harnessing Dionelle.

"You and Spark really should practice together some time, especially since your power is so much stronger," Nandara said.

"Sure. Do you think you can work with Tollar on suppression?"

Dionelle, who had been standing on the edge of their group, stiffened. She wrapped herself tighter in her cloak despite the heat and turned to sit farther away with her back to the camp. Neesha sighed. Spark stared after her, frowning.

"I'll take care of it," Nandara said gently, giving Neesha a sad smile.

Nandara joined Dionelle, whispering softly while Dionelle sat stiff, occasionally shaking her head. Neesha sat in the shade of their tent/gondola with Spark and listened as she described what she'd been able to do.

"Oh, and I find it easier to see with fire if I close my eyes," Spark said. "Maybe that will help you with water?"

Neesha shrugged. Closing her eyes in battle would get her killed. But maybe in practice it could work to get her used to it. For all their practice, they had so little progress—they had things they could do well in controlled circumstances, but nothing about facing Loch would be controlled. Especially for Dionelle and Spark, who had both suffered directly because of him.

They both had to deal with their emotions.

Neesha was grateful that Tollar had taught Spark how to swim—it removed one of Spark's fears about battle. It was easier to chip away at Spark's fears. She was young, had a touch of Neesha's recklessness, and also hadn't suffered to the same extent Dionelle had.

A lot rested on what the Guild could teach them.

The other dragon riders returned shortly afterward, and Spark looked wistfully at Raia. "You can go talk with them. Dionelle has Nandara and the Guild council. Why don't you skip harnessing tomorrow and go fly with them? You need to practice that as much as magic."

Neesha still wasn't worth anything climbing around on dragons. Spark had made it easier, building her a harness with a release cable so she could—very slowly—move around on Abyss in flight without embarrassing falls. It meant better vantage points for her to use magic in battle. But even with what Tollar had taught her, Neesha was not going to be stabbing anyone or throwing anyone off a dragon with anything but her magic.

Spark glanced hopefully in the direction of the dragon riders again. But her expression fell as Tollar approached her and Neesha.

"Want to spar?" Tollar asked Neesha. "We've got a bit of time before dinner, and I'm rested up now."

"I'll be there in a minute."

Tollar went back to Beenala and Spark glared at Neesha.

"I'll lure her away, and you can feel free to go over and talk to your other friends. Go let Raia know you want to train with them tomorrow."

Spark gave her a look but didn't argue. Neesha patted Spark's knee and stood, joining Tollar.

Neesha desperately wished there was more she could do to help Spark get over her fears and adjust. But Spark didn't have Dionelle to rely on, which meant she relied almost exclusively on Neesha. Neesha nearly tripped over her own feet when she realized she'd become the very thing she'd fought so hard against before Spark was born.

Neesha had never minded the idea of being a mother; she just never wanted it to be the *only* thing she was. And here she was, wearing the title of mother like shackles.

"Let's head away," Tollar said, pulling water out of who knew where and giving them watery disc to travel on.

They were well beyond being heard by anyone at camp when Neesha asked, "Blood magic again?"

It was the only reason Tollar ever wanted to spar away from the others. They both knew Dionelle—and probably most of the others—weren't going to react well to seeing Tollar use it, even with consent, even for the purpose of trying to beat Loch.

"Yes. You're still too upset by it."

"Is this really something I can get used to?"

"Well, maybe not. I don't know. I don't use it like this—I don't use it regularly *at all*. But we know he'll use blood magic on you if he can."

"Fine, but what about you?"

Tollar's look turned sly. "He can try. I suspect it will only raise my fury."

Tollar stopped them once they'd cleared another ridge, close enough to the swamps to smell them again.

"I hate this," Neesha muttered.

Tollar looked thoughtfully back toward camp. "Do you think we'll ever get your mother or daughter to work with us on this?"

"Spark, maybe."

Tollar frowned. "This is supposed to be a team effort."

"Two people can be a team."

"A bigger team would be better."

"I keep trying to tell them that."

"Hmm." Tollar glanced back again. "What about Nandara and Dira and her council? Are they trying? Everyone laments the sacrifices you've made—the big one in particular—but you're still doing it, even if on a smaller scale."

"What I lost in those seventeen years doesn't weigh on me the way it weighs on my family."

"Yes, but you're still not making any gains. Don't you want more?"

Neesha wasn't entirely sure what she wanted. Or maybe it was that she didn't know how to *have* what she wanted. She wanted to be with Yenette. She wanted to keep being friends with these people from the other side of the world. She wanted to keep being there for her daughter. She didn't see how those wants could coexist.

"I want to beat Loch," Neesha said. "I'll have some space to think about more when we don't have to worry about him."

Tollar shrugged and stood solemnly. "Are you ready?"

Neesha nodded that she was. But it was still a moment before Tollar did anything. Was it possible that Tollar hated using blood magic even more than Neesha hated it being used on her?

And then Neesha was hit with the sick feeling of not being in control of her own body anymore, but it was far worse than an uncontrolled demon possession. She wasn't aware of much through that. But this? She felt the pull, and if she tried to resist, it was like being torn apart from the inside.

She didn't know advanced enough aquamancy to counter it—to keep her blood where it belonged, not like Tollar could. Neesha had brought a small lantern with her, as she couldn't rely on using her hands to light the flint like this. She pulled fire from it now and tried to throw a fireball at Tollar, but ended up on her face in the grass before she could get much control.

"You need to be faster," Tollar said, her tone gentle.

Tollar's hope with this was that she could desensitize Neesha to it enough that she could launch a counterattack before Loch could kill her with it. Neesha wasn't sure it was possible. She trusted Tollar but still couldn't get over the initial horror of what was happening to her quickly enough.

"You really think this will work?"

"If you're fast enough, yes. He's not really going to expect that you can counter this at all. Of course, there's nothing you're going to be able to do if he cuts off the blood supply to your brain."

Neesha stared at her and went cold. "You didn't think sooner was a good time to mention that's a thing he can do?"

"You're nervous enough."

Neesha dragged her hands down her face. "Tollar, be honest. Is there any point to this?"

Tollar sighed and looked back toward camp. "If we can get your mother to tell us what happened... I know it's hard for her. But any information can help me put together a picture of how Loch fights. We *know* he's going to try this. But maybe he likes the fear. Maybe he won't go straight for killing you or driving you unconscious. I didn't learn much fighting him, except for the strength of his power. He was more focused on the dragons than on me."

Neesha didn't actually want to know what Loch had done to Dionelle or why he'd felt the need to use blood magic on her when she had no hope of escape. Probably the fear. He'd been doing things to intimidate the family before he nearly succeeded in wiping them out.

But information meant strategy. It meant focusing their practice. It would make it easier to use what time they had more wisely. Neesha wasn't sure it was possible anymore—brute strength with little finesse might be their only advantage.

Hopefully the Guild would have the answers they needed.

CHAPTER THIRTEEN

Spark watched the moons shining on the black surface of the ocean and shivered. There were no dangerous wakes visible out there, but that didn't mean anything. Especially when it was so dark. There were two glittering bands from the moons, and the rest was a deadly void.

They'd gone a full day north of the normal crossing and had been resting here an extra day to be sure the dragons could make it all the way across when it was so much farther between shores here.

At least they were out of the marshes and their stink, even if the rocky plateau was cold and windy. Its cold fingers scraped through her short hair and tugged at her robes, sinking into her bones. She should go back to the tent, nestled against Abyss for heat. But she couldn't sleep, not with the weight of tomorrow's crossing pressing down on her. Or the snoring.

Nanny had a whistly nose, which was only a little annoying, but someone nearby was practically roaring in their sleep.

It had been difficult to sleep throughout the journey, but tonight was extra bad. And it wasn't just her. She'd finally managed to doze off when Beenala screamed. That it had been swiftly followed by Tollar's soft murmuring meant it was a one-person emergency, not some kind of attack. Beenala was still battle-scarred from her first fight with Loch.

Spark supposed they all were, in one way or another.

She wished she could have stayed home. She didn't want to fight, but this needed to end. Knowing what Loch was doing not only to dragons but to whole other nations—like he'd tried with Tollar's home, and like he was doing to these islands he'd taken over—was what drove Spark forward. What let her endure leaving Jatt and Ember and the safety of home.

She wished it was enough for her to work with Tollar directly like Neesha did. Wished it was enough for Nanny to pull through and be more like Spark remembered her.

A scrape on stone startled her, and she turned to see Tollar slowly approaching. She stopped a few feet away from Spark, staring out at the ocean.

"I was already awake when Beenala had the terrors," Tollar said. "I know that I should sleep, that I need to be alert for the whole crossing tomorrow."

"The entire thing?" Spark gave her a look.

"It would be best. We'll all have to take turns keeping watch. Raia wanted to scout ahead, but it's really not safe for us to split up. Even if Croves goes with her, one aeromancer isn't enough if those beasts attack."

"Is one aquamancer going to be enough?"

Tollar smiled. "I didn't do so bad on the way here. But no, it'll be your light beams and Neesha's trueflame that'll really make a difference."

"I guess I should try to sleep, then."

Tollar tilted her head, regarding Spark carefully. "You know, if you were at home, you wouldn't be asleep yet. I don't know how you can keep yourself from growing too bored through the night, but maybe you should wait before you try to sleep and then rest through the morning like you normally would. Neesha will be ready if we need pyromancy. You can take the afternoon shift."

Spark blinked, not wanting to admit it was a good idea—but it was a good idea. She should have thought of it first.

"You're not worried about getting across?" Spark asked.

"Well, I can't drown, so no."

Spark rolled her eyes and Tollar grinned.

"Even then, I'm not too worried. I made it with only Croves and Bee for help the first time. Now there are more of us. I *am* a little worried about Bale. She's not full grown and the two-day crossing was a lot, but the winds are in our favour." She shrugged.

Spark glanced back at the sleeping dragons. She hadn't really noticed anything unusual about Bale's size. Maybe she was a bit thinner than Abyss and the other dragonesses?

"We can do it," Tollar said, warmth in her voice. Then she headed back to her tent, leaving Spark to watch the waves and worry.

Spark fumbled blearily around, getting the gondola hooked up to Abyss and trying not to lose her footing while she double- and triple-checked everything. Neesha was with her, both of them holding out fire to see, but Neesha still moving far too slowly. Spark didn't think she'd slept more than a few minutes before Neesha was shaking her awake again. There was the vaguest brush of grey on the horizon ahead of them, and she could just barely make out the silhouettes of the other dragons getting outfitted.

Ice had volunteered to wear the other gondola Spark had made so that she and her family didn't have to cram in with the Guild wizards. It was a lot of work to get all three gondolas ready for flight. And it would be a while yet before Spark could climb back into hers and sleep.

Once the checks were complete, Tollar went to the cliff edge and climbed down. Spark joined Beenala and Neesha, watching Tollar's slow progress. Spark could barely see Tollar in the pre-dawn gloom, but it looked like she had her feet in the ocean. A moment later, she rose up on a column of water and calmly stepped off onto solid ground.

"It's clear for as far as I can see. Let's go."

So no sea beasts, then. At least not yet.

Good. Spark would get some rest after all, and as much as she loved the feel of the wind on her face while Abyss was in flight, it was nice to curl up in the warm gondola and sleep while Neesha and Nandara whispered quietly to each other or watched silently out the little windows at the ocean passing beneath them.

Spark slept—and might have kept on sleeping most of the day, except she thought she heard shouts. Abyss had banked awkwardly, jolting the gondola on an angle so that Spark rolled against the cargo pockets.

"I don't see anything," Nandara said.

"Nothing here," Neesha replied from the other side.

But Spark heard yelling again. She was pretty sure it was Croves.

"I'll go see," Spark said. Of the four of them, she was the only one who could climb from the gondola in mid-flight without worry of plummeting to her doom, even without her flight suit. She was tempted to strap it on before she went out, but there'd been an urgency in Croves's voice that she didn't like.

And then she heard another voice, one they'd only heard once before: Shell. His words were lost to the wind, but also held urgency. Spark understood that Shell had been speaking infrequently, and only to Croves, since Neesha's awakening had returned their voices, but he'd been speaking more since shortly after arriving in the dragon city.

More proof that the dragons and their power were tied up with the power of the fireborn women.

"Ach, it's no use!" Croves shouted, loud enough to be heard clearly this time. She had to get out there.

But as soon as she pushed open the door to climb out, she instantly saw what it was.

"Oh hells!" she gasped.

Neesha was next to her, there to close the flap again once Spark was outside. "Wow," she said.

The seas ahead of them churned beneath towering black clouds that were lit deep purple in their cores from relentless lightning.

Spark turned her attention back to the handholds in front of her and climbed. When she reached Abyss's back to get a better view, she saw the dragons were flying in tight formation, Bale very close on one side and Ice on the other, with Flame trailing them while Shell and Dragon were up front. Eltir and Barlo were still with their dragons, but Raia and Croves had joined Tollar on Bale. Raia waved Spark over when they spotted her.

Abyss angled up and held her wing steady as Spark sprinted across it and jumped to Bale. She slipped, but Bale corrected and kept her up. Spark wasn't as sturdy with dragon-walking as she'd like, but Bale seemed quite used to working with humans.

"That looks bad!" Spark shouted over the wind. "How much will it delay us to go around?"

Tollar bit her lips, and Croves shook his head. "Nah, we can't go 'round. We tried already, and it follows us."

Spark blinked. "How is that possible?"

"Like those storms that tried to drown your home. The Pasdale floods."

"But Loch caused those. Is he—?"

"I doubt it." Tollar shook her head. "It's hard to say where the elementals causing this are."

"How would they know?" Spark's limbs buzzed.

"We haven't figured out how he spies on us," Raia said.

"We suspect those water beasts. Maybe he's got demons themselves watching for dragons to cross." Tollar looked out toward the storm. "Abyss and Bale are both distinctive, though there might be instructions to make things difficult for any dragons over the oceans."

"Do we turn back? Abyss usually takes the northern archipelago when she crosses—it's safest."

"We're going to try to keep going," Tollar said.

Croves growled. "Yer daft!"

Tollar gave him a hard look and turned to Spark. "Now that you're here, I can scout to see what exactly we've got ahead of us."

"Scout?"

"She means to jump into the ocean," Croves snapped, his face reddening.

"I don't need to jump. I can use a water portal. I can go down there, see what's ahead of us and where the elementals are. Then a portal to get back up here. I'm so glad your mother taught me those."

Spark gave her a tight smile. "How can I help with any of that?"

"For starters, you can hold my puddle still while I go down."

Croves looked like he was going to argue again when Tollar pointed harshly at the lines tattooed on her cheeks, and he subsided. Right. Rank lines. Neesha explained that it made Tollar in charge of any sort of battle-type situation, unless there was someone else around with even more lines on their face.

Tollar had apparently earned all those lines by getting people through these sorts of situations alive. Spark had to admit it was kind of nice to have someone who knew what in all the hells they were doing in a fight.

Tollar pulled water out of the air around them and made puddle on Bale's back. She glanced at Spark, who had to focus to keep the thing from blowing away. Spark was still terrible at aquamancy, but at least she could do it at all.

Tollar opened the water portal and dropped into it. Croves hissed out in wordless anger.

"Oi, it'll be all right," Raia said to him. "She's right—if she can find them, we can stop 'em and keep going."

"We could just turn back and go north. We got time."

Raia's expression was longsuffering. "None of us wants to turn back and ye know it."

Before Croves could argue further, Tollar climbed out of the puddle-portal again.

"Still no beasts," Tollar reported. "And I found the elementals. They're in a boat."

Raia grinned and it was a vicious thing. "Well, Spark here is queen of sinking boats. She took down most of Loch's armada."

Spark didn't want to correct her—Neesha controlling the demons had had a fair hand in that—but she *had* sunk a lot of boats. This was only one, and it wouldn't have anyone as powerful as Loch on it.

The storm was on them not long afterward, Tollar keeping a rain-free bubble around them as they transferred Nandara and Spark's family over to the gondola with Beenala, and then unhooked the gondola from Abyss so Bale could carry it. This had been Tollar's idea. Keep them safe and keep the gondola from encumbering Abyss and then she would take them deeper into the storm.

Raia leapt back to Dragon while Tollar, Croves and Spark went to Abyss. Spark barely heard her mother over the storm, insisting she come with them.

It took longer than anyone would have liked for Abyss to carefully position herself under Bale so Neesha could jump. Croves was there to help keep her from falling off Abyss. There were a few straps left, and they all gripped them as Abyss dived into the storm, Tollar at her shoulder to guide her and funnel the rain away from them.

Lightning lashed the air around them and Tollar retreated lower, tight against one of Abyss's spikes. Rain pelted Spark, Tollar having lost her concentration. More lightning flashed by them, the fire in it sizzling across Spark's senses as she tried to redirect it around them, but it was so godsdamn fast.

She pulled herself along Abyss's back until she was closer to Tollar and then stood tall, back braced against a spike, her arms spread. This was probably a terrible idea.

She called to the lightning. Opened her magic to it much like she was summoning a demon.

The lightning answered.

It was like getting punched. And then it buzzed over her. But her fireproof gear held against it. Spark stumbled under the force of it, her feet sliding along Abyss's scales until the after image cleared enough for Spark to see a spike to grab onto. Neesha screamed over the wind, but Spark staggered upright again.

Could she channel it? Redirect it down toward the surface? It was probably possible, but she had no idea how and couldn't risk experimenting anymore than she had by making herself a lightning rod.

Tollar had given her a wide-eyed look for a moment, then grinned and went back to clearing them a path through the rain.

Spark felt like they'd been descending through the storm for an eternity when Tollar stumbled, bumping into the spike behind her before grasping a handhold, and then Spark was slammed with water. She worried for an instant that Abyss had plunged straight into the ocean, but more lightning slammed into Spark.

Tollar was curled up on Abyss's shoulder, a handhold wound around her fist keeping her in place.

"I need help," Tollar called out, her voice barely carrying over the storm even though she was only a few paces away from Spark.

Spark dragged herself up Abyss's back to Tollar, who was reaching out a hand. Spark gripped it and immediately felt cold and empty, the sensation hitting her worse than the lightning had. Her vision blurred and she reeled.

Tollar's grip was strong, holding her in place and the water wasn't slamming into them anymore, but Spark almost wished it was so she could explain why she felt so cold. Spark screamed and jerked away before her brain fully caught up to what was happening.

But in her panic, she had nothing to hold onto and the wind from Abyss's dive slid her across the dragon's back. Until Croves caught her by the upper arm and dragged her in close to the spike where he dragged

Neesha along with him. The water hit them like a wave again, blinding, hard to breathe. Abyss growled.

Spark's cheeks went hot, her eyes stinging, as Croves dragged Neesha past and away, up to Abyss's shoulder and to Tollar. Neesha calmly took Tollar's hand, the larger woman pulling Neesha in and helping her get a grip on the hold. The water cleared around them, the dark blue surface of the ocean coming into view. Tollar had stopped the rain from drowning them, but Spark's cheeks were still wet and she tried to sink down between two spikes like the fool she was, but Croves was back, pulling her to her feet.

"Ye need to be ready with yer light beam," he said, guiding her up to Abyss's other shoulder, ignoring that she was a fool who had panicked and nearly got them all drowned.

She was grateful he'd given her something to focus on other than her own self-loathing. He stood just behind her with a comforting hand on her shoulder, and sometimes she hated how nice these people were. Maybe it would be easier if one of them would just get angry at her for being such a little fool.

She managed to stay calm, even when tentacles of water rose up out of the ocean from around a tiny little blot on the surface. Those water tentacles reached for Abyss, but disintegrated into rain before they got anywhere near.

The little blot resolved into a not-so-little boat. Abyss roared and shot fire down at them. Spark caught that fire and compressed it into a sharp beam, hoping she'd aimed it right because she had to squeeze her eyes closed against the brightness.

Abyss swooped and banked around.

"Ye hit 'em!" Croves called out, pointing.

There was a blaze on the ship, off to one side. There were no more tentacles coming out of the water, instead large waves lapped gently at the fire.

"Abyss, closer!"

She banked hard and Croves's reassuring hand became a steadying one, gripping tight. Spark remembered Raia's stories about his warhammer and hoped he didn't break any bones on her—though apparently Barlo could fix it. It would still fracture her concentration.

Abyss came in fast and hard, Tollar and Neesha disrupting the water tentacles and Croves deflecting whatever other counterattacks the elementals on the boat were trying. When Abyss breathed fire again, Spark directed it into another beam, getting the fire lined up right before it got too bright to look at.

This time when they swooped back around, the boat was in two halves, one almost entirely sunk below the surface. Abyss got in close, and this time Neesha rained trueflame down on what was left. The storm was already dissipating, and she wouldn't need to let Tollar harness her power anymore to keep them safe.

Abyss circled overhead, Neesha raining fire down on the pieces of boat whenever it looked like the fire would go out or like the elementals still alive below would salvage enough for a raft.

Spark couldn't be sure from this height, but there was likely enough small debris that they could, eventually, make themselves a raft and get to safety, but by the time they did, the dragons would be long gone. And that was assuming her mother hadn't incinerated them all.

Abyss finally pitched back up into the sky where the rest of their blaze drifted, waiting. Croves and Neesha swapped shoulders so he could make sure Tollar rested and Neesha could comfort Spark.

"Don't be so hard on yourself," Neesha said. "It worked all right."

"I should be able to do this!"

"Yes, but you need more practice first."

Spark remained curled up against a spike with her hands crammed over her face. She didn't want to think about it. Didn't want to face how she kept failing them all. Hopefully the Guild would have the help they all needed.

CHAPTER FOURTEEN

Tollar stood in the immense cave in the hollowed-out mountain staring at the pile of glittering bones, transfixed. There was urgent whispering behind her. They could be plotting to incinerate her, and she didn't even care. Neesha was there, so she doubted they were up to anything nefarious aimed at her specifically. And besides, Beenala would call out a warning if it was warranted.

When had Tollar become so paranoid?

Spark panicking over the ocean hadn't helped. Ice and Abyss having to carry Bale for the last hour or so hadn't either. Things had been strained and awkward since they'd hit the shore again, and it was even worse now. This cave was apparently about a day away from Pasdale, and the fireborn women were a mess. They weren't actually going to Pasdale, or over it, or even anywhere near it. As Tollar understood, they were going quite a ways north from here to bypass the city.

Tollar half wondered what the other cave looked like—the one where Croves had gone with the Guild wizards and his sister's blaze and their dragons to shelter for the night. This was Abyss's home, and it was her hoard that had utterly captured Tollar's attention.

It was bones. The whole thing was a pile of bones. But calling it a pile didn't do it justice. It was so artfully arranged. And the bones *glittered*. Tollar had never seen anything like it.

The cave itself was lovely, if rather overheated from the fact that it had four dragons crammed into it. Tollar really wanted to ask about that odd fourth dragon—Bale's cousin as she understood—but just could not stop staring at the bones. For the first time in a long time, Tollar wished Toresona was there. What would the old necromancer think of this? Tollar would have to be sure to tell her about it.

"Could I—" Tollar caught herself when she realized what she was about to say. She turned to Abyss, who seemed utterly pleased by Tollar's reaction. "Forgive me, Mistress. I fear I'm about to ask something dreadfully rude, but could I... borrow a small piece of bone?"

Abyss glared and all three fireborn women gasped. Right, so it had been ruder than she'd thought.

"I'm sorry," she whispered. "It's just that I know someone who would be deeply fascinated by this. I don't think she'd be able to make the journey down here either."

Abyss snorted and didn't answer and as far as Tollar could tell, that was a no.

Tollar bowed deeply. "Thank you for the honour of sharing this with us, Mistress. Might I ask how you found these? As you may know, my people hold on to bones, and I've never heard of anything like this."

Neesha snickered and Tollar had a moment to wonder if she'd said something wrong again, and then Abyss launched into an explanation—a well-rehearsed lesson, really—about how under the right circumstances, mostly in certain kinds of caves, bones could crystallize in such a fashion. Abyss had also learned the magic necessary to make these kinds of bones herself.

"There was, of course, some trial and error," Abyss said. "I practiced on spare bones from meals, incinerating the failures."

"Of course."

She went on to explain that the most prominently displayed were the ones that had occurred naturally, and the bear skeleton on the top was the favourite of the ones she'd made herself.

Tollar jumped into a pause and asked, "Do you think you could do that with my granny's bone?"

She held out the pendant to show the dragon, but Abyss only stared in the silent, patient way she did when humans made profoundly rude requests. Tollar subsided and Abyss went on with her lesson.

Most of the bones were animals, including what appeared to be a small dragon skull, but there were four human skeletons that Tollar could see.

She wondered if Abyss knew her cave was likely haunted. She wanted Toresona there even more now. But she also knew better than to ask any questions about ghosts. Maybe it was something she could encourage Bale to ask of her kin.

"Thank you for sharing your wisdom!" Tollar bowed deeply. "And thank you and your family for your kind hospitality. I'm sure we don't deserve it."

Abyss snorted again and Tollar was worried she was only making things worse, but Neesha chuckled and came to stand with her.

"Abyss doesn't love formality," Neesha explained.

"Ah. I'm beginning to understand when you say she is unlike the other dragons. She and Bale both."

A wordless grumble like an unsettled volcano came from the next chamber over.

"Merciless Winter Sky is more of a traditionalist," Abyss said. Tollar assumed the grumble had come from him. "Our offspring are more divided. Our son, Searing Thunderbolt, shares my interest in humans—I assume in part because Spark helped rescue him from Loch and was there when he hatched, much as you were there for Bale. Our daughter Shattered Starshine is more of a traditionalist." Abyss paused to glance back at the odd little dragon curled up with Dionelle, who hadn't stopped sobbing since they arrived. The dragon was slightly larger than an adult male, but nowhere near as large as a full-grown dragoness. And she was entirely white but for a few fire-coloured touches at the tips of all her spiky bits.

"Glacial Sunfire," Abyss continued, "hasn't given indication one way or another. She doesn't speak and rarely leaves our mountain."

"Ah." Tollar smiled politely. "And do Searing Thunderbolt and Shattered Starshine live here as well? Are we crowding them out?"

"They roam," Abyss said. "It is a young dragon's way. They come here when they truly need shelter, but for the most part they travel and meet new dragons and cause trouble and get into fights and look for a new blaze to join."

"Should... I send Bale off to travel then?"

Beenala scoffed from her place next to Spark where she was furiously sketching in her book. Spark was trying her best to console her grandmother, though Tollar wasn't sure that the tears were entirely caused by grief. She'd done almost as much staring at Abyss's hoard as Tollar had.

"The naming ceremony is a dragon's introduction to travel," Abyss said. "Though I don't believe you will have difficulties in that regard."

Abyss gave her a knowing look, and Tollar wondered how much the dragons gossiped. Surely they gossiped about each other, but were humans high enough in esteem to be worth the effort to them? Well, Abyss wasn't exactly normal, and she *had* spent plenty of time with Bale, who knew as well as anyone how Tollar had been just about everywhere.

"Do adult dragons travel much?" Tollar asked.

"Some of us. My rank on the dragon council means that I am required to venture to the dragon city much more than other dragons. There was a time I had responsibilities in these lands, though those have lessened with the fractures in our relations with Pasdale. We have a quiet understanding with the nomadic herders that requires little input from either side, leaving me with less to do than normal. I do perhaps roam more than a dragon my age would."

"And how old are you?" Neesha asked.

"Ninety-four."

Tollar exchanged a startled glance with Neesha. She wasn't sure what she'd expected, but probably should have guessed this dragoness was old—though in reality she was barely middle-aged for a dragon. But Tollar knew she'd been friends with Dionelle since Dionelle was twenty, and the woman was nearly sixty now.

"You should take rest while you can," Abyss said, the tone more command than suggestion. And she bowed in a way that signalled dismissal and then carefully picked her way across the cavern to lie against the far wall, facing her glittering hoard.

Bale had been huddled in the space between the two caverns, and she lay down, stretching her head into the middle of this one, her snout not far from where Beenala still sketched, her tongue poking out the corner of her mouth. Spark still sat between Bee and Dionelle, rubbing her grandmother's back, but leaned to watch Bee draw.

Nandara appeared to be sleeping, though Tollar couldn't quite tell from here. She was curled up inside the gondola, at any rate. Tollar considered joining her, no idea what time it was with no daylight filtering into the cave, but she was tired.

Neesha had started to pace, though. Tollar stood with her hands on her hips and watched. It was weird, usually she was the one pacing, but she felt heavy—limbs leaden—right along with being tired. Neesha was jittery. She kept glancing at her family like she ought to join them and then pacing away. Despite the cave's tremendous size, it still felt cramped, particularly with all the dragons. Previous campsites had been wide-open spaces, and had included a lot more humans.

Neesha was still spreading herself thin, trying to train with Tollar, trying to enjoy having friends, trying to support her family through whatever it was they were going through. And now they were very close to the home they'd all lost.

"Do you want to talk about it?" Tollar asked quietly when Neesha's pacing brought her close again.

Neesha cast a quick glance at Dionelle, who was staring at the ground in front of her and didn't seem to be paying much attention to anything. She still wept, but it seemed to be wearing itself out.

"We're just so close. I miss it and I hate that it's too dangerous to go back."

"Do you want to go back?" Tollar asked.

"I wish I could. But it's hard. Dionelle and Spark don't want to go back. Too much loss. I lost half my family as well, but it still doesn't feel real, even after going back and seeing the house destroyed."

"And then our friends are all in the dragon city," Spark said. "There's nothing left for us to go back for."

"It's easy for them. But I'm torn," Neesha said. "My family is in the dragon city but—"

"Ah, but Yenette is here," Tollar said.

At the mention of the woman's name, Dionelle sucked air through her teeth in a way that sounded an awful lot like a hiss.

Neesha wandered farther away, and Tollar followed her. "Yes," she said, her voice lower. "And her letters sure indicate she's not leaving anytime soon. And I had other friends. They weren't people I was close with, but I don't know, maybe they could be friends, proper ones, again."

"So you're torn."

Neesha sighed and leaned against the stone in the little passage between the two dragon chambers.

"You may enter here," Merciless Winter Sky said.

"Are you certain? We don't wish to intrude," Neesha said.

"You are our guests, and we both wish for you to be comfortable," he said. "Void Behind the Stars is proud of the uniqueness of her hoard, but I have the largest collection of jewels in this entire mountain range."

Neesha chuckled.

"I'm glad I'm not the only one who likes to show off," Tollar said, striding into the chamber and stopping short for the second time that day. Abyss's hoard was certainly the more interesting of the two, but there was no denying the sheer size of this one. If it got much taller, he was going to have to fly to add to the top of it.

Neesha came to stand beside her, both of them staring. It was the only polite thing to do.

"What're you—oh my," Beenala gasped, coming to stand next to Tollar.

The three of them stood there, letting the silence wash over them and appreciating the glittering spectacle.

"I... guess I have something of a hoard of my own," Neesha whispered.

Tollar looked at her, but she'd glanced over her shoulder, then gestured for them to follow her deeper into the chamber.

"Oh, you mean the dragon diamonds?" Tollar asked.

Neesha nodded. "I've got a coin purse full of them with me, just in case."

"What did you do with the rest?" Beenala asked.

"It's in an old rice sack in the pantry."

Tollar burst out laughing. "Not going to keep it on display? It'd look lovely with the lighting in the studio."

Neesha sighed. "I don't even need fire to go anywhere or do anything for the entire rest of my life. And I still haven't thought of a single thing to do with it after two years."

"Sounds like you didn't know what you were missing until recently." Tollar sat against the stone wall, facing the hoard, with her legs stretched out. Neesha huddled against the wall next to her. Beenala had moved closer to the passage between chambers, her sketchbook open again. It looked like she had a good vantage of both the hoard and Merciless Winter Sky gloating over it.

"Everyone, including Spark, has been saying for the last two years that I need things in my life that are just for me. And I didn't really understand what they meant. I had Guild exams to study for, and magic was always my whole life until Spark was born, and recently magic is something she and I have been able to do together. I thought it was enough."

"Ah, and then we dropped in and ruined it all."

Neesha gave her a sidelong look. "And I don't know what to do. I raged against the prison of motherhood through my entire pregnancy, agreeing to marry Stone only in exchange for my freedom—and now here I am, shackled to the role anyway! Every option seems impossible."

"I know and abhor your people's customs, and yet I still find new ways in which to be horrified by them," Tollar said. "I struggle to understand how having a child is a prison?"

Neesha shrugged and flailed her hands desperately. "Mostly, it was because I was expected to marry, *especially* after I became pregnant. So many mothers leave public society once they marry and have children. My own mother was an outlier, in part because she'd managed to become so entrenched in her role before I was born. I've always wanted to be *more*. And now here I am, just Spark's mom and that weirdo who slept half her life away."

After sifting through and discarding half a dozen responses, Tollar carefully said, "But Spark is an adult now."

Neesha sighed. "Yes, but she still needs me."

"I still need my mother," Beenala said, not looking up from her sketch. "But I haven't seen her in weeks. And even when I'm home, I usually only see her twice a week."

"Okay, maybe I'm making excuses." Neesha took a shaky breath and looked desperately at Tollar. "I don't really know what I want, but the shape it's taking is just too big. I appreciate that I can do things like take a fire portal to come visit you for an afternoon or go other places for longer. And now you know you can come to the dragon city any time through the water."

Tollar grinned and then pressed her lips together. That possibility was an absolute delight to consider, though unfortunate that it couldn't include Bee or Bale. Still, pop in on midwinter to see their festival and then head home again before she had the chance to remember why she hated winter.

Tollar remembered how torn she had been for so long—wanting to see the world, to go everywhere and soak up everything, but also so desperate to be with Beenala. And having Bale to help her travel, knowing she always had a solid base to come home to—that she had a proper home in the first place—made her less inclined to leave but happier to return if she did. Tollar felt sure of herself in a way she never had before. Sure enough to do something as irrevocable as become a mother. She understood the weight of motherhood the way Neesha did, even if she didn't understand the limitations of it.

"I understand that you'll need to ease in to whatever shape your life takes next, but what's stopping you from starting small and taking a fire to go see Yenette whenever the two of you want?" Tollar asked.

Neesha startled. She stared at Tollar a moment and then looked at the stone floor in front of her, silent for a long time.

"I could," Neesha admitted, sounding shocked by the realization. "I could use my next letter to her to arrange it. I could see her whenever she wants. But we could never leave the safety of her home. It would have to be a secret thing. And feel shameful. It's… why we didn't keep at things when we were younger."

Neesha's face twisted in pain, her mouth pressing into a thin line and her eyes shining with tears.

"I'm sorry." Tollar rested a hand on Neesha's knee. "But what if it only had to be a secret thing for a little while? What if you knew there was an end date to the secrecy? You two clearly need to start talking straight at the problem instead of around it, but what if she will definitely go with you to the dragon city when her children are grown? How old are they now? How long would you have to wait?"

Neesha blinked away her tears, her brow furrowing. "That's still a lot of uncertainty."

"Right. So be more direct in your next letter. Start making things less uncertain. And things don't have to happen immediately. Beenala and I danced around the edges of our love for each other for *fifteen years*. And even then, it took Croves overtly flirting with me before I realized that what Bee and I had needed to be named and made real. You don't have to decide anything right now, or next month, or even next season."

Neesha gave her a stubborn look, but Tollar was determined.

"Neesha, look, we're going right past. Send her a letter. Start making plans."

Neesha shook her head. "I'll send her something from the Guild."

"I'll go," Tollar said. "I can take the river when we go past it and zip into the city and drop it off personally to her door and be back up the river to Bale in no time. No one in Pasdale knows who or what I am. I've never been there, and not even close—except to the Guild once, and that was years ago. It'd be no danger."

A refusal was building, Tollar could see it in Neesha's expression. But then Bee was standing in front of them, tearing a couple of pages from her sketchbook and handing them to Neesha along with a piece of graphite to write.

Neesha burst out crying again.

Tollar suppressed a chuckle and wrapped the tiny woman up in her arms until she'd calmed down, trying not to think foul things about the rest of Neesha's family—particularly her mother—and how whatever they'd done to her when she was young had resulted in Neesha being unable to handle kindness. Tollar knew well enough what her own family had done to make Tollar doubt that she was worthy of being loved.

While Neesha spread out the sheets of paper and began to write—sniffling and occasionally pausing to wipe tears—Tollar glanced first toward the other chamber and then to Beenala, who looked sad and a bit helpless.

Tollar struggled with helplessness herself. They could certainly continue to support Neesha in whatever choices she eventually came to, but it seemed it would be easier if her family—particularly Dionelle and her friends—would trust Neesha's judgement. How far could she push to intervene on her friend's behalf before she pushed too far?

And the fact that they didn't trust Tollar any more than they trusted Neesha was certainly a problem that would haunt them if they didn't solve it before facing Loch.

She'd have to have a quiet conversation with Beenala about it sometime soon. Tollar hoped reaching the Guild would have the answers they needed.

CHAPTER FIFTEEN

Neesha stood alone in the dragon chamber at the Wizards Guild feeling unexpectedly tense, when this was the quiet place in her mind she retreated to when she needed to win out against a demon. But in reality, the last time she'd been here, her life had changed drastically, and then nearly ended.

It was still a relief to be here and be surrounded by powerful wizards—ones nearly as knowledgeable as Dira and some with deep specialties that would help them find the answers they needed. So far, it had just been a lot of settling in, getting rest, and the more senior wizards exchanging information and trying to find the right place to start.

Neesha had been keeping to herself since they arrived yesterday. Dionelle was still in a mood, and Spark hadn't been to the Guild since the day she was born, so she was off getting into everything and getting in everyone's way. Neesha had initially trailed after her, always enjoying Spark's exuberant curiosity. But then she'd found the Guild's forge and basically hadn't left it.

Neesha didn't feel like she fit with them quite as well as she used to. Or maybe she never did and was only starting to see it now. She wished Beenala and Tollar were there. They should arrive soon, but Neesha wasn't sure how long Tollar would have needed to get through the valley and out again without drawing too much attention to herself.

And then there was the possibility that maybe she had. Neesha had come into the dragon chamber when she realized she'd been hovering around the message centre, expecting bad news any moment.

She turned at the sound of the door scraping open and Croves came in.

"Ah, here ye are! Bee and Toll are back, just getting settled in across the hall from ye."

Neesha barely suppressed the urge to bounce around or do anything as undignified as giggle, but the way Croves grinned at her suggested she wasn't doing much about keeping her excitement out of her expression.

"Come on, I'll walk with ye."

Neesha went with Croves through the labyrinthine passages of the Wizards Guild, which consisted largely of tunnels carved into a hillside with the only daylight coming through skylights, if at all. The last time Neesha had been here, most of the halls and rooms had been lit by firelight, but now there were little glass globes filled with light. The explanation she'd been given sounded like lightning was being harnessed to make little wires glow.

Croves had said they were common in Upalint, particularly in the cities, and a few other places in the south, though they'd started to catch on elsewhere.

They passed rooms meant for training and practice and meeting and teaching. Somewhere deeper into the hill, past the dragon chamber, was the massive library and council chamber. And then one large wing of the complex was personal rooms. The permanent residents, like Dira and the council, had larger suites of rooms deeper in the cave.

But there were small suites meant for individuals, and others ranging in size to accommodate whole families. Neesha and her family were at one end of the hallway in one of the mid-sized suites, next to Croves and his friends. Nandara was farther down the hall in one of the single rooms.

Croves brought Neesha to the room across from hers where Tollar and Beenala were unpacking their things, and then he took his leave. Beenala was setting up what art supplies she had on the central table while Tollar was steaming her dresses to get the wrinkles out—using only her magic—and hanging things in the wardrobe.

"You made it!" Neesha was unable to keep all the relief from her voice.

Tollar and Beenala both smiled. Tollar hung up the latest dress—the black one Beenala and Ember had made for her—and strode across the room to greet Neesha with a hug.

"How was it? No trouble?"

"It was lovely," Tollar said. "No trouble for me. But still not a place fully welcoming to you. Yenette invited me in and was very secretive."

"How is she?"

"Middle-aged and tired." Tollar gave her a wry grin.

Neesha laughed. "But she was well? Did you—?"

Dionelle cleared her throat from the doorway, startling Neesha.

"Oh, hi, Mamma! Bee and Toll just got back from Pasdale and dropping off my letter to Yenette and—"

Dionelle slashed her hand horizontally, as she sometimes did, to signal she'd had enough. Her jaw was clenched and her blue eyes flashed with amber.

Neesha's heartbeat raced and her limbs felt cold. "I really don't understand what part of this is so upsetting. Is it because of Pasdale? I'm not going back there until it's safe, that was the whole reason for Toll going. And who knows, maybe Yenette will come to the dragon city."

Dionelle shook her head vehemently.

"You don't like Yenette? Why? Is there something Nandara doesn't know that you do?"

Dionelle slashed her hand through the air again and then crossed her arms and glared.

"Wait. Is it because Yenette is a woman? Is that what this is about?"

Dionelle continued to glare.

Neesha's limbs went hot. "Really? When Bee and Toll, or Spark and Ember, have not caused the world to end by loving each other, you're drawing the line at me? What in all the hells is this?"

Dionelle shook her head and flung her hands out in frustration before turning away, signalling that she was done with the conversation. Neesha was not. She caught her mother's shoulder, vaguely aware of shuffling across the room from Beenala and Tollar—what must they think of all this?

Neesha gripped Dionelle's shoulder and got right in her face. "You might not remember because it was twenty years ago for you, but it was really only two for me—but you said that people like me had alternate options. I want those options, Mamma. Why don't you support it anymore? What's so different now?"

Dionelle fought to rein in her expression, to bring it to neutral, but there was something like grief in amongst her anger, and Neesha just wanted to shake the woman until she actually started to talk again.

"Don't you—"

A knock on the door startled them all and a moment later Nandara pushed in.

"The council has—oh." Nandara froze, staring at the scene. "Do you need a minute?"

"What does the council want?" Neesha asked.

"I think they may have some of the answers you've been looking for. They're waiting in the council chamber."

"Yes, fine. We need to get this over with." Neesha gave her mother a look that she hoped conveyed they weren't done, shot an apologetic glance to Beenala and Tollar, and then they all followed her mentor.

Neesha didn't like the grim expression on Dira's face as Neesha sat in the bench seating with her family, facing the council table. Beenala sat not far off, but Tollar did not. She paced in the open floor between the table and seating.

"All right, now that everyone is here, let's begin," Dira said. "We've got a lot of ground to cover."

Tollar abruptly stopped directly in front of Dira, hands on hips.

"First of all," Tollar said, "you need a mind healer for Dionelle." She gestured off to the side where Dionelle sat huddled with Nandara.

"Yes, that will be addressed, but—"

"And who have you got to work on suppression with us?"

Dira held up a placating hand. "Tollar, I understand your concerns and your frustrations. Believe me, none of us here wants to see another wizard used as a fuel source the way Karthiry did. We'll work on that."

"But? There's a but. Why is there always a but?"

Dira gave Tollar a lopsided smile. But then she sighed and rubbed a spot in the middle of her forehead.

"While I was in the dragon city, others on the council followed up on old leads as well as the information brought to us by Eltir's blaze. We understand the situation quite clearly now, which is good. But—" She paused to give Tollar a look before addressing them all. "But we have an even greater disadvantage than we initially realized."

"Ah." Tollar resumed pacing.

"Our first concern is Loch himself and how he is so powerful," Dira said. "We have determined with absolute certainty that he is not demonborn. However, he has learned to wield demons in much the same way Spark and Neesha have."

"Yes, possession, we know." Tollar waved dismissively and kept pacing.

"He uses a similar technique to Spark's mind palace. He's clearly able to maintain control in deeply stressful circumstances."

"His power still isn't as stable as Tollar's," Neesha said.

"But ancestors help us all if he gets ahold of me—or any of us—before we learn to resist being harnessed." Tollar glanced at Dira on her way by, but didn't stop pacing.

"Yes, but at this point I question the wisdom of getting so close to him, and whether you'll even be able to."

Neesha's gut clenched at Dira's fallen expression. Her mother nudged Nandara, who crept to the council table to quietly collect a quill and paper before sliding in next to Dionelle again.

Tollar stopped pacing, pointing angrily at Dira. "You still haven't rallied the Guild, have you? All this, and you cowards still won't fight?"

Gasps went up all around, some angry hissed whispers, but Dira remained slightly wilted at her place at the table.

"No, they won't fight," Dira said. "Too many of them have been swayed to Loch's cause."

"Then sway them back!" Tollar snapped.

"He's got a shadow guild of his own," Dira said. "It's something Draxli set in motion before he even moved on Pasdale. It took us far too long to see it."

"A shadow guild?" Spark asked. "What does that even mean?"

"It functions similarly to our Guild," Dira said. "There are no exams, only loyalty to Loch. His connection to the king in Golden Hill allows him to offer them significant advantages in exchange for that loyalty. They are mostly aquamancers, but well connected and deeply committed to their cause."

"Surely the Guild must outnumber them," Nandara said. "There are far more wizards of other kinds than aquamancers alone. And obviously not all of the world's aquamancers are sided with Loch."

"No, and we have a strong contingent of our members who are dedicated to stopping Loch, as you are."

"There's another but coming," Tollar muttered, stopping to stare at Dira.

"The anti-Loch contingent still isn't enough. We are still outnumbered. And the dragons are, as of now, still refusing to get involved."

Neesha's stomach roiled. Spark leaned forward, burying her face in her hands. Dionelle stopped whatever she was writing and trembled, crumpling in on herself.

Neesha got up to stand next to Tollar. "So the dragons won't get involved unless more of the Guild is on board. Isn't that enough to get more of the Guild on board?"

Dira sighed. "Some of them refuse to believe the extent of the harm Loch has caused. Some of them are arguing about nuances and internal politics. Some of them believe we will fail and are remaining neutral so they will have a chance of receiving mercy from Loch."

"Then take some of his people from him!" Tollar snapped.

"Can't you waive the 'only one try at exams' rule? Just for a time?" Neesha asked. "Not for Loch, obviously. But what about his followers? That was Loch's whole thing, wasn't it? Attacking my family was half about his jealousy. You bent the rules for me; bend the rules for others!"

Grumbling dissent started up, but Tollar shouted over it.

"Let the ones who failed the general test take a specialist tier. Give them *something*. Make this cursed Guild attainable to more of us."

"The whole point of the Guild is to retain the most elite wizards," a pink-skinned, silver-haired man said. "If we don't have the best, what's the point?"

"Some of these people following Loch *are* the best," Tollar said. "Loch himself would be a Guild member if you'd had the specialist tiers sooner. And you'd have so many other talented wizards of other stripes. Not to mention the entire southern half of the world you insist on ignoring."

Dira stood, hands held out for calm.

"Tollar, I've told you I will work with you on the necromancers, but that will take time we don't have. A lot of this will take time we don't have."

"You have a quorum," Nandara said gently. "You can decide on the tiers now."

"There's no place in this Guild for monsters like Loch's," the pink-faced man shouted.

"Peace, Aldred," Nandara replied. "Just because they're Guild members doesn't mean you can't investigate them for crimes. But give them the recognition they crave."

"He's got so many misguided fools devoted to his cause," Tollar said.

"Like Draminedes," Beenala said softly, gaze downcast and hands wringing out the hem of her shirt.

"Yes, we've read the report from Cerro," Dira said. "It's a consideration, and part of the reason why our plans must involve preserving Biterna and as many of its citizens as we can."

"You need to extend that to Loch's supporters," Tollar said. "Some of them, like that awful Karthiry, are certainly there for personal gain. But how many Drams has he fooled? How many think they're on the right side and just need a chance to change their minds?"

"We can't put too much energy into that."

"No, but you can waive the one-try rule. With the support of the Guild behind some of them, they may turn on Loch as readily as Draminedes did. And he was instrumental to our success in Port Sawulxo."

Dira glanced along the length of the table. Most of the other wizards looked deeply troubled, like pink-faced Aldred.

"We'll discuss the option," Dira said. "After this."

"And none of that matters," Neesha said, stepping closer to Dira, "if you can't teach us to resist harnessing. With the few dragons we have and the four demonborn able to resist being used against our own people, we have enough to beat Loch."

"I've been working with a team since Dira sent a message back about it," Aldred said. "We haven't had any success yet."

Nandara hissed out something that sounded like a curse and approached Dira, holding out the scrap of paper Dionelle had been writing on. Neesha looked to the bench Dionelle had shared with Nandara, but her mother was gone. Neesha caught a glimpse of her rushing down the hallway just before the door to the chamber swung shut.

"We've needed to know, in part, what kind of man Loch is—how he fights," Nandara said, her voice shaky, as Dira read Dionelle's note.

"My stars," Dira gasped, her colour going grey.

"She couldn't resist being harnessed," Nandara said. "Loch used her power to incinerate other prisoners—some of them her former allies."

Spark let out a strangled cry while Tollar cursed in Upalan. Neesha turned immediately to go find Dionelle, but Spark was on her feet and blocked her.

"Mamma, I'll go talk to her. I'm rubbish at strategy anyway."

Neesha affectionately patted Spark's cheek and let her go. She'd do a better job of comforting Dionelle anyway.

"Damn it, no wonder she couldn't train with us," Neesha said to Tollar.

Tollar had her eyes closed, shaking her head gently. She sank onto the bench Neesha had just vacated.

"He's every bit the monster we suspected," Tollar said.

"A monster who thrives on drama and fear," Dira said. "We may learn to exploit that."

"He's still a monster."

"A desperate, ruthless monster," Neesha added. "We *have* to learn to resist being harnessed."

"It may not be possible," Dira said, sounding grimmer than she ever had. "If Dionelle had a year and still couldn't—"

"Dionelle was a shattered wreck for the entirety of that year," Neesha said. "Shattered and isolated. She may not have even thought to use suppression. Or maybe suppression is the wrong tack to take? At any rate, she had no support, no one to help her, and no way to practice. Clearly, we can't involve her further, but surely we can explore this before we dismiss the possibility."

"I'll work with you," Aldred said. "I agree, the technique needs to be explored thoroughly before we think to dismiss it."

"Thank you," Tollar said. "I'm ready to start working when you are."

"We'll work on the magic we need to beat Loch," Neesha said to Dira. "But you need to work on syphoning off some of his supporters."

Neesha didn't wait for answers, joining Tollar and Aldred at the side of the room where Tollar was already telling him what they'd tried. Neesha was deeply annoyed with the Guild over how little they'd accomplished with all the time and resources they'd had. But giving up wasn't an option, and she'd drag these old fools to reason herself if she had to.

CHAPTER SIXTEEN

Dionelle sat in the cozy chair in her suite, trying to focus on the verses of poetry from the book open in her lap, but her mind buzzed around her recent session with Elima. Someone had told her about Dionelle's written confession to the council, and it had been all the woman had wanted to talk about and the last thing *Dionelle* ever wanted to think about again. The memories stalked the edges of her thoughts like a starving dragon.

"Nanny! Something's going on in the council chamber!" Mita shouted from the doorway, startling Dionelle into dropping the book. "Ondias is here!"

Then Mita was gone again, darting back down the hall. Dionelle clenched. There was no reason—no good one—for Ondias to be here. There were enough wizards left in the dragon city to send a message if there was something urgent, and she had insisted on staying behind to liaise with the dragons while they decided on the best use of their talents and the best way to support the humans in confronting Loch.

Had that attack crossing the ocean spooked Loch? Had he made a rash surprise attack on the city?

Dionelle sat shaking in her chair, thoughts racing as fast as her heart, until a door slamming down the hallway startled her out of her panic. She picked up her book and carefully put it away, took some deep breaths and focused on *now*—on this bright, clean room in perhaps the safest place in the world for her to be.

Once she'd stopped shaking, she pushed out the door and into the hallway.

Tollar was leaning against the wall next to the door to her own suite of rooms—where Neesha had been staying since she'd returned from the last big meeting in the council chamber. Dionelle's desperate efforts to not lose her daughter again were only making things worse. Dionelle wanted to talk to Neesha, but didn't know how without one of them getting angry.

The silence had been a strained relief. Neesha's absence had provided too much space. And no one had told Mita why her mother was suddenly not staying in the rooms provided for them, and she had been tense and quieter than normal, somehow spending even more time in the forge over the last week.

When Dionelle came out into the hallway, Tollar pushed away from the wall and sauntered toward her.

"Can I talk to you a moment?" Tollar asked. "I know you need to get to the chamber—I don't imagine it's quite as urgent for us." Tollar glanced back at her door. "We'll be along once Bee is done cleaning the paint off enough to look half-respectable."

Dionelle stood in place, trying to keep up with the woman's rapid-fire prime.

Tollar waited a beat, but seemed to correctly interpret the silence. She slouched, bringing her gaze closer to Dionelle's, those startling silver eyes intent.

"Look, I didn't want to intervene," Tollar said, switching to her lightly accented Prairiean. "But all of you are suffering, and it's getting in the way of us being able to do what's needed to stop Loch. That's got to be the priority. We *have* to stop him. We're the only ones that can do it. And we've got to work together."

Dionelle stiffened and waited.

"You don't have to like me, but you've got to learn to work with me in whatever capacity is safest for you. And Neesha too. You're drawing further away from her when we need to be more cohesive."

Dionelle felt cold and folded her arms around herself. She wouldn't admit to this stranger the extent to which Dionelle didn't understand her daughter and never had. How much it hurt that she'd thought she understood Mita but had gotten that wrong too. They'd all lost the only home they'd ever known, and Dionelle didn't know how to keep them together, how to stop them from losing out on ever having a home anywhere. The dragon city was a respite—it wasn't permanent.

Dionelle had always been vaguely aware of the social capital being married to Reiser provided, but it hadn't been until she'd lost him that she really understood what it meant. Both Neesha and Mita didn't see the precariousness of their situation.

"I can't pretend to know everything about your family or history or culture, and most of what I know comes through the lens of Neesha and Croves—both of them outcasts."

Dionelle flinched at the word. Didn't mean to but couldn't help it. Tollar leaned away and waited. Dionelle wanted nothing more than to be able to stop drawing parallels between her daughter's life and her sister's. She'd thought she'd lost them both, and had been relieved beyond measure to get Neesha back—for a time, at least. But seventeen years asleep had taught none of them anything, least of all Neesha.

They were chasing the same mistakes in an endless spiral.

Vyranna and Neesha had both spurned marriage. One had died and the other nearly so, and it was hard for Dionelle to separate those facts.

"I know about your sister. And I'm sorry. Nandara told me, and it sounded horrifying. I don't know what you're working on with the healer, but I hope that's part of it."

Dionelle wanted to flee, but she stayed put and met Tollar's eyes. Maybe this outsider—an outcast herself, if the stories were to be believed—did have the perspective to help them all see where things were continuing to go so wrong. Dionelle had not brought up Vyranna with Elima and hadn't even thought to. So far, everything they'd spoken of and worked on had to do with Loch.

"I know you've suffered, but I don't think you're actually so fragile, so I'm going to be blunt." Tollar put her hands on her hips and focused on Dionelle. "You're treating Neesha like a child. It sounds like you never stopped."

Dionelle glared. Neesha kept making endlessly bad decisions. Anyone could see that! It was hardly fair to paint Dionelle as the villain when she'd been trying to get Neesha to be more responsible before she got herself killed.

But all Dionelle's efforts had amounted to was failure. And sometimes retreating into the comfort of those failures was easier than confronting what had happened and all that she'd lost. Sometimes she believed nothing she did would change the outcome—that Neesha and Mita were both lost to destructive paths.

Dionelle had been so certain she'd finally gotten things right with Mita, who had always been bright and kind and helpful. The girl had always stuck to what was expected of her and what was best for the family, even if it wasn't what she wanted most. Until Neesha had come along. Yes, Mita had been resistant to the betrothal Dionelle and Reiser had arranged for her, but Dionelle had expected she'd warm up to it.

It wasn't a coincidence that Mita had become so defiant immediately upon being reunited with her mother. Not when spite and defiance had been all Neesha had ever known.

And Mita was Neesha's child and her responsibility. It wasn't Dionelle's place to interfere. As much as she wanted to, she doubted it would do any good.

Dionelle didn't like the idea of Mita being with Ember any more than she liked the idea of Neesha and Yenette. Giving any indication of that would only hurt Mita, and the poor girl had already suffered so much. It left Neesha with the incorrect impression that Dionelle was somehow singling her out. Dionelle wished the words she needed to explain weren't so heavy.

Neesha would only get angry and hear what she wanted to.

A pattern of blind disagreement had always shaped their relationship, and Dionelle couldn't see how to change that.

"You need to understand that she's her own woman." Tollar's voice softened, sounding sad. "That's something my own mother still can't fathom about me, and so we don't talk or see each other at all. Unless my auntie or brother have said something to her, she won't even know she's getting more grandchildren."

Dionelle's chest tightened, and she glanced at the closed door to the suites Neesha had retreated to for the entire week.

"Family is hard," Tollar continued. "Ancestors, don't I know it. But everyone's got to put in the effort if it's going to work."

Dionelle wondered what effort Tollar thought Neesha was putting in. The extent of Neesha's efforts had always ever been to do whatever the hells she wanted and leave everyone else to deal with the aftermath.

"You've all been through a lot, I know. We're all still going through a lot. That makes it hard to see from another perspective, but you're not going to get anywhere with Neesha until you try to see from hers." Tollar crossed her arms and leaned forward, her gaze intent and uncomfortable. "If you can trust that after all Neesha has been through, she really does know what she wants—if you can let go and do that—you can have a proper relationship with her again. But if not, I can spell out exactly the sort of silence you're going to get in return."

Dionelle swallowed and felt cold. As if she didn't know what was at stake. As if she didn't know she was about to lose her daughter—for good, this time. But Tollar didn't seem to understand that Dionelle and Neesha had never had a proper relationship to begin with. She wasn't going to tell this stranger that. But how could Tollar think she had anything helpful to say without knowing how bad it had always been?

Tollar sighed. "All of you lost seventeen years. You all lost it in different ways because you were all in a different place when it happened. You're waiting for her to grow up, to admit that Yenette was just a phase. I don't know how to convince you it's not. But Beenala and I have loved each other since we were children. That we're both women doesn't make it any different than the love you had for your husband. If your daughter has found someone safe like that, it shouldn't matter what packaging that love and security come in."

Dionelle nodded slowly. Nandara had said something similar once—a shock after how long she'd been siding with Dionelle when it came to Neesha's relationships. And it was Nandara who had helped Neesha reconnect with this other woman.

It wasn't that Dionelle didn't want Neesha to be happy. She desperately wanted her daughter to be happy. The problem was that Neesha's version of happy was impossible—there was no compromise in her at all. Neesha didn't think that Dionelle remembered their long-ago conversation about different options, but Dionelle remembered it clearly. Mostly, she remembered the guilt at not realizing sooner why Neesha had rejected all her suitors—that it wasn't merely spite. That when Neesha had said she'd rather have a wife, she had one woman in particular in mind.

The problem wasn't that Yenette was a woman. In the years since that conversation, Dionelle had met so many people with arrangements that allowed them to have the appearance of a socially acceptable marriage while still being with who they really loved.

Neesha didn't want that. Neesha had never wanted that. Was it because it was safe? Was it another facet of her recklessness?

No, the problem with Neesha pining for Yenette was that Neesha thought she could go back to Pasdale and carry on like Tollar and Beenala did. Neesha refused to see that Pasdale was not Nytaltek.

Pasdale was a powder keg. One already poisoned against the Joasera women. And Neesha wanted to go back with her big flashy magic—no wonder she and Tollar were friends—and spit in the face of social norms. Dionelle couldn't even begin to imagine the trouble that would incite, the kind of danger Neesha would put herself in. It made Dionelle queasy.

She managed not to flinch when Tollar reached out and touched her shoulder. It was a soft, gentle thing, full of reassurance.

"You're all stubborn." Tollar grinned. "But I say all this because you can keep things from going as bad as they did with me and my own mother. Neither of you needs that pain. It's awful. I promise you I'm trying to get Neesha to bridge the gap too. But there's only so far she can come to meet you before she betrays everything that makes her who she is."

Dionelle's thoughts spun, and trying to maintain eye contact made her want to twitch. Just as the panic started to creep back in, Tollar patted her shoulder and stepped back.

"You best get in there." She gestured down the hallway.

Dionelle turned and fled. She didn't care that it was obvious she was fleeing.

Her thoughts were a tangle of concern for keeping all of them safe. Neesha clearly didn't want what was safe, and Dionelle didn't know how to accept that. There was no safety while Loch roamed free. Yet these petty conflicts between them were making it harder to find the path to defeating Loch for good.

Despite Elima's help, Dionelle could still barely think about Loch, let alone the year she'd spent under his boot. But if Ondias was here, it couldn't be anything good. It had to be Loch. What had he done now?

Nandara was waiting grimly next to the door, but took Dionelle's elbow and led her to a seat.

"The city is safe," Nandara said. "Ondias is here with the Dragoness Superior and some news. She didn't say what."

Ondias was at the council table talking to Dira, who kept glancing out into the room.

"We'll begin now, those who this most pertains to are present," Dira said. "Ondias, please give us the message from the dragons."

"The dragons have had a theory for sometime—since Void Behind the Stars laid the unusual white egg—and one that solidified for them after Neesha awoke. This remains a theory, but one they are confident in: that the power of the fireborn women, particularly Neesha and Mita, is inexorably linked to the dragons' power. It is apparent to them that when Neesha pulled all the demons and fire magic—and her own consciousness—back into the fire realm, she dragged part of the dragons' magic with her."

"That's why they all started talking again when Mamma woke up?" Mita asked.

"Not all of them." Ondias shook her head. "The fact that it was exactly two-thirds of them has cemented the theory for the dragons. The fact that Croves's dragon began speaking more upon reaching the city furthers the theory. Dionelle remains silent and so do many of their own kind."

"She's not silent, though," Neesha said. "She speaks when she has to."

"Nevertheless, the dragons are firm in their belief."

"This could have been a message, O. Why are you here?"

Dionelle bristled at her daughter's rudeness, even if she was right. The dragons had decided something, clearly, to send the Mistress Superior herself here with Ondias.

"Not only do they refuse to be involved in a battle with Loch, they refuse to allow this mission you have to go any further."

Neesha erupted to her feet in a fury of fire and cursing. Dionelle startled and shrank back.

Tollar was at Neesha's side quickly. Dionelle hadn't even seen the woman come in.

"There's always a but," Tollar said, a wry smile on her lips.

"Yes," Ondias confirmed. "The dragons will allow this mission against Loch to continue and give it the entirety of their aid, but *only* if Mita and Neesha renounce their power as Dionelle has."

"Absolutely not!" Neesha roared.

Mita drew her knees up to her chest, her mouth pressed against her legs, rocking in her seat. Dionelle wanted to go to her but couldn't move.

"Renounce their power?" Tollar asked. "What does that mean?"

Dira explained to her what had happened to Dionelle, and Tollar's gaze darted between Neesha and Dionelle.

"It's probably something you could do as well," Dira said. "Though we don't have an idea of what sort of implications your power has. You aren't connected to any magical entities like the dragons."

"Well, I'm certainly connected to the dragons themselves."

"But not through their primary element."

"So if Neesha and Spark were demonborn aeromancers instead, this wouldn't matter?"

"I believe things would have gone much differently," Dira said. "Whether that's a good thing or a bad thing, I cannot say."

"Regardless, this is the only way to beat Loch," Ondias said. "You still haven't learned any of the magic you'll need to beat him with what you've got on your own."

Dionelle sighed. Aldred had taught Neesha and Tollar and Mita to suppress to the extent of their abilities, and still none of them had been able to resist being harnessed any better than Dionelle had. Mita was even better at suppression than Dionelle was, but it still hadn't made a difference. Aldred believed that it was still possible to resist being harnessed, and that suppression must be a component of it, but that other magic was involved as well. He was working on it, but they had so precious little time if they meant to stop Loch from attacking the port again.

"Give us more time!" Neesha snapped. "We've got at least a month yet before we need to get to the south. We'll figure out the harnessing thing."

"That's still of small concern to the dragons," Ondias said. "They believe that if one of you is hurt or killed in battle, it would similarly affect a third of the dragons."

"Wait, they think that if Mamma or I is killed, a third of the dragons will die along with us?"

"This is all a theory, but yes. The risk of that happening seems high. The dragons do not accept that risk. Even if you ultimately never face Loch in battle, the dragons wish for both of you to renounce your power."

"No!" Neesha growled.

"So anything that happens to us could happen to the dragons?" Mita said with dawning horror. "And if someone like Loch figures that out, he'll come after all three of us. Get rid of the dragons by getting rid of us."

"It's exactly what he wants," Tollar said.

Dionelle was surprised the woman wasn't pacing the room. She'd been at Neesha's side the whole time, a hand on her shoulder.

"My magic is all I have," Neesha blurted in a horrified whisper.

"It's not, though." Tollar gripped her shoulder and looked into her face.

"Mamma, we have to." Mita got up and staggered to her mother's side. "Nanny still has more power than any normal pyromancer. You're not going to end up with nothing."

Dionelle wanted to comfort them both, wanted to point out how much stronger they both were and how much stronger they'd likely remain. But everything about their lives had been shrouded in mystery. Little more than theories.

But the dragons' current theory made terrible sense.

Tollar murmured something comforting to Neesha, whose eyes were bright with panic and unshed tears.

"There's also the possibility," Ondias said, "that while your own power may diminish, that the dragons will gain back all of what they lost when the fire took you."

"I've sacrificed enough!" Neesha spat, her voice hoarse.

"And we'll all be making sacrifices yet before this is over," Ondias said. Her tone was hard, and Dionelle wished she knew the words to bring back her old friend's softness.

Tollar kept herself between Neesha and Ondias, and Dionelle was really starting to appreciate the woman's awareness for conflict. But Dionelle was on her feet, crossing the room. She took Mita's hand and touched Neesha's elbow.

"I'll go with you," she said, unable to hide how she trembled at the mere thought of that searing, blinding pain.

"No!" Mita gasped.

"Absolutely not!" Neesha snarled. "No one's going anywhere, because this isn't happening. We're playing right into Loch's hands. This is what he wants."

"You won't be helpless," Tollar said.

Dionelle didn't know where the words came from, but they spilled out of her. "It's your ego against the entirety of dragon civilization. You want me to believe you're an adult, but you still insist on being this selfish."

Neesha's expression darkened, but she spun away, storming for the door. Dionelle wasn't sure if that was an improvement or not. But Tollar caught up to Neesha and stopped her, casting an exasperated look back at Dionelle.

"We talked about this," Tollar said.

Dionelle rolled her eyes. Tollar had talked *at* her about this. But Tollar had already turned her attention back to Neesha.

"Your mother's right, though, and you need to accept that if you really want this to get any better. You're still going to be the second most powerful pyromancer in the world. Surely that's enough?"

Neesha glared. "What if being more powerful than my mother means that Spark and I have even more power to lose?"

Mita had drawn closer and pulled Neesha into a hug. "Mamma, we have to. It won't be that bad."

"You can't know that," Neesha said, her voice still horrified and furious.

"And if it really makes a difference, you'll still have access to stable demonpower by harnessing me," Tollar said.

Dionelle had drawn in closer, Ondias and Nandara and the others hanging back.

"Mamma, we'll still have enough to beat him. Especially if we do this and the dragons agree to help. It's a weird sacrifice, and maybe a big one, but it's better than the three of us having to take ugly risks without the dragons."

Neesha sighed and sagged. Watching the fight go out of her dragged at Dionelle, trying to pull her into the floor. No matter how much Neesha's stubborn defiance grated at her, seeing her with no fight left and verging on despair made Dionelle want to vomit. Tollar nodded toward the council table and guided Neesha from the room while Mita offered to go gather all their fireproof clothing. Dionelle finally caught all the way up to them.

"I'll come with you," she repeated.

Neesha shook her head. "I'll do this. I don't want you to suffer that place anymore."

Tollar kept a hand on Neesha's shoulder as she guided her toward their suite. Ondias and Dira were talking about getting the dragon chamber ready, and Dionelle fell into the background again. She wished she could comfort Neesha the way Tollar and Mita could. She wondered if she'd ever be able to. Would they ever get over their history of animosity to trust each other enough?

Dionelle just wished she could make Neesha understand that all she wanted was to clear the obstacles to Neesha's happiness, but that she was realistic about what that meant. Neesha thought Dionelle merely disapproved, which wasn't accurate. Dionelle didn't fully understand, but that wasn't the same as disapproval. What Dionelle understood all too well was how dangerous the people who did disapprove of Neesha's preferences were. She knew some of them personally. She knew the kind of power they had and how they would wield it against her daughter.

She knew Neesha was blind to all of it.

What she wished she knew was how Neesha could possibly be safe if she returned to Pasdale and put her truth on display.

Dionelle had waited in the hallway with Nandara while Mita and Neesha had changed into their fire clothes.

Neesha still shook with fury as they all made their way out of the suite and headed for the dragon chamber. It was cramped when they got there, Abyss and Bolt and Bale all there along with the Mistress Superior. Beenala was nowhere in sight, but Tollar had come, trailing along behind them. Dionelle held Mita's hand, both of them trembling.

"This is a mistake!" Neesha shouted at the dragons as soon as she saw them.

Dionelle closed her eyes and took a shaky breath.

"You've already said you'd do this, so let's just get it over with," Ondias said, gesturing to the dragons.

The dragons clustered together, and Ondias ushered Neesha and Mita forward while directing everyone else to stand much farther back. Still holding Mita's hand, Dionelle moved forward with her. She had her firecloak tucked under her arm, and Mita really took note of her at her side and stopped.

"No, Nanny. You've suffered enough. Mamma and I can do this."

She let go of Dionelle's hand and Nandara was there immediately, pulling her to stand back with Ondias, Dira, and Tollar. Mita took Neesha's hand and the two of them went to the dragons together. Neesha's shoulders shook, and Dionelle realized she was crying. She took a step toward them to go with them to the fire realm anyway, but it was Tollar who stopped her this time.

"She thinks magic is her whole identity, and that's why she's afraid," Tollar said. "I expect she's like me and her fear manifests as rage half the time."

Dionelle blinked. Yes, that was a very apt summation of who Neesha was and had always been.

"What *is* her identity, then?" Dionelle heard herself ask.

Tollar smiled. "I think she's still figuring that out. We can help her with it."

Dionelle let out a breath, relieved for the first time that Neesha did have friends. She never really had before, except maybe Stone. But the new friends she'd made understood her in ways that Stone never could. Ondias and Nandara had been so vital in Dionelle's life, in helping her cope with difficulties and celebrate joys, in helping to keep her centred.

She'd never really considered before how isolated and alone Neesha had probably always been. She'd always held the rest of the family at arm's length, even Sharice and Breen—she'd never been properly close to anyone. She'd always been just a little too different. Neesha herself had confessed, not long after the three of them had been reunited, that she'd taken on so many lovers in her youth in part to try to fill an emptiness. She'd implied that having their full house in the dragon city had finally filled that for her, though it was clear now that she'd been wrong.

"And besides, she's the only one here who believes she's losing it all."

Dionelle wished she shared Tollar's confidence. They were working off a lot of theories, and it was hard to extrapolate what was really about to happen to Mita and Neesha based on what had happened to Dionelle.

"What if you're wrong?" Dionelle whispered.

"We'll cross that bridge when we get to it."

Tollar stepped back, and Nandara and Ondias moved in to flank Dionelle while Mita pulled up a fire and opened a fire portal. Dionelle's heart seized as Mita and Neesha paused and looked back in her direction, both of them still hand in hand. Dionelle tried to keep her expression neutral as she nodded encouragingly.

The flame swallowed up the two of them, and Dionelle held her breath while her heartbeat raged in her ears. This wasn't fair to either of them. Mita didn't stake her identity on her magic the way Neesha did, but they'd both been proud of their abilities. What if they really did lose it all? What if being more demon meant they had more to lose and not more power against what was coming?

The fire portal stayed open between where she stood and where the dragons waited. Time stretched on. A minute, then two. Dionelle wished they'd talked about how long it should take. Had something gone wrong? Did they need help?

She glanced at Nandara, who shrugged. She was about to step forward and go looking for them anyway when the portal flared and the two of them stumbled out.

Dionelle moved quickly toward them. Footsteps behind her indicated the others followed. When she reached them, Neesha was staring at her hands and breathing raggedly while Mita had given her skin a brief glance and then immediately pulled flame out of the air, grinning. So, at least one of them had kept power.

Mita appeared unchanged, but Neesha's unruly hair had auburn streaks, and as Dionelle reached her, she saw that her daughter's white skin had taken on a more natural pink hue.

"What happened?" Neesha gasped, staring at her shaking hands.

Dionelle ran her fingers through her daughter's changed hair, while Tollar materialized next to her with a disk of water like a mirror, tilting it so Neesha could see the changes.

"Not nearly as much auburn as your mother gained," Ondias said briskly. "And Mita barely looks any different."

"I'm pink!" Mita exclaimed, holding up her hands.

Dionelle squinted, and yes, Mita was so very subtly pinker than before. Her hair was still cloud white and offered the slightest contrast to make the difference even notable. But she'd already proven that she could still do the one thing no one else could and didn't share Neesha's worries.

"Your physical changes aren't especially drastic," Tollar said. "Good chance the same is true for your power. Spark has already pulled fire out of the air. Neesha, why don't you try some magic?"

Neesha slowly turned her gaze from the disk of water and her new image to look at all of them in turn. She looked to Mita.

"Give me some fire."

Mita pulled flame out of the air again, still grinning, and Neesha immediately snatched it from her and gasped, flinching away. The fire extinguished.

"Mamma?"

"It hurt."

Dionelle held her breath.

"Not agony, but it stung. Like a paper cut. Has your magic changed at all?"

Mita pulled fire out of the air again and held it this time.

"Oh, that's weird," she said. "It... buzzes? It doesn't hurt, though."

Nandara immediately started giving them little tests. Mita's power seemed largely unchanged, though she seemed to be working slightly harder than normal. Neesha, however, was having greater difficulties.

"It's hard when it didn't used to be," she complained.

But then both of them tried to open fire portals. Mita had no troubles, but Neesha couldn't at all.

"No." The word dropped out of Neesha's mouth like a shattered heirloom, and the cold sinking feeling crept into Dionelle's stomach.

Neesha kept trying, growing more and more desperate. When Mita pulled trueflame from the fire realm, Neesha couldn't control it anymore than she could open a fire portal. Dionelle's breathing came swift and shaky as Neesha kept trying, gasping, "No, no, no!" over and over again, like if she said it enough times, her power would come back.

Fire portals had been Neesha's freedom. Dionelle squeezed her eyes shut against the tears and focused on breathing like Elima had taught her, but it was no use. She turned her back on her daughter's increasingly desperate chorus of denials and fled the room.

CHAPTER SEVENTEEN

Neesha wasn't sure she'd ever stop crying, was half-convinced Tollar had opened water portals in her sodding eyes, and honestly wasn't sure she *wanted* to stop crying. What was the point of any of it?

Oh, sure, she still had some magic. She was at least as powerful as her mother. But she couldn't do any of the powerful battle magic that had made such a difference against Loch the last time. She was *useless*.

Beenala came into the room and sat on the edge of the bed with a hand on Neesha's shoulder.

"Being normal's not so bad," she said gently.

Neesha snorted, doing everything she could not to curse her friend out. She was only trying to help, but nothing could help.

Beenala sighed. "I'm sorry, I'm rubbish at this. There's a reason Tollar is the one having the babies."

Neesha chuckled and finally sat up. "If *I* could figure out how to be good at it, you'll be fine."

Beenala smiled. She had such a lovely, bright smile that lit up her face.

"Where is Tollar, anyway?"

"Um. Practicing. With your family."

The tears came on again, and Neesha nearly flopped back into the bed, but Beenala caught her shoulder, her expression firmer.

"It's really *not* that bad being a boring normal wizard. And besides, you don't really know for sure how much your power has changed."

"But fire portals…" Neesha couldn't bear to say the words.

"They were your escape."

Neesha started sobbing again, and Beenala rubbed her back while making comforting sounds for a moment before she continued. "Tollar was very good at escaping before you ever taught her she could go through the water to do it. Just because the means you thought you had have changed or are maybe gone doesn't mean you're helpless."

"But everyone I'd be escaping to is so godsdamn far away."

"It's five days to Pasdale and eleven to Nytaltek if you go by dragon. That's still not really so bad."

"Bee, that trip is exhausting."

Beenala only grinned at her again. "Yes, it is. And it's absolutely worth it."

Neesha groaned. "I know you're—"

The door to the suite burst open again, and Spark rushed in, breathless from running. Startled, Neesha sprang to her feet.

"Mamma!" Spark stood there flexing her hands. "Ondias caught a spy."

"A spy?" Neesha stared. What in the hells did Spark mean?

"One of Loch's?" Beenala asked, her voice shaky.

Spark nodded. "Right here in the Guild!"

"A spy?" Neesha still couldn't get her brain to catch up with the news.

"He and Karthiry had so many of them in Nytaltek," Beenala said, sounding horrified.

"He got a bird out the window before Ondias took him down."

"She what?!" Neesha couldn't help but be impressed. Ondias liked to be bossy and make other people do the heavy lifting.

"She tackled him!"

Neesha was moving, following Spark out the door and through the halls while Spark kept explaining, and Beenala trailed after them, her hands twisted up in the hem of her shirt.

Ondias had stumbled on the man in the message centre when she was going to send a message back to the dragon city. She didn't recognize him and couldn't figure out why he was using a bird when there were so many wizards to help magic a message to its recipient. He was evasive when questioned and started suppressing her magic when she tried to stop him.

So she'd tackled him, but not before he'd gotten a message bird out the window.

"Did a dragon eat the bird?"

"It was long gone by the time the chaos settled enough to send a dragon after it."

They reached the hall outside the message centre, and it became apparent that some of the chaos came from the fact that Ondias was a touch too old to tackle anyone and had injured herself more than the rogue wizard. She was sitting on the floor in the middle of the message centre, arguing with Dira while a pair of healers tended to what seemed to be a broken leg or hip.

"—not the one who let a spy in!" Ondias snapped. So that's how well that was going.

"Where is he! Let me incinerate the bastard!" Neesha shouted over them all.

Ondias rolled her eyes and Dira ignored her, and Nandara came their way but Tollar reached her first.

"We need to see what information we can get out of him before anyone incinerates anyone," Tollar said, guiding Neesha away. Spark and Beenala both hovered around outside the door, but there was no sign of Dionelle.

"Does it matter? I assume he's fed Loch everything there is to know."

"He didn't get all of his messages sent. There was one he was in the middle of composing when Ondias interrupted. Aldred is still decoding it. But yes, we should assume that he knows your power has taken a hit and that we're coming for him and that I'm with you."

"Does he really know much about you?"

"I expect he does now, if he didn't. He'll know the dragons are willing to help us now too."

"But not the Guild." Neesha glanced around Tollar, down the hall, toward all those senior wizards who hadn't made a decision yet.

Tollar sighed, "No, but even if we manage to convince them, it's hard to say how much of a difference that will make when the dragons have far more power."

"And I guess that spy will have told Loch about the Guild's plans to swipe some of his wizards out from under him."

"Yes, that will complicate things."

"We can't do this, can we? Spark isn't much of a fighter and still doesn't trust you, and I'm useless now. The dragons can still stop him without us, but not while sparing Biterna."

Tollar tilted her head. "You're not useless."

"I can't open portals or control trueflame! That was the only battle magic I had that was worth a damn against Loch."

"I'm not a supercharged demonborn like you and Spark were," Tollar said, hands on hips. "My power is no stronger than Dionelle's ever was, but I still learned how to open water portals."

"What, you seriously think I can still do it?"

"I think you need to keep trying."

Neesha tried to argue but Tollar cut her off. "You haven't really taken account of all the ways your power has changed and tried to adjust for it, to try to do things the way normal wizards do."

"Normal wizards can't open portals."

"Ah, but if they could, *how* would they?"

Neesha groaned, but Tollar was already ushering her toward the training room they'd been using.

"You insist on basing your entire identity on your magic, and on these misguided ideas about not being your mother or trapped in motherhood, and it's not served you well this far. You need more to your life than your magic."

Neesha glared. "Easy for you to say—you get to keep your power!"

"But I've already lost some of it." Tollar stopped in the middle of the hall, hands on hips and giving Neesha that stubborn look of hers. "Hopefully my loss is temporary, but I really am dealing with something similar. My magic not being as reliable as I'd like hasn't changed who I am. It does mean I have to rely more on the people who care about me, but that's not really such a bad thing."

"You'd never have done what you have without your power!"

"In a sense?" Tollar shrugged. "My identity has always been moored in action. In helping people. I was always going to do that. Having the power I do made being the hero I am possible, made it possible for me to do it at the scale I have. But I always wanted to help people. What do you *want*, Neesha?"

She wanted people to stop asking her that. Still scowling, she said, "I want to destroy Loch."

Tollar grinned. "Then let's go do that."

While Neesha had to admit that Tollar had a point, she wasn't sure how much it would help Neesha get what she wanted. Against Loch or anything else. What she really wanted was to be the best. She couldn't really be the best pyromancer anymore—that went to Spark. But Spark didn't have the Guild ambitions Neesha did. Spark wanted to loiter in the dragon city, building gadgets and going flying. Neesha wanted on the Guild council. Hell, she wanted to be Grand Chancellor. Could she still do that?

Of course, everyone on the council was a normal wizard. They were enough. But could Neesha be enough without her flashy tricks?

"Do you think Dionelle could learn to open a fire portal?"

Tollar shrugged.

"And where in all the hells even is she?" Neesha crossed her arms and glanced around like she'd catch sight of her mother hiding just around a corner. "She's never there when I need her. Sometimes I really feel like she hates me."

"She doesn't hate you. She just doesn't understand you. That's the root of the problem with my mother too, but she never even *tried* to understand me. I think Dionelle is trying, but it's as painful for her as it is for you. Imagine failing Spark like this?"

Neesha nearly stumbled over Tollar's words. It wasn't a stretch to imagine. Half the time, she already felt like she'd failed her daughter, even if she had done everything in her power at the time. It hadn't been enough. Spark had still grown up without her. Regardless of why, Neesha hadn't been there for Spark, and Spark had clearly needed her.

"She's worried about you," Tollar continued. "She just doesn't know how to not fight with you and knows that's not what you need right now."

Neesha sighed. "I imagine this hasn't been exactly easy on her either. She came out of the fire realm, halfway through a pregnancy she hadn't even known about, to find her sister had tried to kill her."

Tollar grimaced. "She clearly never got over that. And then everything else that's happened."

They both fell into silence until they reached the training room, where Neesha was hit with an idea.

"Wait, do you think a normal wizard can learn to open a portal? Like, if they're harnessing each other, wouldn't they have the power for it?"

Tollar tilted her head, fingers tapping against her chin. "I've never seen it happen, but Loch can open them."

"But he uses demons."

"I wonder if you can still use a demon?"

Neesha shuddered. "It's not worth finding out."

"Even if it means you can open fire portals again?"

Neesha thought of the seventeen years she'd lost, weighed them against taking days or months to travel to see Yenette. She'd have to move back to Pasdale if they were going to make it work. Losing another seventeen years wasn't worth the risk.

"Why don't you try harnessing my power to see if you can open a portal that way?" Tollar suggested.

"I can't harness you every time I want to go somewhere."

Tollar crossed her arms. "But if it works, it might work harnessing anyone. Don't you want to find out?"

Neesha wasn't sure she was ready for the disappointment of failure. But with that damned spy getting so much information back to Loch, they probably didn't have much time left to linger at the Guild. They'd need to be ready.

Tollar used a match to light a candle on one of the nearby tables, and then Neesha took her hand, giving her magic a gentle tug. She swirled up a fire in the middle of the stone floor and expanded it, being mindful of the size, not wanting it to get too big. Tollar, after all, was not fireproof.

She went through the motions of opening a fire portal the way she normally would, just in case *this time* it actually worked. It did not. She growled in frustration and, still in her fire clothes from the trip to losing her sodding magic, she stepped right into the fire, one hand stretched out beyond it to hold onto Tollar from a safe distance.

The first time Neesha had ever opened a fire portal, she had been furious and terrified and desperate. At the moment, she was mostly just desperate, but she leaned into the frustration and the irritating way the fire stung, grabbing fistfuls of fire and tossing it, like she could tear reality apart. That had worked the first time she'd learned to open a fire portal on purpose. She pulled a little harder on Tollar's power and angrily ripped at the fire again. Something flared, like a portal about to open, before disappearing again.

She gasped. Then growled again and pushed at the fire with the combination of her magic and Tollar's, digging her hand in, not caring how it hurt. Fire caused pain now, but not damage. She poured her fury back into the magic and *pulled* on the fire.

And it opened.

Her breath caught. She lost all focus, and the fire and the portal vanished. Neesha pressed her hands over her mouth, choking the trapped breath out in a sob while her heart pounded and her body felt numb.

"There," Tollar said, somehow managing not to sound smug. Mostly she sounded tired. "Looks like you've got some experimenting to do."

"Mamma, that was great!"

Neesha turned to see that Spark, Dionelle, and Aldred had come in while she'd had her focus on the fire. They were still working to prevent harnessing, and Neesha sat with Spark to watch them at it while Spark nattered about the spy. The message Ondias had interrupted had had details of how their power had changed, so at least Loch was unlikely to know about their new weaknesses. Though it was possible the theory about the connection between the fireborn and the dragons would have been passed along.

"And Ondias can walk again, but she'll need a cane when she does, and to rest a lot. One of the other wizards has gone down into Montberg to find a chair for her to get around in."

Neesha tried not to think about how things might have been better if Ondias had decided to be more hands-on like this twenty years ago. She wouldn't have even broken her damn leg back then.

Neesha had only been half paying attention, but her mother suddenly gasped and let go of Tollar. Neesha buzzed and jerked forward, nearly sprang to her feet, ready to get in the middle of a fight, but Dionelle was grinning. She snapped her fingers and pointed at Tollar.

"What, did she get it?" Spark asked.

Dionelle nodded vigorously, but Tollar looked perplexed. "I didn't have it. I still felt my magic go."

Dionelle shook her head.

"Her magic had to have gone somewhere," Aldred pointed out.

Dionelle shrugged. "Not to me."

"I want to try again," Spark said, getting up.

Aldred spoke with Tollar for a moment, but she kept rubbing her hands over her face and practically collapsed onto the bench against the wall where Neesha watched on.

"So which of you was mistaken?" Neesha asked.

Tollar shrugged. "My magic was gone. I hate that feeling. I wouldn't have mistaken it for anything else."

"But Dionelle is so certain."

"We can try again when I'm feeling a little more alert."

It wasn't long afterward that Tollar's chin drooped to her chest as she clearly fell asleep. Neesha took a quick look around to see if there was anything to cover her with, like a spare robe or something, then thought about waking her and making her go back to the suite to lie down properly, but decided to let her just get what rest she could. If Neesha woke her up, she'd just refuse to rest more anyway.

She'd been doing way too much, on top of being emotional support for the whole lot of them, which was definitely not fair, especially when Dionelle had Elima. Something was working, at any rate. Dionelle had been more verbal than Neesha could ever remember over the last two years. And she'd become so much more willing to work with Tollar.

Tollar jolted awake and cursed softly. "Sorry, didn't mean to fall asleep."

Neesha stood before her and took Tollar's face in her hands. "Listen to me. You are growing two babies. That was exhausting for me when I was half your age and had half the babies."

Tollar's eyes flashed like a ripple on a lake, and she gripped Neesha's wrists. "But there's no future for them if we don't figure this out."

"I said those very exact words twenty years ago, and look where it got me." Neesha's gut clenched. "That mistake means nothing—my sacrifice is useless, if we don't learn from it. Now go rest! Don't make me get Beenala."

Neesha pointed firmly toward the door. Tollar still gripped the wrist of her other hand, and she kissed Neesha's palm, a faint smile twitching at the corners of her lips. She nodded and stood, heading for the door.

Nandara came in so quickly that she nearly collided with Tollar in the doorway.

"Everything all right?" Tollar asked her.

"The council is ready to make a decision."

Neesha didn't wait for the others and pushed out the room and down the hall. It was about godsdamned time.

Neesha was the one pacing in front of the council table, having made sure Beenala kept Tollar in her seat.

"I really don't understand why you're voting on this instead of just doing it," Neesha snapped, glaring at Dira.

"This is how we do it. If we don't follow our own rules—if we have no rules at all—we're no better than Loch and his little cult."

"You need to figure out how to do things faster than this," Neesha grumbled.

"The council is still at odds on allowing any of Loch's people to retest."

"Well, that's simply foolish. Do you want him to continue to win?"

"How can we be certain that allowing his criminal followers into the Guild will give us the numbers we need?" Aldred said.

"You've said yourself that too many other wizards are remaining neutral," Spark said, coming to stand next to Neesha. "You don't have to actually sway any of Loch's people. You just need to make it look like you are to get these cursed fence-sitters to act."

"There's still no guarantee it's enough," Dira said.

"We have the dragons on our side now!" Neesha snapped. "I did that—you're welcome. Another sacrifice out of me, when I've absolutely done enough of that for this Guild. What are you going to give back?"

"Even if we were to change the entrance rules again this very moment, we won't get the word out fast enough," Dira said, sounding tired. "That spy has left us with very little time to act before Loch will be prepared for us."

Neesha opened her mouth to argue, but Dionelle was suddenly there, slamming both hands down on the table and leaning on it hard while she glared at Dira.

"I lost *everything*," Dionelle snarled. "Loch took *everything* from me. And you *let* him! I got some of it back." She gestured to Neesha and

Spark. "But the scars are forever. You will help us!" Dionelle gestured more broadly, taking in Tollar as well. "Or you're going to lose four of your most powerful wizards."

Neesha gasped, her heart rate speeding up. Spark gave Neesha a wild look before reaching out to put a hand on Dionelle's shoulder.

"Five," Beenala said. "I've said this already."

"Six," Tollar said. "Honestly, Croves can barely stand the Guild anymore."

"Seven." This from Nandara.

"Eight," Ondias said, immediately on Nandara's heels.

Dionelle swallowed as she looked around at all of them and nodded. Had this been her mother's plan? Had she known half the room would threaten to leave?

Dionelle turned her attention back to Dira, pointing at her. "You stop him now or this Guild fractures into dust."

Dira sighed and glanced down the table at the others. "We need to deliberate before we can decide."

"There's nothing to deliberate!" Neesha snapped.

"We'll have a decision, one way or another, by the end of the day."

It was a dismissal, and Neesha wished—not for the first or last time—that she could pull fire out of the air like Spark did and just incinerate the entire sodding worthless council. But it was Dionelle with a hand on her shoulder, nodding toward the door.

And so they all filed out, lots of grumbling echoing in their wake.

"We should get back to the training room," Tollar said.

"Absolutely not!" Neesha snapped. "You are going to lie down in a proper bed and stay there until I say otherwise."

"What did I miss?" Beenala whispered, startled.

"I fell asleep in practice."

"Toll! Neesha's right. You need to rest."

Dionelle had already left them, heading toward the training room.

"Mamma, I'm going to go with her and see if we can get suppression to work."

Neesha would not be deterred and escorted Tollar back to their suite, standing arms crossed in the middle of the room until Tollar got into bed and covered herself with a blanket.

"I'm not even tired anymore."

"Yes, you are. You're just too angry to notice."

"Stop projecting," Tollar said, chuckling.

"If we've got Ondias on our side this time, the Guild will either make the right decision, or my mother and her friends will have a very detailed plan on how we're continuing on without the rest of the Guild."

Beenala sighed and sat at the foot of Tollar's bed. "It's not going to look good for Biterna."

Neesha just managed to bite back a comment about sacrifices. Loch had overtaken nearly half the world now, but sacrificing an entire nation, no matter how small, was not worth the price of victory. There were other ways. Hopefully the people with the power to stop disaster would realize it.

"No catastrophizing," Tollar mumbled, clearly halfway back to sleep no matter how not-tired she was.

"She's right. We need to wait for the Guild to do whatever they're going to do and do whatever we can do in the meantime. Tollar is going to nap. I might try some more with fire."

"You should rest too," Beenala said.

"I rested for seventeen years. I need this to be over."

Neesha lit the candle on Tollar's bedside table and played with the flame, not really trying anything big. Just getting used to the way it stung and trying to test out all the parameters of how it had changed.

"So much for not tired," Beenala whispered, barely audible over the crackle of Neesha's little fire.

Neesha snuffed the flame and stood at the edge of the bed, Tollar sound asleep while Beenala watched on, utterly smitten and gently stroking Tollar's ankle through the blanket. Neesha watched her friend sleep, and her chest panged with a sweet ache similar to when she watched Spark sleep. Neesha had known for some time that she loved her new friends. It wasn't anything like the way she loved Yenette, or even Spark or her mother. Her breath caught as she realized it was so much like the way she'd loved Breen, and she found herself perching at the edge of the bed near the intersection of Beenala and Tollar's legs.

And that was how they were—Tollar sleeping while Beenala and Neesha silently watched over her—when Nandara tapped on the door and let herself in.

"Oh good, you got her to rest," she whispered. "This arrived in the message centre."

Nandara handed Neesha a letter, her eyes sparkling and a small grin on her lips. Then she left again with a polite nod to Beenala on her way out.

"It's from Yenette."

Beenala's eyes widened. "Go read it!" She shooed Neesha.

Neesha took the letter and retreated to the other bed across the room. This suite had two beds, and usually Beenala slept alone in one while Neesha shared the other with Tollar. Though sometimes Beenala's anxiety was especially high, and then Beenala would squeeze in with Tollar instead.

She opened the letter and skimmed it quickly, her heart racing and hands going numb. Then she read it again, more slowly. She wasn't sure what her expression showed—the letter was both good and bad—but Beenala was suddenly there, sitting next to her with a hand on her shoulder.

Neesha's last letter, the one Tollar had personally delivered, had been a bold declaration. Neesha had taken their advice and confessed her love for Yenette, and how much she wanted the two of them to be together, preferably in the dragon city, or all the way down to Nytaltek. Yenette's reply had been equally bold, but at odds with Neesha's wants.

"Well, we're on the same page about loving each other," Neesha said, exhaling deeply and slow.

"But? There's always a but," Beenala said, grinning slyly.

"But her children come first. She won't plan anything until later, if I'm willing to wait."

Beenala's smile got a bit lopsided as she glanced across the room to Tollar's sleeping form. "No harm in waiting."

"It's been twenty years already. What's a few more?" Neesha turned the page over, more fiddling with it than anything, and was startled to see more writing on the back of the page, after Yenette had signed off. "There's a section here for Tollar!" Neesha hissed.

Beenala laughed. "She makes friends everywhere, I told you."

"What if her husband has an accident?" Tollar said sleepily, not even rolling over to face them.

"That would be lovely!" Neesha said. "I don't know if it would get her to pack up and move, though. There's no proper school in the dragon city. I think she wants to wait until her children are grown."

"What did she have to say to me?" Tollar asked.

"About necromancy? What were you two talking about!"

Tollar chuckled. "She's brilliant, you know? Was going to be a diplomat. Knew where my ancestors were from. Guessed where I live now based on my tattoos and Granny's pendant. She said she'd like to learn the truth about our necromancers."

"I'm guessing they don't actually eat people?" Neesha said, barely suppressing a shudder.

Beenala sighed theatrically.

"They do not eat people," Tollar confirmed, a smile in her voice. "A lot of them don't eat meat at all."

Tollar sat up now, leaning against the wall and rubbing her face before she got down to the basics of necromancy. It was a kind of bone magic—but only on dead bone, so they couldn't rend the living—and they could speak to the dead, but only if there was a bit of the departed's bone left. The bones were the connection to the living. Neesha wished bitterly she'd known any of this before they'd pyred her father and said as much.

"Yes, what happened to your family is one of the reasons our necromancers are so cherished," Tollar said.

"When there's an accident or sudden death, they can bring closure," Beenala said. "I'm sorry you don't have that."

"And we don't lose the wisdom of our elders after they're gone. They still see what goes on in the world and can advise. Or sometimes they think of something we should know that they never taught us."

Neesha groaned and leaned her head back. She'd overheard some talk of the necromancers being admitted to the Guild, though the Guild, of course, was reluctant to make any changes. But Neesha couldn't stop thinking about how things could have been different if they'd had a necromancer with them that final night in Pasdale.

"It sounds like a lovely practice," she said. "Comforting."

Beenala gave her a sad smile and patted her knee.

"Oh, it's not as wonderful as all that. The dead are just as stubborn as the living," Tollar chuckled. "And the necromancers tend to deliver their messages in riddles."

They were downplaying it to make her feel better, but even a riddle from her father right now would have been a miracle. Still, she appreciated the gentleness both Tollar and Beenala continued to exhibit around her. She could at least accept their kindness without bursting into tears, and she cherished how much they had enriched her life in such a short time.

Neesha half-listened while the pair bantered back and forth about something one of the necromancers they knew had said. She felt a deep longing for Nytaltek and hoped she got to see it some day. But first they had to protect it from Loch, and Neesha needed to find a way to keep her friends safe along with her family.

There'd been enough loss. It was time to do this right.

CHAPTER EIGHTEEN

The training room was exhausting, and Spark never wanted to see the inside of it ever again. There probably wasn't actually a reason for her to keep coming to these. She wasn't really progressing. She could harness and be harnessed just fine, particularly if it was her mother or Nandara. Nanny hadn't really done a whole lot of it.

And Spark's magic hadn't really changed enough for her to need extra practice on things she already knew how to do. But Neesha was still struggling, especially since magic was more tiring than it used to be, and they had to leave soon and didn't think they had all the spellcraft they'd need. No one was ever around for it, but Tollar was trying to teach Neesha blood magic too, in case things got particularly bad in the fight with Loch. They were at least cautious enough not to talk about it around Nanny.

Nanny wasn't with them right now. Spark had no idea where she was, if she was in another session with Elima or visiting Ondias or what.

Currently, Tollar was trying to resist Neesha's attempts to harness her, but still wasn't able to replicate whatever it was Nanny insisted she'd done.

"We've got two days until we leave and over a week after that until we're in the port," Nandara said, joining Tollar and Neesha in the middle of the room. "Dira has some concerns about confronting Loch."

"Don't we all," Neesha muttered.

"Tollar, you know how to remove a demon from a possessed human?" Nandara asked, ignoring Neesha.

"In theory. I did it just fine with those water beasts."

"Right, but they weren't fighting you, trying to hold on to the demon. We don't know exactly what it's like for Loch, but removing a demon from Spark and Neesha has not been the same as with a regular wizard."

Beenala came in with another book on volcanoes, in case they had to stop on that volcanic archipelago again. Spark had played with the lava a little when Neesha brought her to that erupting one, but she'd only been studying it, not trying to do much with it. Beenala was certain Spark could redirect the lava flows and harden them into protective barriers.

But without any lava to practice with here—and no safe space to make some and practice at scale—theory was all they had right now.

"You think Tollar should try unpossessing one of us?" Neesha asked.

"I don't speak fire," Tollar said, her eyes wide. "And a water demon in a fireborn seems like a particularly foolish idea—even for me!"

"What did I walk in on?" Beenala whispered, leaning closer to Spark.

"Probably another bad idea. Nandara's this time, though."

"Oh, well, I guess we've all got to have our turn at them." Beenala turned away from the discussion and opened the book, this one with several diagrams of the inner network of a volcano. This was far more detailed than the ones Spark had seen before, with information about the vents and fissures that could rupture the ground leagues away from the main caldera.

Spark wasn't sure exactly what she'd be able to do. So far, she'd only played in a lava flow, and that was honestly more like a spicy bath than anything strenuous.

She knew she could cool the lava quickly, but not at what kind of scale or how sturdy the result would be.

Spark startled and looked up when she heard Tollar speaking water, and suddenly there was a water demon there and nobody looked happy about it, least of all Tollar. Beenala noticed too, her brow furrowing and hands gripping the book tighter. There was another wizard there Spark didn't recognize, apparently another elemental.

Nandara let the water demon possess her and Spark gasped.

Tollar, however, had the demon out of Nandara again almost instantly.

"That was entirely too easy," Tollar said, banishing the demon.

Nandara looked uneasy. Neesha sighed.

"We need a better idea of how he does it," Neesha said.

Neesha pulled up some fire, and a fire demon, and went through a possession. Spark stared, horrified. It had been ages since either of them had used this kind of magic. There just hadn't been the need. And now, with the harnessing...

But Neesha was still in control, conversing calmly with Nandara even though she kept twitching in that specific demon-possessed way they both did.

Spark tried to focus on the plumbing of volcanoes, but the words kept blurring together. Nandara was trying to pull the demon out of Neesha, and Neesha wasn't letting her.

"But Loch isn't going to have the natural mastery," Tollar said. "It's impossible with Neesha, because of the link, but it can't be that much harder with Loch than just a normal possession."

"We can't count on that," Neesha said.

She shoved the demon out and started coaching Nandara, as best she could, on how she and Spark were able to control demons.

"It's almost like a reverse safe space," Spark said, not meaning to. "When they take over, we retreat somewhere safe. But when we're in control, it's like we've stuffed them in a pocket or something, ready to use when we need it."

"You really shouldn't encourage this," Beenala said gently.

Spark shrugged. "They're going to do it anyway. Might as well give it the best chance of success."

Spark went back to studying the diagrams and flipping through the book some more while Nandara worked on visualizations.

"This pyroclastic cloud thing could be a problem, couldn't it?" Spark asked. "It's not just fire and seems like more than a dragon or aeromancer could handle. Maybe if we had a demonborn aeromancer, but even then..."

Beenala frowned down at the pages. "I think... the islands are the wrong kind of volcano for this? Hmm... Maybe we should find one of the council's terramancers to ask."

Spark shrugged and flipped around the book a little more, overwhelmed by how little she knew and how much was left to learn in such a short amount of time. They'd all been struggling with it, and Spark thought she'd finally gotten a handle on it, but then Beenala had started talking volcanoes with her.

"I think I'm ready," Nandara said softly.

Spark let the book rest in her lap and watched on as Tollar called another demon, and Nandara let it possess her again, her face pinched with the concentration of trying to hold onto it. It took a brief moment for Tollar to have the demon out of her again.

"I don't think I had it," Nandara said.

"It was still easy," Tollar said.

Beenala was holding her breath as Tollar called up another demon, and Spark briefly rested a hand on her shoulder, the contact reminding her to breathe. As she understood it, Beenala had a dog back in Nytaltek who'd been trained to help her manage her anxiety. With the dog left at home, she had to rely on those around her to help keep her grounded.

Nandara's contorted grimace changed, going blank, her hands twitching.

"Shit," Tollar hissed.

Beenala gasped.

"Try to hold it!" Tollar said to Nandara. Spark had no idea how much her mentor was aware of, but the air in the room grew dry, a puddle forming in front of Nandara.

"Shit, it's using her," Neesha said.

The spare elemental, an average sized man with rust coloured skin and thick black hair in elaborate braids, was on his feet, trying to suppress Nandara and the demon so Tollar could do the unpossessing. The air continued to dry, though not as quickly. Neesha lunged and grabbed his wrist, going still as he harnessed her power. Spark leapt to her mother's side, taking her hand and feeling the magic sap out of her.

It was the worst feeling. Cold and empty and like she was trapped in the moment between sleep and waking.

But then the demon was out and Nandara collapsed to her knees, Tollar both trying to catch her and banish the demon at once. Spark let go of Neesha and Neesha let go of the other elemental while Tollar tried to tell Nandara it was enough.

"No." Nandara shook her head. "Try one more time. I think I know what I need to hold onto it this time."

"Let her try," Spark said before anyone could argue.

"She knows her limits," Neesha added.

They'd both practiced dangerous magic with Nandara enough to know she would say when she couldn't keep going.

Tollar looked between the three of them, biting her lips. She nodded. "One more time, and that's it."

Spark sat beside Beenala again, both of them holding their breath as the demon disappeared into Nandara. Her face pinched up in concentration, her gaze hard and focused in the middle of the room, her whole body clenched and still.

Tollar went through the spell again. "Huh."

Nothing happened.

She made a fist and hissed something in water, and Nandara swayed. Tollar repeated the command, this time with a tugging gesture, and finally the demon reappeared. Nandara crumpled again, slowly, curling in on herself and breathing hard.

"Yes, that's enough," she said.

"Whatever you did, it was certainly more of a challenge."

The other elemental helped Nandara up and insisted on bringing her back to her room.

"Please, go rest," Tollar said. "I think I've got what I need."

When Nandara reached the door, Spark noticed for the first time that Nanny had joined them. Her eyes were wide, and her lips were pressed into a thin line. She touched Nandara's arm as she passed. Nandara murmured something reassuring and then was whisked away by her escort.

Nanny watched Nandara disappear and then strode purposefully into the room.

"Everything okay?" Neesha asked.

Nanny held her hand out, palm up, holding something. A blue gem. Spark gasped when she recognized it as a love stone and thought for a brief, horrified moment that it was Nanny's own. Spark hadn't seen that one since the night they'd given a pyre to Pappy, Bren, and Breen.

But this one was a raw stone, not a polished piece of jewellery. And it swirled with inner light. Nanny's no longer did, its light released in the fire.

"What...?" Neesha started.

"I want to see," Nanny said, holding the stone out to Tollar.

Tollar glanced at Neesha, who was smirking when she nodded. Tollar took the stone from Nanny, and Spark realized Nanny was testing them.

"Bee, come hold Tollar's hand," Neesha said, her tone holding some amusement but also an edge of something sharp. She knew it was a test too, and she didn't like it.

Spark went cold. Was she going to test Spark and Ember too? Spark couldn't figure out why Nanny was so weird about this.

"Hold the stone between you," Neesha instructed as Beenala reached Tollar.

Spark was expecting the light that flashed up out of the stone and swirled around them, but was startled all the same.

Tollar and Beenala were exclaiming delightedly, and Neesha started explaining the stone to them, but Nanny had retreated, sinking onto the bench near the door, her eyes shining with tears. Spark went and sat next to her, rubbing her back and absently listening to her mother talk about the love stone. She'd apparently researched them after the pyre.

"—soulmates is an old theory. Newer speculation is that it measures love in a more general sense. I think there's been some experimentation, with widows finding love again later on."

Spark tilted her head. "So the soulmates thing isn't true?"

"Or maybe just that you can have multiple soulmates."

"Oh, I wonder what happens if I hold this with Croves," Tollar said, her eyes sparkling.

"You don't love him like that," Beenala said.

"No, but..." Tollar gestured at her growing belly.

"I think Bee's right," Neesha said. "I don't know how it works, but it really seems to measure the intensity of certain kinds of love. It doesn't do anything when Spark and I hold one at the same time, and you can't argue that I don't love her intensely. I almost died to keep her safe."

Spark felt her cheeks grow hot.

"And while I've never really had friends before, I love the two of you like I loved the brother I lost," Neesha added quickly, her cheeks getting pink. "But look." She put the stone in Tollar's hand so the both of them held it together, and once again nothing happened.

Nanny was listening as well, her head tilted, frowning. Spark wished she knew what Nanny was thinking. There was a time she'd been good at reading her grandmother.

Neesha came to stand in front of them both, arms crossed, glaring at Nanny.

"Do you want to test it on me and Yenette too?" Neesha's tone was hard.

Spark held her breath.

Nanny shook her head.

Neesha sighed and deflated, the fight going out of her.

"I know you're trying to understand, and I appreciate that you're trying, but I wish you'd just take us at our word."

Nanny was still shaking her head, glancing at Tollar and Beenala, who had set the stone aside and were watching from a respectful distance. She wiped her eyes and took a deep breath.

Nanny looked right at Neesha and said, "Pasdale isn't Nytaltek. Who will protect you?"

Spark's eyes widened, and she glanced at her mother.

"We protect ourselves," Neesha said, her expression softening more. "And we protect each other."

Nanny was still shaking her head, and the sheen of tears had returned. Spark took her hand, and Nanny squeezed but kept her focus on Neesha.

"I've lost too much already," Nanny said.

Spark swallowed and closed her eyes. If she wasn't careful, that loss took on shape, carried sound. She was better at blocking it all out now. And she knew Nanny had lost more than just Neesha before that bitter night.

When she replied, Neesha's tone was sad. "I know."

Spark opened her eyes to see Neesha kneeling in front of Nanny, having taken Nanny's other hand.

"I know it started with your sister when you were practically still a girl. But keeping me from living my life doesn't help anything."

Nanny sighed. "I don't want you to deny who you are, but I want you to be safe."

Amber firelight chased itself around Neesha's irises, and her expression grew determined.

"Guess I'll just have to make myself so indispensable that they have no choice but to change their ideas of acceptable."

Spark grinned. Nanny rolled her eyes.

"You can't bend reality to your will."

"Maybe not, but I'm damn-well gonna try."

Tollar approached them then, a hand on Neesha's shoulder.

"Your mother's right," Tollar said. "You can't expect it to go the way it has for me and Bee, and Upalint is out of reach for the time being. I'm not saying don't try, but consider the danger and how you can be ready for it. Consider making them love or need you first, then shatter reality."

"Is that what worked for you?" Nanny asked and Spark was surprised by how hard her voice was.

Tollar shrugged. "To a degree, yes. I didn't tell the people close to me about being demonborn until they'd gotten used to my big flashy magic. And then I used that big magic to save them all."

"We weren't so lucky," Spark said, trying to keep her tone even.

Tollar looked sad. "I'm sorry for that. You should have been celebrated. I'm certain if any of you choose to come to Nytaltek that you will be."

Spark sighed and Nanny shrank. It was possible, had Neesha not lost control and then slept for seventeen years, that the three of them might have been embraced. Nanny certainly had been at one point. Maybe knowing exactly what she was missing made it that much harder for her.

"All three of you are heroes, even if your home doesn't see it. You need to remember that." Tollar's voice was firm, looking between the three of them before settling her gaze on Neesha. "You need to be careful when you go back. But I think if you can play it right, you can make them see the truth."

"Let's just deal with Loch first and worry about Pasdale later."

"I'm not going," Nanny blurted.

"What? To Pasdale? Of course not," Neesha said.

Nanny stood, vibrating, that panicked look Spark hated to see returning to her face, like she was on the verge of another flashback.

"Loch. I'm staying here," Nanny said, not looking at any of them.

"No!" Spark gasped, jumping to her feet and putting a hand on Nanny's shoulder, trying to get Nanny to look at her.

"I can't," Nanny whispered, her voice breaking.

"But we need you!" Spark said.

Nanny shook her head, jerked out of Spark's grip, and fled the room.

"Nanny!"

Neesha grabbed Spark's arm to keep her from going after Nanny. "We were always planning for her to not be anywhere near the battle," she said, frowning.

Spark forced herself to keep looking at her mother when she answered.

"It's not about the battle," she said softly.

Neesha's expression started to crumple, but she pressed her lips together, tamping down whatever emotions rocked her, and squeezed both of Spark's hands, making her daughter keep looking at her.

"Spark, I know. This was maybe not the best time for me to start figuring out exactly who I am outside of being your mother. But I can be more than one thing, all right? I need you to keep talking to me and to keep trusting me."

Spark nodded shallowly, glancing out the door after Nanny. She wanted to believe her mother, but the whole trip Spark had felt so alone. She couldn't help but feel bitter that her mother had her friends with her. Even Nanny had her best friends here. Not having Ember and Jatt around had been hard enough—not having Nanny with them for the rest of the journey would be unbearable.

CHAPTER NINETEEN

Beenala held Tollar's hand and stood respectfully outside the door of the forge while Neesha went to collect Spark, who did not want to be collected.

"You're not sitting in here by yourself brooding," Neesha said.

"I guess you can stay with me."

"No. Spark, we're heading into danger again tomorrow, so you should enjoy yourself while you can."

"I enjoy the forge."

"You're working."

"Sometimes work is fun."

Neesha made a strangled noise. "I have never in my life wished harder that I had been around to raise you." But there was laughter in her tone.

Tollar squeezed Beenala's hand and grinned at her, eyes shining. She wondered what sorts of arguments they'd end up having with the twins, knew Tollar was thinking the very same.

"I guess Nanny did her best to make sure I turned out the opposite of you."

"You're allowed to have fun. *Real* fun, Spark. Not work dressed up as fun. Now come on, it won't be that much different than when you go watch Jatt and Ember drink with the apprentices."

"Mamma, that's not actually any fun. I just do it because they like it."

Neesha sighed. Even Beenala could see her resolve faltering.

"Right," Beenala found herself saying, taking a step into the room. "Sometimes that's what friendship is. Or love and family, or whatever. I don't like travelling. I hate it, actually, but I do it because Tollar loves it. Tollar does not care about mulch day, but she does it with me because she knows I find it soothing. I don't enjoy drinking, but I do it now and then because Tollar and Croves have so much fun with it. I don't like kissing, but—well, that's none of your business. But do you see?"

Spark's face did something complicated that said she understood but wanted to argue anyway.

"You're stuck with us for the next, oh, month or two," Neesha said. "I don't expect you to be friends with my friends just the same as I'm not friends with your friends, but I get along with them just fine. That's all we need, all right? So tonight, we're bonding. Now. Let's go."

Spark sighed and relented. Beenala stayed with Tollar, following Neesha and Spark out, and felt bad about making Spark come, but she understood what Neesha was trying to do. They weren't under any pressure here, tonight, at the Guild. It was the last opportunity they'd have to make any progress with Spark, to get her to warm up to them so that the journey ahead was less taxing on her.

Croves was at the main doors that led out into the valley and the city, Montberg, below the Guild.

"What took ye so long?"

"Spark doesn't like fun," Neesha deadpanned.

"Mamma..." Spark said with the put-upon airs of every young person with a parent who made terrible jokes.

"The forge will still be there when we get back." Neesha patted her arm.

"And we won't be out that late anyway," Beenala said. "Tollar has promised to get a reasonable amount of sleep tonight."

"Pfft." Tollar gave Beenala's hand a squeeze. "We can always sleep in the gondola tomorrow."

"Don't we need to be on the lookout for danger?" Spark asked.

"Not this close to the Guild," Neesha said. "We'll get at least a couple of days before we really need to pay attention."

"Enough of that," Tollar insisted. "We're supposed to be having fun."

Spark sighed, but it was loud and exaggerated. Maybe this would work after all? Of course, Beenala had a good enough relationship with Spark. But Beenala didn't have to do any sort of magic with her, not when Beenala was heading straight home from Port Sawulxo. Something she dreaded the thought of, but also looked forward to with relief.

It would be easier for her to go home without Tollar if she knew Tollar would be in trustworthy company.

Neesha called it a group bonding outing, but Beenala knew it was really about getting Spark to be more comfortable around Tollar. And Tollar was particularly lovely tonight, her hair cascading loosely over her shoulders and wearing the simple black dress Beenala and Ember had made for her.

Croves fell in on the other side of Tollar, and they headed down into the city. The road sloped gently and Beenala was a little surprised it wasn't lined with stalls or shops or even homes for the staff who worked in the Guild. The ones who were also Guild members lived in the hillside complex, while the rest were down in the city. But the road was clear all the way to the valley floor. Beenala asked about it.

"Oh," Spark said. "It's because sometimes there are people foolish enough to attack. Obviously a fight with this many wizards is, um, messy. So having the city a good distance away is for its own safety."

"Has anyone attacked this place recently?" Tollar asked, startled.

"I don't think so." Spark shrugged. "From what I read, it was back when the Guild was newer."

The city sprang up suddenly on the valley floor, shops with apartments above them appearing first and then a market sprawling out beyond that. Despite the late hour, with the sun well set and the moons just cresting the horizon, the market was buzzing with activity, growing busier and louder and more extravagant the farther they went. There were lights strung on lines, the rich scent of many kinds of food, and music ringing out over the general murmur of the large crowd. Most people were dressed up, some of them wearing vests or sashes or skirts with bells.

"A festival?" Tollar asked.

"Oh, it's the final moons of the summer," Neesha said. "Gods, I used to get so drunk at this back in Pasdale. It's where I met Yenette."

"I love a good festival," Tollar said, her eyes gleaming.

"Tollar, you said we should go to a quiet inn," Beenala said.

"Yes, of course, but can't we take in the festival for a bit first?" Tollar turned her attention to Neesha, who was leading this little outing. "It'd be nice to see some of the more pleasant side of northern culture."

"I've never been to a festival," Spark said, sounding startled. "Not one for humans, anyway. Just dragon festivals back in the city."

"Well, I think that means we *have* to check this one out," Neesha said.

Neesha started deeper into the throng of people with Spark at her side and Beenala just behind them. Tollar had stopped with Croves on the side of the wide avenue, and he had her wrapped up in another one of those kisses. Sometimes Beenala gave them privacy, and other times—like now—she watched on with horrified fascination. And relief. Tollar had been right that this was not something Beenala should be trying to provide for her.

Tollar was unsteady on her feet when Croves released her, so Beenala sidled in, a hand on Tollar's elbow, and gave Croves a little wave. He'd only ever planned on escorting them into the city. He was headed off to the comfort house while one was still available to him.

The council had thought it best they stick to wilderness as much as possible on their way south to avoid Loch's spies. No one was particularly looking forward to it. If things went smoothly, Neesha would get to pass her thirty-seventh birthday with her uncle and brother in the south, but it was more likely to be in the middle of nowhere—part of the reason they were doing this now.

"Do you think we'll get home by my birthday?" Beenala asked as they caught up with Neesha and Spark.

"We had better. The midwife at the Guild warned that twins often come early."

Beenala stopped. Her skin felt cold and her insides too hot.

"Take a breath," Tollar said gently, a hand on Beenala's shoulder. "That's at least two months away yet. We'll be in Sawulxo in about a week. We've got time."

"Oh." Spark turned to them. "My birthday's in a month. Am I going to be celebrating it in a battle?"

"With a bit of luck, we'll be giving you a victory for your birthday," Tollar said.

"And a future," Neesha added quietly.

"A future for all of us," Beenala said.

Tollar absently ran her hand across the swell of her belly. That particular future was becoming more and more real.

"No brooding," Tollar whispered, leaning down with her lips near Beenala's ear.

"Yes, right. We're having fun!"

Neesha rolled her eyes. "In point of fact, there's some sort of magic competition or something going on. We're so close to the Guild, there's a bunch of wizards showing off."

"Perfect!" Tollar said. "Let's go show off."

Spark rolled her eyes, but she was smiling at least.

Tollar found the food vendors and got a round of treats for all of them, including ice cream served in bowls made of cookie. Tollar went back for a second one of those while they watched the wizards perform. It wasn't any sort of competition, just anyone stepping into that particular gap in the crowd to do some kind of magic trick.

"All right, time to show off," Tollar said, wiping her hands and standing.

"Oh, here we go." Beenala rolled her eyes but smiled after Tollar as she strode into the crowd and immediately opened a water portal and summoned three water demons, which she then made dance—to the gasps of the transfixed crowd—before sending them away again. Then she pulled a blob of water out of the air and made it into some shapes.

Neesha joined her, dragging Spark. Spark's cheeks burned a furious pink, but she pulled fire out of the air to delighted gasps. Tollar stepped to the fringe next to Beenala while Spark opened a fire portal, channelling a bit of trueflame before closing it and slinking away, leaving Neesha to do some tricks with fire. She seemed at ease and enjoying herself—maybe finally opening a portal again, even with help, had done her some good.

Neesha echoed the same shapes Tollar had made, but using fire.

"Maybe I shouldn't have opened with trueflame," Spark said, standing on the other side of Tollar.

"Oh, Neesha will find some way to reclaim the spotlight." Tollar chuckled.

And Neesha did. First, she let the fire play across her bare arms and wore it like a crown. Then she danced in it. Beenala wondered at that. She wasn't wearing anything fireproof and all her focus must be in keeping her clothing from igniting. And though Neesha couldn't open a fire portal without help, she could still make a really big fire.

So she made a really big fire.

It spiralled up into the sky with a roar, blooming out overhead like a vast burning umbrella. And Neesha stood, head leaned back watching it and arms outstretched, grinning as the firelight danced in her eyes.

"Spark," Tollar said, wary and firm. "Spark, you're all right. Take a breath."

Beenala turned to find Tollar standing with her hands cupping Spark's face and the younger woman's expression gone inward with a sheen of panic.

"We're at the Guild, Spark. This isn't Pasdale. There are no dragons. Dionelle and your mother are here and they're safe. You're safe, Spark."

Tollar switched to Prairiean, presumably repeating what she'd already said. She kept her voice calm and gentle and firm, just like she did when Beenala woke screaming from night terrors. Clarity finally returned to Spark's expression, though she still trembled.

"Tollar?" Spark's voice was broken with emotion—terror, but also confusion and relief.

Tollar wrapped Spark up in her arms for a hug. "I'll always keep you safe, the same as I would my own."

Beenala moved closer, a hand on Spark's shoulder. But her stomach was in knots. As often as it was that Beenala was the one in a panic, she never quite knew what to do to help someone else going through it.

"What's going on?" Neesha said, coming closer, done with her fire display.

"Flashback," Beenala said carefully.

Neesha rushed in, arms outstretched for her daughter, and Tollar folded the smaller woman into her embrace as well while Neesha crooned reassurances to Spark. It was easy to forget sometimes just how much smaller Neesha was than the rest of them, but that didn't stop her from somehow managing to expertly gather her daughter into her arms.

"Maybe it's time we bring you back to your forge?" Neesha gently suggested.

"I dunno. Maybe I can handle a little time in a quiet pub." Spark managed a smile then, her amber eyes shining with mischief.

Neesha kissed her forehead. "Sounds perfect."

"Let's go have fun," Spark said.

Beenala's pulse rushed in her ears, and she doubted again her ability to do any mothering at all, regardless of what anyone else said. She was pretty sure she was done having fun for the evening, though Tollar did buy them all more ice cream on their way out of the market. It was good to have a distraction, no matter how brief. They had a long hard road ahead.

CHAPTER TWENTY

Tollar stood on Abyss's shoulder, gripping one of her spikes, and squinted into the rain and wind. Spark was on the dragon's other shoulder, with Croves somewhere behind them both. Neesha had wanted to come, but none of them were kidding themselves about her abilities with dragon-walking. Her confidence in her magic was also still lower than Tollar would have liked.

And besides, Spark still being utterly fireproof and not feeling the pain of it meant she was better suited for what Tollar had brought her along for in the first place.

"Anything?" Tollar called over the wind.

If they replied, she couldn't hear them. When she glanced back, Croves shook his head.

"It smells wrong," Abyss said.

It looked wrong too, but Tollar needed to be certain before she could make a decision.

A bolt of lightning came out of nowhere, and Tollar had no time at all to react to it. Spark, somehow, did. She screamed, but it was an angry, triumphant sound, and when the afterimage cleared from Tollar's vision, she glanced over to see Spark climbing Abyss's neck to stand behind her horns.

Making herself a lightning rod.

Tollar grinned. Croves was laughing.

"Give me your hand," Tollar called back to him. He crept forward, engulfing her hand with his big meaty paw.

And Tollar tugged on his magic. Less for the aeromancy, though it certainly helped smooth out the turbulence so Abyss could fly steady, and more for the boost. It was so much easier on the ocean, when Tollar had so much water to help her spot her foes.

Even with the boost, she couldn't really sense anything.

"Mistress, take us right into the clouds."

Rain was too diffuse for Tollar to really use it to see, but clouds were a good bet.

"Spark, be ready!"

Tollar had barely finished calling the warning when another flash snaked toward them. This time, Spark didn't take it. She redirected it. The bolt passed through her and shot groundward.

"Holy shit. Did ye know she could do that?"

Tollar shook her head. The girl was full of surprises. And at least they wouldn't have to worry about the lightning anymore.

Once in the clouds, Tollar tugged on Croves's power again and followed the scattered water around her. This time, the magic in the storm stood out.

She cursed.

"It's them, is it?" Croves grumbled from her side.

"It's someone. They're on a mountain deeper into the range."

And now she had a call to make: go in there and pummel them, or take her crew the long way round, heading west to the shore and skimming it south. The direct route, clearly, was being guarded.

Loch knew they were coming.

"We should save energy," Croves said.

Both of them flinched when Spark caught another lightning bolt and redirected it away from them.

Tollar wanted to go fight. But Croves was right. They had a small team, with the bulk of the Guild and the dragons waiting for her to scout the path south. She could go down there and fight this team of elementals, but there would be more. She had no doubt Loch had them planted throughout the lands between the Guild and the southern shores.

It was entirely possible he had them all the way to the western shores as well. But she'd worry about that battle when they came to it.

"All right, Mistress, let's head back to the others and bring them the news."

"You don't want to send a message to these ones?" Abyss asked.

"It's possible they haven't sensed us, even with Spark's light show. It's better if they don't know exactly where we are. Let them think we're still coming straight down the centre so they're less likely to chase us down the western shore."

Tollar knew that was a big ask. She expected they'd be fighting Loch's forces the entire way to Port Sawulxo.

After losing four days to backtracking and then swinging west, Tollar wished she had Spark's talent for pulling fire out of the air because she could just about spit lava right now. They'd been skimming along the western shore for half a day, and now, from her place on Bale's shoulder, she stared at a large storm that came right down out of the coastal mountains into the ocean.

"It could just be normal weather," Croves said.

"We both know it isn't."

Coastal storms were normal here. In the winter. It was very much not winter. The only way there was a winter storm in their path was if someone had put it there.

There was the tiniest chance—and Tollar was clinging to it—that Loch didn't know exactly where they were and had merely stationed his people at random intervals all along the northern continent to cause problems for them whichever route they took. If that was the case, there was a chance they could give this storm a wide berth out over the ocean and remain undetected. This could be the only magical storm waiting for them on the coast.

Abyss appeared suddenly like a slice of night sky, spiralling down in front of them and growling something dragonish to Bale, who then banked hard, nearly throwing Tollar clear off her back. She caught a handhold at the last instant and Croves, also struggling, got both of them in close to the spikes on Bale's back.

"What in the name of every cursed ancestor was that!" Tollar shouted.

"Auntie says trouble," Bale said, spiralling after her kin.

They had pulled hard away from both the storm and the ocean—Shell, Dragon, Flame, and Ice banking at speed to remain in formation behind them. They went inland, into the mountains first, and then pulled north a few leagues before landing in a valley.

Spark was already on Abyss's shoulder, Neesha struggling up the rigging to join her as Abyss spoke.

"I saw wakes out in the deeps, not far from the edge of the storm," Abyss said.

"More of those water beasts?" Tollar asked.

"Godsdamnit." Neesha joined them, breathing hard and glaring back the way they'd come.

"This was a trap?" Spark asked.

Tollar rubbed her face. "Likely. Croves, go warn Bee."

Tollar had never been so grateful that he didn't argue with her. The other three dragons landed, and Tollar caught them up on the situation.

"So let the storm drive us into the water and those beasts drown us," Raia said.

"You got a plan?" Eltir asked.

Tollar appreciated that while Croves liked to argue with her, at least his blaze didn't. They tended to look to her for guidance.

"Storm's headed this way," Neesha said.

So that entirely ruled out the possibility that the storm was a natural freak occurrence. At least Tollar was having a good brain day, even if she was feeling a tad queasy and more than a tad exhausted. The twins were growing fast, her centre of gravity was in shambles, and she was having a harder time with dragon-walking. And just about everything else.

She climbed out onto Bale's shoulder and leaned out to get her attention.

"You're going to stay here with Bee and our gear." She then pointed at the two fireborn women. "Spark, get suited up. Neesha, in your harness. You three help Croves get all the unnecessary gear off the dragons."

"So we fight?" Croves asked, most of the way back up from the gondola.

"I'll warn Bee. But we've got no choice. We'll get the elementals in the storm first, and then we'll deal with those water beasts."

Beenala was indeed unhappy when Tollar told her the plan.

"Tollar, what about those elementals?"

They were certainly going to be a problem. And out in the middle of nowhere, with no wizards to spare to bring them to the Guild, they couldn't take them prisoner. But she couldn't leave them to cause trouble for them all the way to the southern coast.

"I'll think of something."

"Think fast, Toll. Croves won't be forgiving. I doubt Neesha will either."

Tollar sighed. She couldn't blame either of them, after what Loch had put them through, but didn't want to see anyone die needlessly. It was not lost on her how many of Loch's followers were lied to and manipulated. Like Draminedes had been.

Beenala kissed her hands, and Tollar kissed the top of Beenala's head. She hated leaving her behind, but they both knew Beenala couldn't be involved in the fight anymore than Dionelle could. She climbed to Bale's shoulder, feeling heavier than usual, and then turned cold when she saw that Croves had his warhammer with him.

She pulled him aside while the others finished unbuckling the gondola from Abyss.

"I know you want revenge after what they did to you and Shell, and if death is our only option... It is what it is."

"Aye. Ye know I think of Dram, same as you. But what can we do with 'em?"

Tollar stood straighter, struck by an idea. "We take their supplies and leave them tied up somewhere unpleasant."

Croves scratched his beard. "Ye think that'll be enough?"

"It gives them a chance to reconsider their choices. If they chase us after that..." Tollar shrugged. "You know I don't want a part of it."

"I'll do what needs doing. Raia will help."

Tollar didn't like it—hated being left with nothing but bad and worse choices. Hoped the damned fools didn't try to make trouble for them. She walked with Croves across Bale's wing to stand with the fireborn women on Abyss's shoulder.

"Am I a lightning rod again?" Spark asked, seeming eager.

"Yes, and that's brilliant by the way. Can you aim it at all?"

"A little."

"Once we figure out where these elementals are, aim it near them. Don't hit them, but give them something to think about."

Spark climbed up between Abyss's horns again. Neesha was in her fireproof clothing and a harness, already latched at Abyss's shoulder in what remained of the rigging. Raia and Barlo had just finished stowing it all with Beenala and Bale, and were heading for their own dragons.

Croves, knowing what was needed of him, was heading for Shell.

"So what do I do?" Neesha asked.

"Whatever we need. Keep an eye on Spark for now and be ready to let me harness you." Tollar wedged herself between two spikes next to Neesha and whistled, signalling for the dragons to take flight.

"Straight into the clouds so I can find them," Tollar called to Abyss as she gained altitude.

And just like last time, the magic in the storm stood out once she was surrounded by clouds, the source easy to locate.

"Southeast!" Tollar called. "Highest peak."

Abyss banked and the other dragons followed in formation, Shell just off her shoulder so that Croves would be in position to help Tollar clear the storm and make it easier to see. For now, letting the clouds conceal them worked to their advantage.

"South a bit!"

There was less lightning farther inland, the worst of the storm at the shore. Which made sense if this was indeed meant to drive them out into the ocean for the water beasts to finish off. Spark wasn't bored, at least, though how could anyone be bored soaring through the air like this? Terrified, sure. But not bored.

Tollar kept calling out instructions to Abyss until they were directly in front of their target and only a couple of leagues out.

"Dive now! Straight ahead!"

Tollar bunched her fists around a handhold as Abyss sliced through the cloud. They broke through into the rain and Tollar cleared them a dry path, improving visibility. There was a craggy peak just ahead with a strange plateau not far from the summit.

"They'll be there!"

And then thunder boomed and lightning exploded around them. Spark's startled cry barely carried over the din, but she caught it, staggering and nearly losing her balance. She was ready for the next one though, which came immediately on the heels of the first. Spark turned the lightning away and it struck near the foot of the mountain.

"Shit, they must see us," Neesha said.

The next bolt she redirected higher but nothing quite close enough to the enemy elementals to be considered a threat. The wind around them grew stronger, Croves unable to counter it.

Just as Tollar reached for Neesha to counter with some water, Abyss tilted her wings and shrieked a battle cry. The rest of the blaze followed suit.

And Spark stiffened and lost her grip, tumbling backward.

Neesha cursed something particularly filthy as she lunged and caught Spark's foot before Spark could fly out into the storm. Neesha had all the strength of overcooked noodles, but it slowed Spark's fall enough for Tollar to get into a better position and drag the girl in against the spikes with them.

"It's okay, baby," Neesha said, wrapping Spark up in her arms. "We're safe. Well. The dragons aren't angry with *us*. These are our dragons, and they're here to protect you. Just take a deep breath. There you go."

Spark buried her face against her mother's shoulder and gasped raggedly. The dragons still shrieked all around them, but there hadn't been any more lightning. Tollar focused and cleared the rain so she could see, and Abyss was already swooping past the plateau.

Looking behind them, she spotted the cluster of elementals, Shell and the other dragons diving for them. Tollar pulled a torrent out of the storm and washed them off the mountain and down into the valley. Her vision blurred with the effort, and she closed her eyes a moment to clear her head.

The other dragons circled until Abyss could land, the demonborn working together to suppress the magic of the entire group. But Croves hopped from circling Shell to land next to Tollar.

"She threw someone off the mountain." He gestured to Abyss.

"I saw what he did," Abyss growled. She pointed a long claw at the group, and one woman in particular. "That one comes with us. Do as you will with the rest."

Tollar blinked. Hostages had not been part of the plan. She wanted to argue, but... when it came down to it, Tollar was in charge of the humans and Abyss was in charge of, well, everything. Tollar was not about to argue with this specific angry dragoness. Balipar would be proud.

Croves sprinted down Abyss's back and across her tail to join the others and keep the indicated woman from being tied up with the others. Neesha was still ready with suppression, but the rest of them drew nearer and Tollar got there just as Croves drove the blunt end of his warhammer into one man's leg.

"Croves!" she snapped, getting in his face and grabbing his arm.

"Just giving 'em something to think about. Ain't gonna follow us on a mangled leg and it ain't gonna kill him."

Barlo had gagged the group. There were four in total, not counting their new hostage and the one Abyss had killed—though one was unconscious and the rest were bleary. The hostage was bedraggled and unkempt, even considering she'd just taken an impromptu journey down a waterfall off the side of a mountain. Her curly brown hair was matted and her olive skin stained with old dirt. She was a little bigger than Neesha and glared warily at them with moss-green eyes. The woman screamed and flailed away when Croves approached, and absolutely lost her mind when Abyss tried to draw near.

Tollar had a sinking feeling and made a quick decision.

"Neesha, go to her."

If Beenala had been with them, Tollar would have sent her, but Neesha was the least threatening among them. While Neesha knelt in front of the woman and murmured softly, Tollar caught Abyss's attention.

"Not a hostage?" she whispered.

Abyss shook her head.

Tollar rubbed her face as the sun came out, the artificial storm rapidly dissipating.

"Raia, all of you, back to your dragons and wait by the coast. Croves, you too."

Croves looked like he might argue, but his sister gripped his shoulder and tugged. They grabbed up all the supplies they could carry and went back to their dragons. By the time they took off, Neesha had extracted the woman from her huddle and gotten her away from the group of Loch's elementals.

"Oh gods, you're the fireborn," the woman gasped in Prairiean, panic in her tone.

"Hey, you're all right," Tollar said gently, making herself as small as she could and moving Neesha to go stand with Spark. This woman wore a scarf despite the southern heat and that sour feeling in Tollar's gut solidified.

"They been using you as an energy source?" Tollar asked. "Harnessing your magic against your will?"

The woman burst out sobbing.

"Listen, you're safe from them now, but you need to come with us."

"With dragons?!"

"That dragon just killed a man for you."

The woman blinked and looked at the group behind her, comprehension filling her expression.

"Hey, what's your name? Where are you from?"

"Um, I'm Meriella. From Sweet Rock."

"That's in Stonarel, right?"

Meriella nodded, eyes still wide, taking in her surroundings.

"I don't know how you ended up tangled up with Loch, and that doesn't matter. You're safe from him too. We've all handed him some embarrassing temporary defeats, and now we're working together to make that more permanent. You understand?"

Meriella still looked terrified.

"Look, we can get you home, but it'll be a roundabout way, all right? We'll make sure you get to the Guild—"

"No! They'll have my head!"

Tollar sighed and explained about the recent changes.

"But I'm not good enough—I'm strong, but I've got no control."

"Ah, and that's why they used you for the energy." Tollar was going to personally make sure all of Loch's insides ended up on his outside.

"So we get her a good mentor," Spark said. "She can still get in, she just needs practice, right? Isn't that the whole point of the Guild and their lessons and exams?"

"Meriella, you're going to be okay, but you've got to come with us. And that means letting the dragon pick you up—just for a short time, we've got better accommodations just over the range."

Spark butted in with her youthful enthusiasm, explaining the gondola and the rigging, and Tollar realized that Meriella was likely not much older than Spark. But Meriella kept glancing over at the group of struggling elementals that they really needed to get away from soon.

"We've beat him already," Tollar said. "You'll be safe coming with us. Look..." Tollar crouched, getting eye level with Meriella. She gestured to her own eyes, pointed out the colour of her skin. "I'm like them, part demon. But water demon. Do you understand?"

Something like hope entered Meriella's expression for the first time. "You're stronger than he is."

"Yes. Now please, come with us, before your friends cause more trouble for us. Croves'll come back and break more than their legs." That startled Meriella. "The dragon will just cup you in her hands. You don't have to hang off the side of her like we do."

"And I'll stay with you," Spark offered.

Tollar was worried Meriella would keep refusing, but while she was hesitant, she finally agreed. Abyss set Neesha and Tollar back on her shoulder and gently scooped up Meriella and Spark before heading toward the coast to find Bale and join the rest of their blaze.

Tollar had only the beginnings of a plan for dealing with those water beasts and now had to figure out how to account for Meriella's presence.

CHAPTER TWENTY-ONE

Tollar stood with Neesha and Croves on a water platform out on the ocean and wondered if this day would ever bloody well end. Her growing headache, a throb behind her eyes threatening to turn into a spike, would put an end to things soon if Tollar didn't figure it out. Neesha had a hand on her arm so Tollar could harness her while Croves was playing lookout as Shell and Flame, the two fastest with them, circled overhead as bait.

And there were several wakes racing toward them, the knobbly backs of the sea monsters just visible cutting the surface.

"Five," Croves said. "No, six."

Neesha's hand gripped her arm.

"It's not too many," Tollar said calmly.

It was definitely too many. But she had to do something about them sooner or later, and she was still having a fairly good day in terms of her abilities, so it seemed wisest to use it while she had it, headache be damned.

It would be best not to have to worry about these things trailing them along the coast or lying in wait when it was time to make their crossing to the southern continent.

She whistled and signalled. Flame, who had Spark on his shoulder, broke away to fly out farther over the water, away from them. Two of the beasts turned to follow him. Tollar had hoped it would be more.

"Open a fire portal and be ready," she said to Neesha.

Once the woman had fire ready, Tollar broke her grip and harnessed Croves instead.

"Just like last time," she told him.

When the beasts were in range, Tollar solidified the water directly in their path so that they slammed into a wall of water. She immediately summoned the demon in the beast in the lead and Croves banished it. While she called the demon from the second, a third lunged at them, but Neesha opened up with trueflame. She still couldn't do much more than pull it straight out, but that was enough to open a gap and keep the beasts back while Tollar and Croves worked.

"Seven," Croves said through gritted teeth.

"What?"

"Eight, godsdamnit, how are there this many of 'em in the whole world?"

Tollar caught sight of the new beasts coming in from the side and cursed. Pulled another demon out, but the fire keeping the fourth back vanished and Neesha inhaled a sharp, ragged gasp.

The beasts farther out had three water whips around Flame and had nearly pulled him and Spark right into the water.

Tollar cursed herself. She hadn't properly considered the ramifications of making Neesha watch her daughter in peril. She trusted Spark's capabilities but hadn't counted on there being so many of these water beasts.

"Nine," Croves breathed.

At last, fire erupted from around Flame and those light beams of Spark's cut through the water whips so Flame could gain altitude again.

"Really, we're back down to six," Tollar said.

"It's too many," he said.

"Neesha, summon Flame. Both of you hold on."

Tollar pulled in the edges of their water platform so that it was a disc just big enough for the three of them and shot across the surface back to the shore. Shell first went out to help Flame and then both of them raced back to the coastal mountains where the other dragons waited with Beenala and Meriella and the other humans.

Meriella was thankfully asleep in the gondola. Beenala was pacing in front of Bale when Tollar brought them in closer. Back on solid land, Tollar let go of all the magic and sat abruptly on a smooth, seaside boulder, while the ache behind her eyes grew teeth and made itself at home. She dug the heels of her hands into her temples and breathed deep. Then stood.

"So what now?" Eltir asked as the two dragons, bearing Spark, landed nearby.

"Should we send to the Guild for reinforcements?" Neesha asked.

"We're supposed to be scouting," Tollar said.

"We've scouted, it's impassable, we need help."

Tollar grumbled and paced the rocky shore. "I don't want to have to fight the entire way south. There's got to be a better way."

There was. Tollar had been mulling it over since Spark and Neesha had made their dramatic trip to the fire realm. No one was going to like it. But if it worked, it would clear the ocean passage for them and make any future water battles much easier.

Tollar stopped pacing with a hand on Neesha's shoulder. "What's the worst that happened to you and Spark from being in the fire realm in utero?"

"No!" Beenala gasped. "Absolutely not."

Tollar sighed. She'd hoped to get an answer before anyone started arguing with her. She pointed at her rank lines. Everyone shifted uncomfortably.

"It's too dangerous," Neesha said.

"*This* is too dangerous!" Tollar gestured to the writhing mass of sea monsters just beyond the shallows. "They almost got Spark and Flame!"

"The only risk is you getting trapped there," Spark said.

Neesha cut her a dark look and Spark shrugged.

"It's a big risk," Neesha said.

"But the twins will be safe? It might make them more powerful, but that's it?"

Croves, thick as mud sometimes, fully caught on to what she meant. "Absolutely not!"

"Not your decision." Tollar pointed at her rank lines again.

"Now wait a minute, those are my babes too!" he protested.

Tollar closed her eyes for a beat. She supposed this conversation had been long in the making, and she might as well get it over with.

"Oh, are they?" she shot back. "How do you propose to keep them alive for the next three months?"

"That's *yer* job."

"You're right, it is. You've put, what, two minutes into this so far? Right now it's my body being stretched, my resources being used, my internal organs being pressed into places they have no right being."

Croves went a bit grey. The others shifted uneasily. She'd have definitely preferred to have this conversation in private, but she supposed Raia overhearing it would be beneficial when he needed reminders later.

"And now, here's you, not even able to handle me talking about it. So let's get one thing straight: you helped make this happen, yes, but until these babies are on the other side of my skin, all the responsibility, all the risk, and therefore all the choice, is mine."

"But—I didn't—Ye can't—" Croves sputtered.

A small smile played at the corners of her lips, and she touched his arm, meeting his eye.

"I value your input," she said. "You are always welcome to advise, but in the end, decisions are mine. And right now, these two—who have done this many times before—are telling me it's safe for the twins."

"The danger is to you," Neesha said. "And as you say, those babies are relying on you for months yet. If something happens, it happens to all three of you."

"But will something happen?" Spark said. "Mamma, I know it went badly for you and Nanny. But it's not the same for you more recently. It's never been a threat for me. Tollar is even less inclined to stay there."

"What if they don't give her a choice? Like with Dionelle? No one can help her."

"The harness," Tollar said. "Can't I put it on and you can yank me back out if you think I've been too long?"

Spark ran to fetch the harness and the longest bit of lead while Croves tried to argue and Raia ultimately dragged him off with the help of Barlo and Eltir, so it was just Neesha and Beenala left arguing with her, which was an improvement.

"Bee, I have to."

"No. We should just wait here for reinforcements. Even just more dragons. They'll be here in a couple of days."

"Loch knows we're coming. Every second we waste out here spells doom for Biterna."

"Gods, I wish Nandara was here," Neesha said. "She knows the most about what my parents went through. But listen, you need to be quick and you need to get yourself to whatever passes for leadership among them. The fire demons have something like an emperor."

Beenala gave Neesha a wounded look.

"Bee, information is how I stay safe. So I can just think the portal to their leader, right? That's how these work?"

"Best I can tell." Neesha shrugged.

"It'll have to do."

Spark returned with the harness and a coil of rope.

"I can't believe this," Beenala said.

"If she's quick, the risk is low," Spark said. "We've been through the fire realm dozens of times. It's been fine."

"I don't *want* to be there, Bee. I'm not going to stay, and there's not really anything they can do to hurt me." With the harness buckled on, Tollar handed the other end of the rope to Spark. "If I tug three times, you haul me out as fast as you can."

"I'm stronger," Croves said from a distance. "Shouldn't I—"

"I need you back here guarding the portal in case one of them comes out. Spark's plenty strong, but she can't banish water demons. You need to help Neesha. Everyone else needs to stay clear."

Beenala was still stiff and angry when Tollar gave her a quick hug. She hoped Beenala would forgive her when she came back unscathed. She didn't give any of them time to argue more, or for her to change her mind. Tollar opened a water portal on the beach and jumped in.

It was a lot brighter than the only other time she'd been there. There were visible currents making whorls like roadways and there were pillars of ice just in front of her, all lit up in greys and blues from a light source she couldn't see. The pillars supported a throne.

Water demons outside their own realm often took on vaguely animalistic shapes, but they looked much different here. More like puddles. Puddles inside of puddles, which was a thing that made her brain itch if she looked at them too long. And to call the thing in front of her a throne wasn't quite accurate. It was more like a bowl on a pedestal. A shallow bowl and a wide pedestal.

Tollar was overthinking it and she really needed to get out of here.

"You're in charge?" she said, trying to keep her language as close to theirs as she could. "You need to stop listening to that human. To Loch."

"He brings us mischief."

She hadn't expected much in the way of an answer, but she definitely hadn't expected that.

"He'll bring you all doom."

"Doom, perhaps, but not ours."

"You know what, I don't have time for this. If you don't stop interfering where you have no business—particularly if you don't stop taking marching orders from Loch like a bunch of brand-new guppies—I'm going to come back here and I'm going to stay here until the worlds rip apart. How's that for doom?"

Okay, so threats weren't what she'd been planning on either, but it had been a long day and this really had been a terrible idea.

She didn't wait for an answer. She had no idea how long she had before the others got spooked and Spark dragged her back out. The shimmer of the portal was right behind her, a little more than an arms' length away.

Tollar did what she had really come here to do. She summoned all of the demons currently topside. She hadn't been sure she'd be able to do it until she'd been back here. One thing she'd latched onto in listening to the fireborn women talk about their trips to the fire realm was how energized they were both in their realm and afterward.

Aquamancy was startlingly easy here. And her headache was entirely gone.

So Tollar summoned every single water demon back to the seat of their power. At the very least, it meant Loch was going to have to individually put demons back in all those water monsters.

Dozens of water demons funnelled in from all over, gathering before her, and that was perhaps going to be a problem. She'd interrupted whatever fun they'd been having.

She gave the rope three tugs. It went taut a moment later, and then the quick release snapped. Tollar really should have thought of what the pressures of this place would do to it. She sighed, bubbles drifting around her head. She gathered the pieces and used magic to propel herself back out.

Where the others were positively losing their minds over the empty rope and broken quick release.

"It's fine!" Tollar called, closing the portal behind her.

"What the hell happened?" Neesha demanded. She pointed out to sea, where the beasts all currently thrashed.

"Ah." So she explained.

"You threatened the water king?" Beenala said.

Neesha burst out laughing. "Of course you did."

"It's done and over and everything is fine."

"But my quick release," Spark said.

"Yes, you enchanted it to withstand a dragon. But water is an entirely different force of nature. When this is over, someone really needs to teach you aquamancy. I think you can do some brilliant things with it."

"You act like this was nothing!" Beenala snapped.

"It *was* nothing. At no point did I feel like I was in danger. I don't know if they were going to attack me for recalling them all or not. I didn't stick around to find out. Because that would be foolish."

Beenala pressed her hands over her face, and Croves was staring off into the mountains. Neesha was still laughing.

"And it worked!" Spark said.

Tollar wasn't sure if her sudden support was part of her desperate attempt to patch over how tense things had been or if it was more academic interest. Spark was terrified of aquamancy but always entranced by new information about demon magic. And really most things.

"Yes, it worked!" Tollar looked around at the others. "We're not going to have to worry about ocean crossings for a while, so let's make use of that. We're still two days out from Baymouth Shores and five days behind schedule, so let's get a message to the Guild and head out. We need to get Meriella somewhere properly safe, these nonsense delays have ruined Neesha's birthday plans, and quite frankly I miss real beds for maybe the first time in my life."

This at least got a chuckle out of Beenala. And all the wizards gathered round—even Barlo, who couldn't do much but could still lend a little power to a harnessing. And with Tollar bursting with water energy at the moment, it made it that much easier for Neesha to harness the lot of them and send an update—her image projected on a wall in the Guild message room along with the sound of her voice.

It was at least safe enough for them to come west and down the coast. Tollar and her crew needed to keep scouting ahead, but it was nice to know reinforcements wouldn't be far behind now.

CHAPTER TWENTY-TWO

Neesha did not love the walk into Baymouth Shores—and hadn't ever done it before, only ever travelling there by fire portal—but Tollar insisted they remain as inconspicuous as possible in populated areas. So the dragons had dropped them off on the other side of the mountain earlier that morning and they had to follow the road in. And gods, it was hot, even for morning. She resented the fact that fire couldn't hurt her but hot air could still make her terribly uncomfortable. It was all the water in the air. Like walking through a boiling swamp.

Tollar and Beenala didn't even seem to notice. Upalint was apparently one big boiling swamp, and they both liked it that way.

Meriella was red-faced and sweating, her dishevelled corkscrew brown curls plastered to her forehead, still refusing to take off the scarf or long robes even though all of them knew damn-well what she was trying to hide. Neesha's only regret in Abyss's actions was that she hadn't known what the dragon was doing. She'd have liked the satisfaction of watching the monster who did this to Meriella plummet to his death.

The demonborn women plus Beenala flanked their new charge, less a cage and more a protective wall, and if Meriella noticed, she didn't seem to mind. Spark was right next to her, nattering her ear off like she had for the past two days. It had pulled Meriella out of her shell a handful of times and even made her laugh once.

Croves and the others had gone ahead already, both to give Meriella more space as the numbers overwhelmed her, but also they'd look less conspicuous arriving as two smaller groups than one large one. And it wasn't like they were the only ones on the roads. There were other clusters of people, carts and wagons and mules, all heading into the city from outlying areas for trade or whatever it was people did.

Neesha supposed she'd regularly made a similar but not nearly so long and hot trek into Pasdale from the family's outlying farm.

But Baymouth Shores was much bigger than Pasdale, something made evident as they came around the mountain's shoulder and the entire city came into view, climbing up the side of the mountain. It was a steep city. It wasn't much of a bay and didn't exactly have shores, as the land more or less dropped straight into the ocean. The road they took was elevated, the surf crashing against the cliff a good distance below.

Ahead, the land flattened out and met the sea more gradually with some reclaimed areas that jutted out into the water. Those areas were primarily industrial, with factories and warehouses, and docks to accommodate merchant ships.

Neesha was only vaguely familiar with the city, but knew approximately where the remnants of her family lived. She'd sent Croves and the others into a safer but more worker-friendly part of the city to find them an inn to stay at—her uncle couldn't accommodate them all and none of them thought it was a good idea to split up for longer than this particular errand would take.

They'd meet at one of the squares. Not the big central city square—too conspicuous—but a smaller one to the southeast of it. It was also closer to their approach, so hopefully Neesha and her group wouldn't have to do a lot of walking or waiting to meet back up with the others.

It was mid-morning when they reached the square, which thankfully had a good deal of shade from trees and scattered pavilions, and they took refuge at a cluster of benches under a tree.

"Never been here before," Tollar said, her eyes drinking in her surroundings.

"So Neesha's ahead of you on the friend count on this one?" Beenala grinned.

"I'm afraid only family. And an enemy, if you count my brother."

"Is it really that bad?"

"He's worse than your mother." Neesha gave Tollar a significant look. "He's like my father was."

"How unfortunate," Tollar murmured, most of her attention still on the city around them. "How do they get carts all the way up there?"

She was facing vaguely north, where the city climbed the steepest.

"Pulleys, mostly. I think. Probably a lot of wizards magicking things up for anyone or anything that can't climb the stairs. Lots of stairs. A few ramps. Fine for people but less so for carts."

Tollar was twitching in a way Neesha had learned to interpret as wanting to get moving. She was somewhere new and wanted to explore.

"My family lives about halfway up the mountain," Neesha said. "You'll get to see a good amount of the city on the way."

Spark had been quiet, mostly watching, sitting on a bench next to Meriella, her arm around the other woman's shoulders. Meriella had her hood drawn up, her face in shadows, and she shook, hugging her knees to her chest. She wasn't as bad as Dionelle had been. Or maybe she was worse? Neesha supposed it depended on how you looked at it. Dionelle had been so damaged by Loch, she'd utterly disappeared inside herself. It had been gut-wrenching, but she'd been malleable and easier to care for. Meriella was like a frightened deer about to bolt. Or sometimes something more vicious, on the verge of lashing out.

Another benefit of leaving her with Neesha's extended family was that her aunt was a nurse. And the Guild knew what kind of care she'd need when they came to collect her. Neesha wasn't sure how much she trusted the Guild, but they'd found the right person to help Dionelle.

"Ah, there's Raia!" Tollar bounced to her feet and intercepted the approaching dragon rider.

Neesha supposed it was also a good idea they'd split up to keep these giants apart. Croves and Raia together was enough. Spark and Tollar as well was quite a lot.

"Barlo and Eltir already started drinkin'," Raia reported.

Neesha could guess that Raia had also had a quick drink before heading out to meet them.

"It's not far." Raia waved indiscriminately down the street and gave them the directions and the name of the place.

"The Drunk Mermaid, really?" Beenala huffed with feigned indignance.

"And what about Croves?" Tollar asked.

"Eh, he's gone off to find a comfort house."

"Ah." Tollar rolled her eyes, amused.

"So much for sticking together," Neesha said.

Tollar shrugged. "Good luck to anyone who tries to make trouble for him, may they still have all their limbs attached at the end."

Raia cackled and Meriella flinched.

"Aye, no point in worryin' about him. He'll be fine. I'm heading back to catch up on the drinking. See ye this evening?"

Tollar glanced at Neesha.

"If it all goes well, we'll stay for dinner with my family and be back a little after dark."

"You still want us to come?" Tollar asked, touching Beenala's arm.

"I'd appreciate it."

Raia left them to it, and Neesha, loathe to leave the shade of the park, brought them deeper and higher into the city, stopping at another smaller neighbourhood park with street vendors so they could eat. It was nice to have real food after a week of terrible rations. It would be nice to sleep in a real bed. Two whole nights! Tollar thought it would be best to give the Guild and the dragons some time to catch up, and also Tollar was really starting to feel the burden of carrying two small humans with her everywhere she went.

Neesha was just relieved that Tollar was listening to her and Beenala when they counselled her on the amount of rest she should be getting.

It was a long climb through the city, the east–west roads the only break they got in the aggressive incline. Neesha's legs ached, even with finding as many of the switchback ramps as she could. There was one large lift, a big box on pulleys, that they took, which was a deep relief, though Neesha seemed to be the only one tired.

She tried not to be too cranky about that.

It was early afternoon when directions she had to stop for finally brought her to her brother's house. She supposed it was more her uncle's house. Cusec and his family had come out here first and then, once established, Bly had joined them. They all lived together, including Bly and his wife and their children, in this three-level, narrow stone building, pressed in against all the others along the row.

Everything was stone, much of the city carved from the mountainside. The south side of each building had deep awnings over the windows, letting in bright light but protecting from the harsh heat of the sun. There were a few trees lining the streets, but most of the greenery was on rooftop gardens.

According to her uncle, the city boasted some of the world's best floramancers to maintain the house gardens. Neesha couldn't do plant magic, though it sounded mostly like aquamancy with a bit extra. It seemed like Tollar could do it to some extent, and it really made Neesha question the nature of Tollar's power. It really did seem that she was more than just an aquamancer, just that everything else had been overshadowed.

Her shoulders felt tight as she knocked at the door and waited. She really did not want to see her brother, but they definitely needed the family's help.

Bly's wife, Onnali, was the one to open the door and greet them, and Neesha hoped she kept the relief off her face.

"Ah, here you are!" Onnali opened the door wider and ushered them all in. She was about Neesha's height with straight brown hair, dark-brown eyes, and light-brown skin. Neesha had sent a message ahead before leaving the Guild that they'd be stopping in but with vague details.

"Great to see you!" Neesha and Spark hugged Onnali and introduced their companions.

"Oh, Nee! Did you do something to your hair?" Onnali ran a fingertip over one of the darker locks of Neesha's braid.

"Uh. Yeah."

"Her magic's changed a bit," Spark said in a hushed whisper. "Mine too, sort of. Look, I'm pink now!"

Onnali squinted and smiled uncertainly but thankfully didn't ask any more about it.

"If Seina is around, I think it would be helpful for her to have a look at Meriella," Neesha said.

Meriella was still huddled as deep into her robe as she could get.

"Yes, of course." Onnali smiled warmly. "Seina's home—most everyone is except Bly and Inara. We don't usually do much in this heat. Come in and let me get you something cold to drink."

Neesha had forgotten that they took most of the afternoon off, in part to stay cool. Having not experienced the full force of the heat before, she hadn't really given it much thought. She'd expected Onnali to be home because she was a teacher and the schools were closed for the summer, and Uncle Cusec was a professor and likely to be home for the same reason. Bly was a minor politician and worked all sorts of hours, so it was hard to say when he'd be around, but at least he wasn't here now. She started to hope maybe they could get in and out without seeing him at all.

They weren't far into the house when three dogs came bounding up to them, all large—larger than Shadow—and one of them very nearly the size of a small pony. Beenala and Spark both relaxed and pet the dogs, though Meriella tensed, until she spotted a cat on the stairs, a big fluffy grey thing, and scooped it up. The cat, surprisingly, did not seem to mind this at all.

Onnali chattered about the family as she led them down a flight of stairs to the kitchen and dining area. Cusec's daughter Cavvi was a builder, and would probably notice their presence and join them soon. His other daughter, Serra, was married and lived with her husband's family on the other side of town. Onnali's son, Bevir, was done school and off apprenticing now, and her daughter, Inara, was also recently done school and a wild thing always out with her friends.

"Sounds like someone I know," Neesha laughed. "Bly must love that."

"They do rather lock horns," Onnali said. "But Inara has a good heart. She'll be fine."

"I guess if nothing else, what happened to me can serve as a dire warning."

Onnali put a hand on Neesha's arm. "You lost some years, but it looks like it's working out for you. It is too bad you didn't make it in time for us to celebrate your birthday."

"We celebrated on the way here. I got extra rations that day." Neesha smirked.

"Well, I think I can do a little better than rations."

Onnali brought a tray of glasses and three pitchers—one with plain water, one with wine and one with a cool fruit juice—and set them out, serving her guests. Cavvi appeared, shorter like Neesha if not quite so pale, her sandy blonde hair cut short, and hazel eyes sparkling as she grinned at their guests. Onnali sent Cavvi to fetch Seina for Meriella, and Cusec, since he'd be pleased to visit.

Tollar took a glass of the juice and paced around, the dogs trailing her, her gaze taking it all in while she listened to Neesha and Spark chat with family. Spark stayed with Meriella and the cat she still cradled, sitting close to her while Neesha and Beenala sat across from them. Onnali took a spot near the head of the long table, asking them about their trip. Cavvi came back with Cusec, whose auburn hair was greyer than Neesha remembered but he still gave the same shy smile when he saw them. While Spark introduced everyone to Cavvi and Uncle Cusec, Neesha took Seina aside to explain what they knew and suspected of Meriella.

Seina bit her lips, her pale cheeks flushing and glanced at Meriella, her blue eyes drawn in concern.

"I'll do what I can," she whispered, and then went to introduce herself and lead Meriella (and the cat) off to another part of the house.

Neesha and Spark spoke a bit about their journey and more about how Dionelle was doing, and Cusec was relieved to hear his sister was improving.

"We'll bring her back as soon as we can," Neesha promised. "You might even get a few words out of her."

Cusec smiled. "It would be nice to hear her voice again after all these years."

Onnali asked Beenala and Tollar about their home, and Beenala smiled politely while Tollar talked a bit about their farm.

"Farmers, really?"

"Well, not only. Bee's an artist and I have a penchant for trouble."

"Solving trouble," Beenala amended with a fond smile. "She saved three entire nations from Loch and very nearly did it by herself."

Tollar waved a hand and paced around the table. "It took all of us, but I'm the one who gets the blame." Tollar smiled wryly.

The front door clattered and Neesha had a brief moment to hope it was Inara before Bly called out.

"Down here," Onnali called. "We've guests."

"Ah, did Nee and Mita finally make it?"

Bly came down the stairs, so much like their father with his height and broad shoulders, olive skin and brown hair, and Neesha half-wanted to hide under the table. Onnali had been in the middle of introductions, but Bly took one look at Tollar—whose pacing had brought her next to Onnali—sniffed derisively, and glared at Neesha.

"All this time and all that's happened and still nothing changes with you. Still keeping questionable company?" Bly sneered. "Though I suppose the likes of you run together."

"Of course we do!" Neesha slapped the table and stood, pointing an accusing finger at him. "How else are we supposed to keep each other safe from people like you? Spark has a girlfriend—are you going to throw her away like garbage too? We're the best pyromancers in the entire world, Bly, but somehow that's not good enough because we don't have *husbands*? Do you hear yourself?"

Without a word, Cusec slipped past Bly and up the stairs. It was dizzying how quickly her fool of a brother could make her feel like she was trapped in the old farmhouse, impending marriage looming like a noose. Cavvi, at least, stayed off to the side, watching with open interest.

"And I suppose you're fine with this one running around in her condition?" Bly gestured at Tollar, whose pregnancy was undeniable these days. "Clearly she's got no husband to talk sense into her."

Neesha opened her mouth to fire back, but took note of how much more space Tollar suddenly took up without seeming to have moved at all. She leaned forward a touch, and with her height, Neesha had to assume she loomed over Bly.

"If you must know," Tollar said with exacting deadly calm. "This is my wife." She gestured to Beenala. "And you're upsetting her."

Neesha hadn't even noticed, she was so focused on her brother, but Spark had sunk into her chair with her hands pressed over her face, while Beenala sat stiffly, her hands gripping the edge of the table.

"*Your* wife promised us hospitality," Tollar continued, pointing at Bly. "Do you plan to embarrass her?"

"Your wife?" Bly was still glaring. "Please! You're not married."

"No," Onnali said evenly, hands on hips. "They clearly come from the southern continent, where *no one* gets married. They just love each other, and that's enough."

"And I suppose," Tollar went on, before Bly could reply, "that you'd invalidate what Bee and I have because of my relationship with my babies' father? That's what's important to you, isn't it? That there's a man involved."

"Uncle," Spark said, extracting her face from her hands. "Nanny gave them a love stone at the Guild before we left. The light swirled around them, just like it did for Nanny and Pappy before. That was good enough for her."

"Yes," Neesha snapped. "Our father, bless him, didn't live long enough to learn to be better, but Dionelle has. She wants us to be safe, but doesn't try to deny who we are or act like we're monsters for it. Gods only hope you can do the same!"

"And we're plenty safe enough, obviously," Tollar said. "Is that what upsets you so much? That we don't need men like you? I don't see how that affects you when you're happily married to a wonderful woman who you clearly don't deserve."

Onnali burst out laughing and the tension snapped.

"He does not deserve me," she agreed, still chuckling fondly. "And I tell him that every day. And we speak of this now and then, how he clings to the worst of Pasdale because there isn't much good left in it."

Bly crossed his arms, looking positively miserable. "I didn't want to leave. I hate that I had to."

"But you know you would be dead if you had stayed," Onnali said gently, her hand on his arm.

"I wish Nanny had taken us all here with you. Uncle, it was terrible."

Neesha focused all her attention on Spark, who was shaking, her eyes having taken on a sheen of panic. She put a hand on her daughter's shoulder.

"I miss them too. We're safe now. We'll make sure we all stay that way. But why don't you take a break? Maybe Cavvi can show you around?"

Cavvi brightened up and came all the way around Bly, beckoning to Spark.

"Your friend seems to have absconded with my cat, but it's about time to bring the dogs outside. Why don't you come help with that?"

Spark was out of her chair in an instant, and Neesha thought Beenala might follow. But she stayed put, either too panicked to move or understanding that Spark needed some time with her kin.

Onnali guided Bly into a chair. "Please remember your manners around our guests. Not everywhere is Pasdale, and you don't have to like the customs of other places, but you do have to respect them, particularly when they cause you no actual harm."

Bly's face puckered up but he remained silent.

"I like you," Tollar said, flashing Onnali a grin before she resumed pacing.

"So you're going after Loch again?" Bly asked. "Why these two?"

"Oh!" Neesha beamed. "Tollar is the world's best aquamancer! She's a demon hybrid too."

"Of course." Bly blinked a few times. "How many of you are there?"

"Just the four of us, as best the Guild has been able to tell," Tollar said. "They found me, recruited me, because of your family. So they're looking. Could be they've missed one or two, but it seems awfully rare."

"Yes, well." Bly gave his wife a hesitant look before continuing. "You may want to keep that bit, and any of your magic, really, to yourselves."

"Oh?" Tollar leaned on the back of Beenala's chair, giving Bly her full attention now.

"Elementals aren't held in particular regard at the moment. And a lot of us saw your dragons this morning—that'll have people on edge. We don't get a lot of dragons through here in general, particularly not lately."

"Oh no," Beenala gasped.

"Have your people rather suddenly turned on dragons and wizards?" Tollar asked, urgency in her tone.

"Yes. How did you know it was both?"

Tollar dragged her hands down her face. "This is what Loch does. He divides people, turns them against the dragons and the wizards so no one's got any allies and everyone's at each other's throats. Makes you easy pickings when he rolls in to take over."

"Shit," Neesha hissed.

"He's done this across most of the continent," Beenala said.

"We managed to drive him off our lands," Tollar said. "But it was hard won."

"So he's expanding this way?" Neesha asked, horrified.

Tollar pointed at Bly again. "Onnali says you're a politician? You need to warn your people. Loch is targeting you."

"How's he still got the resources?" Neesha asked. "You killed his general."

"He's got more." Tollar sighed.

"And the king in Golden Hill," Bly said, deflating.

Neesha stared at the middle of the table, clenching and unclenching her fists. It had taken this long just to get the Guild to move against Loch. Would they be ready to move against the king?

"So stopping Loch won't do anything?" Beenala said, her voice small and shaking.

"Loch's been the king's lapdog for well over a decade," Bly said. "Stopping him will do plenty good." He glanced at Neesha. "You sure you *can* stop him?"

"I did once already." She glared at him. "We told Dionelle we'd keep each other safe, and that's what we're godsdamn going to do."

While they'd been talking, Onnali had put together a selection of meat cutlets, cheeses, and fruit, with little nibbles of bread and dips, and set it all out before them. It was a good distraction and right on time. Cavvi and Spark came back with the dogs, who definitely got a lot more nibbles than they probably should have, both Spark and Beenala paying plenty of attention to them. The biggest pony one came and set its big shaggy head right in Neesha's lap, looking mournfully at her until she gave it a bit of her bread, which it was surprisingly gentle in accepting.

Seina reappeared, though Meriella did not.

"She's resting," Seina said. "Got her cleaned up and in fresh clothes, gave her some tea that will help calm her but make her sleepy. I'll take care of her till the Guild comes. I'll have Bly drop a note for them when he heads back to the citadel."

Onnali continued to play hostess, filling their cups and bringing out more light fare, including some baked goods she'd prepared for Neesha's birthday. Cusec eventually came back, grabbing something to eat before he had to head back to the university where he was overseeing some research.

Neesha went with him to the door, wanting to apologize for how things had initially gone.

"You're not wrong about your brother," Cusec said with a sad smile. "It's just hard for me."

"Well, hopefully my next visit will be a peaceful one."

Cusec smiled and hugged her before leaving. Bly and Cavvi were both preparing to head back to work late in the afternoon, and Neesha supposed it was as good a time as any to rejoin the rest of her travel companions. She and the others followed out as Bly left, thanking Onnali profusely for her hospitality. Neesha brought her brother aside before they parted.

"Mamma is doing a lot better since we reached the Guild. I tried to convince her to come this far and stay with you, but I think she needs to be with Ondias and Nandara a little longer. But she's talking again. And we're here with her dragon. You remember the large black one? Would you like to say hello? I can bring her to the local dragon chamber when she comes to pick us up day after tomorrow."

Neesha couldn't read her brother's expression and hoped he wouldn't pick a fight with her when she was trying to give him grace he honestly didn't deserve. At last, he nodded slowly.

"Yes, that would be interesting, if nothing else. And I suppose hearing directly from the dragons a little more about what Loch has been doing here will help me make sure we can start to undo it."

"They managed it in Upalint," Neesha said. "Tollar got warning in enough time to pull her people together."

Bly didn't really say much to that, but at least he wasn't fighting with her anymore.

"You can stop him?" Bly asked again.

"Yes. We already have. We just need to make it permanent this time."

Neesha wished she believed her own words, but Bly was right that they had to stop Loch, regardless of what other challenges lay ahead of them. And there certainly were enough of those if Loch controlled everything between here and Port Sawulxo. She'd sincerely hoped that when Tollar had knocked the demons out of the sea monsters, that it would give them some breathing room. She did not want to have to fight the entire way south.

CHAPTER TWENTY-THREE

S park stood on Abyss's shoulder, watching ahead where the armada gathered, feeling strangely grateful that Tollar had taught her how to swim. She was still rubbish at it, but did better than just uselessly sinking to the seafloor now. Abyss circled with Bale just above the shallows around the southeast-most island of the archipelago, the one they'd been following south for a day and a half. They had to cross here to get to Port Sawulxo.

Loch clearly knew that. Spark wondered if he was out there or if he'd just sent some more of his minions to do his dirty work.

A dragon from the Guild contingent had caught up with them first thing this morning with the message that the rest weren't far behind. Tollar (and honestly all the rest of them) was eager to attack and get this over with, but insisted it would go better if they waited for backup.

So they circled and waited, and Spark got increasingly nervous.

They knew what they had to do. They'd done it already, again and again. She had to wonder if Loch's people had anything to counter her light beams and Neesha's trueflame. They'd had some time since that defeat. And had they figured out how to beat Tollar? *Could* they beat Tollar?

Tollar didn't seem to think they could.

But she was also exhausted, sleeping more and more, clumsy while climbing around on Bale, and just generally irritable. Spark was once again relieved that she'd chosen long ago not to have children of her own, though she now worried about what sort of monster Ember would turn into when she finally got around to having the babies she said she wanted.

Seemed like a truly miserable process. Spark had no idea how people chose to keep doing this. Really, humans should have gone extinct from a lack of anyone wanting to have babies millennia ago. The dragons certainly had the right idea. Lay a tidy little egg that feeds on magic and grows independently of either of its parents.

Abyss roared and banked hard toward the north, changing direction so abruptly Spark would have been thrown off into the sky if not for currently being tethered next to Neesha.

Once Spark regained her footing, she squinted at the horizon, and there were definitely a whole lot of shapes coming their way. It wasn't all of the dragons left in the world—some of them were staying in the city because someone had to, while others still had the very young or the very old to protect. But aside from the ones on the horizon, there were the ones who lived in the south who were meeting them in Port Sawulxo, and then all the ones from the western continent would join them soon. But the northern contingent, several dozen at least, was heading their way now.

And Abyss kept calling to them at regular intervals. But it wasn't only the regular greeting call. There was a component to it that Spark hadn't heard before.

Tollar landed on Abyss's other shoulder, and Spark shrieked, not sure how she missed the fact that Bale had caught up to them and flew overhead.

"Finally!" Tollar said between dragon calls. "I want this over with by sundown. We can rest back on the island tonight and head for the port at dawn."

"Just like that?" Spark asked.

"Of course!"

"You're not worried about this?"

"We could have taken them even before the rest arrived."

Spark had no idea where this woman got her confidence from. Neesha said it was because Tollar had been through plenty of situations like this and didn't have a penchant for losing.

"Holy shit, look!" Neesha shouted, pointing.

There was a brilliant white dragon near the lead, the blaze getting closer, and Spark was shocked, momentarily thinking it was the former Dragoness

Superior. And then the dragon's markings became discernible, and Spark was even more shocked than she would have been if it had been the Superior back from the dead.

It was Glacial Sunfire, Abyss's daughter. Spark had thought she was largely unable to fly, but here she was keeping up with her father and brother. The blaze reached them, and Abyss did a whole lot of roaring and spiralling around the members of her family, Tollar jumping back to Bale to avoid being thrown into the ocean.

At last, they banked into a recognizable formation, the whole lot of them circling back where Tollar had originally been holding position. This contingent of dragons didn't have any wizards with them, but they did, shockingly, have weapons and armour. All of it things Spark had been making for them over the years.

The Dragoness Superior must have cleared out the armoury before leaving for the Guild. Jatt and Ember had probably helped. Spark felt a pang of longing she didn't have time for.

Abyss had been giving instructions to the rest of the blaze, giving them the plan Tollar had come up with last night. It wasn't much different than what they'd done before: demonborn using their magic to keep everyone safe from water whips, harnessing whenever they could, routing out the elemental clusters doing most of the magic against them, and either killing or unpossessing the sea monsters. There'd been signs of magic from them again, so either whatever Tollar had done a week ago hadn't worked or Loch had put new demons in the ones they faced now.

"Glacial Sunfire had an influx of magic that coincided with you two renouncing your power," Abyss said.

"I really didn't think that was going to actually do anything," Neesha said.

"Glacial Sunfire won't get any bigger, but has the strength and magic she should. Bolt and Merciless Winter Sky have been teaching her to fly and to fight. Shattered Starshine stayed behind to guard the Guild, should it need defending."

"Will it?" Spark asked, startled.

"While Loch is the king's strongest general, he's not the only one."

"Great."

"Ready?" Tollar called from above, Bale circling back around. Tollar leapt back down to join them.

"The dragons are ready," Abyss confirmed.

"Not sure about the people," Spark said.

"You'll do fine," Tollar said. "No lightning this time even!"

Spark didn't want to admit that she was disappointed they weren't trying a storm. She kind of wanted to fight a storm again and see what she could do with lightning. She'd tried to turn fire into lightning but hadn't quite gotten it to work. She and Neesha had both been practicing plenty.

"I just need you to track where Croves and his crew end up," Tollar said. "Make sure you don't accidentally light them on fire."

That was the one part of the plan that Spark didn't like. Croves, Raia, Barlo and Eltir were going to try to get onto the enemy ships to fight the elementals there directly. Part of Spark and Neesha's job was to use their fire to clear a path for Shell and Dragon to deliver the group of humans to a boat.

Spark half-wanted to go with them, but mostly wished they'd stay on their dragons with her. But after Tollar and her people had liberated Port Sawulxo, they'd freed most of the dragons Loch had left in captivity. It was likely he would keep any that remained on Biterna to hold the island.

Spark would have preferred an air battle. This one would get awfully close to the water.

"Let's go then!" Tollar pitched backward off of Abyss, diving away into the ocean.

"She does that," Neesha said, smirking.

"Mamma, your friends are crazy."

"She just wants this over with because she's worried about Bee."

Spark was worried too. None of them liked leaving Beenala alone on the island with the gondolas. Well, not totally alone, she was just outside a settlement after Tollar had negotiated with the people who lived there. Spark had no idea how much those people could be trusted. But they also all agreed—especially Beenala—that she would be a hindrance if they brought her into battle. The closer they got to her home, the more desperately she wanted to return to it and be free of this fight.

Ahead of them, the sea monsters started screaming like they had off the coast a week ago.

"Oh my gods, did she go back to the water realm?" Neesha gasped.

"Maybe you shouldn't have taught her to do that."

Neesha laughed. "You were the one who encouraged her to do it."

"It's time, hang on," Abyss said, and dived.

Even if Tollar had gone back to the water realm to unpossess all the sea monsters at once, they'd still want to stay and fight the dragons, particularly with so many of them around. There were no water whips from the monsters, but there were plenty coming from the ships.

"Portal time!" Neesha called over the air rushing past as Abyss dived hard toward the boats.

Spark pulled fire out of the air and made a portal for her mother, then took Abyss's dragonflame and concentrated it into light beams. She cut one of the sea monsters apart and put a big hole in the first boat as they passed overhead. Neesha dropped trueflame on them from above. Spark caught glimpses of some of the other dragons dropping the huge spears she had made, letting gravity carry them pointy-end-first down into the water and the monsters below.

That was definitely not what she had made those for, but it was an interesting tactic. And it was working. Too bad they'd never be able to recover the weapons.

Great spouts of water shot up here and there, sometimes seeming random, sometimes capsizing ships, and Spark supposed that was Tollar doing whatever it was she did.

Any dragons that could get close enough to the boats would shred any humans they could reach. There were fire and steam everywhere. Croves clearing the flames was the only thing that allowed Spark to track where he and the others were. He was cutting a path along one of the biggest ships.

There was no sign of Loch, and Spark was strangely disappointed. If he'd been here now, could they have finished this here? It would certainly be easier than trying to battle around an island full of innocent people.

As the dragons and Croves's team tore through the elementals and the boats and the sea monsters, the response became weaker and more chaotic. It was almost too easy.

Was it some sort of trap? Was Loch waiting, somehow hidden, with an even bigger force nearby?

A blast of water shot up next to Abyss, and Spark screamed and fell backward, nearly off the dragon because she wasn't tethered. But it was Tollar, riding the spout to hop onto Abyss's shoulder.

"Spark, quick, I need to harness you."

Spark stared at her, at the steam evaporating around her, and couldn't get herself to move.

"I've got it," Neesha said, pulling to the end of her tether and grabbing Tollar's wrist.

"Abyss, close to the water, if you would?"

Abyss started her dive and Tollar turned back to Spark.

"Keep an eye out for those water beasts. Be ready with your light beams." And then she turned away, harnessing Neesha, with all her focus on the ocean drawing nearer below them.

The water steamed and bubbled, and Spark had a hard time focusing on sea monsters, though there didn't appear to be any around. There had been one near Abyss, but it streaked away from the steaming water, getting fainter as it dived deeper.

The steaming water bulged, like a giant bubble. Spark took a quick look around, just in time to see Dragon swoop in and pull Croves and the others off one of the sinking boats.

And then the bubble burst into a giant wave, with more of those boiling spouts shooting out all over the place. It rose up, capsizing the remaining boats, boiling the last of the sea monsters that hadn't yet fled. The roaring steam from the huge boiling wave drowned out all sound, even the dragons.

At last, there was nothing left but calm, steaming water, and Abyss banked away, back into the sky.

Tollar let go of Neesha and staggered. Neesha crumpled at the end of her tether and slid along Abyss's back, driven by the winds. Tollar stumbled and then fell. Spark got her brain and her body agreeing with each other again and lunged forward, catching Tollar by the arm before she slid away out into the sky.

Spark knew falling off Abyss into the ocean wouldn't hurt her. She'd heard the story about how Tollar had spent a night at the bottom of a river after falling off of Bale. But Spark had no idea how they'd fetch her if she sank to the bottom of the ocean.

So she got her arms around Tollar and hauled her in between two spikes, near Neesha, and helped her find a handhold. Tollar's expression was as unfocused as Neesha's, but she did grip the hold when Spark brought her to it.

"Next time," Tollar wheezed, "I think I'll use some demons as well."

"Wouldn't it be better to just not have a next time?"

Tollar blinked and focused her gaze, looking at Spark. "Till Loch's gone, we've got a whole lot of next times ahead of us."

Spark didn't like to think about that. Or about how she'd have probably been more help than her mother had been. They were both right there, but Tollar had asked for Spark because Spark was stronger. Only she'd frozen. And now Tollar and Neesha were both exhausted.

"Don't be so hard on yourself," Tollar said, patting Spark's arm. "I knew that wave would finish it, and it didn't matter what shape any of us were in afterward."

"You almost fell off a dragon again."

"Bee would never forgive me." Tollar chuckled. "But Bale would have caught me. I appreciate you not letting me fall, all the same."

Spark looked back and saw that Bale wasn't far behind them. Of course she would be, probably trailing behind Abyss the whole time. All that remained of her kin was here in this fight.

And Tollar had probably been exactly as calculating with the magic as she said, but it still would have been better for everyone if Spark had been the one to help her. Spark didn't even know why she'd frozen. All the forced bonding and Tollar's incessant patient kindness had worn down Spark's fears. It was like Neesha had said—Spark didn't have to be friends with the southerners, but now she got along with them the same way Neesha got along with Jatt and Ember. Tollar would likely need Spark's help like this again before it was over, but Spark couldn't stop worrying that she'd let them all down when it mattered most.

IN THE SKIES

As Tollar's aquamancy burst around the enemy armada, Void Behind the Stars began her dive, leading the charge. She knew only that Brooding Cloudwall was directly behind her, and Heart's Blood was probably on the other side of her. Like many of the humans, Void Behind the Stars had longed for this confrontation for two years, but she suddenly did not want to stare at these boats and these awful humans.

Glacial Sunfire was flying! That was all in the world that mattered.

Void Behind the Stars had to hold herself rigid through the dive, but tried to glance, moving only her eyes, to see where Bolt and Glacial Sunfire and Merciless Winter Sky were. She caught only a fleeting glimpse of black and cerulean—that would be Bolt—and then she was upon the boats and needed to focus.

Spark used her fire to make more light beams, searing beast and boat alike. And then Void Behind the Stars reached the other side and spiralled into the air, looping back around to hit them again.

Just ahead of her, Merciless Winter Sky dropped a large spear onto one of the boats, puncturing it with a massive hole. Spark had made these spears in the unfortunate case that they would need them to fight other dragons, but they were doing wonders now. For the most part, the spears were being dropped on the sea beasts, and while it would take many hits to kill any of them, it gave them something to think about.

Void Behind the Stars did not necessarily want to kill the creatures, not like she wanted to incinerate every last one of these cursed wizards doing Loch's bidding.

So Void Behind the Stars hovered a moment to watch Glacial Sunfire and Bolt dive at a boat, talons out to shred their enemies, and then she dived again to do much the same while the fireborn lit more fires.

Blasts of superheated water capsized boats and seared the beasts. Void Behind the Stars looked for Tollar, but couldn't see her as the seas boiled and frothed.

Void Behind the Stars pitched into the sky to lead another dive, Brooding Cloudwall calling out from behind her, while Merciless Winter Sky, Glacial Sunfire, and Bolt zipped ahead, targeting the remaining wizards that might pose a threat as she, Brooding Cloudwall, and Heart's Blood raked the ships with fire once more. And Void Behind the Stars marvelled at Glacial Sunfire, at the joy she took in flight and the destruction she wrought upon the people who had caused them all so much harm.

Bolt and Glacial Sunfire spiralled down in tandem, fire engulfing everything before them.

It was unfortunate that Shattered Starshine had chosen to remain at the Guild to protect it should trouble head north. Had she been here, it would have been the first time their whole family had taken to the skies together.

As she circled, she noted one ship swiftly retreating south and thought to warn one of the males, but its speed was terrifying, and she suspected that only Tollar herself would be able to catch it. Something to note for later.

Heart's Blood was also ferrying handfuls of the enemy elementals back toward shore. Prisoners? Void Behind the Stars wasn't certain how much she believed that these people were being manipulated. Not these ones, who would have clearly been so close to Loch to be trusted with something like this.

Smoke rose all around her, partially shrouding the battle below. Smoke and steam obscured everything but the small patch of boat where Croves cleared it for his team to do their work. These humans were focusing on efficiency rather than revenge, which was probably for the best, though Croves with his warhammer could achieve both at the same time.

A blast of water erupted from next to the boats, and she nearly sliced away from it, noticing only at the last moment that Tollar herself rode the column of water. Void Behind the Stars held steady, and the woman landed on her shoulder, calling for a harness.

Mighty Alpine Evergreen swooped in to snatch his humans from the boat just as Tollar called out to her.

"Abyss, close to the water, if you would?"

She dived, vaguely aware that Brooding Cloudwall and Heart's Blood were still with her. She levelled out near the water and slowed, circling and watching as the water around the boats bubbled and boiled, rising on a massive wave that hissed and roared and drowned out all other sound before rolling over what remained of battle.

She pitched skyward again, going easy as she became aware that the humans were having difficulties, mindful of the fact that Tollar did not have a tether. Brooding Cloudwall would undoubtedly catch her mother if she fell, but Void Behind the Stars thought it best to keep the demonborn together until she was certain they had a victory. At the moment, she could see nothing but steam below.

She called to the other dragons to use their wings to clear the air. Unsurprisingly, there was little more than debris with a few remaining humans clinging to it in the waters below. Even the beasts had fled. The day was late enough that they would not venture farther south now, and Void Behind the Stars hoped to drop off these humans on the islands so she'd have the opportunity to fly with her family in victory.

CHAPTER TWENTY-FOUR

Tollar set her sword down across the bartop in front of her, and the room got very quiet. The cacophony of hammering and the grumbling hum of terramancy filled the otherwise silent space, sounds of the city still rebuilding—and now desperately trying to fortify. They'd done a bit over the summer right after the attack, but there was so much to rebuild and only so many people to spare to do it. The Nishram and Upalint and even people from the Tinitan Plains and beyond had come to the port to help them rebuild and defend them if it was necessary.

Word of the battle had spread. Everyone on the southern continent knew they were at risk if Loch's people managed to get a foothold.

"You don't trust my friends?" Tollar said softly into the silence.

There was a lot of uncomfortable shifting.

On the other side of the bar, Tollar's longtime friend and primary ally in the port, Chalky, leaned forward on her cane and gave Tollar a hard look, her tawny complexion going paler even if her brown eyes scowled hard and dark. Chalky had trimmed her brown hair even shorter, little more than stubble.

"I suppose we deserved this," Spark said, pressed in next to her mother, the two of them protectively between Tollar and Croves against the bar in Chalky's newly rebuilt inn. Croves loomed silently, his warhammer on display.

"Speak for yourself," Neesha muttered.

Tollar tried really hard not to smile, especially since they were speaking Prairiean while Tollar had insisted on speaking in prime even if none of the others here would.

"These ones are fine," Chalky said quickly, in prime now too. "If you trust them enough to call them friends, then I trust them. But you're not friends with the whole damn lot of them, Tollar. You don't even know half of them. And the rest are *Guild*."

She spat into the sawdust on the floor to emphasize what she—and pretty much the entire port—thought of the sodding Guild.

"I'm still not sure I trust the Guild," Tollar admitted. "Definitely not all of them, but they've made changes and they're finally willing to listen and act."

"Tollar, they let thousands of people die."

"Yes, and at some point we'll hold them accountable. Right now, we need them to keep thousands more from dying."

"Do we really need them?" someone in the back called.

"Really, it's the dragons we need," Chalky said. "And they're here."

"*Some* of the dragons are here," Neesha said. "And I'm not sure they'd come without the Guild. The dragons alone probably could have ended this years ago, but not without losing more of their kind than they can afford to risk. This is a human problem, so they expect us to do most of the solving."

Chalky leaned back, still braced against her cane, but looking less like she might hit someone with it.

"How much of this is your usual bluster?" Chalky asked Tollar in Upalan. "How much do you really trust these people?"

"These two?" Tollar replied in Upalan. "I trust them with my life, same as I would you or Croves or Bee. Well, Spark's a bit jumpy still, but her heart is true and her magic is sound."

Chalky tapped one finger against the handle of her cane, she and Tollar staring each other down.

"You trust me," Tollar said, back to prime. "I won't take anyone *I* don't trust into the thick of it. When it's time to get right up close to Loch, I'm not bringing any of those bumbling fools from the Guild. We'll need all the hands we can get, including theirs. But they don't touch the most important parts of this."

Chalky let out a deep breath and came around the bar, gesturing with her cane at one of the tables that had a couple of empty seats. The occupied seats there quickly emptied, and Chalky sat with Tollar, Neesha, Spark and Croves.

"So tell me your plan," Chalky said.

"The dragons bring us in. We've got tethers to keep even the frailest wizards on them. We use the dragons and the Guild wizards to deal with whatever forces Loch's got—and I can neutralize those sea creatures now—and then I take a small team directly to Loch and we finish this."

Chalky pointed at the rest of them around the table. "This is your small team, I take it?"

"I might add one or two more, but yes."

"Their power's that strong?"

"Yes," Neesha snapped. "We're like Tollar, but with fire. Spark, show them."

Spark was clearly uncomfortable about putting on a show for strangers who didn't trust her, but she snapped her fingers and a small flame appeared in the palm of her hand.

There were gasps. Neesha picked up the fire and let it wreath her hand, not flinching.

"My daughter is the strongest pyromancer alive."

"Sister," Chalky said.

"What?"

"What? In prime, the word is 'sister'."

"There's nothing wrong with my prime." Neesha bristled.

Spark jumped in then to explain Neesha's magical accident. "So that's why she looks like my sister, but she's really not."

"I missed her growing up, almost died and lost *half* my life to this," Neesha said. "I'm not messing around. And I'm not doing this by myself. So are you going to work with us?"

"We'll fight him anyway," Spark said. "It's what we've been doing all along. But without help we have to use big destructive magic."

"Remember that giant wave at the end last year?" Tollar said. "Imagine that but fire."

Chalky went pale. There was even more uncomfortable shifting and some muttering from the assembled rebels—or whatever Chalky's little cadre of trusted fighters was. Chalky had said people kept trying to make her chief or something, but she just wanted to run her damned inn. And she didn't want to deal with people she didn't trust, which was still almost everyone after how Loch had turned them against each other before.

The port was rebuilding, but there was still a lot of healing left to do.

"We want to stop them from coming back here," Neesha said. "But we want to do it without destroying Biterna."

Chalky sighed and looked around the room. "I'm not sure that's possible anymore."

Tollar sat up straighter. "What do you mean?"

"We've managed a bit of scouting. Just keeping an eye on him since I got your message. Last few weeks, there's been a lot of activity. Yarrow!" Chalky called, beckoning over a woman who was like a block made of muscle, skin darker than Tollar's and criss-crossed with scars, long black hair in a crown of braids around her head and hard dark eyes but an easy smile. "Yarrow's one of our few remaining wizards. She came back from a scouting mission two days ago. Tell them what you saw."

"They've had terramancers or something to pile up the beaches and shoreline like a wall," Yarrow said. "Good thing you got a way in from the air. It's the *only* way in."

"Do they have dragons?" Neesha asked.

"There were seven dragons left behind in Meeri Bay when he moved us here," Croves said.

"I've not seen any dragons except the ones you brought with you."

"There's still a way they're coming and going then."

"A tunnel, I think," Yarrow said. "Haven't really been able to get close enough. But it's one that'll be full of water till Loch don't want it to be."

"Pfft." Tollar shrugged.

"Right," Chalky said. "Anything he can do, Toll can do better."

"Still won't be easy getting on the island without dragons to drop people in," Yarrow continued. "And then there's the weather. Lots of unusual storms."

"Loch likes to use storms to conceal what he's doing and make it harder to get close," Tollar said.

"We can deal with that too," Spark added, her amber eyes shining.

"If you say so." Yarrow shrugged. "But the thing that was most worrying is how empty the island looks. Like it's deserted."

"Has he killed them all?" Tollar asked, horrified.

"Not all of them. There's a bunch of cramped encampments, raggedy tents, all around the palace. It's surrounded by a wall too."

"Shit."

"Human shield," Croves said. "He's done it before."

Tollar closed her eyes and took a long breath.

"I'm sorry, Tollar," Chalky said. "If you can think of a way to stop him without making it worse, you know I'll follow you. But for now we need to focus on fortifying the port."

"He's been loading ships," Yarrow said. "He doesn't have nearly as many as last year, but it's still a concerning number."

Tollar nodded. "We know this is his real target. Taking and holding the port is his way farther inland. And he's mad and embarrassed that a bunch of bumpkins like us stopped him."

"Wait," Spark said. "Are we not going to Biterna?"

"We need a new plan if we are," Neesha said.

Tollar nodded slowly.

Spark blinked a lot and stared at her. "After all you've done, all the people you've helped, you don't know how to stop him now?"

"I've never fought anyone who'd lost their humanity before," Tollar said. "Until a year ago, I'd never seen anything so depraved as Karthiry with all those wizards strapped to her as a power source."

Tollar shook her head and shrugged helplessly. The flaw in her leadership—if she could even call it a flaw—was in never being able to think up the kind of cruelty these people sank to. She'd seen a lot of awful things in her years of travel, but she'd never think to use wizards against their will.

"And even if she'd seen people use human shields before, it's hard to counter without riskin' the people yer tryin' to save," Croves said.

"Dira will be here in a few more days," Tollar said. "Hopefully she gets here before Loch's forces set out and we can reconfigure our plan."

"I'm heading back there," Yarrow said. "To watch for them to leave."

Tollar shrugged. They'd stop him either way. They had dragons and more wizards and knew what they were dealing with now. They'd stop him from taking the port.

"Toll," Croves said. "There's nothing stopping him from loading half of Biterna onto those boats. If this is the track he's taking, we gotta be extra careful in anything we do to fight him."

Chalky hissed something particularly foul. Tollar sighed.

Abyss had seen a boat speeding away at the end of the battle, and it had gotten far enough away that Tollar hadn't been able to sense it from the archipelago once she learned of it. Neesha had refused to let her try tracking it through the water realm—and Tollar had been so exhausted, she knew Neesha had been right. But it meant some of Loch's people had not only survived the battle, but got back to him with information on exactly what they could do and how they'd fight. He'd be ready.

"I'll talk to Dira. We'll figure it out." But Tollar felt cold and wasn't sure she trusted her own words.

"It's late," Chalky said. "And you've had a long trip. Go get some rest."

As soon as it was clear that plotting was over for the night, Neesha and Spark disappeared up to the room Chalky had given them. Tollar looked wistfully at the barrels of ale behind the counter.

"When exactly did this happen?" Chalky asked, pointing her cane at Tollar's middle. "Not exactly a good fit for war."

Tollar sighed. "Right after we got back to Nytaltek. I was gonna settle down, Chalky. I really was. Gonna just be a farmer with Bee for a couple of years—be a mom, have a little family, rest a bit. And then right after I find out I've got twins on the way, the dragon city summoned Bale and, well..."

"Did he help with it?" Chalky asked, gesturing to Croves with a sparkle in her eye.

"Yes, but not like that." Tollar rolled her eyes.

Croves chuckled. "Don't I wish!" He teasingly kissed her shoulder and went to get himself a drink.

"Sounds like your plans keep getting thrown into disarray," Chalky said.

"I'd prefer not to make a habit of it. We need to figure out how to stop Loch before the twins come. We've got about a month left."

"Should be enough time. Look, Toll, you've had a long trip. Go find Bee and get some rest. We'll figure it out."

Tollar stomped up the stairs, trying not to stomp but too frustrated not to. She needed to unfrustrate herself as much as possible before she got upstairs to Beenala. Beenala was leaving in the morning—Bale and her kin taking her back to the farms and Dram, and Tollar wouldn't see her again until Loch was no longer a threat.

And if she couldn't get these sodding people working together and helping her with better plans, she'd end up having her babies right in the middle of an unending battle. She didn't want to fight on two fronts, and she was tired of being the adult who had to unify everyone. Hopefully Chalky would see that and use more of her pull with the locals to smooth the way.

If the situation on Biterna was as dire as Yarrow suggested, they couldn't let it go on any longer.

CHAPTER TWENTY-FIVE

Neesha stood in the square not far from Chalky's inn and stared across the city to the patch of deforested mountainside next to the dam, trying to give Tollar and Beenala some privacy as they said their goodbyes. Bale took up most of the rest of the square, the gondola strapped to her once more. Half a year of work by local terramancers and floramancers to restore the mountain had certainly helped—it was covered in greenery. Nothing tall, not like the towering trees along the edges of the desecrated patch.

It would be a while, possibly another year, before they had the area stabilized enough that erosion and mudslides wouldn't be a major concern. And that was provided Loch didn't slide back in with his human shield and wreck it all over again.

Neesha didn't like to think about all the other patches like this left in the wake of Loch's forces. She knew the others were worried about the state of Biterna, not just the people but the environment itself. So much destruction. And it had been going on for so godsdamn long.

"I wish we could just go home together," Beenala said, her voice a broken whisper.

"I know, love. I shouldn't be too far behind you."

"But you don't know." Beenala buried her face against Tollar's chest, Tollar with an arm around her shoulders, Beenala resting one hand on the swell of Tollar's belly.

Neesha understood that it was always hard on Beenala when Tollar went adventuring, but Tollar hadn't really done it—nothing more than a quick, aborted trip—since the two of them had become more than neighbours. Now, with Tollar pregnant and all the plans for their future together in jeopardy, Neesha suspected it was damn near intolerable for Beenala.

But going home had been Beenala's idea. Since they'd left the Guild, she'd insisted she was going home, and then she'd tumbled out of the gondola as soon as they landed in the port and promptly threw up. Her nerves couldn't even handle being in the city. Never mind back in actual battle.

She wanted to be with Tollar but was going out of her mind here. She knew she'd get in the way if she stayed and tried to help them fight. And she'd said multiple times on the journey that Tollar had all the firepower she needed with Neesha and Spark.

But none of that made it any easier. For any of them.

Neesha was going to miss having Beenala around. Tollar was going to be a mess without her. Neesha's shoulders went tense just trying to imagine the emotional turmoil it must be for the both of them. It had been bad enough just to send a reply to Yenette before leaving the Guild to let her know how bad things were. That Neesha might not survive. Permanently this time.

Because as much as Neesha cherished this brief second chance, she would do everything she could to protect Tollar and continue protecting Spark.

Tollar kissed the top of Beenala's head and let her go. That was Neesha's cue to come over for a quick hug goodbye. Beenala held Tollar's hands for a little while, and then Bale helped her into the gondola.

Bale stretched her neck down so her face came in to nuzzle Tollar. Tollar stroked the end of Bale's nose while Bale said something dragonish to her.

"Just get Bee home safe."

Neesha and Tollar both shielded themselves, waving, as Bale lifted off to join her aunt and uncle and cousins who'd been circling overhead the whole time. When Bale reached them, they zipped off to the south, disappearing quickly.

Abyss had insisted they could get to Nytaltek and back in four or five days. Tollar had been less certain. Bale had done an awful lot of travelling this season and she was still growing, still not as strong as she could be. And Glacial Sunfire's abilities were still a complete mystery.

But Neesha trusted Abyss. She knew they could still fight if tired, and they really needed all the dragons with them before whatever was going to happen happened.

Tollar let out a long, shaky breath, and Neesha closed the distance between them to take her hand.

"Bee worries too much," Tollar said.

Neesha politely ignored the way Tollar's eyes shone and her lip trembled. "You'll get home to her."

Tollar gave a half-smile, her voice hollow when she said, "I always do. But she'll still worry."

Something in Neesha broke and the rest of her hardened around it. "No. You're going home to her. I'll damn-well see to it myself."

Tollar gave her a sharp look. "No more sacrifices."

"That's for me to decide." Neesha crossed her arms and squared up in front of Tollar like she wasn't half Tollar's size. "I'm a ghost wandering through a life I don't fit into anymore, and all I've got is some vague ideas and half-promises. You've got an entire future, Tollar, and you're going to have it."

"You can't just assign extra Worth Points because I've got babies on the way! What if they both grow up to be little toads and I never speak to them and take up drinking again but get *mean* about it and just go back to running like I did before Bee taught me better but I quit helping people while I'm at it? You're going to sacrifice yourself for that when your half-promises might lead you to becoming Grand Chancellor where you can get that sodding Guild to recognize people off the northern continent and stop anything like this from happening again and save millions of people in the process?"

"That's all hypothetical!" Neesha snapped.

"So's this." Tollar put a hand over her belly.

"Your babies aren't going to be toads. I'm sure they'll be lovely."

"Or all three of us could die when I'm trying to birth them. I've got a wonderful midwife and world-class healers at home, but sometimes things like that just happen anyway."

Neesha pressed her hands over her face and growled in wordless frustration, wondering how anyone ever got anything done with Tollar when she was so godsdamn stubborn. And then Neesha burst out laughing.

"Shit, is this what it's like for everyone else trying to argue with *me*?"

Tollar put a hand on Neesha's shoulder and gave her a very stern look. "Let's save talk of sacrifices as a last resort. Let's find a plan that doesn't need it."

"Plans always go wrong." Neesha crossed her arms again. "Tollar, this is what I'm good at. It's always been what I'm good at. Playing it safe is what gets me into trouble. Trying to do it everyone else's way is how I lost seventeen years. I didn't travel all this way to let Loch gain more ground. We're not letting him off that godsdamn island and we're not letting him destroy all those people to keep himself safe."

"Neesha..." Tollar sighed.

"No. I know what I want, Tollar. I want to *live*. I want to go back to Pasdale and marry Yenette and make them see me for what I am and accept it. I want to hand Loch his ass if it's the last thing I do. I want to be *a disaster*, one that rolls right over him once and for all. I want to do something big and flashy and *stupid*. And I know you do too."

Tollar's eyes sparkled while she struggled to keep a smile off her face. "We promised your mother we'd keep each other safe."

"Let's figure out how to be safe *and* stupid, then. *This* is what's been missing from my life, Toll—someone to be stupid with. That was Yenette a lifetime ago, and I've been alone ever since. I don't need caution—I need someone who has my back." Neesha grabbed Tollar's hand. "Come on. Yarrow made notes on Chalky's map, didn't she? Let's figure out where Loch's water tunnel is, and you can figure out how to take me with you through it."

"That's going to need a diversion," Tollar said.

"Well, we've got a lot of people good at those."

Tollar grinned and they headed back to the inn.

As Tollar burst through the door to Chalky's ahead of Neesha and grabbed the map of Biterna to spread out on a table, some of the tension in Neesha's gut uncoiled. She didn't have to take the risks alone. She didn't have to sacrifice—maybe none of them did. The idea of storming the island with Tollar filled her with a giddy rush that even the best pyromancy never could.

And for the first time since waking up, she saw a clear path forward.

CHAPTER TWENTY-SIX

Tollar woke to darkness, blanketed in the gentle sounds of home and swaddled firmly in Beenala's arms. The babies were dancing on Tollar's bladder. She'd been able to sense them with her magic almost right from the start, but at some point since reaching the dragon city, she'd been able to feel them moving just like a normal swib would. She wished she'd had more time to enjoy this part of it, because she was certainly not doing this again. Overall, she didn't love being pregnant—especially lately with all the aches and the way her swollen feet barely fit in her boots—but there was certainly a kind of magic to growing a pair of humans. And it was occasionally useful, this time waking her right on cue, though Beenala was wide awake and watching her.

"You didn't sleep at all, did you."

"I have no idea how you did."

Tollar snorted. She'd learned to sleep the night before a battle decades ago, when she was still young and stupid and hadn't fully grasped all the stakes. Knowing better hadn't thrown her out of the practice, which was for the best, particularly for *this* battle.

She went to the loo, started braiding her hair on her way back to Beenala's room. There was still no light at all in the east, but she couldn't linger. Neesha had promised to fetch her if something happened in the night, but it would be better if Tollar was there with them.

She sat next to Beenala and one of the twins spun, causing a ripple effect visible across the tight skin of her belly and through the light fabric of her shirt. Beenala gasped, still mesmerized by this, even as she insisted she wasn't anywhere near as interested in motherhood as Tollar was. Beenala splayed a hand over Tollar's belly. The twins had gone quiet, but Tollar used a touch of aquamancy to get one of them to bop against Beenala's hand.

Beenala started crying.

Well, that was not the desired effect. Tollar gathered Beenala in her arms.

"You know I can stop him, Bee. You know I can do it by myself. And you know that I don't *have* to do it by myself."

"It's so dangerous," Beenala sobbed.

"It was more dangerous against Karthiry, honestly, and that worked out."

"You almost died!"

"*Almost.* As you can see, I did not, in fact, die."

"Tollar!"

One of the twins spun on its own again, and Beenala pressed her face against the spot.

"I've decided on names for them," Tollar said. She'd known early on that she was having a boy and a girl, and names had come to her almost immediately, though she'd kept it to herself. She hadn't actually given it much consideration since, what with the adventuring and the danger.

Beenala sat up, watching her expectantly.

"What do you think of River and Rain? River for the girl and Rain for the boy?"

Beenala teared up again. "Sounds perfect."

Tollar kissed her cheek. "I'll come back through the water as often as its safe to from now until I can come home for real. And we'll get the house properly ready for River and Rain, all right?"

"Maybe that's something I can start while you're gone. To keep my mind off the danger."

"If you think it will help." Tollar smiled and held Beenala's face in her hands. "I really need to get back to them."

"It'll be today, you're sure?"

As long as Yarrow was certain about her intel, it would be today.

"I'll bring you news as soon as I can. I promise."

Tollar tried not to draw out the goodbye, but couldn't stand for it to be brief. She felt confident that she'd be home, victorious, in as soon as a week. But it still felt all so different. It wasn't just the hormones making her an overly sentimental sop, either. She had a home now. She'd never had a home before and leaving it was the worst kind of agony.

Neesha had warned her against the emotional upheaval of using a water portal to come home. She was right. But Tollar couldn't imagine not using the new trick to offer Beenala a tiny bit of comfort, and to find a bit for herself. Sleeping in her own home the night before battle was a new experience. A good one. Hopefully she'd never have to repeat it, but it was certainly more restful than cramming into the gondola with Neesha and Spark or sleeping under a dragon wing with Croves.

"I'm sorry, Bee, I really do have to go now."

"Time to be a hero." Beenala smiled, both brittle and sentimental.

Tollar kissed the back of her hand and scratched Ash behind the ears where the dog still slept at the foot of the bed. Then she used the water from the bedside basin to make a water portal in the middle of the room, taking the water realm to the shallows around Sharp Island.

It was the westernmost island in the Biternan archipelago and the oldest, formed by violent eruptions that left it with a steep, jagged coastline that rose into even steeper and more jagged summits, like the jaw of some particularly vicious earth giant. It was uninhabitable by people, but the deep valleys between the high peaks made it a good place to hide some dragons and a small army.

Before surfacing to join the others, Tollar extended her senses into the water. There was one large boat just at the edge of Tollar's awareness approaching the main island rapidly from the north. Most of the boats had taken up anchor, the sea serpents had moved to the waters in the south, the storms around the main island had grown particularly intense and tall, and Loch's little secret tunnel under the newly erected walls was once again full of water.

So yes, the fight would come today.

Tollar surfaced and rode a disk of water to a dry gully on the northwest side of the island that split the mountains and offered access to the interior. Croves was the one on guard at the moment, calmly watching her approach.

"How's everyone?" she asked him.

"Mostly asleep. How's Bee?"

"Worried. I didn't get to see Dram, but I told her to pass along the message about his family."

One of Yarrow's contacts was the woman who had helped Draminedes escape. She'd been delighted to find out that her efforts had paid off and that Draminedes was alive and well. His family was still safe—as safe as could be given the circumstances—and she'd asked Tollar to let Draminedes know.

"Ye seem rested. Goin' home was a good idea, then?"

"Yeah. Bee is still a mess, but I think it helps her to know how quickly I can be home with news."

"And ye can use it to escape if this goes ass up on us."

Tollar nodded. She and the fireborn women had briefly spoken about the potential for escape. Neesha had made Spark and Tollar promise they would use portals to get out if it all went wrong. Tollar didn't like it, but there was also no sense in being captured or dying needlessly if she could easily escape to regroup with whoever was left and come back to hit Loch again with a new plan.

Croves unexpectedly grabbed her up in his thick arms and squeezed her close.

"Oof."

"I don't like this," he whispered into her hair.

"We can do it."

He took her face in his hands and kissed her hard and urgent, leaving her gasping and unable to tell which way was up when he was done. She hated it when he did this and somehow wanted him to do it again. He hadn't let her go, and she was worried and hopeful that he might try again. She got her arms between them and planted her hands firmly on his chest.

"You can kiss me all you want once we're done sending Loch into oblivion."

"What if ye pull him into the water realm with ye?"

Tollar stared at him in the starlight. "Croves, do you know what happens to something deep in the ocean that's not meant to be deep in the ocean?"

"Don't it drown 'em?"

"No. I wish that was all it did. Croves, water is heavy. Same as earth."

She stared and waited.

"Oh gods," he muttered in a horrified whisper.

"Yes. So no, I will not bring him into the water realm."

"Bet we could get Neesha to pull him into the fire realm."

Tollar strangled a laugh. "The Guild wants him alive."

"Fools," Croves growled.

"Maybe. But I'm not going to be the one to kill him."

"Neesha would like the chance."

Tollar sighed this time. He wasn't wrong. If *he* could open an elemental portal, he'd shove Loch into it without a thought. Tollar loved him—loved Neesha—but wished they weren't quite so eager to end a life. Even one as vile as Loch's.

She hoped the Guild knew what they were doing, insisting on capturing someone as powerful as Loch. Cerro had come back with the dragons—and Cerro and Tollar's elemental friends Tavalu and Macana and Eratona as well, ready to help with the fight—and he was the only member of Guild leadership here on the island with them. He was here to help fight but also to oversee Loch's capture. Of the Guild leadership with any battle experience, he had the most and was the youngest.

Tollar didn't fully trust him, but he'd been as useful as anyone else the last time they faced Loch, and at least she knew how to work with him. She was bringing him and Neesha and the other three with her underwater and through Loch's secret tunnel so they could be another layer of distraction while she and Neesha hunted down Loch, but also so they could try to free any residents still on the island and not loaded onto the boats.

Neesha and Tollar, with some input from Croves and Chalky, had come up with their plan that very morning Beenala had left, and then Neesha had helped her practice keeping people safe underwater until the rest of the dragons with the Guild council had arrived.

Dira had been gracious enough to approve the plan without trying to stop them. She'd even given them the idea of a further diversion on the island. Tollar still wasn't sure if that was sincere or just a way to keep Cerro at the centre of things—Dira's eyes where she couldn't go.

But it had been a good suggestion, and Tollar didn't find it worth arguing over. It wasn't like Cerro could stop her if he decided he didn't like what she was doing.

"I need to go prepare them," Tollar said. "Are you going to stay here?"

"Nah. If you're back then I reckon it's about time to go."

As much as she hated (and wanted) him to kiss her again on the walk to the valley where the others camped, he didn't. He did keep her close, holding her hand and sometimes his arm around her when the terrain allowed. While Tollar never felt particularly unsafe in a general sense, she hadn't ever before experienced the sort of safe comfort she did when folded up in Croves's giant arms.

She wondered how much of her attraction to him was just that he was bigger than her. Bigger than her and capable of making her feel small. But he didn't.

"Yer sure about this?" he asked, stopping her just beyond earshot of camp.

"We have to. You know that."

He sighed. "Ye feel okay?"

"Everything aches, and I feel like I've got a moon on my bladder, but my mind is clear and my magic is strong, and that's all that matters right now."

"I know I don't have no right to tell ye what to do—it's just that I don't expect to live much longer. Kinda shocked I made it this far, to be honest. Those babies'll be all that's left of me when I'm gone."

She smiled sadly into the dark and touched his face. "I know, Croves. I know. But I can do this."

"All right then." He kissed her, gently this time, and headed into camp.

Some of them were already stirring, Spark the one waking everyone and getting them ready. Had the girl slept at all? Probably not. Normally, she'd be going to bed right about now. Hopefully that wouldn't affect her performance.

Spark wasn't only waking people—she was handing out little glass balls. She called them venom balls, and they were filled with dragon venom and flint so they would burst into flame when smashed. There wasn't a lick of fire anywhere on the island. Yarrow had said so, but Tollar had taken Spark in closer on a water disk after dark so she could check. The only source of fire in the entire archipelago was a volcano to the northwest of the main island. That would make it trickier for Neesha and anyone without a dragon.

They had flints to start little fires for pyromancy, but they were sometimes going to need bigger fires. Swibs might need fire too. So Spark had spent the days between making the plan and waiting to head out making dozens of these little balls.

Spark reached Tollar and held out the crate, surprised when Tollar only took one.

"I can't do anything with fire." Tollar shrugged. "I just need one in case I need you or your ma."

Spark nodded and moved on. She hadn't loved that part of the plan—honestly, Tollar didn't either—but they needed contingencies because Neesha had been right that things never went according to plan. Tollar tucked the ball into her belt, where she could get it easily but it would be safe. Along with her visible weapons—sword and dagger—she had the pouch of spiky water-filled balls Spark had gifted her.

She went into the gondola and got out the rest of her gear, which Beenala and Spark—back at the Guild—had altered to fit her changed body, with a vest of overlapped little metal plates that looked something like scales to go over her growing belly. It was flexible and could accommodate her putting on a couple more inches around the middle before it would need adjusting again. Tollar swallowed against the tight hot feeling in her throat. She'd wept at the thoughtfulness—and the need for it—when they'd first presented her with it. And Spark had also made her an underlayer of dragon skin armour to act as extra protection.

She pulled it all on silently, being as methodical as she could, trying not to think too much about what was about to happen and all the ways it could go wrong.

When Tollar was certain that everyone was awake, she stood on a boulder near the edge of camp and addressed them all.

"We're all tired and worried—"

"I feel pretty good," Neesha called from somewhere in the middle of the crowd. That got a chuckle, bless her.

"Oh good, you get up here and give the speech. I hate this shit."

That got another laugh.

Neesha didn't take the bait, not that Tollar had expected her to.

"I know there's still some hard feelings and mistrust. The northerners let this go too far for too long, but they understand that and that's why they're here. What we're not going to do is forget who our real enemy is or what he'll do to us if we don't stop him. We're about to have a very trying day followed by a stretch of trying days. But we're going to beat Loch. This is where his tyranny ends, make no mistake. We've got half the dragons, half the Guild, the world's best aquamancer and the two best pyromancers. What's Loch got? He's outclassed, even if he doesn't know it yet. Beating him isn't a concern. It's the people on those islands. They're our neighbours and our friends. They're victims in this, and he will use them against us in any way he can. We all know our strengths and our roles, and that's what we're going to stick to. Just do your best."

"Can I do my worst?" Neesha asked. It was a joke. But also it wasn't.

Tollar sighed while others chuckled. "The Guild wants Loch alive. We're going to do our best to honour that, but not by sacrificing innocents. Interpret that however you need to in order to get the job done."

Tollar gestured to Croves. "You're all ready to move out?"

"Aye, and we best get moving."

"You haven't got much night left for cover. Go quick, be silent. And good luck."

The humans who were going with dragons rushed to whichever dragon they'd been assigned. All of them already in harnesses and getting buckled in with the tethers Spark had made extras of while they'd been at the Guild. Only a handful of wizards held back, Neesha moving to stand next to Tollar.

Spark, who should have been with Abyss, came over to them.

"Are you sure I shouldn't come with you?" she asked. "I'm stronger."

Neesha was the one to answer, a gentle hand on her daughter's arm. "It's not about power right now. It's about a different kind of strength and about trust. I will uselessly fall to my death the first time Abyss does a spiral. And you will react badly the first time Tollar needs to syphon your magic. Are you going to be able to act without hesitation? I trust her and her magic. She and I are friends in a way you aren't. And you work better with the dragons. You know them in ways I don't."

"Trust the plan," Tollar said. "I've got you all assigned to where you'll best succeed. The dragons will need you and your light beams, especially at the start."

Tollar hadn't removed the new demons from the water beasts. It was a dead giveaway that she was nearby. She wasn't sure there'd be a good time to do it at all. One of the fireborn *had* to stay with the dragons to help protect them.

"Come, Spark," Abyss said, frightfully close by and invisible in the dark.

Spark didn't argue further and went, the dragons leaving silently—Croves with Shell, Raia with Dragon, Barlo and Eltir with Ice and Flame, other wizards with them all, plus more dragons with them like Abyss's family. As many dragons as they'd been able to hide on the island. They'd fly silently south and close to the water where their silhouettes against the stars and the soon-to-brighten sky wouldn't give away their position until they swung around back toward Biterna and Loch's armada making its way toward Port Sawulxo.

She wanted Loch to think these dragons had left from the port. Keep Loch's attention focused on the south and away from the west and anything Tollar got up to. She was about to get up to a whole lot.

CHAPTER
TWENTY-SEVEN

Neesha stood on the shore facing east, hidden from view by some rocks, not that anyone could see them from the main island, but no one wanted to risk blowing the plan so soon. Tollar huddled with the Upalintan elementals who had volunteered to come help her. They'd been instrumental in securing victory against Loch the last time.

Cerro tried to pretend like he was in charge, but the middle-aged Guild wizard with the greying blonde hair was equally pink-faced over the excessive heat, even this early in the morning, and the way Tollar was just ignoring his entire existence.

Both Macana, a blocky woman with dark-brown skin, and Eratona, a lanky russet-brown man, stuck together and largely remained quiet, only ever speaking to Tollar. It didn't seem that either of them were especially strong at speaking prime. Macana was a powerful terramancer and Eratona was a talented elemental.

And then there was Tavalu, who was like Tollar's brother—a man who'd been mistaken as a girl when he was a child—only Tavalu was the reverse. She was a tall, broad-shouldered woman with sparkling blue eyes and her brown hair pulled back into two braids, who was either smitten with Tollar or worshipped her like some kind of goddess and never really stopped talking, though mostly about how great Tollar was. While Neesha was inclined to agree, she was less in the mood to hear about past exploits and more interested in just getting on with this whole mess. Though while

Tavalu was mostly talking up how great Tollar was, her own role in how they'd beaten Loch before was impressive—especially her proficiency with harnessing magic.

Dawn broke and Tollar stuck a hand in the water to see what was going on beyond the fog bank and storms surrounding the main island. She reported that some of the boats were on the move, but not all. They needed to let the boats get far enough away that they couldn't double back easily to help Loch.

Neesha's worry was that Loch was going to go with them. If he was on a boat and not the island, that would make things trickier.

Tollar was still confident. In fact she liked her odds better surrounded by water, but Neesha didn't like it. The sun was well up when Tollar stuck her hand in the water and finally noticed a change.

"They're moving fast," Tollar said. "He's still got a lot of aquamancers."

"Can you tell if he's with them?" Tavalu asked.

Tollar shook her head. "There are four boats left—one leaving the volcano and headed for the main island, and three still docked. He'll go with those."

She was guessing, but given everything they'd seen from Loch, it was a solid guess. The last time he'd attacked the port, he'd come in only after it became clear Karthiry couldn't get the job done. Did he have a new lapdog with that kind of power?

Yarrow hadn't heard anything, but also her intel was limited. Neesha was uninterested in any more surprises.

"All right," Tollar said. "They're far enough—they'll be even farther by the time we get there. Let's go."

Tollar waded out into the water up to her waist with a piece of dragon rigging full of handholds draped over her shoulders. Neesha was worried about this part, no matter how much Tollar insisted it would be fine. When they were practicing, Tollar frequently had coughing fits any time she forgot to focus on keeping her breathing water completely free of salt. And then Neesha would end up losing her air bubble and freaking out.

It had been a complete disaster until about three days ago. And even then, Tollar hadn't had to do it maintaining this many air bubbles while dragging people through the water nearly as far as they actually had to go. They could barely see the main island at all from here.

Neesha gathered with the others around Tollar, all of them grabbing onto handholds. Tollar had just sort of carried Neesha around when they'd been practicing, but she definitely could not do that with five of them. The handholds had been Spark's idea, and they would definitely cut down on the amount of work Tollar would have to do to drag them all across the ocean.

"Ready? Under."

Neesha hadn't realized that Tollar had stopped right on the edge of a significant drop, but as she tugged them all forward, the ground disappeared out from under Neesha. She took a deep breath and held it as Tollar pulled them all under. Everyone else was too.

But then there was a bubble around her face. It only had an air supply of a few minutes, so Tollar needed to remember to keep pulling oxygen out of the water and replenishing it for them. While she kept salt out of her own water. And pulled them all through the ocean.

It sounded an awful lot like Neesha trying to control a ton of demons in battle.

Of course, if Tollar lost track of anything here, she wasn't going to end up consumed by demons. They'd all just have to swim to the surface and start again.

Wait, could all of them swim?

No one who couldn't swim would be stupid enough to volunteer for this, would they? But everyone here trusted Tollar completely.

Tollar was going slow through the water in part because it made it easier to concentrate on what she was doing, but also because she couldn't bring them all down to the seafloor like she would if she was alone. She had to try to mimic natural water creatures if they didn't want to attract attention.

Neesha wasn't sure if it was better or not that the air bubble around her face meant she could see a bit under water. If one of those sea monsters came for them...

She decided to close her eyes.

Every now and then the current would make her bump shoulders with Tavalu or knock her into Tollar. It took a lot longer than Neesha liked. She'd been ready for the fight this morning when the sun had barely risen, but when she opened her eyes, she could see it was getting awful close to midday. And they were travelling through a forest of kelp.

A school of large grey blobby fish-things got close, and while Tollar didn't seem particularly troubled, Neesha decided to close her eyes again.

She didn't open them until Tollar stopped.

They were not in Loch's less-than-secret tunnel. Tollar was gripping a wooden post, near the surface, three large dark shapes bobbing nearby that looked like boats.

Oh shit. Were they attacking?

Tollar made the water do something swishy to get the attention of her team. She motioned for quiet and then broke the surface, bringing them all with her.

Neesha tried really hard not to gasp for air or sputter or do anything else undignified. The others were having about as much luck as she was. Tollar, meanwhile, was perfectly silent as water poured from her mouth and she took a quick breath of air.

The storm around them was loud enough, rain battering everything and wind gusting, that they could probably shout at each other without being noticed. But Tollar remained silent as she left the rest of them with the handholds tied to one of the dock's support columns and rose up on one of her water disks, drawing her sword.

"Oh shit," Tavalu whispered.

Neesha tensed, wishing Tollar had given them any indication of what was going on. But she didn't get near either the boats or the dock, instead using the sword to swiftly cut the ties securing the boats. They immediately began drifting.

"Is that really going to do any good?" Neesha asked when Tollar got back.

"Any chaos we insert now delays them that much more later." Tollar shrugged, took up the rigging again, and brought them back down into the water. It was only a few minutes until they were in the tunnel, and then she slowed down to nearly a standstill.

She'd told Neesha beforehand that she was going to have to go slowly, check for traps and monitor for any magic. The tunnel itself was below the waterline and filled with seawater naturally, so the only magic really used on it was to push all the water out so Loch's minions could use it to come and go. But there was a chance he or someone else would be monitoring it.

Tollar could counter that, but she had to catch it in time.

They reached the end of the tunnel and a stairway carved out of the bedrock. Neesha's stomach clenched as Tollar left them once again—this time on the stairs above the waterline but out of sight—and went to scout ahead.

CHAPTER TWENTY-EIGHT

The blots on the water ahead marked Loch's armada, and Spark wasn't sure if she felt relief or dread. After several hours of flying—first straight south and then banking back to the north at dawn—she was exhausted and ready for this to be over. She'd just started to doze off when the time had come to prepare for battle. She'd tried to sleep on Abyss, but she was too jumpy.

While fighting Loch on the plains hadn't exactly been easy, they'd been free to rain down as much fire as they could. *This* battle was going to take forever. Tollar seemed to think they could capture all the boats in a day, but Spark was not convinced. There were *a lot* of boats. They had to go through them one or two at a time to find all the Biternans and free them first.

And then there were the water beasts protecting the boats.

The armada must have spotted the approaching dragons because the surface had exploded with tentacle-like water whips, ready to pull the dragons to a watery death. Without Neesha or Nanny to help with fire magic, it was largely going to be Spark's responsibility to deal with the water beasts.

Other wizards could call fire demons to drop on the beasts, but that would only do so much. Spark's light beams were going to be the only real weapon they had until Tollar recalled the demons in the beasts.

She hadn't given Spark a clear timeline on when that would happen. Tollar hadn't known exactly when she'd be able to safely return to the water realm to deal with the demons. But Spark hoped it would be soon. She had no idea how they were even going to get close to the boats. Spark with her gliding suit was the only one who would be able to drop from the air and land on a boat without dying. But she really didn't think she could fight a whole boat's worth of wizards on her own.

The dragons had some idea of what they were doing. Abyss called out to them in dragonish, and they were forming up above her with Shell and Jin's dragon following directly behind. Jin and her crew had come up from Port Sawulxo in the night with more southerners to help in the fight.

"Spark, be ready with your light beams."

Abyss dived toward the surface, skimming only slightly higher than the decks of the boats. There was not a lot of warning before water whips shot up toward them. Abyss was ready with fire, and Spark responded immediately, cutting through the water with her beams of fire.

They were nearly over one of the boats when Abyss roared and peeled away into the sky at a jarringly steep angle. Abyss banked hard, throwing Spark against her tether, and spiralled back down toward the water, where Shell was tangled in water ropes, nearly disappearing under the surface.

The dragons who had remained above spewed fire, their wizards dropping fire demons uselessly into the water.

Abyss opened up with fire again, and Spark honed it into another beam. But it wasn't enough, even with Abyss still spiralling and the fire cutting in a circle, the ropes appeared again almost immediately.

Shell carried Croves, Raia, Barlo and Eltir. Spark's skin felt tight and her insides like ice at the thought of losing all five of them.

With a deep, steadying breath, she split Abyss's fire into two and then three beams, angling them all slightly differently, so that they spread out around the struggling dragon, slicing through the water in tandem.

And then just as Spark was certain they were going to slam into the water, Abyss hauled herself out of the dive. Just as she angled skyward again, she jerked like she'd hit a wall, her progress slowing. Spark pulled fire out of the air and ballooned it out to the sides, ready to slice the fire at any water she could see.

But then they headed skyward again, Abyss flapping furiously, and Spark realized she'd grabbed onto Shell, dragging him and his humans out of the water.

Spark didn't relax until they were well clear of the water, and Shell, flying under his own power, shot up past them to circle with the other dragons. Jin was up there already, having aborted the attack when Shell had been snagged.

The dragons were conversing again. Spark tried to keep an eye on the boats below, wishing she had a target to drop a fire demon on. She couldn't attack the boats, not yet. The beasts were staying far enough under the surface that even a hundred fire demons wouldn't do any good.

"Spark, go to Shell. He is faster."

Abyss angled herself up so that she circled above Shell, just far enough for them to not tangle their wings. Spark leapt, landing in the middle of Shell's back, and Raia came to her quickly.

"Are ye all right?"

"Yes. Are you ready?"

Raia helped Spark up to Shell's shoulder and got her tethered. Then he spiralled back around and came in fast, just above the water as Abyss had tried. When he breathed fire, Spark first ballooned it out in front of him, an obscuring wall of flame. She hoped it would make him a more difficult target.

Raia, Croves, and the others untethered and all moved to Shell's side, near his wing.

When they reached one of the boats, Shell roared and the others jumped. Spark caught the barest glimpse of the other four hitting the deck before he banked away, pitching back into the sky as water whips rose up around them. Spark was ready with her fire beams again, cutting them apart until Shell was clear.

Back up in the air, Abyss sent Spark to join Jin and her crew on her dragon, Jewelled Waters.

"We're not trying the same attack, are we?"

Jin shook her head. "They'll be ready for that. Abyss says she will go ahead as bait, that we stay just above her and let her block their view of us."

"No! They'll catch her!"

"And my dragon will bring you back around to free her."

Spark went numb and stumbled. If she hadn't been tethered to Jewelled Waters, she might have tumbled right off his back and out into the open air.

"That's too risky."

"Abyss trusts your ability. Stay focused."

Spark wanted to argue more, that there had to be a better way, but then Abyss roared and started her dive, Jewelled Waters banking to follow her.

Spark's heart raced and her skin felt icy. Ahead and below, Abyss spiralled and banked to avoid the whips coming at her. They'd nearly reached another boat when one wrapped around her back legs. She fought it with fire, and Spark tried to get a couple of fire beams in to help her, but Jin had released all the tethers.

"Now, go!"

Jewelled Waters banked hard just as Jin's crew left his back. Abyss was still struggling, her fires enough to keep her above water. But one of the water beasts closed in on her, jaws wide.

"No no no!"

Jewelled Waters came in fast and hard, breathing fire that Spark used to sear the face of the water beast. She split the beam again, cutting a circle around Abyss. It wasn't quite enough, and just before Jewelled Waters swooped past to avoid a water whip, Spark leapt.

She wasn't particularly adept with her gliding suit yet, but she hadn't had far to go, slamming into Abyss's back and scrabbling to hang onto one of her spikes. Now she could use Abyss's fire in a more targeted way and really see what she was doing.

Dragons shrieked overhead and Bale, Zephyr, Bolt and Glacial Sunfire all dived toward them, all of them breathing fire out ahead. Spark directed it as best she could, but also used the abundance of flame to open a fire portal and bathe herself and Abyss in trueflame.

And finally—*finally*—Abyss pumped her wings and climbed from the water. Bale was there, grabbing onto her as she swooped past to help drag her up just as Abyss had dragged Shell.

And then they were clear.

Spark collapsed against Abyss's shoulder panting and trying not to cry.

"Let's not do that again!"

But they'd gotten the two teams of dragon riders onto ships so they could start clearing them and securing the Biternans. Spark would just have to throw fire at any good targets she saw and wait until Tollar had the chance to deal with the demons.

While Abyss circled with the other dragons above the boats, Spark tethered herself in again and sat back against a spike, eyes closed, trying to get herself under control. She'd been through so much with only Abyss to help, and now they had other dragons and even other wizards! But she'd gotten so used to having her family with her over the last two years that she was not at all prepared to face all this danger without Neesha and Nanny.

She hated how they were all split up. How necessary it was. How she wouldn't know if her mother was okay until everything was over.

Abyss banked suddenly, turning north, and shrieked a particularly furious battle cry. Spark screamed and jumped to her feet, peering down over Abyss's shoulder to get a view of the ocean below. Nothing there had changed. But Abyss broke away from circling and flew north.

They were closer to the island than she'd expected. Had they moved closer as the battle had gone on?

But that wasn't the most concerning part. There were shapes of five dragons just coming over the island toward them.

"Are they from the Guild?"

"Not any of ours!" Abyss snapped and shrieked again.

The red Superior and all of Abyss's family had joined her.

"Wait, you mean these are more captives? How is that possible?"

"We have many unaccounted for that we have assumed dead. That assumption may have been incorrect."

"Should we do this without Croves or Jin's crews?"

"Getting them off the boats will be as difficult as getting them onto the boats was."

"We should at least go back for Croves. I'm not very good at this on my own!"

Abyss called out and slowed, Zephyr catching up to them. "He will take you."

Abyss dipped her wing and dropped below Zephyr, who plucked Spark from her shoulder and turned to race back to the boats. Because he blended in with the sky, he dived straight down at the boat containing all the other dragon riders. Spark hadn't realized that Jin's crew had ended up on the same boat as Croves's, but it was probably for the best, especially right now.

Zephyr angled at the last moment to swoop over the boat and pluck Croves from the midst of battle.

"Watch for the water behind us," Zephyr said as he climbed.

Spark had to cut through one water whip that came up after them almost as an afterthought, and then Zephyr had zipped beyond their reach.

"What in all the hells!" Croves called up.

Zephyr put the man up on his shoulder with Spark as he raced to catch up with the other dragons.

"We've got company." Spark pointed north.

Croves used a word that Neesha was fond of.

"So what do ye want me for?"

"It would have been better to have more of you, but we could only make one pass." Spark sighed. "I'm not good enough at this. I need your help."

Croves looked at the blaze of enemy dragons approaching. "Our dragons can handle this."

"Yeah, probably, but it will go faster if they have some help. I'm still not worth much in a fight, but my axe can cut through the chains around the dragons if you can keep Loch's people back long enough for me to do it. It's... it's how we freed Shell back on the plains."

"Ah." Croves watched her thoughtfully for a beat. "Raia said you cut the chains, and it brought all Loch's people off the dragons with the rigging."

"Yes. I can do it again if you can distract them."

"I dunno that I can do it all on my own."

"Croves, you're like half the size of a dragon already."

He laughed and then called to Zephyr, "Can ye get us to Abyss so we can have a plan before we reach those dragons?"

Zephyr didn't answer, but somehow managed to go even faster, calling out, presumably for Abyss. After a few calls back and forth, the whole blaze banked around to circle in place until Zephyr reached them. He dropped Croves and Spark back onto Abyss's shoulders before pitching up and away. Spark lost track of him against the sky. He would probably drop in from above at some critical point.

Spark explained to Abyss what they would try.

"One dragon at a time," Abyss said. "Our blaze can distract theirs while you do your work."

Spark had no doubts that the blaze could free these five dragons. They had done it back on the plains two years ago. But Spark working with the other dragon riders had sped things up significantly and also got the chains off the dragons, which was critical in getting them fully freed from Loch's influence.

Abyss had been leading the charge, but she hung back now, letting the red Superior take the lead. The dragons ahead of them slammed into the captive dragons, snarling and thrashing and biting and shooting fire at their riders. The Superior quickly knocked one of the humans off a dusty orange and grey dragon, and Abyss swooped in to deposit Croves and Spark in the empty space.

Croves charged down the dragon's back and slammed his warhammer into the legs of the first person he encountered. That person fell sideways and was then carried away by the wind.

Spark conjured a ball of fire and threw it at another of Loch's people coming at her from the other side of the dragon's spines. Croves jumped between two spikes to reach the man and knock him off as well. They were near the back of the dragon's head and Croves stayed where he was, blocking others from coming closer, as Spark hacked at the chains.

Three strikes did it. She'd found that there were three critical spots to hit and had told Croves about them on the approach.

"Clear!" she shouted and they moved to the next, right above the dragon's wings.

Loch's people didn't have the same sort of riding gear with handholds the way Spark and the others had, but they did climb up the chains from somewhere to attack. Spark kept her head down and let Croves handle them. For the most part the wind screaming past and the roar of dragons covered the noise it made when Croves's hammer collided with a target.

She cut the second chain and there was only one more left near the base of the tail. There were chains criss-crossing the dragons, but the three looped over their backs were critical infrastructure holding the whole thing in place.

By the time she reached the third chain, there was only one of Loch's people left on the dragon, and he was losing control of it. The dragon pitched and twisted, trying to dislodge them all, shooting flame down its back at them that Spark had to deflect.

At last she severed the third chain and the whole thing fell away. She and Croves immediately jumped. The red Superior had been circling nearby and dropped down onto the orange and grey dragon to help subdue it, while Shell shot up from under to catch them both out of the air.

Spark didn't see Abyss anywhere, but they apparently had another target already. Shell spiralled down to drop Croves and Spark onto a dragon that had only one human left alive, but near the head. Spark easily cut the chain near the tail, but then Loch's rider noticed them and the dragon tried to burn them and knock them off.

Spark gripped her axe in one hand, the chain in the other, and hacked away at it even while she was flung around. There was no sign of Croves. She couldn't worry about him being thrown clear. Shell or someone else would catch him.

She cut the chain near the wings and got flung out away from the dragon. With her only options being trying to climb a chain on a furious dragon trying to kill her, or falling away for an ally to catch, it was an easy choice to make.

Just before Bale plucked her out of the sky, Spark spotted the storm cloud covering the island directly beneath them. Something about falling onto land rather than water seemed more terrifying, even though she knew rationally she'd be just as dead either way.

Then Bale dropped her onto the second dragon's shoulder, while Bolt dropped Croves onto the other side. He lunged in with the hammer, knocking the final rider off and giving Spark plenty of space to cut the final chain.

It was going about as well as it could, but Spark didn't like the way each dragon they freed took two of their own out of the fight to contain. It was past midday and they still had the entire armada to battle after this. Spark did not have any of Tollar's confidence in the plan. And of course, the plan hadn't accounted for Loch having any dragons of his own.

CHAPTER TWENTY-NINE

Neesha huddled between Tavalu and Macana on the steps just above the waterline, Cerro and Eratona on the step just above, all of them out of sight from anyone passing by the tunnel entrance. Tollar hadn't returned yet and Neesha's skin was hot and buzzing. Was this what it felt like for normal people to be on fire? She didn't like it.

Dragons shrieked from directly overhead and that was particularly worrying. All of the dragons were supposed to be attacking the armada in the waters to the south. The armada should be far enough away by now that they shouldn't be able to hear the dragons at all.

Tollar finally reappeared, her face pinched.

"What in the hells is going on out there?" Neesha asked.

"No idea what's going on with the dragons." Tollar shook her head. "We've got our work cut out for us getting across the island. The palace is northish and not far from here, but there's no cover. They've cut down all the trees and shrubs and there aren't even any buildings. I don't know what this section of island used to look like, but there's only some rocks, not even any hills."

"He's really made it impossible to get in unnoticed."

"Or to escape," Cerro said, pressing his lips together.

"I can give us cover," Tollar said. "But they'll know we're here once I do."

"If he's going to know we're here, it's probably the best time you've got to deal with any water demons," Neesha said.

Tavalu muttered something that sounded like dismay. Neesha didn't love it either. But Tollar sank into the water again, gone only a moment before returning.

"All right, let's go. I can pull fog out of the storm around the island to give us some cover, but I'll need help spreading it. I can move it, but it'll be easier if someone can use some aeromancy to spread it faster."

"Pull it from as far from here as you can," Macana said. "We'll spread it out over half the island."

"Right," Neesha said. "Make them think we dropped in on dragons, not that we snuck in through the back door."

They stayed huddled on the stairs, and Tollar took Neesha's hand, drawing on her power to pull fog from the storm from clear on the other side of the island. Cerro harnessed Eratona to help spread it, sending it toward the hill where the palace sat before dragging it their way to give them cover.

And yeah, that made sense. Block Loch's view of the whole island before putting cover where they needed it most.

And then they were up and out of the tunnel, all of them somehow dry as a bone despite having just climbed from the ocean and now surrounded by thick fog. Neesha couldn't see more than a few feet in front of her, but she kept Tollar in her sight, knowing the other woman could navigate just fine. She went slowly all the same, letting Macana and Cerro stop and scout, using terramancy to see if anyone was coming.

Something hit the ground nearby with a thud that made Neesha's stomach lurch.

"Stay here," Tollar whispered and disappeared into the fog.

Her face was even more pinched than before when she returned.

"Now what?" Neesha asked, not sure she wanted the answer.

"One of Loch's people just fell from the sky. Dead before he hit the ground. The side of him not embedded in the ground had a wound consistent with Croves's warhammer."

Neesha blinked a lot.

"What...?" Tavalu stared up, not that there was anything to see.

"Godsdamnit, Croves said there'd been captive dragons left." Neesha tried to remember everything he'd said but couldn't come up with anything useful. "Are they here now?"

Tollar let out a long, slow breath. "That must be it." She glanced up. "If he's up there, he'll have the others with him."

"What about the boats?" Cerro asked.

Tollar shrugged. "We have to trust they know what they're doing. There's a lot of dragon riders and dragons and wizards out there. We've got our own task."

Tollar kept going toward the palace. They got a lot farther than Neesha expected they would before Macana cursed in Upalan.

"Here they come."

"In your pairs," Tollar said. "Fan out."

Neesha stayed with Tollar. Tavalu went with Cerro while Eratona and Macana went off in the other direction. Neesha pulled out one of her venom balls and handed it to Tollar, who pitched it as far as she could out in front of them. When it landed, Neesha ballooned it into the biggest fire she could manage.

There were cries of alarm.

Neesha knelt to touch the ground, sending her awareness through it as far as she could. The two teams stood out nearby, heading away from her. There were clusters heading generally their way. Loch's elementals would be using terramancy to similar effect, so Tollar got a water disk and helped Neesha up onto it, using water now to sense where the others were.

Neesha wanted to throw more fireballs, but Tollar didn't want to catch any of the locals in the fight. She brought them closer on the water disk, going slow and careful, while Neesha gripped another venom ball, waiting.

The disk stopped and Tollar gasped. Neesha could hear Loch's people approaching. It sounded like they were having a hushed argument. Someone was whimpering.

"They have prisoners," Tollar whispered, barely audible. She brought them out and around this group, approaching from behind.

Neesha held her breath, certain Loch's people would be able to hear her raging heartbeat despite Tollar's silent approach. Then the group loomed out of the fog, and they were close enough to see that there were people tied up, being driven ahead.

Loch had done her and Tollar the huge service of bringing mostly pale northerners with him, so that they didn't even need to see the bindings to know who they needed to stop and who to save.

Tollar drew her sword, a furious snarl on her face, and for one horrifying moment, Neesha was certain Tollar would take off the head of the man directly in front of them. Instead, at the last moment, she pivoted low and swung the blade out, cutting through one of his legs.

When he screamed and the chaos started, Neesha threw her venom ball at the nearest northerner. Tollar had some kind of warrior code about not killing if it wasn't absolutely necessary.

Neesha did not. And she wanted seventeen godsdamn years worth of blood.

Not that she gave them a whole lot of opportunity to bleed. She couldn't open a portal to wield trueflame, but she'd learned to make fire very near to those beams of concentrated light Spark used. She cut them down quickly while Tollar went to their prisoners, cutting their bonds and instructing them to take cover.

The two of them repeated the process with one more group before Loch's people retreated. She hadn't seen any sign of the other two pairs who'd come with Tollar, but they seemed to be having some success. The storm around the island was weakening. And with Tollar's focus elsewhere, the fog had lifted significantly.

Tollar grinned. "Tavalu is good at a number of things, but she decided the thing she would excel at is hunting Loch's elementals."

Neesha heard a weird rumbling, something vaguely familiar she couldn't quite place, a moment before the ground beneath her shuddered and heaved.

"Shit!" It felt an awful lot like that erupting volcano she and Spark had adventured to earlier in the year. Neesha immediately turned to look for the nearby volcano. They were on a rise, giving her a decent view of it, especially as the storm continued to weaken. It hadn't ever been particularly strong on the north side of the island to begin with.

The volcano was just a big mountain, sitting there doing whatever volcanoes did. Neesha had sworn it had been leaking out its one side when they'd scouted last night. Leaking was definitely not the right word. Spark would probably know what it was. But it had been... leaking fire but not actually erupting. Or whatever. Maybe she should have paid a bit of attention to whatever Beenala and Spark had been doing.

But the earthquake subsided and the volcano continued to do nothing, so Neesha hurried after Tollar, who was heading into a gully that led toward the palace. It had probably been Loch's people causing the earthquake. Trying to scare them? Or using it to find them?

She supposed it didn't matter one way or another. She'd come here for a fight, and Loch was godsdamn going to get one.

CHAPTER THIRTY

Spark stayed low on Abyss's head, waiting for lightning that didn't seem to be coming. The main island was covered in thick fog, but the storm that had once been ringing the island was mainly to the south and looking pretty sad. She tried to not be disappointed. Wanting to be struck by lightning was absolute lunacy.

But it was *fun*.

After freeing the five dragons and returning Croves to the boats with the others, Spark was even more jittery and getting tired. And she kind of felt like she was going to throw up. With the water beasts neutralized, she had even less to do.

Abyss swooped at another boat, spewing fire that Spark directed toward the masts and any oars she could see. She really wanted to just sink the boat. Well, she'd gotten to sink one earlier. That had been right after the water monsters had fled.

Tollar must have taken their demons. She wondered if Loch was the only one who could put the demons in them? Probably. Or maybe he had a minion who could do it, but from what Spark had seen of Tollar's power versus normal elementals and aquamancers, it was going to be a rare ability.

Anyway, Spark had gotten to sink a boat, and she'd probably get to sink a few more before much longer. The dragon riders plus some of Chalky's people and all of the Guild wizards who knew how to fight, were down on the boats.

The dragons dropped them in, they did whatever they needed to separate the Biternans from Loch's people, and brought them all to the one boat Croves and Raia had cleared and taken command of at the start.

That had been Dira's idea. Spark had been pretty sure Tollar would cry from relief at the suggestion. One thing Spark had in common with Tollar that Neesha didn't was her disdain for hurting people. It wasn't so much that Neesha enjoyed hurting people, she enjoyed hurting *bad* people—people who had caused her harm first.

Neesha didn't really see the difference between Loch's people and Loch himself. Spark wouldn't *enjoy* hurting Loch, but she definitely wanted to stab him in the face all the same. She did not want to stab anyone else anywhere.

Croves and Raia though? Lots of stabbing. And smashing.

Spark was glad to be up in the sky and far away from it. She'd been close up only briefly and hadn't fully understood what she'd seen—weird smears and a bad smell after Croves had taken his warhammer to someone. And then Abyss had swooped on by, and Spark stopped looking after that.

It had been easier up in the aerial battle when anyone Croves hit fell off the dragon before Spark could register the damage he'd done. Spark had also had a lot more to focus on.

But the plan was for the dragons to target anyone they could see who definitely wasn't a Biternan, while the riders and the wizards cleared the boats one by one. When a boat was cleared, Croves or Aldred would be the last off, summoning the dragons before rushing to the one safe boat.

And then whichever dragon was closest would swoop in and light the boat on fire. If it was Abyss, with Spark's help, they would bore a hole right through it so it could burn *and* sink.

Abyss banked suddenly like she did when there was a summoning, and Spark got a good view of Croves leaping from one boat to the other as they approached. But then Abyss growled and pitched into the sky, slicing around quickly. Spark looked back and saw that Zephyr, who stayed close, went in to finish off the boat.

"What is it?"

"Summons from Yarrow."

Spark blinked. Why would she do that? Abyss circled the island and went in low, right into what was left of the storm, coming down on the southeast side, furthest from Loch's palace.

"Is this a trap?" Spark asked.

"If it is, she will regret it," Abyss said.

She glided in to land on top of the wall in the middle of the storm, half her body hanging over onto the island, with her talons gripping the wall and her head stretched way down to look at two women in a small wooden boat near the shore.

Maybe Spark would get to play with some lightning after all.

"Mistress! Bad news!" Yarrow shouted.

The woman with her was the one they'd met last night—Tollar had spoken to her, but Spark had been there and recognized the woman's inexpertly cropped brown hair and the way her clothes, the same she'd worn last night, hung off her. She'd helped Tollar's friend escape and had been pitching messages with information over the wall for Yarrow to find. Yesterday, she'd gotten herself over the wall to finally properly escape and was now with Yarrow until this was over.

"Peniope, tell them," Yarrow said.

"He's weaponized the volcano!" Peniope cried in heavily accented prime.

The what? Spark blinked a lot, waiting for the explanation.

"He's had teams on it for weeks," she continued. "He instructed them to clog up all the vents and flows if the island was attacked. They're all back here now, all of them off the volcano, it's going to explode if you don't leave!"

Spark blinked a whole lot more and gripped Abyss's horns. "We need to tell Tollar!"

"No," Abyss said. "We will deal with it."

"You can't! It will explode!" Peniope's voice was desperate. "Have you seen that before? Do you know what it will do to this whole archipelago?"

"Yes," Abyss said, her tone gentle. "But we can handle this. Find safety, if you can."

Abyss took to the air again, screeching into the battle as she sought out her family. Abyss roared something in dragonish, and Shell peeled out of the nearby dragon formation to dive toward Croves. Abyss turned and headed for the volcano with Zephyr and Bolt out ahead of her and Bale and Glacial Sunfire trailing behind. They flew straight over the island—and there was a bit of magic directed their way, but not much, and Spark could see at least two fires burning in the middle of what was maybe a field. That was good.

If Loch's people were leading any sort of proper counterattack, they wouldn't leave any fire for Neesha to work with.

Spark couldn't worry about her mother now. She had to worry about *all* of them. Why would Loch do this? He had to have some kind of escape plan or secret safe place if he'd planned on blowing up an entire volcano? Maybe it was a bluff?

But no, even from so high above and at this distance, Spark could see that the lava flows that had been running strong and healthy into the ocean last night were gone. Just solid black streaks on the landscape.

"Oh. Oh shit."

Zephyr and Bolt had been circling the volcano, but all three dragons landed on the side of it when Abyss reached them. Bale and Glacial Sunfire continued to circle while Shell came in with Croves and a couple of Guild wizards. As soon as Spark set foot on the volcano, she felt it shuddering beneath her feet. A near-constant tremor, nearly a hum.

That was probably bad.

"What in all the hells is this about?" Croves asked, once Shell had deposited he and the wizards next to Spark on the mountainside. Volcanoside?

Spark explained what Peniope had told them. "But Abyss says we can handle it. Somehow."

"The lava itself, even flying rocks, cannot harm us," Abyss said. "We use something like your elemental magic to make our homes in the mountains, to build the dragon city. We can use that here."

"Right." One of the Guild wizards stood next to Spark. "We can just use terramancy to open the vents again, same as Loch's people closed it."

"No!" Spark tried not to imagine what that would do to the geography. "It's been building pressure for however long now. We've got to... hold that back somehow and let it vent off slowly."

"That's not possible."

Spark flexed her hands, glanced at Abyss. "I can probably do it."

"No one who isn't fireproof should be anywhere near this volcano," Abyss said.

Croves shared a concerned look with the two wizards who'd come with him.

"Bale kept us safe from lava flows," Croves said. "When we was on our way to the dragon city. Active volcano was the only place to land."

"Yes, we can shield you, but it is still a risk."

"Yer gonna need more magic than just Spark's got. I don't reckon even *she* can hold the volcano for long."

"Shit," Spark gasped. "No, probably not. We're going to have to find some of the vents and one of the old fissures and get them all open near simultaneously."

"Can your magic reach the fire from here?" Abyss asked.

Spark pressed her palm against the rock, startled by how warm it was, and she could sense the lava, but it was a long way down. If she could see with dirt the way she could see with fire, she'd be able to see the weak points, know where to focus. She couldn't see with dirt though. She could only see with fire.

"Oh shit on the moons for all eternity!" Spark stood again and looked around desperately, feeling jangly and a little cold. This was so many hells worse than getting struck by lightning.

"I have to go in there," Spark said. "I can't control it from out here."

"That's madness!" the other wizard gasped.

"At this point I'm pretty sure madness is my specialty. I probably get it from my mother. I don't think this will be that much different from being in the fire realm?"

"We have no time for arguments," Abyss said. "We must find the vents immediately."

Spark opened her mouth to start coming up with a more detailed plan when a dragon screamed from behind her. She leapt toward Abyss and turned—an absolutely massive dragoness, filthy and in chains, charged over the shoulder of the volcano toward them.

Abyss snatched Spark up off the ground so quickly it rattled her before depositing Spark on her shoulder. Shell grabbed the other humans and took flight while Bale dived out of the sky and Zephyr launched himself at the dragoness, knocking her sideways.

Spark had only enough time to note that her wings were chained at her sides before Abyss leapt into the fight.

"Put me on her back so I can cut her loose!"

"She will roll over and crush you."

Abyss collided with the other dragoness, biting at her neck and raking her talons along the other dragon's sides. Not anticipating any dragon battles, Abyss was not wearing her armour.

Spark crouched between two spikes on Abyss's back, her fists wrapped around handholds, hoping not to get thrown clear.

Bale dropped into the fight, landing on the chained dragon's back and clamping her jaws around her neck near the side of her head where the spikes were shorter.

"Can you hold her down so I can cut the chains?"

"There is no time."

The volcano agreed by rumbling, the ground shaking even worse than the dragon battle had made it. Spark gasped.

Zephyr came back in out of nowhere, and while he and Bale had the chained dragon partially immobilized, Abyss raked at her underside with her talons fully extended, ripping a long, bloody gash down her body. The chained dragon screamed and tried to flail against Bale and Zephyr's grip, but the gaping wound slowed her down enough for Abyss to lunge in and rip out her throat.

Spark curled up deeper behind the spike, squeezing her eyes against the hot tight feeling in her throat.

"I could have cut her loose," Spark said, her voice breaking with emotion.

"It would not have saved her. There are no humans here controlling her behaviour—attacking us was her choice. We have seen this before and dragons in this state cannot be helped," Abyss said. "A swift death is the only mercy."

Spark inhaled a shaky breath, but the ground beneath them shook again.

"We do not have time. Spark, you must act."

Spark nodded even though Abyss couldn't see it. Shell returned with the other humans, forcing Spark to get herself together. They had an explosion to stop.

"Abyss, you come with me down to the fissure we could see last night." Spark thought about the locations of the lava flows and paused. One of them had been pointed right at the main island. "Wait! That one around the side facing the main island—we need to leave that one alone until this mountain is stable."

"I thought the whole point of you going in there was to control it," one of the Guild wizards said.

Spark pressed one hand to the top of her head. They were arguing and didn't have time. "I probably can. We can't risk the island on probably. Leave anything facing that island alone. There was a fissure around the other side. We'll use that one to relieve pressure. We need to vent steam and fumes, though, too. I'll use a summoning to signal to the dragons when it's safe to open things up."

"The rest of you find those points. Go," Abyss commanded.

Then Raia and Dragon zipped overhead.

"You've got company!" Raia called.

"Boats from the island," Bale added, circling around behind them.

"Shell and I will help Raia keep 'em back," Croves said.

"Everyone else to the vents," Abyss said.

It was a short, rough flight down to the old lava flow, and Abyss immediately began digging at the point where the flow had originated. She was scooping it away like mud, which didn't seem possible. Spark wanted to sit there all day and watch Abyss use her magic.

"Go, Spark. We do not have much time."

Right. Spark opened a fire portal and zipped through it, the fire realm overbright and roaring mercilessly. It seemed louder and brighter than normal. Did that have anything to do with where she'd come from? She concentrated on an area not far from Abyss and opened a new fire portal.

CHAPTER THIRTY-ONE

Neesha nearly dropped the venom ball she was about to lob at the latest batch of Loch's people when Abyss went screaming overhead without so much as a glance their way. She had her entire family with her, Shell not far behind. There hadn't been any dragons overhead for some time, not since a mass of chains with a couple of Loch's people tangled in it had fallen out of the sky. The ground rumbled and pitched under Neesha's feet again, and she watched with dismay as the dragons all headed for the volcano.

"Toll, something's happening."

"Looks like they're on it."

"Should we be worried?"

"Probably. Nothing we can do. *This* is our fight."

Neesha shrugged, let out a noisy breath, and heaved the venom ball at Loch's people. She flared the fire in their midst, sowing confusion to make it easier for her and Tollar to attack.

But Tollar caught her shoulder before either of them got any closer.

"Consider maiming them? Revenge won't give you your years back."

Neesha's heartbeat roared in her ears, her skin prickling with heat, and she opened her mouth to snap at Tollar, but the other woman was already sprinting into battle, sword up and water whip lashing at her side. Neesha had a pang of furious and irrational jealousy at the fact Tollar could move as fast as she could as pregnant as she was when all Neesha could do by that point had been an undignified waddle. Honestly Neesha couldn't even move that fast *now*.

Neesha had one deeply uncharitable moment where she was tempted to just stand there and watch Tollar fight the whole group by herself. She'd probably be fine. This group didn't even have any Biternans as human shields.

But grumbling under her breath about maiming, Neesha got closer, pulled a lance of flame out of the ground fire, and ran it through the meaty part of one woman's leg. Tollar was also primarily aiming at legs.

One of the men in the group tried to run. Neesha took out *both* his legs.

And then Tavalu appeared out of the dissipating fog at a full run, hand clamped over her mouth and tears streaming down her face.

"Tollar!" she called. "Neesha, Toll, you have to come!"

Tollar cut off one more leg, and they were left with screaming and unconscious wizards on the ground around them. Both of them met Tavalu on her approach.

"Cerro and the others are trying to suppress it, but you've got to come," Tavalu panted.

"Suppress what? What's going on?" Tollar put a steadying hand on the other woman's broad shoulders, but she burst out sobbing.

"They're killing all the locals!" Tavalu sucked in a gasping ragged breath. "There were already no local wizards left on this island, and now they're just indiscriminately killing everyone left."

"Still want me to only maim them?" Neesha snapped at Tollar, stomping off in the direction Tavalu had come from.

Taller and in infinitely better shape than Neesha, both Tollar and Tavalu got ahead of her quickly, so that she was struggling to keep up and not be left behind. Tollar paused when they could hear the screaming nearby and turned to Neesha.

"Stay out of sight. Whatever happens, help from somewhere unseen. Don't make it obvious you're here."

Neesha wanted to argue because if Tollar was keeping Neesha out of the way, it was to enact Neesha's least favourite backup plan. But yes, she could pull her hood up over her head and stay in the back and let the others harness her energy to do whatever it was they needed to do.

So she pulled up her hood and was slow and cautious as she drew nearer. They'd made it to the side of the palace that faced inland and appeared to be the main entrance. Most of the area surrounding the palace was crammed with tents, but it was a wider open space here. There were a lot of bodies on the ground.

Tavalu was explaining as they approached, and Neesha could just hear what she said to Tollar. Loch's elementals had started using the ground to smother people, or blood magic to rupture their hearts. Just indiscriminately. Whoever happened to be closest.

Loch's people also claimed to be manipulating the volcano and that it would explode and destroy the archipelago if the contingent from the south didn't surrender. Neesha gasped and looked around for the volcano, but the view was obscured by the palace. Was that what Abyss had raced off to?

Spark would be with her. Was there anything Spark could do about a whole entire volcano? Neesha felt cold. The escape plan weighed heavily on her mind. Could they save anyone here? There were so many dead already, and Loch's people just would not quit.

Cerro was harnessing Macana and Eratona and directing a wall of suppression magic into the throng. But Loch's people had weapons, while the islanders had sticks—if they were lucky.

None of these wizards could fight a physical battle. That's what Tavalu had come to get Tollar for. Cerro would keep the wall of suppression going, so Loch's people couldn't use magic, but neither could Tollar.

Tollar drew her sword and stormed into the fray.

Tavalu took Macana's hand to lend her power to the effort. Neesha took Tavalu's other hand to do the same and kept crouched half-behind the group of them, peering around to watch Tollar.

Who was somehow swinging that giant sword with one hand—Neesha could still barely lift it with two—and had a dagger in the other. Tollar wasn't focused solely on legs anymore, but Neesha suspected none of the body hits were getting anything important. Just big and terrifying wounds in places that *looked* important.

Cause them pain. Make them afraid. Just enough to stop the fighting.

Neesha had three venom balls left. Well, four—but that last one was supposed to be her escape. Potentially. She couldn't throw that far, but she was betting Tavalu could. Neesha offered them to Tavalu, touching her other arm to keep contributing to the harnessing. Tavalu heaved them out at anyone trying to sneak up on Tollar.

But there were so many of them.

And Tollar was sloppy. Even Neesha could see that. She'd practiced with Tollar enough to know.

Tollar threw the dagger and got a man in the chest. That'd probably collapse a lung. Good. She had only the sword left, moving it quickly, but there were a lot of them.

With all the attention on Tollar, at least locals were slipping away. Neesha watched them slink behind tarps and into tents or just slowly vanish into the background. Also good. Tollar was still winning, even with pretending to be exhausted. Maybe Neesha should try to sneak in and find Loch. Could she face him on her own?

She still had that last venom ball—she could use it to start a fire in there, to do the summoning Tollar was supposed to so Spark could join her.

Neesha leaned forward, looking for a route, and that was when she saw the woman with the ropes.

"Shit!" Tavalu had seen her too.

Neesha offered up her final venom ball and watched it arc through the air—another fantastic throw from Tavalu.

But too late.

The woman had made a loop and thrown it around Tollar just as she'd lunged with the sword. The woman yanked, and Tollar dropped her sword and nearly fell backward. The venom ball hit the woman and she dropped the rope, flailing. Tollar regained her balance but was still in trouble. They were out of venom balls, and another of Loch's people rushed in to grab the rope the burning woman had dropped.

Tollar was doing her best, staying on her feet and dancing away from their attempts to tie her up. Neesha doubted Tollar had expected that part.

She was wearing long sleeves—thin fabric, but still covering most of her skin except for her palms and face—but if they tied her up, they could easily grab her hands or touch her face to harness her magic.

If those wizards harnessed Tollar, Neesha and the others were absolutely doomed.

Another one got a loop of rope around Tollar from the other side. But Tollar was big and strong, and even though her centre of gravity wasn't what she was used to, she was *solid*. Even working in concert, they couldn't get her off her feet. But the more she tried to evade them, the more tangled up she became in the ropes.

"Shit, shit, shit..." Neesha muttered.

Was it worth it to get Cerro to stop suppressing magic so Tollar could really fight back? Or was the suppression the only thing stopping Loch's people from harnessing her and destroying them all?

Loch's people swarmed Tollar as she struggled and seemed to be reaching for something in her pocket. There was a lot of shouting, and someone got kicked right out of the cluster and into a tent. Neesha got a glimpse, and they'd gotten Tollar's wrists bound in front of her.

"Cerro, stop—"

A mind-splitting roar echoed across the island, emanating from the side of the palace. Neesha forgot anything she was about to say and had to struggle to stay on her feet. That had been a dragon. A *profoundly angry* dragon. Entirely too close.

Fighting back every instinct screaming at her to run and hide, Neesha looked around and spotted a chained-up dragon charging toward them, a complement of Loch's people on its back and shoulders driving it onward.

Neesha swore.

"Ancestors save us all," Tavalu whispered, staring in horror.

Macana shouted out a warning in Upalan, and Tavalu grabbed Neesha's arm to get her attention.

The crowd was dragging a still-struggling Tollar into the palace.

"What do we do?"

"I'll handle the dragon. Just keep disrupting them! Keep these people safe!" Neesha hissed. "This is what she wanted. She's bringing the fight to him."

Tavalu said something in Upalan that Neesha had to assume was a particularly terrible curse. The dragon roared again. It had come all the way around the side of the palace and spotted them.

"You're sure? This is what Tollar wanted?"

"Well, no, she wanted to walk in and hand Loch his ass with minimal fuss." Neesha crossed her arms. "But this was one of her more backed up backup plans."

"We didn't authorize this," Cerro said.

Neesha shrugged. "File a report. If we survive. Which if we do, will be because of whatever she's doing!" Neesha pointed the way Tollar had been dragged, the group subduing her had gone all the way inside now. There were still a lot of wizards left.

"Just protect these people! I'll see what I can do to keep this dragon out of your way."

Neesha pulled some of the fire from the smouldering remains of the woman who had roped Tollar and dashed toward the dragon, fireball in hand. So this was probably it, this was how she was going to die. Spark should be the one out here fighting a dragon. She at least had an axe. What in all the hells could Neesha do with fire against a dragon.

She ran at the dragon on an angle, toward it but away from the palace, hoping to draw its attention. Surely a fireborn woman would be an ideal target. She crested a ridge and turned to see if it was working. Horrified when she realized it was.

But this dragon had come through the storm, the dust and grime partially washed away, and though she'd never seen him before in her life, she recognized him from description. Black as the darkest night and streaked with white, a pattern so very much like Bolt's.

This was Summer's Eve Lightning. This was Abyss's brother. Bale's father.

"Oh hells. Oh shit."

Could this get any worse? If this dragon didn't kill her, Abyss was going to.

Neesha took a deep breath and flared the fire around her, making herself as obvious a target as she could.

CHAPTER
THIRTY-TWO

Tollar put up exactly the right amount of fight—dragging her feet and making like she was trying to shrug off the ropes—to make them think they really had her. None of them were smart enough—or stupid enough?—to try to harness her yet, even after they'd moved beyond the reach of Cerro's suppression.

Tollar had desperately wanted to look back and make sure they weren't doing some fool thing like trying to rescue her. Or to see what in all the hells that roaring dragon had been about. She had to stay focused on what was to come.

They dragged her kicking and muttering curses down a hallway. She managed to twist sideways and kick one of them in the side of the knee, taking him down. Two of the others grabbed her legs and the ones at her arms hauled harder and then they were carrying her.

Tollar wanted to laugh. She knew exactly how heavy she was with her height and this armour and these babies. Good. Let them do her work for her.

They dropped her on a stone floor, probably thinking they'd do some damage, but she managed to land right. She rolled onto her side, pivoted on her hip, and kicked out one more knee.

"Enough!" a man shouted in Prairiean.

Tollar's captors backed away, remaining at a wary distance, some of them drawing weapons, one of them holding onto her sword in a way that made her confident he had no idea how to use it.

Shoving with her elbows and not nearly as dignified as she would have been a few months ago, Tollar got first to her knees and then her feet. Despite the fatigued ache in her limbs from all the sword use and the splitting headache from the magic she'd done, Tollar stood tall and unbothered. Sitting in what could only be described as a throne was a gangly pale northerner with stringy blonde hair and sharp blue eyes.

"Ah, you must be Loch," she said, also in Prairiean. "Good. Let's get this over with."

"And just who, exactly, are you?" he sneered.

"Oh, your spy didn't tell you? I'm Tollar." She took a bow.

"That should mean something?"

"Come on, Dram told you all about me!"

He stared, expression blank. Dawning horror rose in her gut, and she had to suppress hysterical laughter.

"You have no idea who I am. All of us are just bugs to you. Why would you bother remembering our names? You don't even remember Dram, do you? Karthiry's little pet before he escaped?"

That got a flicker of recognition.

Tollar grinned. "Maybe you'd be pleased to know he's living quite happily on my farm in Nytaltek?"

"You talk entirely too much. I grow weary of this."

Loch stood and gestured, hitting her with aquamancy, an attempt at blood magic that she quickly repelled, her anger rising.

"Oh no you don't!" Tollar snapped.

Loch's eyes grew wide. "What—How—?"

"I guess Ondias interrupted your spy before he could answer those questions?" Tollar's grin returned, savage and full of teeth. It was nearly enough to stave off the headache. "The what is that I'm half demon like your friends in Pasdale."

Loch roared and lunged forward, but Tollar threw some aquamancy of her own, pulling water straight out of the humid air to punch him with it, and he staggered backward, nearly falling.

"And the how? Well, being a half-demon aquamancer just means that I'm better at this than you."

"Another one of you freaks," he snarled, back on his feet.

"I might be a freak, but *my* magic is stable. No need to cling pathetically to demons. Good enough to get into the Guild on those new tiers they'd never let you in on."

"I don't need the Guild."

"Yes, of course. You've got your own little operation. How's that working for you? Seems you've suffered some humiliating defeats. No more Karthiry to help you out. Who've you got doing your dirty work these days?"

Loch studied her closely. "You were the one on the dragon. In the port."

"Yes! A dragon I stole from you—twice!—by the way!"

Loch was clenching and unclenching his fists, and she wondered what magic he was thinking of trying to use against her. "What happened to Karthiry?"

"I was better than her."

"You killed her. All your moral superiority, but you're still monsters."

"Oh, but the Guild wants *you* alive."

Loch threw back his head and laughed. "Those old cowards?"

The ground beneath them shook before Tollar could throw any more verbal barbs. Loch's people shifted uneasily as bits of dust rained from the walls.

"That would be the rigged volcano about to go off," Loch said casually, like he was commenting on a lovely summer's day. "Now that I've captured one of you fools, you can get the others to surrender, or I'll let the volcano do whatever it is they do when you plug them up. My terramancers assured me it would be spectacular."

Tollar stared. "You expect me to believe that? The volcano will wipe you out along with the rest of the island."

He waved a dismissive hand. "Of course I have a fortified bunker."

"For you, I'm sure. What about the rest of your people?" She glanced around the room, more nervous shuffling from her would-be captors.

"Those who have shown me utmost loyalty know they have a place safely at my side."

Tollar had never heard thicker oxshit.

"Well, that's dull and you're boring me. Let's get this over with."

Hands still bound, Tollar flung more water out of the air at him, freezing it into deadly shards as it raced toward him. But he was quick, parting the attack around him and using the moment to try blood magic on her again.

Tollar kept resisting his nonsense, even if it made her vision blur around the edges. She pulled the ice shards back around, melting them into one long bar that she rammed into the back of his legs. Just as he hit the ground, the floor beneath her feet shuddered and jerked. Tollar had hoped he'd been lying about the volcano. She wasn't sure there was enough aquamancy in the world to stop something like that.

CHAPTER THIRTY-THREE

S park barely had her fire portal to the volcano open when lava immediately burst into the space, slamming her backward. Spark screamed. It startled her enough that she lost control of the portal and it closed, leaving her surrounded by lava.

Right. Lava was heavy. And she'd be coming out under a whole mountain's worth.

"Shit. Oh shit."

She took a deep shaky breath and called up everything she could remember about both terramancy and volcanoes. This was nothing like what she'd expected to need the information for.

She opened a portal again and immediately shoved her hand out in front of her, using two kinds of elemental magic at once to heave the magma out of her way and leave a bubble in it big enough for her to fit. She came out of the fire realm to something much darker than she'd expected. It was reddish-orange fire, and she wasn't entirely sure if that was from all the pressure or something else.

She couldn't breathe—choking on fumes, she had no time to really consider it.

Right. There wouldn't really be any air down here.

So. She needed to use three elements, focusing on aeromancy for a moment and filtering out the fumes. There was still not a lot of oxygen for her, so she would need to be quick.

She pressed her hand against the side of her lava bubble and focused on the shape of it. Or the fiery bits of it, anyway. A clear picture erupted in her mind, the angry fire pressing at the sides, prodding for weakness, desperate to get out.

Wait, that was entirely too much emotion for something that wasn't sentient. Were volcanoes sentient? The books hadn't said anything about that.

And then fire erupted out of the lava, coming straight for her, and she screamed and lurched away, her bubble nearly collapsing on her.

A fire demon? What in all the hells?

She managed to catch it and hold it, and she searched the fire again. There were at least half a dozen of them, all moving toward her. They were trapped in here, angry they couldn't escape. Something to speed the eruption along?

Spark used her mother's favourite swear word.

Well, Spark had known she needed to be quick. She opened a fire portal and shoved this one through, trying desperately to keep her focus on what the volcano was doing and track the incoming demons at the same time. But she'd gotten herself close enough to the clogged-up fissure to find it easily. She planted her feet against the wall of the magma chamber and directed terramancy at the magma toward her feet.

The result was that using the magic made this part of the ground soft, compounding the effect. It was the fastest way to make a hole in the ground.

A pair of fire demons reached her, and she had to pause to shove them through a new fire portal. Just as she was finishing, the entire blob of magma surged up and sort of to her left.

"Gah!"

Spark gripped the whole damned thing in her mind and dragged it back down. It made her woozy. She was taking too long. Had the others got a vent open? Weren't they supposed to wait for her signal?

Okay. She could still do this.

And then a trio of fire demons broke into her little bubble and it nearly collapsed on her, and she nearly lost control of all this godsdamn lava.

Spark repeated her mother's favourite swear. Louder this time.

She held onto the magma, just barely, but one of the fire demons went and possessed her before she could do anything about them, and whatever, it was fine. It was all fine.

She summoned Abyss because things were about as under control as they were likely to be, and they couldn't keep wasting time.

She shoved the demon into a box in her mental kitchen and used its power to get rid of the other two while *not* losing control of an entire godsdamn volcano. If she didn't die right here, everyone was going to hear about this every single day for the rest of her life.

Hey everyone, I'm the best pyromancer in the world, and I fought an entire volcano!

The fire demon was a risk, but it also made it easier for her to separate patches of gas from the main body of the lava and float it up to the surface. Where hopefully there was a vent for it to escape. Several vents would be better, but she just had no way of knowing without playing with the lava in a way that even *she* thought was lunacy.

She could also see the last pair of demons clearly, closing in on her location. So she waited. Not that she really had the time. She was running out of air. Her skin felt tight and itchy. They broke through to her at long last, and she shoved them through a portal.

And then she used the final demon to just *hold* all this lava, because it really, really wanted to go up. Up and out. So the others were doing *something*.

She was getting tired and gasping. Was she almost out of air? Was it time to get back to tunnelling? Worried she'd pass out with a demon still in her, she shoved this one out and through a portal. No sooner than she got the portal closed, her little bubble of lava sprang a leak, almost exactly where she'd just been trying to go.

"Shit!"

She did not have much control over the lava now, trying to keep it at a steady flow instead of a massive explosion out of whatever hole had just opened in the mountainside. But it pulled her along with it on its escape. It was like trying to swim through rapids. (Which she had in fact done. Thanks, Tollar.)

She was about as successful with it now as she had been in the water.

For one brief, glorious moment, she got it all to just *stop*. If Tollar had stopped an entire river, Spark could hold this still.

But she was still short on oxygen, still gasping and getting lightheaded. She lost her concentration again and got sucked into the lava tube. All she could do was keep herself in the middle of the flow so she didn't get slammed into rocks and hope for the best.

She continued to encourage the rest of the lava to maybe just relax a bit and stay put a bit longer, but she had no idea if it was working, and also she was dizzy. That was probably bad.

Spark was certain she was about to pass out. Would she survive that? She could breathe in fire, but not molten rock. That would be bad, right?

As she was debating switching her focus to finding more air, she shot out of the fissure, tumbled along the lava flow, and finally got her head up to take one good proper breath.

Still trying not to drown in lava—no one was going to believe her—she also kept trying to get the lava to slow down and stay put. It had ripped an awfully large hole in the side of the volcano.

And then she tumbled over, and everything was very wet and steamy and hard to breathe again.

So she was coughing and sputtering and trying not to drown in two different liquids at once when Abyss finally fished her out of the ocean and lava.

"I need to keep my hand in it!"

Abyss moved farther from the water before lowering Spark close enough to keep working with the lava.

"It appears to have worked," Abyss said calmly, like an entire mountain hadn't been about to turn into a very large, noisy crater, and take everything in sight with it.

Lava suddenly exploded out of the side of the volcano to the east and slightly farther up, and Spark noticed for the first time that Bolt and Zephyr were both over there, apparently digging an entirely new fissure. And there were steaming vents in a couple of places toward the summit.

Spark kept some of her attention on keeping the lava at a steady pace and not just ripping out the entire northern side of the slope, but spared some energy to summon Bale.

"You have an idea?" Abyss asked.

Spark was already crafting some of the lava into a large ball and cooling the outside of it.

"Loch wanted an explosion? Let's give him one."

IN THE SKIES

Bale is on the other side of the volcano with Glacial Sunfire, trying to hit the boats with fire without getting caught by magic from the people on the boats. Bale wishes they had some of those spears to drop. Toll-mum dredged them all up out of the sea after the last fight, but doesn't want them used in this one in case they hit anyone who doesn't deserve it.

Bale still isn't sure any of them don't deserve it, but she will listen to Toll-mum all the same.

She's circling, looking for a weak point, when Spark summons her. So she skims along the edge of the volcano and sees Bolt and Merciless Winter Sky digging holes in the volcano while Auntie Void is with Spark.

"We must continue to guard the volcano," Auntie Void says. "Spark needs to guide the lava flow until enough pressure has been relieved."

"I've got something for you to take to Loch," Spark says, sounding a lot angrier than Bale has ever heard her.

Spark is sitting in Auntie's hand with her bare feet in the lava flow, using her hands to guide something that looks like a large black rock. But Bale can sense the fire in it.

"I've cooled the outside enough that it should hold," Spark says, using her power to raise the ball up closer to Bale. "You'll probably want to rotate it around so the lava inside can't eat through the bottom before you deliver it."

"The other dragons can use them against the boats," Bale says. "We can't get our fire close enough. One of them used magic and almost pulled Dragon out of the air."

"All right, you tell the others. I'll make more."

Bale takes her lava rock and heads up the volcano until she's high enough to easily take flight. She doesn't get too high, though, and veers straight for the nearest boat. Glacial Sunfire comes in above her, breathing fire at Loch's wizards to keep their attention. Bale banks suddenly, letting go of the lava ball.

She spirals back around to see it crash into the middle of one of the silly little boats, ripping it in half and setting both halves on fire.

Loch has done them the favour of sending out people who can't be more obviously northerners—they even have matching uniforms that look a lot like the ones the people who'd kept Bale prisoner had worn.

Bale hopes Toll-mum won't be too mad if she drowns all of these ones. But these boats aren't big enough to hide people in. These boats aren't shields. And Bale doesn't care about hurting these people.

"What was that?" Glacial Sunfire calls. "I want one!"

"With me!" Bale calls back, and loops around to Spark, who has five of those balls, gently rotating them in sync while her feet are still in the lava flow.

Bale dives in and grabs one, Glacial Sunfire right behind her, and Shell has seen what they're doing and dives in after them. Glacial Sunfire tells the other dragons about the lava balls while Bale drops this one on another boat. It hits a person, crushing them even worse than Croves's hammer does, before it smashes the boat to pieces.

After Glacial Sunfire drops her lava ball on a boat, some of the farthest turn and try to escape, but Shell and Dragon are there, dropping lava and blocking their path.

Bolt and Merciless Winter Sky are banking around the volcano with lava balls of their own, when Bale dives in for a fresh one from Spark. She gets around the volcano in time to see Bolt drop a lava ball on a boat. She's looking for the right boat to hit when a dragon roars from the island.

Bale turns toward it like it's a summoning. It rattles in her bones and pulls on her insides like it sometimes does when Auntie Void calls out, only this is so much stronger. She glides toward the island, searching. There are the last straggles of wispy storm cloud left, and when she banks around one of the bigger clouds, she sees a dragon not far from the palace.

But this dragon is impossible. Deepest black with white lightning markings, this dragon is supposed to be dead. Impossibly, it's Summer's Eve Lightning. It's Bale's father.

Her scales buzz like when she flies through a thunderstorm. She both wants to somersault through the air and cry like a human.

Bale dives closer and sees her father is charging the speck of a human standing on a ridge. At this distance, the human is only a blob of purple and white, but instantly recognizable. It's Neesha.

Summer's Eve Lightning fires at Neesha, who disappears behind the wall of flame. The buzzing gets louder—in her head as well as on her scales. Why is her father attacking Neesha?

And then Bale sees the chains criss-crossing her father's body, holding his wings tight at his sides. Loch has done this. The buzzing goes hot like Bale is on fire, and she tucks her wings, picking up speed, diving before people she cares about hurt each other.

CHAPTER THIRTY-FOUR

Neesha's life tried to flash before her eyes, but she simply did not have time for that. The dragon—Summer's Eve Lightning—roared again as he stampeded toward her. His fire washed over her and she let it, holding some to use later.

When the fire cleared and Neesha was completely unharmed, the dragon slowed. They were always stunned by her lack of being dead. It wouldn't last. The humans on him were already shouting for him to kill her.

Neesha planted her feet and squared off, close enough now to see the gleam of his teeth. Putting as much fire language into her voice as she could, getting it as close to dragonish as her human capabilities allowed, she shouted his name. And once again, the dragon slowed, taken aback. Something in his eyes cleared, if only for a moment, before one of those bastards on his shoulder lashed him in the face, screaming for him to kill her.

Summer's Eve Lightning breathed fire on her again, but this time she directed it right back at him in tight lances of fire. Not quite the light beams Spark was capable of, but enough to cut a human to dust. Or three humans, as the case was.

The dragon slowed even more. Neesha held her ground.

"Summer's Eve Lightning!" she called. "I know you. I name you! Summer's Even Lightning, I am friend to both your sister and your daughter. I am not your enemy."

The coherency returned to his expression. Neesha had the briefest moment to hope that she wasn't about to get crushed to death by a dragon. By her friend's kin.

And then one of Loch's people, who she hadn't seen—probably hiding somewhere near the dragon's wings—climbed into view and cracked the dragon in the head with a length of chain.

"Shit. Oh hells."

Neesha shuffled backward. Was there any point in running? Her only hope was that the dragon would go for fire again, and she could use it to kill this human too. She tried to remember how many riders Loch usually sent on his dragons, but the only thought she could hold onto was that she was about to die.

Alone.

They were supposed to keep each other safe, godsdamnit, and here she was, about to die with nothing to show for it. She'd thought she was ready for it, had come here willing to sacrifice herself to protect Tollar and Spark. But if she was being honest, she'd envisioned something a bit more heroic and spectacular. There was nothing heroic about getting ground into paste. Spectacular? *Maybe*.

A huge black ball slammed into the back of Summer's Eve Lightning's head and exploded into fire and molten rock, Loch's rider disappearing beneath it all. The dragon stumbled and slowed. Neesha dashed farther back and saw Bale overhead, looping back around.

"Oh shit."

Did Bale know this was her father? If Neesha could tell, Bale would know, wouldn't she? Whose side would she take?

Bale tilted into a dive, moving faster than Neesha thought she could. She slammed into Summer's Eve Lightning, the two of them rolling across the open ground. Neesha sprinted. She might have noodle arms, but there was nothing wrong with her legs.

Bale had her father pinned. Neesha drew near just as Bale used her jaws to pull what appeared to be the final rider off Summer's Eve Lightning. The man's mangled corpse hit the ground not far from Neesha.

"Bale! I can get the chains off him!"

Neesha had no idea if that was actually true, but she would do what she could. Again, this should have been Spark's job. Spark had brought her enchanted axe in part because of how useful it was for cutting dragon bonds. Bale hissed at her father in dragonish as Neesha reached them.

"Summer's Eve Lightning! This is your daughter. One of your eggs survived," Neesha said, pouring more fire into her words. He was still snapping and struggling.

"Bale, tell him I'll get the chains off."

Neesha was looking for some way to scale the angry dragon when Bale slammed him on his side right in front of her. Neesha screamed and fell back, afraid she was about to be smeared across the ground. And then she saw. A lock on the chains right between his wings. Bale had rolled him so that it was right in front of her.

Neesha grabbed the lock and poured fire into it, hoping. It was tempered, of course, to withstand dragonfire. And probably all kinds of fire. Removing the enchantment was something Neesha wasn't especially good at, and they didn't have anything even remotely like enough time for that. She looked around desperately, like a key would fall out of the air. She thought to go check the body of the one rider that hadn't been reduced to ashes.

"Water?" Bale said. "Toll-mum uses water to open locks."

Neesha wasn't going to tell her that Tollar could see with water and Neesha could not. There was also the problem of not having any water on hand.

But there was an awful lot of blood dripping from Bale's mouth and staining her teeth from the man she had killed.

"Sure, why not."

It wasn't exactly like using aquamancy on water, but it wasn't so different either. Neesha tried not to think too hard about what she was doing, pouring the blood into the lock and sticking her fingertip into it. Neesha held her breath, channelling her focus and hoping that all her training with the world's best aquamancer would amount to something.

But it didn't. Neesha was just standing there, trying not to get crushed by a struggling angry dragon, with her finger in a dead man's blood, feeling stupid.

And then she had another really bad idea.

"Bale, fire."

Bale, thankfully, did not question or argue and snorted a fireball at her, which she used to summon a fire demon. Gods, this was such a bad idea. They were supposed to stick together and harness each other.

Neesha sighed and invited the demon possession. She stuffed it in her mental safe box and stuck her finger back in the bloody lock, trying to see with it like she could with fire, like she could when harnessing Tollar.

With the demon's boost in power, the shape of the lock bloomed in her mind. Neesha gasped. She pressed the blood against tumblers until she heard the click.

She shoved away the demon and pushed herself back away from the pair of dragons. Summer's Eve Lightning had been trembling as he struggled against the hold of his much larger daughter. But the lock opening had renewed those struggles.

Bale leapt clear of him and snatched Neesha up as she darted into the sky. When she circled back around, Neesha saw that Summer's Eve Lightning had shaken off the chains. Well, the ones on his wings anyway. He'd need help with the rest. And then he was airborne.

"Shit. Bale!"

"I have told him where to find Auntie. He doesn't believe who I am, but I think he senses she's here."

Summer's Eve Lightning didn't come after them, aiming for the volcano instead. Smaller and faster, he got ahead of them, though Bale followed.

"Bale, I need to be on the island!"

"I need to get more lava from Spark. For Loch."

Neesha couldn't really argue with that, but she did need to get back there. Bale set Neesha on her back. If Spark hadn't gone to the fire realm already, Neesha supposed the two of them could go together.

Bale jerked in the air, her head turning toward the island like she meant to turn back before she shook herself and kept going for the volcano.

"What? What is it?"

"Summon from Toll-mum."

"Shit. She needs our help. Bale, I have to go back!"

"A fire portal is faster than I am."

Neesha wanted to argue, but Bale hit her in the face with a fireball. Neesha gathered it in her hands before the wind carried it away.

How would a normal wizard open a fire portal?

Tollar had asked her that approximately a million years ago. Neesha had practiced every chance she got but hadn't been able to do it without harnessing another wizard. Could she risk another demon possession?

Neesha had been terrified and furious the very first time she'd opened a fire portal. Would it help that she was once again terrified and furious? It had to. Otherwise her best friend was going to die.

Neesha snarled at the fire and plunged her hand into it. She tore at it like the fire had personally offended her. She took a breath to focus, putting her anger into it, pressing for the edge between realms. She narrowed her focus like she did when she made those fire lances, condensing all her power into one point. And it flared. She drove her hands into it like she meant to part a curtain and *pulled*.

The fire stretched. The fire's entire reality stretched. In the centre, it tore—an ugly, glorious part in the flames, brighter than the rest.

Stifling a sob, Neesha pulled the fire portal open wide enough to fit through and plunged in.

CHAPTER
THIRTY-FIVE

Loch bared his teeth in a snarl and threw more aquamancy at Tollar. Shards of ice flew at her face. She batted it away, bits of ice shattering on the stone floor around her. Her pulse rushed in her ears and the pain behind her eyes grew worse, but she gave him a sternly disappointed look, like he was a child who'd just wet his pants.

"Yes, you've got some nice little tricks. But did you miss the part where I'm better than you? So how about you just surrender already and make this easier on both of us?"

Loch roared wordlessly and flung out his hands. Water ropes sprang up out of nowhere, wrapping tightly around her throat. Tollar rolled her eyes. Loch was storming toward her, but she shrugged the water off, letting it splatter around her feet.

"You're just not listening to anything I say. I know my Prairiean is quite good, so this isn't a language issue."

He lunged, hand out, possibly meaning to strangle her? Or harness her power. Cold fear crept in between her shoulder blades, but even with her tied up, he was easy enough to evade with a side-step and quick pivot. He came back around, reaching for her exposed wrist, and she jerked away again. Hot rage pushed down her fear, buzzing across her skin, and she sought out the water in his veins. Used blood magic to hold him still.

"Where I come from, we ask permission before touching someone," she snapped.

Wrenching her arms around, twisting painfully and straining against the ropes, Tollar fished out the venom ball from her pouch and heaved it two-handed at a clear space behind her.

Loch gasped, and she felt him wrench out of her control like a frayed rope snapping in her mind. He threw water at the little fire she'd started, and she pushed the water away—anger and fear keeping her focused despite her growing bleariness. He lunged toward her, breaking her concentration when she had to pivot away from his grasping hands. The fire went out.

Well, shit.

"Trying to summon help?" Loch sneered. "All your talk of being better than me and you want that fiery little monster here to do the job for you?"

"What, you mean Spark? She's got her mother with her, you know."

"Neesha died twenty years ago!"

Tollar blinked once. "You need better spies. Oh, or did you use all your good ones on Upalint? We caught them all, you know."

She gave him a tight, taunting smile and tried to keep the panic down, even as he drew a dagger from his robes.

"This ends now." He pointed the blade at her.

"Well, yes, but if I don't have a bit of help, I'm not sure I can do it the Guild's way. Did I mention you should surrender?"

Loch advanced on her and she backed away, having to move in a circle as the people who had dragged her in were still standing around the edges of the room, watching. Which was honestly foolish. If they had any sense at all, they'd be attacking her in unison, but she supposed Loch hadn't told them to do anything and clearly they had no gumption.

"Gods, who let you out of the nursery?" Loch said in disgust. He was now pointing his blade at her belly.

If there had been any fear left in her it was incinerated under the white-hot rage. Her headache crumbled to ash under the power of her fury, blazing across her skin. She stopped backing away and stood as tall as she could under the circumstances. Loch halted, watching her warily but still gesturing with his knife.

"Someone needs to cut them out of you. I suppose they'll have your magic? It'd be easy enough to take."

Well. If the Guild wanted him alive, they had better godsdamn get here in a hurry. She went very still and watched him.

"Oh, no more banter? I thought we were having fun," he said, grinning like broken glass.

She let him gloat, thinking he'd rattled her. And in a way, she supposed he had. She was tired of this. Just tired. It was time to end it. While his focus was on how clever he was, Tollar summoned one of the water-filled spiky balls from her pouch and ran it through the ropes binding her.

Loch only took notice when she flung out a hand to direct the ball at him. He flinched but her aim, guided by aquamancy, was impeccable, and the spikes tore through his hand holding the dagger. He shrieked and dropped it.

Tollar used it to her advantage and did a quick summon of the dragons.

And then Loch was in front of her, grasping her wrist with that same greedy look Karthiry had had. Tollar startled and her gut clenched, and she went straight to trying to suppress everything before he could take her magic.

And it worked?

Instead of the dreadful empty feeling of her magic going somewhere else, it felt heavy, stifled, like it had when Dionelle suppressed her.

"Holy shit," she gasped.

Loch's eyes were wide with horror. "What have you done? Where's my magic gone!"

Tollar laughed, high and wild and ugly and tore her arm from his grip. Had it really been this easy all along? Aldred and the rest had been right about suppression. She'd only been sending the magic out instead of inward. She suppressed herself, and there was no magic for him to take.

Loch screamed again, this time because a water demon launched itself out of him and made for the nearest elemental on the side of the room.

Well. She hadn't really expected that.

Tollar tsked at him. "That's just embarrassing, really."

She kept up with the suppression though. None of them could use magic, but she'd already seen she was a better fighter than anyone in the entire room combined. Maybe better than anyone left on the island. These were all soft academics used to battle magic.

Tollar was scanning the room to see who had her sword when Loch lunged for her again. This time with a fist. Which she batted aside and then punched him square in the face. He stumbled back, screaming, and then tried to tackle her. She pivoted around, because he was slow and clumsy and letting him just fall on his stupid face was less work.

He got halfway up when Tollar kicked out the back of his knee, and he went down again.

"Don't just stand there, you fools—get her!"

Tollar sighed. She spotted the goon with her sword and went straight for him. He held the pointy end out at her. Good for him. He jabbed and she deflected it with her bracer and kicked him in the gut. He dropped her sword and crumpled in on himself. She rammed her knee into his face, knocking him backward and probably unconscious, before picking up her sword.

Her back complained, and this was absolutely not the time for her condition to catch up with her. She tightened her core, fixed her posture, and reminded herself she could rest all she needed if she could just do something about this sodding fool of a man.

Through all of this, she kept suppressing their magic. The woman near the door ran. Tollar let her. Smartest one of the lot of them.

Something thwacked into the armour on Tollar's shoulder, and she turned in time to watch Loch's dagger fall to the floor. Someone had thrown it at her. Someone with absolutely no skill because it was the side of the hilt that hit her. And anyway she was wearing dragon skin under all this and good luck to them trying to stab her with *anything*.

She glared across at the man who had been the one to throw the blade. He paled, going a bit grey-green.

"Did you not bring a *single* fighter?" Tollar said, turning fully to Loch. "Even the Guild has proper soldiers among them, honestly!"

"River!" Loch screamed down the side hall. "Where in the hells is that fool of a boy?"

Someone hit Tollar in the back. Cowardly and sloppy. But it wasn't anyone with any kind of leverage, and she stumbled forward a couple of steps before getting her feet under her again. He'd tried to get his arms all the way around her, but he was on the short side, didn't have much in the way of reach, and the babies were awful big—meaning so was she.

Tollar twisted around and hit him in the head with the pommel of her sword.

There was another right behind this one, and she was out of patience and swung the blade low and hard, cutting off his foot just above the ankle. There was a lot of screaming. And running. More of these bloody northerners coming down a different hallway than the one who had wisely run off.

And then a very large man, not much more than a boy, charged into the room from the hallway Loch had just been shouting down. Tollar went cold. She had never met him but recognized him immediately in his resemblance to Stone. Neesha had mentioned River's betrayal, how he'd fled the dragon city to join Loch.

Tollar took a steadying breath and adjusted her stance and her grip on the sword. River held a battle-axe. He was slightly taller than Stone, though Tollar had some height and heft on him.

She now regretted taunting Loch about his lack of real fighters. She hoped handing River his arse wouldn't complicate things with Spark or Ember.

And then Tollar realized she'd let herself get distracted and had stopped the suppression spell. She pivoted quickly, searching for Loch, only to find him as he pulled the demon back in.

Shit.

CHAPTER THIRTY-SIX

S park couldn't sense any fire in the palace near Tollar but tried to open a portal there anyway. One opened, but she could feel that it was farther away, something out on the island. Abyss said Tollar had summoned them. Why would she do that if she didn't need help? She was supposed to use the venom ball.

Spark tried the portal again, still not opening anything in the palace. Should she go through one of the ones farther away and just run to the palace? Would that be quicker?

And then a portal opened next to her, and Neesha dropped through it looking stunned and crying.

"Mamma! I didn't know you could open a portal!"

"I couldn't." Neesha stood and flung her arms around Spark in a big hug.

Spark nearly started crying too, so relieved to see her mother was still okay.

"But you finally figured it out?"

"Yeah. What a day."

"I can't get a portal into the palace."

Neesha threw her a startled glance, tried to open a portal of her own.

"Shit!" Neesha shouted.

"What if we go to the fires farther out?"

"There's a battle going on between those fires and the palace entrance. I don't know, we might still be able to fight our way through."

"Should we wait?"

Neesha stared at the fire around them, an expression of open horror on her face. Waiting could get Tollar killed. But it sounded like trying to fight their way in from the outside wasn't going to go much better.

"Let's give her a couple of minutes, okay?"

The two of them went back to trying to open portals into the palace. Spark's skin buzzed with the need to do something, anything.

CHAPTER THIRTY-SEVEN

Tollar shuffled so she had a visual on both men at the same time. She did not like the angry gleam in River's eyes. This was a man who would gleefully spend the afternoon hurting her in every way he could imagine. And he moved like he knew how to use that axe.

Just as River charged toward her, Loch shot another ice spear at her. Tollar sloppily turned it into water an instant before it splashed into her, most of her focus on River, trying to assess what kind of fighter he was and how much of a threat he posed. He was not especially quick, but didn't provide any openings either, not swinging the axe until he was within range.

Tollar raised her sword and stumbled when the blood in her body sloshed in ways it wasn't meant to. She didn't have the focus to fight both Loch and River. She slammed down suppression, blocking everything in the room, and took the axe against her sword, but wasn't braced for it. She went back to one knee, not especially gracefully, the landing jarring her hips and lancing pain through her whole body.

She held the sword firm and the axe at bay, using River's momentum as she pivoted on her knees. He stumbled forward and she swung the sword around, trying to take his legs out from under him. He did a fumbling leap over her sword, catching the blade's edge on the side of his boot before slamming onto the floor on his side.

Tollar kept the swing going, letting the weight of the sword bring her all the way around with one foot planted on the ground. Grunting with effort, she got all the way to her feet and faced River, who had avoided landing on his axe but still took a self-inflicted cut across his shoulder. He was back on his feet, but not ready to fight.

Tollar lunged in, her knees screaming in protest, and brought her sword down hard across his forearm, severing his hand halfway to the elbow. He screamed and dropped the axe. It was a big, mean weapon, one too heavy for most people to swing with only one arm. River might have been able to, but the shock and the pain was enough to take him out, at least for the moment.

The suppression had gotten away from her again, though, and Loch was back in control of his demon. Staring him down across the room, Tollar sheathed the sword and gathered water from the air.

And then Bale roared from somewhere overhead and the ceiling collapsed. The dome of water Tollar had been gathering deflected most of the debris. Thankfully, the bulk of the collapse had been in the hallway where Loch's backup had been approaching.

Tollar scanned the room quickly and saw that none of them had made it in, which meant... Oh. Well, the Guild hadn't said anything about keeping them *all* alive. River had been hit by a support beam and was either unconscious or dead, though she didn't have time to see which. There was a lot of fire, the wood and palm fronds roof ablaze, with chunks of cooling lava scattered amongst the mess. Lava? Tollar went cold.

Oh sweet ancestors, is the volcano going off?

Loch was screaming again and a large blob of water headed right for the biggest of the fires in the debris. Tollar knocked it off course and then used more blood magic to knock him over. From the ground, he kept trying to put out this newest fire, but even as he did, the fire exploded with light. And Spark crawled out of it, glancing around warily, Neesha emerging just behind her.

Tollar very nearly sagged with relief but knew better than to let her guard down.

"It really doesn't look like you needed our help," Neesha said. And immediately had to dodge a spear of ice.

"You're supposed to be dead!" Loch screamed. He'd been doing a lot of that.

"You first," Neesha snarled, drawing from the fire behind her.

"Alive!" Tollar reminded. "If I can't kill the bastard, neither can you. The Guild wants him alive!"

"To hell with what the Guild wants!"

"Mamma…"

More ice shards. Neesha dodged them again, and Spark flung a fireball in front of herself to melt them. They pinged uselessly off Tollar's armour.

"Shit!" Neesha pointed frantically at Loch. "Portal! Tollar, stop him!"

Right, yes, they needed to stop arguing and just do something about this pathetic fool of a man. He had a water portal open and Croves's suggestion of tossing him in one flashed through her mind, and then she used more blood magic to knock him on his arse again.

The fire behind Neesha and Spark flared. Tollar braced for a fire demon and was not at all prepared for what she saw instead.

Dionelle. Hastily securing fireproof robes and pulling little fireproof slippers out of the pockets.

"Holy shit!"

CHAPTER THIRTY-EIGHT

Dionelle was vaguely aware of Tollar swearing and everyone staring at her in utter disbelief. She was just about as shocked that she was here as they were to see her. But when the Dragoness Superior had told her about the summon, Dionelle had acted without thinking.

She was vaguely aware of Loch doing some kind of magic off across the room, and she held her breath, trying not to vomit or scream or pass out. She was in a large bright room, with a large hole in it to outdoors, and she could see several dragons in the sky outside. This was a vastly unsafe situation, but she was not helpless.

That was the mantra Elima had been drilling into her for the last several weeks. *She was not helpless.* And she was not alone.

She had also spent the last several weeks learning a lot more than magic and to control her own emotions. Tollar was still watching her wide-eyed, open mouth forming into a grin.

Dionelle lifted a hand and signed, "Let's end this."

Tollar's grin turned vicious and she nodded.

Dionelle snapped her fingers and pointed at Neesha, then Tollar. Gods, if ever she needed any of them to read her mind it was now. She still wasn't sure she could find the right words, but Loch being able to hear and prepare a counterattack would not be to anyone's benefit.

"Tollar!" Mita screamed, and the panic in her voice nearly drove Dionelle to her knees. She hadn't heard Mita so afraid since the night Loch's dragons had killed half their family.

Reiser's screams echoed in her mind. Her skin went cold.

She gasped a breath, then another, but they were coming too quickly, too harsh, none of it seemed to be getting into her at all. Like she was somehow breathing water. And the water was rising swiftly around her. Already at her knees, her hips, her waist.

Too much too fast.

Loch had a water portal open, and it was a beast, like a great waterfall crashing into the room.

Just like in the cell. He'd tried so hard to get her to tell him where Mita was. Threatened every day that he'd find her and bring her to that dark and terrible place and take her apart in front of Dionelle.

Darkness and water rising around her, stealing the air. Water to her chest, the current trying to pull her off her feet.

And then Tollar was there, in front of them all, pushing the water away and bubbling it out and around them, forcing it to drain away outside. But the roar of water didn't cease, the water portal growing and growing like Loch meant to drown the entire island.

She supposed he did.

And then Neesha, bless her, was at Tollar's back, a hand resting at the side of Tollar's neck—Tollar had wisely covered most of her skin against unwanted harnessings. Neesha closed her eyes and sagged in the way they all did when great amounts of their power were pulled away.

The portal shrank, the gush of water slowing.

But a spear of ice flew through the wall of water between them and Loch, and it caught Tollar in the shoulder. She grunted and staggered into Neesha. But neither of them lost control of the magic.

Then water demon after water demon poured through the water toward them. Mita shrieked and Dionelle moved in closer, sending the demons back through the portal. But the demons were the problem. Particularly the one inside Loch.

"Demon!" Dionelle called to Tollar. "*His* demon!"

Tollar glanced back and nodded, urged Mita over toward Dionelle, who was still rapidly banishing water demons while Tollar and Neesha kept the water portal from getting any worse. Mita drew near and Dionelle gripped her hand and directed the full force of their combined magic at Loch in the form of a suppression spell.

The others could suppress, and they were good enough at it, but none of them had had to raise a fiery little girl—or two—and constantly put out and prevent fires. They could be strong or they could be targeted, but only Dionelle was both.

The portal disappeared, the demons went with it, and Loch roared in horror.

"Ah yes," Tollar said. "That would be Dionelle and Spark with the targeted suppression. You're the only one here who can't use magic now. So reverse the volcano and—"

"Oh, I already did that!" Mita said, grinning. "I was brilliant. I had to go right *inside* it! But it's not going to blow up anymore."

Dionelle had no idea what that was all about and wasn't sure she wanted to know.

"Right, yes, that *is* brilliant." Tollar turned back to Loch. "You've got nothing. Surrender now and—"

He screamed and charged at Tollar, a blade in his hand aimed right at her belly, and while Dionelle didn't lose her grip on the suppression spell, she lost her grip on just about everything else, including her ability to feel the floor beneath her. Mita leaned into her, squeezing her hand and keeping her on her feet.

Loch sailed across the room, landing hard on his back. Dionelle didn't see what Tollar had done, but it had been deeply effective.

And then Tollar was angrily speaking the words to end a water demon possession. Loch's screams grew shrill and he fought. Oh how he fought to keep that demon. But he had nothing but his will, and Tollar's was stronger.

The demon came out, and she banished it immediately.

The ground rushed up under Dionelle's feet again, and she pulled free of Mita's grasp and stormed across the room. Her body trembled like a leaf in a storm, but her blood raged like the volcano her granddaughter had apparently just fought. Dionelle kept all of her focus and rage into suppressing Loch, and she beat even Neesha to stand over him.

Dionelle profoundly wished that she could shower sparks the way Mita used to, as a stolen lifetime's worth of grief and fury poured through her and her magic.

She leaned right down, her face an inch from his. He flinched but didn't move, and Dionelle suspected Tollar was using blood magic to hold him down. Good. Suddenly, from this end, it didn't seem so frightening.

"You took everything from me," Dionelle said, a low growling whisper. "Now you're going to watch me strip it all away from you."

CHAPTER
THIRTY-NINE

When Cerro led the team into what was left of Loch's throne room, Tollar damn near collapsed. She hadn't realized how bone-weary tired she was until there was no more adrenaline left to power her. Every ache of battle rushed in—growing bruises from where she'd been hit with blades and shards of ice, the throbbing of her feet in her too-small boots, and the twinge in her lower back had grown into a monster, searing through her hip and halfway down her leg. She sank to the floor, huddled in on herself, breathing hard through how many times that awful hateful man had threatened her babies.

Empty threats. He'd never had the slimmest chance. But it left her feeling cold and hollowed out.

"We kept each other safe," Dionelle said.

Tollar looked up as Dionelle crouched in front of her, hands held up in proper greeting. Tollar grinned and then sobbed and then took the woman's hands. Dionelle knelt next to her, arms around Tollar's shoulders.

"You were sodding brilliant," Tollar said, giving Dionelle a squeeze. "I really did not expect to see you here."

"Neither did I," Dionelle said, a smile in her voice.

"I keep telling you all that you're stronger than you think."

"Maybe we'll listen one day."

Tollar signed to her, "Your bravery is an inspiration."

Smiling, Dionelle replied with, "So is yours." Then she leaned forward and wiped Tollar's tears with her thumbs, gave her a kiss on the head and stood.

"I'm going with them." Dionelle gestured to where Cerro and Tavalu were properly securing Loch. "To watch and make sure he stays caught."

"Nanny, no!" Spark gasped.

"They'll need help suppressing him," Dionelle said. "I'll do it as long as I can."

Tollar put a hand on Dionelle's shoulder. "If you're certain. You know your own limits. But shouldn't you get back to the Guild? Do they even know you're here?"

Tollar tried not to chuckle at the way Dionelle blinked a lot before responding. "I'm sure the Superior mentioned something."

"I'll let them know you're with us when I report," Cerro said. "It's not like you can't just go back through a fire any time you want."

Cerro and Tavalu hoisted up Loch, who was shackled and also appeared to be half-unconscious, and dragged him out.

Tollar must have been staring with some kind of expression on her face.

"They've sedated him," Neesha said. "Heavy sedation for now, then suppression. Blood magic if they need it. It's going to be a slog getting him back to the Guild."

"The dragons aren't going to help get everyone back?"

"Some of them will. I don't know how many."

"We'll need to get back to the port, right?" Spark asked. "Back to Dira so she can organize the return?"

"Gods, what a mess," Tollar said, running her hands over her face. "I hate this part. I used to leave for this part."

"This part?"

"She means cleaning up," Neesha said. "Rebuilding."

"Sorting out the dead," Tollar added. "Figuring out who's to blame for what."

Neesha helped haul Tollar to her feet, much as she wanted to lie down and sleep for a month. Surveying the partially destroyed room, Tollar realized there would be a lot of bodies under the rubble Bale had created. And then she saw that the people she'd maimed in the fight earlier were all dead. Drowned where they'd fallen. Including River.

Spark saw him at the same time Tollar did. She gasped and took a half-step in his direction.

"Mamma...!"

"Weeping ancestors. He killed his own people trying to stop us."

"Let's get out of here," Neesha said, ushering them all toward the exit.

Croves came charging up the stairs toward them.

"They said ye were all right but I had to see for myself," he said. He swept Tollar up into a quick hug, but was mostly searching her for injuries.

"I'm fine." She managed not to wince at the way his bear-hug made her back ache even worse. She wasn't injured, just a strained body doing what strained bodies did. "Just tired."

"Aye. Well I saw 'em draggin' Loch off toward a dragon. That a good idea?"

"Dionelle is going with them."

Croves nodded like that made all the sense in the world. "I don't trust the Guild."

"Hey now, Neesha's going to be Grand Chancellor some day."

"Aye. But she ain't yet."

"Tollar..." Neesha protested.

"What?" Tollar draped her arm around Neesha's shoulders. "You don't want to be Grand Chancellor?"

"Of course I do!" Neesha playfully pushed Tollar away.

"Well, I've heard it takes about forty years. I expect you'll do it in thirty?"

Neesha laughed, but quickly gave Tollar a serious look. "They're restructuring the high council so there are always two specialists on it. When I'm Grand Chancellor, I expect you to have a seat there with me."

Tollar thought that sounded like a nightmare. But likely a necessary one. And anyway, she had thirty years to prepare. "You save me a spot."

Neesha grinned and went off to find her family, who had gone ahead, likely so Dionelle could continue to keep an eye on Loch. Hopefully Elima had her prepared enough to face this challenge, though seeing him in bonds and unable to hurt her or anyone else was likely very good for Dionelle's recovery.

Tollar turned back to Croves and found herself swept up in his arms again, his lips crushing against hers, his beard rough against her cheeks. Her legs were as good as noodles, and she was still clutching his arm and gasping when he released her again.

"Ye said I could kiss ye all I wanted when this was done."

Tollar heard dragoncries to the south and saw they were still in battle formation out over the ocean. Of course, Loch's people wouldn't have learned of his defeat yet and would still be fighting like they had a leader. Or a chance of winning.

Tollar pointed toward the battle. "Get back out there and help your sister!"

"All right, fine. As long as yer safe." He took her face in his hands and kissed her again, gave her belly an affectionate pat, and started to walk away.

"And Croves, we've won now. Show them mercy."

He stopped and looked at her, grumbling wordlessly.

"Make. Good. Choices."

He laughed, kissed her one last time, and then whistled for Shell, who had apparently been circling the island the whole time. Bale was up there with him. Shell swooped in, plucking Croves up as he went, and Bale came in low, tilting her wings in something like a wave, before chasing after him.

The fireborn women and Cerro and the rest had gone out to the middle of the island to hand off Loch to one of the Superiors and start the process of getting all of them back to Port Sawulxo. Tollar didn't see Yarrow and Peniope anywhere and hoped they'd be along soon. Tollar headed back toward the palace, struggling not to limp as the back and leg pain got worse. It was hard to maintain posture when the weight of babies and weariness kept trying to pull her into a sag. She went through the hole in the barricade around the slums the island's people had been forced into around the palace.

The rest of the island had been cleared of most vegetation, and she didn't see many buildings left intact either. And if the intel was correct that all their wizards had been killed... Tollar rubbed her face again. She'd have to make sure people from the Guild stayed to help with the worst of the weather when storm season came.

But Tollar wasn't sure the remaining locals knew what had happened or understood they had their freedom again. She wasn't sure how much information Yarrow and Peniope had been able to exchange, or if it had only gone in one direction. Did they know Port Sawulxo had turned Loch away? Did they know these dragons were here to help them?

She couldn't see anyone at all. The bodies from before had been moved, but there wasn't a soul in sight.

At the sound of footsteps behind her, she turned to find Neesha drawing near.

"What are you doing?" Neesha asked.

"Looking for someone." There was one person in particular she had in mind, but literally anyone who called this island home would do in the meantime.

Tollar had learned enough of the Biternan dialect from Draminedes to stumble her way through it now, as hearing their own language was her best bet for getting anyone to listen. She doubted any of Loch's people had bothered to learn it.

"I come from Upalint, courtesy of Port Sawulxo. Your island is yours again," she said, as loudly and slowly and clearly as she could. "Loch is captured and goes to the Guild to face justice."

"The same Guild who let this happen?" a woman's voice called from a nearby tent.

Tollar couldn't see anyone. Realizing she was still wearing her dagger and sword, she unbuckled both and handed them to Neesha, who sagged under the weight but managed not to fall over or drop anything.

"Bring this back out to the others, will you?"

"I imagine they don't want to see any northerners right now anyway."

Once Neesha was gone, Tollar turned, dug the heels of her hands into her lower back to brace herself, and faced the tent that had addressed her earlier.

"Has Sariledes survived? I'm friend to his son, Draminedes."

"Dram died!" the same voice snapped.

"Is that what the northerners told you? Did they tell you no one would come? That no one could help you? The Guild certainly has blood on their hands for this, but they came. Too late, but they came."

The tent remained silent. No one else spoke up. No one came out of hiding.

Tollar sighed. "I'm Tollar Lipraxo, from Nytaltek. I've been fighting Loch for nearly two years now, since he decided my people's lands ought to belong to him. I don't trust the Guild much more than you do, but I trust the dragons who came with us." Tollar spotted Bale swooping nearby and pointed. "I raised that one myself."

Still nothing from the tent in front of her, but a scrap of wood off to Tollar's side shifted and a scrawny young boy crawled out from a space between two crates.

"I saw you fight them," he said. "I saw her fight them! You had to have seen!"

The tent flap twitched back. One dark eye peeked out and grew wide, and then a dishevelled, shorter woman took a hesitant step out.

"Yes," she said. "I saw. They're really gone?"

"The ones the dragons haven't killed are being loaded on to boats, heading back where they came from and, hopefully, jail."

It took some convincing, Tollar showing them her magic, explaining what she was—what her friends were—and how they'd used that plus the help from the dragons to finally stop Loch for good. Then there was weeping and some celebrating. And finally—*finally*—Peniope joined them, backed up everything Tollar had said, and helped her find Sariledes, who was in fact still alive.

The resemblance to Draminedes was clear, though the man was a lot thinner—haggard and gaunt—than she'd expected given how portly Dram was. But Loch had probably been starving them out since his defeat in the port nearly a year ago.

"You're one of those southerners my son put his trust in, aren't you?" Sariledes asked.

Tollar gave him a polite bow and introduced herself. "Your son did put his trust in me, and I've got him tucked away safely on my farm. Well, it's his farm now. He's building a life there." Tollar spotted Shell zipping by and pointed him out. "There. Do you see the large man on that dragon? That's Croves. He's the one Draminedes is building a life with."

Sariledes watched Croves and Shell until they were out of sight again, his eyes shining with unshed tears. He nodded once.

"Still alive. Good. I wasn't sure he'd make it. Bit naïve, that boy."

Tollar grinned. "We're working on him. He's something of a hero. We'd have never known what Loch was doing in time if he hadn't warned us."

Sariledes nodded, but the gentle smile on his face seemed haunted.

"We'll work things out so you two can talk, but I already got a message to him that you were alive."

Peniope took over then, and Tollar gave them all a nod in farewell before heading back out to the field beyond the palace that had become something of a staging area. Cerro spotted her and came over immediately. Tavalu was right behind him, the fireborn women gathering in as well.

"What exactly—" Cerro began.

"How did you—" Tavalu burst out.

"That was—" This from Neesha.

All of them were talking over each other, trying to get answers and give compliments and whatever else all at once. There'd been a time Tollar had loved this part. She was a hero. She knew it. She embraced it. And part of that meant being adored and part of that meant having to answer questions. But she was so exhausted that she was pretty sure even her hair was tired. The ache in her lower back had grown into a roar.

"Shut up," she said softly. And blessed ancestors, they all did. "I'm going home now—I'll be back! But for now, I'm going home to sleep next to Bee until I'm damn-well done sleeping. I'm going to eat until it feels like there's *four* babies in there. Then I'm going to sleep some more! And *then* I'll come back—only through the days, mind you—but I'll come and answer your questions and receive your compliments and help clean things up and rebuild until there's no rebuilding left or these babies come. But I'm tired and the fight is over, and I'm out of it."

"Yes, all right," Cerro conceded. "You've certainly earned a break, and I think we can do some minimal cleaning up and organizing for a couple of days until you're rested. But Dira's going to want you more involved with the Guild."

Tollar nodded wearily. "And she'll get it, but later. Say about a year? Because I'm spending that time with Bee and the babies and sleeping and relaxing and reading books and being a godsdamn farmer, and anything that tries to interrupt will sorely regret it."

"Yes." Cerro straightened his robes. "I think a year will be the right timeframe, once we get this all sorted out and start implementing changes."

He went back to the dragon still waiting in the field. Tollar gave Tavalu a quick hug and thanked her for all she'd done, promising to chat more soon. Once Tavalu and her team had rejoined Cerro, it left Tollar with the fireborn women.

"I can't believe this is over," Tollar said. "I don't know what normal looks like after this, but it will be interesting to find out. You three will be all right here?"

"We've got Abyss," Spark said.

"And Bale and Croves," Tollar said. "Unfortunately no one can come with me through the water."

"We've still got fires," Neesha said. "Toll, I got a portal open!"

"You did?" Tollar nearly crushed Neesha in a hug. "How wonderful! And that certainly changes some things. I know Spark can open portals for you if you need them, but that's your freedom back."

Neesha glanced at her mother. "I bet you can do it too. Want me to teach you?"

Dionelle smiled but didn't answer.

"Well then, we've got lots of space and beds if you want to join me in sleeping a good long way from all of this." Tollar gestured to the barren island and the dragons still shrieking and sinking boats to the south. "Food is plentiful, our home is quiet. I'll have Bee leave a fire on for you—for all three of you. You're welcome any time."

Tollar hugged all three of them in turn and then slipped through a water portal home.

AFTER

Neesha emerged from a fire portal, leaving the roar of the fire realm behind for the cacophony of the jungle. Beenala was standing there waiting for her, as she often was—Neesha came at the same time on the same day of the week and had been for a month now, except two weeks ago when she'd changed the day to come for Beenala's birthday. Today Beenala wore the biggest grin Neesha had ever seen.

Beenala grabbed Neesha's hands. "The babies came! Two days after your last visit!"

She tugged Neesha along, around to the shady side of the house where a cluster of hammock chairs hung from the veranda. Tollar reclined in one of them, blobby brown babies in the crook of each arm, one sleeping and the other nursing. Beenala ushered Neesha into one of the hammocks, kissed Tollar on the head, and took the sleeping baby from her.

"This is Rain, and he's a perfect delight," Beenala said, and then deposited Rain into Neesha's arms. "I'll bring some coconut rice."

Beenala bustled off, Tollar smiling as she watched her go.

"This little monster," Tollar said, gesturing to the baby she nursed, "is River, who is already a wild thing and screams if she's not asleep or eating. Unfortunately, she does not sleep nearly as much as any of us would like."

Tollar sounded exhausted, but smiled as she spoke, her silver irises shining.

"So I feed her first, in hopes she will sleep so I can feed Rain." Tollar grinned. "That's my job—I feed babies, and I sleep. It's delightful."

"Beenala has taken to being a mum after all?" Neesha asked.

"Yes, and Croves and even Dram! And while I would never admit it to my auntie, I do sometimes let Bale take her sister for a little fly around when she's especially screamy."

Neesha smiled and looked around. There was no sign of Croves or Draminedes, though they'd both been around last week when she'd visited. She'd come with Dionelle and Spark right after Tollar had gotten the rest she'd demanded after Loch's defeat. They'd stayed the night, and then Dira had taken Loch and some Guild wizards and the dragons and headed north. Dionelle and Spark had both gone with them. Neesha had stayed with Chalky, trying to help the islanders but mostly feeling like she was in the way.

Tollar had kept coming back for two weeks, but the help the island needed wasn't the sort she really had to offer—they needed terramancers and floramancers. They'd have a desperate need for aquamancers soon, when the storms started, but Tollar wasn't sure she'd be able to help much then.

So Croves, who also wasn't much use, had headed home. His sister and her friends were still around, though not living out here at the farms. When Croves left and Tollar stopped coming around, Neesha had taken a fire portal first to the Guild and then back to the dragon city with Spark, where Neesha had had to tell Stone about his son, and Spark had broken the news to Ember. Spark was still in the dragon city.

Neesha looked down at Rain sleeping peacefully in his swaddle. Her chest panged with a hollow ache. She hadn't held a baby, peaceful and sleeping like this, since Spark had been a newborn.

"You okay?" Tollar asked. "Want me to get Bee?"

Neesha shook her head and swallowed against the tight feeling in her throat. "I never got to do this. I got a handful of hours with Spark, and they were all fraught. I only ever fed her once. And then I woke up and she was a woman."

Tollar leaned over and squeezed Neesha's arm. The wristband she wore glittered with her grandmother's bone—Abyss had crystallized it for her when they'd all come with Bale. Abyss had wanted to see how her kin lived, and the dragons had decided it was a good place for Summer's Eve Lightning to take some rest, spend time with Bale, and heal from his time as Loch's prisoner. Abyss had used her magic to make the bone glitter so that

Tollar could show the technique to the old necromancer without needing to borrow any of Abyss's hoard.

Neesha met Tollar's gaze.

"You want that again?" Tollar glanced at the baby in Neesha's arms.

"I think I might."

Well, that was new. Neesha had felt the vague shape of all the years she'd lost, but aside from Yenette, it hadn't really been clear what those years might have held. "I gave Dionelle and Spark pouches from my diamond hoard. I think all three of us are still putting together what we do with our days, now that the world's a little safer for us, even if we can't go back to Pasdale just yet. Spark loves the dragon city, and I don't expect she'll properly settle anywhere else, though I think she'll do some adventuring. Despite it all, you certainly rubbed off on her."

Tollar laughed. "Well, if she'd like to join me—you know, later, once the twins are bigger—I would love to have a sidekick."

"Dionelle's going to stay at the Guild until the trial, and then she'll go back to the dragon city, but I don't know if she'll stay there. It's still a rustic place, and hard on her the older she gets. She's starting to think about going to Baymouth Shores. She's not her old self and might never be, but she's getting stronger, and the diamonds will give her the freedom to do what she wants."

Tollar watched her for a long moment, and then leaned back in her hammock again.

"You should do the same. Use those diamonds to buy back as much of the lost years as you can."

Neesha grinned. "I've been accumulating a list. Looks a little different than I thought it would. Involves more travel than I expected."

"Ah, seems I've rubbed off on you too."

"Well, things have certainly been interesting."

"That's always been it, hasn't it? You get bored easily. Pasdale wasn't quite big enough, and so you got into trouble."

Neesha nodded slowly. "I think so, yes. I've got some hindsight to help make better choices with my boredom. To tolerate the boredom more than I used to. But with the portals... I've got a lot more than Pasdale available to me now. I like attention, but it turns out I like being important too. And

I knew if I survived Draxli, that I'd want to do more like that, to use my magic to help people."

"So are you and Spark both going to come adventuring with me?"

Neesha laughed. "I'm not sleeping on the ground."

Tollar snorted. "Now that I can portal anywhere any time, I'm never sleeping on the ground again either."

Beenala returned then with halved coconuts full of sweet rice for both of them. Tollar managed to balance the bowl and hold the baby so they could both eat uninterrupted. Beenala took Rain so Neesha could have her rice.

"But you're thinking of Pasdale first, aren't you?" Tollar asked.

"I've been sending and receiving letters from Yenette through the Guild. It's faster than the dragon city. We're trying to figure that part out. I'm finally going to see her—through the fire—the middle of next week."

"You're both welcome here," Beenala said. "Nytaltek would be good for you both, and you can stay with us if you want."

"Thank you. I like that I have that option." Neesha finished her rice and set the coconut shell down. "But I'm not leaving Yenette, and she's not leaving her children."

"It'll be dangerous," Tollar said. "But you knew that."

"I have to go back. Despite the danger—or maybe because of it. I have power that makes it hard for them to touch me, so maybe I can make them see. I have to go back. I have to try—for the girls Yenette and I were, and for everyone suffering because of this foolishness."

River had finished eating and immediately started scream-crying. Beenala deftly swapped babies, and then took screaming River up into the house while Tollar roused Rain enough that he could have his turn.

As Tollar was readjusting her wrap dress, Neesha noticed some new tattoos on her chest and took in for the first time that Tollar had new stripes on her face.

"When did those happen?"

"Yesterday, if you can believe it! The Keeper wanted to be sure I'd be here, and I guess heard about the babies and, well, I'm certainly not going anywhere for a while." Tollar pulled back her wrap a little bit. "This one was for Biterna." She pointed to a medium-sized swirl on her side near her breast. "And this one"—she pointed to a small dot near her collarbone—"is for Meriella."

"Oh, she's back at the Guild now too! Elima and Dionelle are both working with her, and Dira herself has taken on mentoring her."

Tollar smiled.

"Been a lot of changes at the Guild," Neesha said. "It might change things in Pasdale too."

"Well, you're better at taking risks now. And you know that if things go wrong, you don't have to do it alone."

Neesha smiled and leaned back in the hammock, enjoying time with her friend and thinking about her return home. She hadn't ever expected to feel this kind of peace and belonging, hadn't ever expected to feel safe enough to really take the right kind of risks.

Tollar started up one of the many tales of her adventures, and Neesha half-listened and half-daydreamed about starting some adventures of her own.

Scan here or visit thodestool.ca/news to learn more about Vanessa's work or to sign up for her newsletter.

ACKNOWLEDGEMENTS

It's hard to know what to say anymore. The future looks so bleak. It's so hard to keep making art when it's just going to get gobbled up into a plagiarism slop machine to enrich some shitty techbro, drain a lake, and put more artists out of work. Please don't use generative AI! It couldn't be more unethical, between the environmental disaster it's causing and the fact that it's entirely built on stolen work that it doesn't look like any of us will ever be adequately compensated for. As I write this, the shitty AI companies are getting sued, but most of us still won't ever see a dime for having our work stolen.

I can't overstate what a struggle it is to keep going. I'm having inarguably the best year of my career! I'm the first self-published author to win a Nebula Award! I made my first short story pro-sale! ("Billionaire's Tears" in *Escape Pod*, go read it!) People are finally, actually reading my work and seem to be enjoying it! I occasionally make enough royalties to pay some bills! But I'm exhausted. I was planning my exit from publishing entirely when I won the Nebula. It's forced me to reconsider. I still don't know what I'm going to do. Finishing this series gives me a clean break.

But I have so many stories left I want to tell! I have a trilogy that means so much to me that I want to share with everyone. It's got a "depression is the real enemy" but fun sort of vibe like Thunderbolts* has. There's a fun spooky novella I want to write. While the *Fireborn* series is done, I still have *so many* fun ideas for some of the characters.

But I'm tired. I'm so tired. Everyone is so tired. Hopefully this isn't the last book I publish! It's weird to be putting something out without a sneak peek at the next thing in the back. But I don't know for sure what the next thing will be. Or when. I *want* to keep sharing stories. I just don't know if I have the energy anymore.

I hope you'll sign up for my newsletter or keep an eye on my website for any news I might have. And I hope you'll keep telling people about these books if you love them. Leave ratings and reviews online. Request them at your local bookstore and library. Every little bit really does help!

You write a book and you think the hard work is done. But actually making a book professional and then putting it out into the world takes tremendous effort. Thank you to Write Club, my Wednesday write-in crew, and the Sunday afternoon SFWA writing date folks for supporting me through the writing parts. Thank you to the Bluesky writing community for the emotional support. Thank you to my spouse and kid for picking up my slack with chores or letting me be a miserable little goblin in a hole when I need it. Thank you to my dogs for always being so good. Thank you once again to Kris for keeping track of lore and being the cheerleader I desperately need. Thank you to Sydnee for helping me keep from making an ass of myself. Thank you to Chelle for helping make sure these sentences actually say what I want them to say. Good copy editors are heroes!

And once again thank you to all my Kickstarter supporters, without whom this book wouldn't be possible.

ABOUT THE AUTHOR

photo by Mike Thode

Vanessa is a word sorceress and Nebula Award-winning fantasy author whose life seldom strays from the world of books, especially during winter hibernation. Even her volunteer work revolves around the literary world, currently volunteering for SFWA and as co-founder and events director of KW Writers Alliance.

When she's not being bookish, she's into astronomy, hiking, gardening, and has a personal goal to visit all the national parks. Don't ask her about her love of trees unless you've got some time. She loves Halloween and hates to be cold. Vanessa lives in Waterloo (no, the other one) with her spouse, daughter, and very good dogs, where she can be found in her butterfly garden, achieving her final form as a garden witch.

To learn more, visit thodestool.ca or follow her on social media @VRicciThode